Royal Pain

ROYAL PAIN

MARINA HILL

AUTHOR'S NOTE

It's recommended to read *Roaming Holiday* prior to *Royal Pain*. While *Royal Pain* can be read as a standalone, the main couple from *Roaming Holiday* makes frequent appearances.

Content note:

This book closely discusses pregnancy and motherhood with a person close to the female main character. There is no trauma surrounding this topic, but if it is sensitive to your experience, please proceed with caution.

This book also mentions childhood sexual abuse. It is off-page and does not include either of the main characters. Again, if this is sensitive to your experience, please proceed with caution.

Royal Pain discusses the reality of extreme wealth that can be damaging to the environment and many groups of people. In efforts to avoid directly using the struggles of real people as fodder, the town of Lukinda is completely fictional. Sources for some claims made throughout the book will be listed at the end.

For
the girls who have always been called "too much."
May you meet your match.

CHAPTER ONE
MAIA

"Yes, I'm a nightmare, nothing new."

I toss the tabloid magazine across the backseat of the car, a knot of anger twisting my gut from that stupid headline. I glance over my shoulder. "Why do you even have this?"

My best friend stiffens as she climbs into the car behind me, and I regret not masking the clip in my tone. "I stole it," Lyla says, "from a guy in a cafe when he wasn't looking."

"Wait—" I choke out a laugh, my agitation disappearing. Leave it to Lyla to steal a magazine before someone can read about my many disappointments as deemed by the media. I shouldn't be surprised.

She smirks. "You know I got you."

At least the tabloids stopped calling me a witch because of all the healing crystal jewelry I used to wear. My team convinced me to dilute my hippie style since it led to rumors I worship the devil, and I'm sure it didn't help that I dressed up as a witch for Halloween that year.

Not a good look for the princess of Maldana.

The car pulls from the curb and I kick my heels off,

dropping my head back with a groan. "Remind me why we went to that stupid breakfast."

"For money."

I grimace and shut my eyes for a sliver of sleep. Stuffing my feet into heels and putting on a full face of makeup before eight a.m. feels like a crime, not to mention objectifying since we're only looking pretty so the donors want to keep giving us their money. I can't screw it up the way I have so often before. Art galleries, green corporations, universities—they're the few businesses clean enough for donations, and we need to keep the garden in their best interest. At least Dr. Pagoda was there to do most of the heavy lifting. She's way more diplomatic and educated than I am.

I reach for the cloth bag on the floor and take out my padded piggy slippers. They give my feet a fuzzy embrace after hours of tight heels. Twenty minutes later, the car pulls through the security gates of Felicity Gardens.

"Just a few reports and then movies at your house?" Lyla says. I don't know why she has to confirm it, considering it's been our routine every Friday for the past five or six months.

"As long as we watch *The Proposal*."

Her eyes brighten as she shimmies her chest. "I say yes to anything Ryan Reynolds."

"Are you kidding? I'm watching for Sandy B."

We both laugh. My head of security opens the door before I have a chance to finish putting my shoes back on, so I stick with my slippers. I usually beat him to it and insist on doing it myself, but Mason is a by-the-book kind of guy. Always has been.

"Pick me up at three?" I say as I climb out of the car. I

normally drive myself to work, but Mason picked me up for the event this morning.

"You got it."

He helps Lyla out behind me before leaving us. She stares at the retreating car until I force her around. "Will you stop?" I say with a laugh. "He's not going to date you."

"But he's so sexy," she whines, dropping her head against my shoulder. "I'm not saying we need to date. Just hook up."

I shake my head. I've explained it a dozen times, but she won't accept how loyal Mason is to his wife, even though she died. He still hasn't revealed much and I keep trying to pry him open like a stubborn clam. All I managed to squeeze out of him was that his wife's sister had taken custody of his kids after her death. He's still such a mystery—and it low-key drives me crazy. But I know what it's like to have your privacy stripped, so I don't push him like I used to.

It nearly broke my heart when he resigned as my bodyguard a year and a half ago. Even though he's head of my security and oversees certain events, Zeke accompanies me in public. Mason needs to stay out of the public eye because of his government history, and it makes sense.

We step inside the building and before I can head to the closet holding my spare clothes, I spot a figure in the waiting room ahead. Lyla catches me lingering and follows my stare.

"And who the hell is *that*?" she whispers. "Damn, he's fine."

Lyla needs a man for a night—or a better vibrator. Although yes, this man is fine as hell, I know exactly who he is and he's no one good. Still wearing my fitted, knee-length black dress and piggy slippers, I stomp over to the waiting room.

"What are you doing here?" I ask, then instantly bite my tongue as his eyes land on me. Dammit, he's even prettier in person.

He outstretches a hand. "Hi, I'm the new donor. I'll be shadowing for a bit. My name's—"

"I know who you are. Thank you, but we pass on your donation."

There's not a chance in hell we'll accept money from him. Not from a man whose company displaced thousands of families. Not from a man whose company destroys acres upon acres of land for mining.

I haven't found a single redeeming quality about Tristan Farrugia.

Okay, fine. He's a chiseled specimen of human perfection and it makes him so much more hate-able. His dark eyes are framed by unfairly long lashes and his skin is a smooth tawny shade. He's dressed impeccably in a white dress shirt and black slacks. But no amount of good looks can make me forget what Space Technologies has done. Just last month, I signed a public letter urging Maldana to raise the minimum wage. The company that lobbied against it? Space Tech.

He's the definition of a handsome devil.

"I'm afraid it's too late for that," Mr. Farrugia says.

"Excuse me?"

He watches me with pity and I want to slap the look off his face. More importantly, I need to know what the hell he's talking about. "Bridget! Where's Bridget?" I call, searching for the financial director. I turn down a hallway and head straight into her mind-numbingly bland office. "You did *not* accept a donation from Space Tech."

She rises from her seat, lips pursed. She really tried to sneak this by me. "I did. Our funds were quickly—"

"Does Dr. Pagoda know about it? Does the *queen*? Let's start there."

"Well, once the—"

"It's a yes or no question."

Her face hardens. "No."

I let out a harsh breath, flexing my hands to try to grasp this level of absurdity from a coworker. This was the *first* thing she was taught in this role. *The most important thing.*

"Every single penny donated to an official royalty project must go through the queen. Do you even understand the hypocrisy of a botanical garden accepting money from one of the world's worst polluters?"

Mr. Farrugia—whom I hadn't known followed me in here—steps into view with a halting hand. "Now, those statistics—"

"Back off!"

"Your Majesty!" Bridget exclaims, horrified that I spoke to a CEO like that. "Money doesn't grow on trees. We have to be realistic if we want to keep this place up and running."

I don't trust a single billionaire. *No one* can obtain that much money without stepping on the necks of others.

"This garden's existence hinges on our ethics. The queen has worked tirelessly to show this country we will not accept a penny of political donations or perceived political donations. You want to help our budget? Congratulations, you just increased it by eighty thousand a year."

She blanches. "I—Your Majesty, with all due respect, Dr. Pagoda—"

"We both know Dr. Pagoda doesn't bother with any of the garden's administrative work. Your things should be out of here by the end of the day."

CHAPTER TWO

TRISTAN

This is going worse than I thought it would.

The princess is a tree hugger; everyone knows that. I hadn't expected her to fire the finance director for trying to accept what she describes, verbatim, as "blood money" from my company. After she storms out of the office, I stupidly follow to argue our donation.

Truth is, Felicity Gardens is one of the few organizations that fits Grandfather's ridiculous terms.

"This is meant to be a private donation, Your Majesty."

"That doesn't matter," she calls over her shoulder.

I gnaw the inside of my cheek. "Technically, we're paying for a service."

Princess Maia stops in place, and if not for the dimly lit corridor, I'd be dragging my gaze down her lithe body. She stomps back over to me, hands planted on her hips. "And what service would that be?"

"Shadowing."

"For who?"

"Me."

Her brows lift, giving me a full view of her sparkly

brown eyes. "I'm sure you have better things to do with your time."

"That's true," I admit, "and I'm still here."

Her gaze narrows.

I open my mouth, then close it. With a shrug, I add, "Space Tech can stand to learn a few things about the environment."

"Space Tech can read a book." She steps even closer, her pig slippers nearly brushing against my dress shoes. Although I'd already known what she looks like, the pictures don't compare to what's in front of me. "I don't trust you or your donation. Felicity will have no part in whatever you're offering."

Her tone is filled with contempt and her eyes, which I had thought were sparkling, turn out to be embers building into fire. I intended to charm this donation through, but she torched me before I could speak. It doesn't make her button nose any less adorable nor is it easier to rip my gaze from her pouty lips. Bloody hell, I need to regroup.

I blink, steeling my shoulders. "I'll be in contact."

"No need," she says before storming off down another hallway.

I bite back a sigh. My ten-thirty meeting was canceled for nothing. Watching the princess of Maldana have a fit was entertaining, but I don't like being behind schedule.

My focus is nearly ruined for the day. The work is straightforward—an almost monotonous routine of checking reports and emails. The only highlight was reaming out one of my employees on their delayed and poorly written proposal.

With the potential of my inheritance being delayed again, I was irritable.

Celine passes along through our assistants that she will

handle the Felicity Gardens situation. She succeeded in paying off her volunteer hours for her part of the inheritance, but hers can't be released until mine is complete. But if there's one thing she's consistent with, it's her drive to trample over people. Being a good parent? Not so much. But I squashed my expectations of her before I turned double-digits.

All I can think about is the princess. She's crass, has virtually no professionalism, and all but told me to piss off when faced with a million-dollar donation. I respect her on the grounds that she's right to do so; my intentions are not pure of heart. Grandfather taught me to evaluate the consequences of any white lie or swindle. Felicity Gardens won't suffer. In fact, they'll be richer by the end of it. It's a mutually beneficial transaction.

I spent far too long scouring the internet to learn all about Maia last night. She and her older sister Nina—now Her Majesty the Queen—were born and raised in the United States until discovering their mother had been the late Queen Ophelia. I remember when it was first announced, mainly because Celine wanted me to get close to the future queen to expand Space Tech's influence. I shut it down, mistrustful of any plan she put forth.

Maia reads as more of a socialite than a princess. She may not have a reality show like the Kardashians, but younger generations hail her as *the* it-girl of today while the older refuse to take her seriously. She's elbowed the paparazzi in the face and her declarations regarding injustice are... strong. I already knew she wouldn't be open to Space Tech's donation, but I'd hoped to change her mind in person.

Felicity Gardens will get me what I need.

The only thing standing in the way is a self-righteous

hothead who would give any Victoria's Secret model a run for her money. Her long brown curls have hints of honey gold, the same shade as her skin.

Truth be told, it's easy to separate business and pleasure; any desire I need sated can be fulfilled the same night. But fuck, this will be harder than I thought.

My reverie snaps when the intercom on my desk buzzes. Augustus's distant voice says, "Ma'am, I will ask if—"

"He's my son and I'll see him now."

A moment later, my office door bursts open and Celine stomps inside.

"Have you seen our February stats in China? Production has dropped for the third month in a row."

"Good afternoon to you, too."

She crosses her arms, her blue eyes narrowing at me from the other side of my desk. "We're losing money."

"I'm meeting with the team in twenty minutes."

"Were you planning on telling anyone? This is something for the board to know."

"No."

Her face twitches in anger before she schools her features. "You're too soft with them. You believe every bloody excuse they give you when the entire division board needs to be replaced! Give them a choice. If they—"

"You are not important here, Celine!" I snap, exhausted by her presence. "*You* report to *me* and I have no obligation to include you. At this time, this is not a matter for the board. *And whenever that happens, I will make that decision.*"

Neither of us likes the fact that I'm my own mother's boss. But I stopped seeing her as my mother a long time ago. I was never her son, only a pawn in her ploy for dominance over everything she could get.

I'm not eager to fire a man my grandfather hand-picked for China's director. They'd known each other for decades. Celine doesn't think of that. She doesn't consider the importance of relationships in business. Grandfather taught me that having a few confidants—no more than three—prove to others that you're trustworthy. If no one is willing to walk through fire for you, even fewer people want to do business with you. Celine has no one but herself.

I'm pleased she was absent from my childhood. I saw her a few times a year; Grandfather raised me instead. To this day, I don't understand why he didn't cast her out of the company and our lives. She's done plenty of horrible things, starting with Danica. The worst one of all.

Ever since she told my father to take my younger sister and leave for reasons I still don't know, she would use my desire for a mum to encourage me to eavesdrop and steal from Grandfather. She wants power over everyone she meets. There isn't anything she won't do to negotiate the strongest deal, strive for the most money. It wouldn't be such a horrible thing if she weren't willing to trample over her family to do so.

Celine clenches her jaw. When her intimidation doesn't work, she turns to her final card. "Your grandfather never shut me out like this."

"Because he foolishly had hope that you care about anyone other than yourself."

"I care about this company—"

"You care about power," I sneer, leaning back in my chair. "If you'll excuse me, I have a meeting to prepare for. Shut the door on your way out."

CHAPTER THREE

MAIA

As soon as I step inside my house, thoughts of incompetent employees and stubborn billionaires vanish. Daisy and Poppy trot to the door with happy panting and tail wags—well, as much as Daisy's little stump will wag.

"My babies!"

After peppering me with love, they turn to Lyla, who walks in behind me. The foyer still smells like the coconut incense I burned yesterday.

"Where's my Sagey-boo?"

I find my three-legged feline on her cat tree, lying on one of the faux mushrooms. She exposes her belly in a deep stretch.

"How's my little monster?" I say in a squeaky voice as I give her scratchies and lift her into my arms. Her cat tree is designed to resemble a real tree, and her many perches look like artist conk mushrooms. I admit I went a little crazy when decorating my house, but that's what any twenty-something with an obscene amount of money would do.

I bought a dream: ten acres of land and had an 8,000

square-foot single floor house built using wood from the land and cob material. My house is fenced within an acre so my pets can roam safely, but I can take a short, scenic hike to my private lake.

I bought paradise to cope with the terrifying world.

I pepper Sage, short for Blood Sage, with kisses as I head to the back door.

"I'm gonna go check on the ducks," I call to Lyla.

"I'll get the popcorn!"

As I open the back door, my dogs come storming out from behind me. Poppy is sneaky and quick, but Daisy's big body nearly takes me out as Sage leaps from my arms, kicking my chest in the meantime. The commotion sends Elliot and Olivia into a fit of wild quacking.

I groan. "All I did was open a door."

I scoop up my ducks to shower them with kisses as well before tossing out their dinner. Esme, my friend, house-keeper, and overall helper, stops by nearly every day while I'm at the garden to let my animals roam free.

My crew is Poppy the Shiba Inu, Daisy the Rottweiler, Blood Sage the Somali cat, and Elliot and Olivia the Saxony ducks. I have yet to get a horse or two, but I'm still doing research.

Once the animals are taken care of, I head back inside to change into sweats and plop on the couch. Lyla appears behind me, a bowl of popcorn in one hand and an ice pack in the other.

I accept the ice pack with a grateful sigh. "You're the best."

Yesterday, my upper back was bothering me. Today, it's my lower. Who knows? Tomorrow, it could be my neck. Every day is a surprise. I don't like people to know about my condition, but I'm with Lyla so often that she was bound to notice.

Sage curls up in my friend's lap and Daisy hops onto her end of the couch. She has her own sofa, but the blanket-covered section of the couch is also dedicated to her.

Yes, I'm a dog lover, but that doesn't mean I have to sacrifice my couch's cleanliness. My dogs roll in dirt.

I try to get Poppy to cuddle with us, but she settles for chewing on her bone.

Partway through the movie both of us have watched a dozen times, I spot Lyla tapping away on her phone for the third time. She cringes at the screen.

"Who are you texting?" I ask with a snort.

"Some guy." She tosses her phone to the other end of the couch. "He's boring me, though."

He sounds new. "What happened to Marco? I liked him."

Lyla shrugs, fluffing up her wavy black hair. "He had a wife."

"A wife?" I screech.

She huffs. "I *know*. He had a small dick, anyway."

I wince. "Oh, not the small dick."

Lyla always has a man on her roster. You'd think it's from daddy issues, but her parents have been happily married for like forty years.

She's in a PhD program—the reason she started working at Felicity Gardens in the first place despite growing up in Ohio. I admire her energy to jump from man to man; I need at least a month of rest between each one.

"What happened with that sexy ass donor?" Lyla asks suddenly.

As soon as we'd arrived at the garden, she was whisked

away for a meeting. Our day got busy enough that we forgot about this morning.

"I told him to fuck off."

"Really?"

"Not exactly that. I fired Bridget, though."

"What?" she wails, snatching the remote to pause the movie. "You *fired* Bridget?"

"She tried to accept a donation from Space Technologies without talking to anyone."

Her jaw drops even more. "Not even your sister?"

"No!"

"What the hell is her problem? We'd lose all credibility!"

"That's what I'm saying!" My regret eases at the validation. I did the right thing, but it could have been handled better. Not the situation with Tristan Farrugia. If anything, I should have *actually* told him to fuck off. But I embarrassed Bridget, even though she made a colossal decision that anyone would have fired her for.

"And the guy tried to argue the donation in, too."

"Wait—the guy in the lobby? He's from Space Tech?"

I nod, stuffing my face with popcorn. "He runs it."

Lyla's eyes widen, but she quickly deflates with a groan. "But he's so hot."

"I know," I whine. "Such a shame."

She's exactly like me in our hatred of what we call the lazy rich. People who can do so much good with their money and choose not to every day.

Two years ago, Dad thought it would be a good idea to bring my sister and me to a Mediterranean island under the guise of a family vacation. Our birth mom, who died when I was a toddler, had been queen of said island—and we hadn't known a single thing about it. The monarchy was crumbling, and the Higher Court wanted us to save it. Instead of prolonging a system that oppresses its people, we decided to accept the crown only to properly dismantle it. We've reallocated funds, negotiated terms of our inherited estates, and started campaigns to encourage deeper change across the institution.

I gesture toward the remote, indicating to turn the movie back on. "Okay, enough about men. I want to see Sandy dance to *Get Low*."

"Maia, you can't just fire people like that," Nina chides from the other side of her couch.

"She would have tanked us and you know it."

"Obviously, but now she can run to the media and say the princess fired her effective immediately. It's bad press." She sighs, watching me pout with crossed arms like a child. "I know how protective you are of the garden. I'm about to meet with Mr. Farrugia and the board on Monday."

"When should I be there?"

My sister tenses and avoids eye contact. "I need to be impartial. Your blatant hatred isn't a good look for the institution."

"Wha—" I cut myself off, the argument dying on my tongue. The board of Felicity Gardens will be there, and even though I'm technically a co-founder, I'd go in guns blazing.

I've had plenty of mishaps with the media, including assault charges. But hey, if the guy didn't want to be elbowed in the nose, he shouldn't have grabbed me. At the end of the day, it was more a bad look for Nina than me. It may have been my case, but *her* approval ratings went down. She was never angry with me, only concerned about how I was dealing with the press calling me a nightmare in ten different ways.

I became the object of their criticism. Nina does the heavy lifting of meetings, tours, and handling the estates. They compared me to her and brushed over my work on implementing environmentally sustainable architecture in Kosita. The family homes we repaired originated centuries ago. We preserved tradition and history for families who were trampled over by capitalism.

Everyone was paying attention to me, but not a single person truly saw me. They focused on my nights out, on who I was dating. Nothing that really mattered.

I finally had the sense to leave the city for Tropoli, a mountainous village with olive trees splattered every- where. It's not far from Felicity Gardens and it's even closer to Nina.

"Just—keep that guy away from the garden, *please*," I say. There's no good way to be a billionaire. Becoming rich only made me realize how *easy* it is to be a better person. Morals cost money. The way the ultra-rich hoard money is straight-up depravity and any association with Space Tech- nologies will reflect poorly on us.

"I know, but he requested a meeting and it would be rude to decline."

I grunt, but I can't get too annoyed. With anyone else, I'd tell them they're only accepting the meeting because he's rich, but Nina would accept a sit-down with anyone. Because that's my sister. Perfect. The gift that keeps on giving. People expect me to fuck up, and I'm not sure what's worse: the world expecting you to be perfect or expecting you to fail.

Similar to my day with Lyla yesterday, my sister and I

started to watch a movie, but paused at a random point and began chatting. Nina's house is like being in the Swiss Alps with a Mediterranean view. The floor-to-ceiling windows reveal the sea dotted with rock formations. It's cozy and luxurious with a lot of stone accents, unlike my plant-infested house.

Wesley appears behind the couch and leans over Nina, kissing her cheek and then nuzzling his face in her neck. I cringe.

"You're not alone," I remind them.

He ignores me and asks, "Want me to make you some tea?"

"Yes, please."

He plants another kiss on her temple before heading to the kitchen. My sister looks at me. "Do you want anything?"

"Ice cream," I say instantly.

Nina glances toward Wesley's retreating frame and calls, "Babe—"

He cuts her off with a small wave of his hand, saying, "I got it."

Once he enters the kitchen, I turn to my glowing sister. "How's married life going?"

"It doesn't feel that much different."

"He's still being good to you, I hope." Their fairytale wedding was less than a year ago and even though it was very private, it was all the country—and most of Europe—could talk about.

Nina snorts. "One thing you never have to worry about is whether Wesley is being good to me. Everything is perfect."

My heart squeezes as a grin spreads across my face. He's still the brooding grump from our first summer in Maldana. In the beginning, I pitied her for being assigned a bodyguard who looks like he'd murder you in your sleep. And since he's a former hitman, he's probably done it. But with Nina, he's just quiet, obsessed with Daisy, and dotes over my sister. In a way, it's like he's never stopped being her bodyguard.

She has her tea and I have my ice cream and my brother-in-law sits at one end of the U-shaped couch as we chat.

"I got you something!" Nina exclaims, reaching under the coffee table.

I drop my spoon into my now-empty bowl and set it on the table. "Aw, what for? My birthday isn't for another few weeks."

She doesn't respond and instead hands me a perfectly wrapped box. Her gift wrapping has always been impeccable and I'm scared to rip her handiwork. Once I unravel it, I lift the top to reveal a—baby onesie? It reads *I love Auntie Maia* and I instantly drop the box with a gasp. Her anxious smile greets me.

"Are you serious?" I ask, tears already springing to my eyes.

She nods. "Yup. Three weeks."

My big sister is pregnant. She's gonna be a *mom*. *I'm going to be an aunt!* I dive across the couch to capture her in a bear hug as the ugly sobbing breaks out in full force.

Nina singlehandedly raised me. Dad worked the majority of our childhoods and his few present moments were either drunk or complaining he had somewhere else to be. My sister did everything—down to cooking dinner every night and stealing Dad's credit card to pay the bills.

And now she's going to have a baby of her own.

Her chest vibrates with gentle laughter as I cling to her, still crying, while she pats my back.

"Maia," she coos.

"You're going to be the world's best mom," I say, sitting up and wiping at my cheeks. "Speaking from experience. And you're not gonna do this alone like you did growing up. I'm gonna help you."

Nina grins and laughs, taking my shoulders in her hands. "Did you forget I'm married?"

I jolt, turning to my eerily quiet brother-in-law who chuckles when I look at him. "Holy shit! You're so freaking quiet I forgot you were there!" I hop up from the couch and bear hug him, too. "Congratulations, oh my god. This is the best news ever!"

With the way Wesley protects and cares for my sister, I know there's no one better to be a parent with her. I feel safe knowing that, even though they're already married, he's linked to my family forever.

After I'm done crying my eyes out, we—*I*—have more ice cream to celebrate. She understandably doesn't want anyone to know she's pregnant for as long as possible. Numerous times throughout the conversation, I cry again. On one hand, it still feels like both of us are way too young to even consider kids, but she's genuinely excited, and with the way she and Wesley keep looking at each other, I know it's because of *who* she's having a baby with.

I've never been a huge fan of kids. In increments, sure. And toddlers, not babies. Every baby I've held started wailing the moment I carried it in my arms.

The thought of loving someone enough to have a baby with them is chilling. I'm not one for serious relationships —mostly because of how picky I am. Most men are useful for a limited time, and I'm happy to be cool Auntie Maia.

CHAPTER FOUR
TRISTAN

I flick on my jazz playlist before changing into sweats. Saxophone melodies fill my warehouse studio. The floor-to-ceiling windows display the orange sunset blanketing the city. It's only five o'clock, but daylight saving time ends later this month. I certainly don't miss the England weather.

Fridays are the only day of the week I leave the office with the sun still in the sky. If I don't, nothing will get done. I trust the advisors and division leaders, but they lack the initiative I'd like them to have.

Nonetheless, Friday evenings are typically reserved for sculpting. I prepare the clay and examine where I left off on this hand sculpture.

The base of the sculpture is already completed, letting me focus on the details. It's roughly the size of my torso, with two hands curved around each other as the base spreads out like tree roots. I add glue to the clay mixture for strength and lose myself in the details. The only time I stop is to turn on the lights once the sun fully sets.

I stretch out my fingers and back, and before I can continue, my phone rings. I hit answer and put my oldest friend on speaker as I get back to work.

"Hey, mate. It's been a while," I say.

"Hey, yeah, been busy," Romèo replies. "You in London for that conference yet? I'm out here on business."

I scrape the angled edge of the tool along the sculpture's knuckle for more definition. I've been redoing it for the last half hour. "Nah, that's not for another month or so."

"Then how about I fly to you for the weekend?"

"Yeah, it's been a while since I hit up a club."

"Great, I'll give a ring when I land," he says and hangs up without so much as a goodbye. But that's how Romèo works. I've known him since grade school in London and he's my closest friend, even though he has a whole other life. It's been nearly twenty years and I've never met his family. It's not like they're estranged; most of the Amantes lives on a Sicilian compound with their riches from their chain of restaurants.

It may have been almost a year since I last saw him, but he'd disappeared at one point. Thirteen years ago, out of the blue, he sent me an email saying he had to return to Sicily.

And then I didn't hear from him for four years.

When he resurfaced with a phone call, it was like nothing happened. We've been distant since then, only meeting up two, maybe three, times a year.

I've lived in London most of my life. It wasn't until Grandfather's health declined that he moved home to Maldana for his final years. Our operations shifted to the capital, Kosita, during that time, and I just never left. It's been two years since his death and five years since I've been in London longer than a week.

Once Romèo's jet lands from England, we meet at the Lynx Room, one of the few clubs I like in the city. Phones aren't allowed and anyone who attends must be previously approved by a committee. We can bring guests, but they can be turned away at the discretion of staff and must relinquish any cameras or devices. Privacy is their most important policy.

I'd rather be sculpting than here, but I try to enjoy myself. I don't enjoy being around people. There's nothing wrong with a work event; it's easy to snap on the business version of myself. Afterward? I try to speak to no one. I can go hours without saying a single word. Typically, the only person to speak to me outside of work hours is Augustus. And now Romèo. I'm glad, though. It's enough to sustain me. I've never been one to have many friends and I don't plan on changing that.

Every time I consider it, I think of Danica, though she was my sister and not my friend. *Is* my sister—if she's still alive. The two of us were close as children. We had our own secret handshake.

Before I spiral down memory lane, I turn to Romèo as we lower into armchairs in The Lounge. Music thumps from the room on the other side of the wall—The Bar. Another thing I like about the Lynx Room is that there are two separate rooms so we can hear ourselves think.

I nod to the glass in his hand. "Wine, mate? Seriously?"

Romèo shakes his head. "Don't let hubris get in the way of a good drink."

I laugh and toss back another sip of bourbon. He may be a bachelor wherever he goes, but to me, he's the geeky kid I grew up with. He reads *a lot*. Anything and everything and it's quite annoying, really. He's laidback but brushes off everyone. He has a rudeness that no one really likes.

After he resurfaced those years ago, I almost didn't recognize him with his sleeves of tattoos. He never seemed the type. By now, more tattoos snake up his neck and down his hands but most of them are covered by long-sleeved shirts he constantly wears, even in the height of summer.

"How've you been?" Romèo asks. "We haven't hung out in ages."

"It feels like forever," I agree. "But all I do is work. I'm afraid I've no news to share."

"You still sculpt?"

I jerk my head back. I habitually hide my interest in sculpting since Grandfather thought it was a waste of time. I didn't start taking it seriously until around the time Romèo dropped out of my life.

"I told you about that?"

Romèo laughs, sipping his drink. "Last time we were here. You were shitfaced, but you went into great detail about wanting to sculpt the perfect pussy."

I bust out laughing at the memory slamming back into me at full force. Yes, I remember that and yes, I'm slightly embarrassed about it. I drag my hands down my face. "Fuck. I did, didn't I? But yeah I still sculpt. Never did create that, though... You still in the restaurant business?" I ask, eager to change the subject.

He lifts a shoulder. "Yeah, nothing's changed on that front."

"Has your family considered expanding locations to other countries?"

"No," he says fiercely. "We only help Italian economies."

I snort. "Says the bloke who went to school in England."

He doesn't reply, and after we chat about the Italian economy, we move from The Lounge to The Bar.

The techno music thumps so hard I feel it in my chest. It doesn't take long for Romèo to find a woman to take to the dance floor, but I find a seat. I'm not in the mood for dancing. I thought coming out tonight would give me a boost; all I feel like doing is going home.

I notice a woman staring at me. She's attractive enough to hold my attention: long, dark hair, olive skin, and a skintight blue dress. She saunters her way over and I shamelessly let my gaze wander down her body.

My life is busy and I have no time to waste; humans are machines and have requirements for certain outcomes, and my needs for sex are simple.

For me to consider fucking a woman, she should have manners, curves, and respectable clothing—respectable enough that nothing pops out with the wrong angle. I quite frankly don't care what color skin or hair she has, but this woman meets all of my requirements.

"Is this seat taken?" she asks in Maldanian, pointing to the spot I saved for Romèo. I set my drink aside and pat my knee. Her eyes light up.

"You're not even going to ask my name?"

"I figured *the breathtaking one* would suffice."

She smiles and takes the seat on my lap. I settle one hand on the small of her back, the other brushing her raven hair over her shoulder to expose her pale skin.

"What's your name, beautiful?"

"Elena." She stares down at me with a smirk playing on her red-painted lips. Her hand runs up my chest, and I can appreciate her brazenness matching my own. But there's something off. On an average night, I'd be planning on seducing her into my bed. Even as I grip her tight, even as she shifts her plump arse on my lap, my dick barely twitches.

"Elena," I echo slowly, tracing the hem of her dress, "what do you want to happen tonight?"

"I want to know if it's true," she purrs.

"If what's true?"

Her hand runs up my thigh and she hooks a finger over my waistband. She leans in close, her lips brushing my earlobe. I keep waiting to get hard; nothing happens. The fuck is wrong with me? I'm not even thirty. Way too young for ED.

"My friend says that African men are the biggest."

Any wisp of desire I had for this woman burns away within a second. While there's much less racism in Maldana than England, it's inescapable. Not that it matters, but I've never even been to any African country before.

Elena is my final straw, my final excuse to get the hell out of here.

I grip her by the waist and lift her off me with ease. "Find someone else."

She balks. "What? Is it false?"

"You won't be finding out from me."

"If you have a tiny penis, just say so." Elena flips her hair over her shoulder as she fixes her dress.

A wicked, amused smile pulls at my lips. I rise from my seat into my full six-foot-four size, and the woman in front of me stumbles back. My looming frame speaks enough as I leave her behind. I pull out my phone to shoot Romèo a text.

> Headed out.

> Breakfast before I leave tomorrow?

Done. Name a time and I'm there.

TBD

I suppose it depends on how it goes tonight with whatever woman he found. It's a good thing I'm the boss and can rearrange any meeting, but I'm grateful to finally be going home.

CHAPTER FIVE
MAIA

Despite my protests until I'm nearly blue in the face, both my sister and Dr. Pagoda decided to let Mr. Farrugia—Tristan—volunteer here.

Apparently, there's an initiative for Space Technologies to become more eco-conscious, and the way to do that is to take it to the highest chain of command: CEO.

It doesn't make any sense. Nina and Dr. Pagoda are convinced that he genuinely wants to learn about the environment, and I'm convinced he sweet-talked both of them.

I frown at Dr. Pagoda over my salad bowl. She may insist on calling me Your Majesty, but she never lets me forget who's in charge. She's my mentor and I trust her knowledge and skills. She has my respect and earned every ounce of it.

It doesn't mean I don't complain.

"I can't believe you're okay with this."

She grins. Her accent is heavy and thick when she says, "Me and Her Majesty the Queen discussed it with Mr. Farrugia and his mother—"

"His *mother*?" I spit. "Why would she be there?"

"She leads the European side of the company."

"It doesn't make any sense," I repeat for the twentieth time today. "It's clear *I* don't like him—why would he keep trying to convince you guys?"

"The best way to learn is by someone who will not lie to you. Here at Felicity, we won't lie." She gestures toward me. "And it's good for you. You learn to behave."

I grunt, stabbing at my salad. "I can't make any promises."

Dr. Pagoda laughs as she pushes herself to her feet, huffing out a cough in the meantime. She pats me on the back like a pet. "Trust me. This is good. He will be with you during your fieldwork today."

I roll my eyes once her back is to me. There's not a chance in hell I won't end up telling Tristan Farrugia exactly what I think of him and his billions. If he really wanted to learn, he would read a book. He'd hire experts to do the work for him. Yet over the next five months, he's carving out half a workday each week to be here. *Why?*

It. Doesn't. Make. Sense.

Community service, maybe? There's more to it. I know there is. I'm not sure I care to find out, I want to protect Felicity Gardens. Associating with him would make us look hypocritical. It wouldn't just hurt my career—it'd hurt Nina's.

At least my sister had the sense to require an NDA and that his time be confined to private sections to avoid public sightings.

I sling my messenger bag over my shoulder and head to the east side of the surrounding woods. Felicity Gardens is only a year old, and even though most of our records come from universities and Tropoli's archives, we still don't have all of the data. I've been exploring, sampling, and researching the grounds to best improve the region.

The garden is my second home. One of our public greenhouses has a pond with huge lily pads and a fairy fountain. Flagstone paths wind around the property, and the one that leads to the woods is lined with boulders every few feet.

My stomach fills with dread at the sight of Tristan waiting before the steps that lead up the hill and into the woods. There's absolutely no reason he needs to look this fine right now. His white button-up reveals just enough of his brown chest and tattoo of vines on his collarbone. Every part of him is so refined and trimmed yet he's still effortlessly handsome. Big hands, modest watch. It makes me hate him so much more.

"Do you prefer Your Majesty or Maia?" he asks, and fuck, his deep voice sounds ten times sexier with his British accent.

I prefer you jump off a cliff.

I bite the inside of my cheek. Dr. Pagoda wouldn't be happy if I said that, so I'll have to be somewhat civil. I need to set an alarm to remind me to cuss out Nina for letting this happen.

"Maia is fine," I bite out, heading up the stairs to enter the woods. I hear him behind me, and on instinct, I whirl around. "Just so we're clear, I don't want you here—"

"Believe me, I know." He may be looking up at me, but he still has a smug face that pisses me off. I hate the ultra-rich. They're too cocky and need to be humbled. Hopefully my boss will forgive what I'm about to say—assuming Tristan is a snitch. He looks like one.

"You might have convinced my sister and the board

that you actually give a shit about the environment, but not me. I don't trust a damn thing you say. You're a greedy pig."

Unsurprisingly, Tristan doesn't flinch. His smugness is gone, but he doesn't back down. "What have I ever done to you to warrant your hatred?"

I cross my arms. "Consider my hatred on behalf of the earth."

"Space Tech's carbon footprint dropped nearly forty percent over the last three years."

"While electronic waste rose by *twenty-five* percent in that same time frame."

"These things take time, and we're trying for the best methods."

I scoff. "Those methods are available, you're just not using them because you're picking profit over the environment."

"The earth was hit by a meteor and survived! Whether I listen to a couple tree huggers won't change the fate of the universe."

There it is. I toss my hands in the air. "Maybe try hugging a fucking tree for once!"

He glares at me. "Real mature."

It's not about the earth's survival. He's right about that. Species that cannot keep up with the ecosystem will die out, and we as humans are digging our own grave by damaging the ecosystems essential to our survival. But then he called people like me, Lyla, and Dr. Pagoda tree huggers, which diminishes all of the research we do. So yeah, my temper snapped.

"If you're not concerned about the earth then why are you fucking here?"

"You curse too much," he points out.

"You exist too much."

He whistles. "The tabloids are right. You *are* toxic to work with."

I fall silent, my stomach caving. The last thing I need is a reminder of how the media paints me. He struck a nerve and I don't care if he knows it. I shove his shoulder aside to make room.

"I'm not doing this," I say, heading down the steps and back the way I came. "I'm telling Dr. Pagoda that she'll have to fire me before I can work with you."

"Wait—" He bites back a groan and walks toward me. "I'm sorry. I really am here to learn about the environment. Specifically through an unfiltered lens." He extends his hand. "Truce?"

I barely suppress the roll of my eyes. It doesn't change the truth that he's a greedy billionaire who lied to slither his way into the garden—I may not know why, but my gut tells me to dig.

Throwing a tantrum would only make those tabloids true, and though I'm not letting up on my hatred of everything Tristan stands for, I'm tired of being the trouble-maker. Sure, it's important to ruffle feathers in order to make change. But I've been told to be more agreeable my entire life.

I knock his extended hand aside and return toward the stairs. "Whatever. Just don't distract me."

Tristan doesn't say a single word as I work, but it doesn't stop him from distracting me. It's nothing specific; it's his presence. It doesn't matter that I'm five-foot-eleven; he's still much taller and broader, completely shadowing me whenever he's near.

It's infuriating.

I unfold a copy of the decades-old map from the town archives and do my best to pinpoint where I am. I search around for markings such as an old oak tree, but I can't even find that.

"What are you looking for?" Tristan asks, his deep voice cutting me. I can't hide my surprised flinch.

"Didn't I tell you not to distract me?"

"I can help."

"You can't," I bite. "So stop talking."

After a little bit of wandering, I finally spot the mark and work my way out. Without previous field notes, there's no way to tell specific ways the ecosystem changed. Trees are just starting to bud, the cold is beginning to break, and the air shifts in a way that only happens in springtime.

If I didn't have a stupid billionaire whose company is responsible for so much pollution, I'd be able to appreciate the moment more.

I unpack my bag and use rocks on each corner of the map to keep it down. When I lay out my small blanket, I'm pleased that Tristan doesn't take it as an invitation to sit beside me. There's no room, anyway. I start jotting observation notes from the conditions of the forest floor, how much lichen is on the trees, what kinds of birds frequent the area, and the bugs I spot.

I wander the area, taking more notes, and spot the horribly beautiful English ivy. People marvel at the vines that wrap around trees, but they choke the life out of everything they touch. After taking the note, I return to my bag and take out my gloves and pocket knife.

It's awkward to have him watch as I slice through the stubborn vines wrapping the hemlock tree.

"What is that?" he asks, standing beside the oak tree,

hands in pockets. He looks entirely out of place. I'm wearing work pants and a Felicity Garden hoodie, and he's dressed, well... rich.

"English ivy."

"Why are we taking it down?"

I drag a scowl up and down his face. "*We? Lower your expectations." I return my focus to the task. "It's invasive. It'll spread and choke the life out of everything else here."

"There has to be a machine that can tear all this down."

I snort. "We grow a lot of things here; money is not one of them."

The worst part about hand-cutting the vines is that they're a lot stronger than they look. I spend five minutes just trying to slice one part from the trunk. I huff, trying to drag it upward to separate it from the tree. I step back for a break and Tristan takes the opportunity to butt in.

"Here, let me."

"Hey—"

He grabs the hilt of my knife and pushes up. In a couple of efforts, he's sliced through enough roots for him to pull. His sleeves are rolled to his elbows to reveal a few tattoos on one forearm. But damn, his veins are enough to look at. I bite my tongue as he suppresses a grunt with each yank.

No. Don't forget he's a greedy pig.

I didn't think a pig would be sexy, but to each their own. He can only manage a couple more feet above until it's too high and we'll need scaffolding. He backs up and dusts off his hands. One vine yanked, many more to go.

I pat his shoulder condescendingly. "Doesn't even scratch the surface of all the shit your company has done, but it's a start."

He sighs, and the sound pleases me. I hope I piss him off enough to quit.

My phone buzzes in my back pocket and I scoff at the name. Why is everyone bothering me today? Am I getting my period or am I just being a natural bitch? I decline the call as we head back to my supplies.

Halfway there, it rings again.

I bite the inside of my cheek to stifle a grunt. He won't give up.

"Hello?" I say, my tone clipped. I put distance between Tristan and me because there's no reason for him to listen to anything regarding my personal life.

"Hey," Diego replies. "Everything good?"

I can't hide my exasperation. As if I'm the one constantly calling *him*.

"You called *me*. What's up?"

"I haven't heard from you in a while. I miss you."

"I already told you we're not going any further."

"But we had a lot of fun together—we *have* fun together. Why end a good thing?"

"Because you're an asshole."

While yes, we had fun when we hung out and had great sexual chemistry, he's been thoughtless our entire situationship. At some point, I felt like a straight-up booty call. I never really wanted to be in a relationship with him, but the longer I kept it going, the less respect I had for myself.

"Okay, that's harsh—"

I roll my eyes and hang up. He's abandoned me multiple times in my time of need. I don't feel bad about hanging up on him.

Despite the distance I attempted to put between Tristan and me, he asks, "Boyfriend?"

I glare at him as I lower onto my blanket. "Just someone poking their nose where they don't belong."

CHAPTER SIX
TRISTAN

Frustration.

All I feel is frustration. Every kind of it.

The princess detests my very existence and I don't know how to win her over. All I need is to get through these volunteer hours and I can move on. But I'm far too frustrated to do anything but lean into her arguments and make comments that get her riled up. It pleases me more than it should.

After my failed conquest at the Lynx Room, I called Valentina. She's not an escort, per se, but after our encounters, she asks for a few things I'm happy to provide. Debts, tuition, a new outfit from Gucci. The sex is good enough that I'd buy her a car if she asked.

But none of that mattered.

Minutes after Valentina arrived, she left. I tried kissing her, gripping her, touching her—all with eager consent—but it did nothing for me. *She* did nothing for me. I gave her gas money for her time and spent the rest of my night at the studio wondering if I have erectile dysfunction.

All of my questions are answered when I pull into the parking lot at Felicity Gardens on Tuesday morning.

It's unusually warm for April today, and Maia's taking advantage of it by wearing shorts. They're high-waisted and even a little baggy, but her long, slender legs remove any previous worries that I have ED. She's still the princess—and I ought to be more respectful. But *how?* Her skin is literally glowing. How can I not crave it? Maia stands in the sun, talking to a care team as they replant the landscape in front of the research building.

I start rearranging the stuff in my center console to distract my growing erection. The source of my frustration is standing twenty feet away, and I have a feeling it's only going to get harder. Literally.

When I'm composed enough to step into the sun, I spot Maia staring at my car with her face cinched.

"If you're nice to me today," I tell her, "maybe I'll take you for a ride."

She blinks, a scowl replacing her curiosity. "Why would I do that?"

"Be nice to me or ride in my Lambo?"

"Both."

"You were staring at it."

She rolls her eyes and starts walking off. "If I want to ride in a Lamborghini, I'd get my own. But I don't want a car that looks like it was squashed by a giant foot."

I clench my jaw at her rosy scent wafting before me as she passes. "Always a pleasure, Your Majesty."

She shows me little interest throughout the day, and in spite of my little remarks, she doesn't rise to the bait. Not like she did last week.

So by the time next week comes around, I have a new method to get her attention.

I pull into the same parking spot as before and kill the engine of my new Maserati MC20. My stomach lurches in anticipation when I see Maia waiting with her hip cocked and a notebook pressed against her chest. Her brows lift when I open one of the butterfly doors.

"What the hell is that?" she asks.

"A Maserati. Were you waiting for me?"

"What happened to your Lambo? Did your girlfriend crash it for not buying her a fourth mansion?"

"I figured I'd upgrade for you." *But it's good to know she's fishing about whether I have a girlfriend.* "Now, my question."

She tilts her head. "You bought a new car to impress me?"

"No," I lie, "I've had this for a couple of years."

"That's ridiculous."

"You're telling me you don't find this cool?" I reach up to close the door before sauntering over to her, and she sizes me up with assumption and judgment in her earthy brown eyes.

"So you *did* get this to impress me."

"I told you—I've already owned this. And you still haven't answered my question. Were. You. Waiting for me?"

"How many cars do you own?" She looks up at me, and I think it might be the first somewhat civil question she's asked me.

"Six," I reply.

"That's—what? A million's worth?"

I consider for a moment. With my new one costing almost five hundred thousand—having to pay extra to get it on short notice—one mil is too low. And the reality of spending half a million euros to impress a woman dawns on me. I suppose I'm that desperate for her attention, and I'm not sure that bothers me.

"Closer to two," I admit.

She scoffs and heads inside with me trailing behind her. "Two million spent on cars doesn't impress me when the same amount could put thousands through college."

"The great thing about being a billionaire is I could do both."

She waves a hand over her shoulder. "Then do it."

"Who says I haven't already?"

"I believe actions, not words, pretty boy. And yes, I was waiting for you." She turns and slaps the notebook into my chest. "Dr. Pagoda wants you to start taking notes to track your progress."

My stomach lurches again. This time, at her new nickname. "Pretty boy, huh? What happened to rich boy?"

And again, she rolls her eyes, though she doesn't reply.

Maia actively ignores me most of the time. If she's not insulting me, she's doing her best to act like I'm not there. It's adorable, really. She'll make a comment—something not in the spot it should be or another grievance—all in a manner that doesn't indicate she's thinking out loud. She still blames me for forgetting she's supposed to ignore me. After sending a scowl my way, it's another twenty minutes of silence.

I don't mind, though. I watch her water plants and take notes. I never thought those two things would even be remotely interesting, but there's something about the sight that makes it impossible to look away. Something about the way her golden brown curls fall down her back, the way that crease between her brows eases, the way I finally notice how she has doe eyes because she's so often glaring at me.

I follow her around one of the smaller greenhouses

dotted around the property. On the right side, there are dozens of tiny potted plants. Most of them have sprouted green seedlings; some are wilted, fully bloomed, or not bloomed at all.

"What kind of plant is this?" I ask, reaching toward the alien-shaped flower.

Maia whacks my hand away. "Don't touch it." She points to a little plaque listing the name.

"Barbaric-ee-nah—"

"Barbaricina columbine," she says fluidly.

"And all of these are barbar—*that*."

"You catch on quick, huh?" She catches my glare and quickly deflates. "They're endemic to Sardinia, but thanks to habitat loss, they're critically endangered. So we care for and propagate as many as we can hold."

"To do what with?"

She huffs, and I can't tell if her agitation is with me or Italy. "We're *trying* to work with the Italian government to invest in restoring some of their habitat, but they won't cooperate. They'd have to enforce laws to limit overgrazing and over-collecting and they're not happy about that. So, we grow what we can here and try to propagate the strongest ones. Eventually, we'll try to integrate them into the habitat here."

"What do they do?"

"What do you mean?"

"Is it edible, medicinal...? If they don't offer anything, then why are you trying to keep it alive?"

"Believe it or not, people invest time and energy and money into things that don't provide monetary value."

That's the opposite of what I've been taught. Grandfather told me multiple times that if something wasn't working toward my success, it was working toward my demise—that stagnant men go nowhere. My instinct is to discover its purpose.

"They're not in any displays or being sold in pots or something. It just doesn't seem wise."

"And that is exactly why we won't accept donations or funding from people like you," she says. "It's not up to you or any other rich asshole to determine what we care for and conserve in the name of monetization."

"I—"

"Felicity Gardens is not a store. We are not a business—"

"Okay, I—"

"We don't do what we do in the hopes someone will buy it. We do important shit because it matters and not because—"

"*Maia!*" I snap. If she would get off her soapbox, she'd know that I'm trying to *concede*. And she would love that, but she can't get out of her own way.

"Hey, you're the one who started asking all these questions and wanted to volunteer here in the first place which, mind you, is still not lining up with how critical you are of everything we do here."

At this point, there's nothing to do but sit there and take it. I like watching the fire in her eyes as she demands the validity of her beliefs. And I'm the only person she does this with. I've seen her with her friend Lyla and Dr. Pagoda. She doesn't always agree with them, and she often concedes to their preferences.

With me?

It's like Maia would rather die than agree with me.

Felicity Gardens is my best option for getting me what I

need, but this is only my third time here. I thought I could handle the arguments I knew were coming, but she doesn't pull her punches even a little bit. And I still have way over two hundred hours more to do.

I'm going to lose my mind.

CHAPTER SEVEN

TRISTAN

The following week isn't any easier.

It's nearing the middle of April and Felicity Gardens is getting way more visitors now that flowers are being planted and beginning to bloom. Not that it matters since I'm forbidden from being around the public while I'm volunteering.

In spite of the happier weather, the princess still keeps her attitude. I'm quite impressed with how strong it remains. Halfway into my shift, we find ourselves in the break room for a snack. Maia chats with Lyla across the room and I sit at the dining table as I type away on my phone, sending emails.

Maia rises and crosses the room, appearing to clean and tidy the area, but I sense her underlying tension. Her body is taut and her movements are slow. I don't say anything, although I'm enjoying the view of her bending over to put items under the cupboard.

Eventually, she turns to me with a narrowed gaze. "I'm going to try this again. What are you *really* doing here?"

"Physically or existentially?"

She's unamused by my attempt at a joke. "At Felicity Gardens."

"It's already been establish—"

"The *real* reason. Not the one you gave my sister."

"I am here to volunteer and learn for our eco initiatives," I lie. "I have influence among others of my standing; I can inspire them better if I have a hands-on experience that helps my understanding of conservation efforts."

Across the break room, Maia and Lyla look at each other incredulously, but it's the princess who looks pissed. "Inspire others of your standing," she echoes, folding her arms across her chest. "You think you're inspiring?"

I square my shoulders, bracing for what I know is about to happen. "Occasionally."

"So, your granddaddy gave you a billion-dollar corporation that *he* started and *you* think you're inspiring?" Maia leans against the counter and drags her gaze up and down my body from my seat. "You are not self-made."

"Enlighten me, then. What am I?"

"Exactly like the rest. Entitled, greedy, and undeserving."

I flinch in surprise. "Undeserving? That's bold for someone who inherited an entire country."

"I didn't inherit a country, you twat. My sister is dismantling an institution because she, nor I, could stomach what it does to its people."

Twat? Agitation flares inside me. I clench my jaw to withhold any regretful remark. "Bravo, love." I clap slowly, fighting the roll of my eyes. "You're so much better than the rest of us."

"I'm so glad you finally noticed," she quips. "And don't call me *love*."

"It's ironic that you act as though you're not rich. You have more privilege than most of the world."

"I *am* rich. I just don't fit your idea of a rich person because I don't hoard it the way you do."

"You barely know me!" I snap, rising to my full height. "I am not hoarding money."

With every bullet-like argument, we step closer to one another.

"Bullshit! I know you have more money than you know what to do with. Meanwhile there's, what? Two dozen countries suffering from famine?"

"No one is stopping *you* from hopping on a plane and solving—"

"This isn't about me. *I'm* not the billionaire."

"Am I sensing jealousy?"

She scoffs loudly, her eyes sending daggers straight through me. "You know what? Yes. I'm jealous of the options your wealth gives you and I'm *disgusted* by what you don't do with it."

"My god, do you have *any* manners? I don't understand how you've made it thus far in your professional life by speaking—"

"What, the truth?"

"We've had a handful of conversations and you've"—I begin counting on my fingers—"cursed at me, yelled at me, called me entitled, greedy, undeserving, and a twat."

As if proud, Maia tosses her head and plants a hand on her hip. "Would you like to hear more?"

"You're vulgar. I don't take advice from vulgar women."

She releases a sharp breath. "Careful; you're about to add *misogynistic prick* to that list."

"Would you like to hear *your* list of descriptions? The first is *self-righteous hypocrite*."

Maia gasps, and my chest constricts at the hurt flashing across her eyes, but it's quickly replaced with fury. She opens her mouth to argue—

"Enough!" Lyla barks. "Holy shit. You two need to either fuck or shut the fuck up because you're driving me *crazy!*" She bites out the last word, making to rip out her hair as she hops off the stool and marches out of the break room, salad in hand.

Maia and I don't look at each other. I turn away, my face heating. It's not that I haven't thought about it; I don't want to see what I'm sure is her disgusted expression.

I return to the table to retrieve my phone. There's nothing I can say that will please her—nothing that will make this relationship easier. She would hate me even if I won an award for Nicest Man on the Planet. Although I wouldn't even make the cut.

Rather than returning to my emails, I send Romèo a text about going to the Lynx Room again. I need another night out. Another chance to eradicate traces of Maia from my desires.

CHAPTER EIGHT
TRISTAN

My only friend is too busy to catch a jet to Maldana this week. Instead, Augustus finds out that one of our executives is having a yacht party. Rob something. I feign just enough interest to attend, and Rob appears ecstatic to have befriended the boss.

The yacht is modest to my standards and the Friday night crowd is just enough to get lost in.

"Mr. Farrugia," Rob greets, extending a hand with a shit-eating grin. "Glad you could join us."

"Thank you for having me."

He introduces me to a slew of his friends who are no doubt moguls in their own fields. Their names don't stick longer than a few minutes and I manage to slip away to the bar for a drink. The yacht floats around Kosita Bay, the cityscape a myriad of lights against the dark sky.

At the bar, I find myself in conversation with a hedge fund manager who confesses his admiration for my grandfather. It takes me fifteen minutes to break away and reach the edge. I watch the water below lap against the side of the boat. This is much harder when you don't know anyone. My wealth means it's easy to find people willing to have a conversation. Annoyingly enough, it's more power-hungry men than horny women.

And blissfully, beautifully, the universe answers my prayers.

"That was brutal."

A woman appears to my left, her face sweet and her chest huge. The red dress she wears doesn't reveal enough for her tits to fall out, but it's tight enough to show just how big of a rack she has.

"What was?" I ask.

"That conversation with DJ."

"Who's DJ?"

She laughs. "The hedge fund guy you were just talking to." Without asking, she slides right beside me and leans her arms against the railing. "I could see you were uncomfortable."

I shrug. "I was being polite."

"I don't see you at a lot of Rob's parties."

"I didn't know Rob had a lot of parties."

She snickers and even rolls her eyes at my ignorance. The sight reminds me of Maia.

No.

"What kind of gatherings does he have?" I ask, forcing myself to pay attention. The goal is to get Maia out of my mind and looking for every reminder of her isn't helping. The woman talks about Rob's rowdy parties. Before yesterday, I didn't know who he was, yet it sounds like one of my highly paid employees is engaging in morally questionable behavior. I'm not one to judge, but he represents the company.

Although this woman seems genuine, she doesn't hide her flirtatious hints. Her hand often brushes my arm, her lashes batting often, her chest poking out more than necessary. When she catches me staring at her mouth, she smiles. I'm not thinking of kissing her. I'm thinking of what her lips would look like elsewhere. She boldly reaches out to brush a finger along my jaw.

"Would you like to find a private room?" she purrs.

I nod. "Absolutely."

I sling an arm around her slender shoulders and guide her to the edge of the crowd and beyond. Her arms lasso around my waist, a hand brushing over my groin. She told me her name; it didn't stick.

We find an empty bedroom and instead of heading straight for the bed, I bring her over to the couch. I might be forward, but I'm a gentleman.

Or because I'm trying to convince myself I actually want this woman.

She sits beside me, and before she can lean in, I say, "No kissing."

She drags a finger down the side of my neck. "What about your body?"

I reluctantly nod. Kissing has never been my thing; it's too intimate for my taste. I usually entertain it for the woman I'm with at the time. Tonight, I'm completely turned off by it. The woman—Jenny, I think?—begins kissing behind my ear. As she works her way down, I close my eyes and fight the revulsion rising inside me. I clench my jaw, sliding my fingers through her hair. There has to be something I find more arousing about this woman. She checks all of my boxes.

Manners.

Curves.

Respectable clothing.

That usually turns me on, and I need to trust what's always worked. My instincts.

I shut off the doubtful voice in my head to stay in the moment. It's been nearly two months since I had sex; there hasn't been a gap that long since before I lost my virginity. I'm practically starving for a woman.

I pour my focus into the moment.

I inhale the scent of coconut and roses and feel spiral curls twisting around my fingers. I anticipate the feel of her teeth tugging at my skin because, fuck, I feel like she's a biter. My semi turns into a full hard-on.

I wrench back her pillow-soft hair, aiming for her mouth, only to be startled to see blue eyes staring back at me. Not an earthy brown. No curls, either, just blonde strands that fall through my fingers like water. No coconut-rose scent. Just cigarettes and vodka.

Shit.

I was thinking of Maia. Foul-mouthed, always-angry Maia.

"What's wrong?" Jenny asks, eyeing my lips.

I blink and pull back, gently shifting her off me. "This isn't working, Jenny. Sorry."

"My name is *Jessie*," she snaps.

I shift away from her, but she jabs her palm against my shoulder and scrambles to situate herself while mumbling about me being a dick. The night isn't going how either of us imagined. She slams the door behind her and I re-button my shirt.

Maia doesn't check anything off my list, except perhaps the clothing part—sometimes. She's happy to show off what little cleavage she has when clubbing. She—

I drop my head in my hands. This feels stupid. Why

does my list, which has proven useful every single time, suddenly seem so juvenile? *Making lists about women?* Maia is... she's so much more *woman* than a few bullet points could ever summarize. Not in terms of tits or ass. All at once, her femininity soothes me and her ferocity slices me.

When I let instincts take over, Maia was there.

No. Not a chance.

I rise from the couch and head for the room's minibar. There's no way I'm letting some self-righteous princess inconvenience my life more than she already has. I unscrew a bottle of whisky and throw back a gulp.

Is it really so bad if I think about her that way? It feels disrespectful. It's supposed to be a working relationship, but it's never felt that way. Not once. It's difficult to build a professional relationship when one party calls the other greedy all the time. Maia infuriates me. I barely know her and she's telling me how to run *my* company. Who does she think she is?

No matter how hard I try to push her from my mind, she appears uninvited and with more vigor than before. I shut my eyes, finally giving in to the thoughts of everything I want to do to her.

I imagine myself eating her out until her constant arguments fade away, replaced by moans that are muffled by her thighs clenching around my head. I imagine sinking inside of her so deep I get lost—but it wouldn't make a difference. I wouldn't be searching for a way out, anyway. Before I know it, my trousers are unbuckled and I'm stroking myself to these thoughts I can't escape from. I imagine her on her knees in front of me, sucking and licking and incapable of calling me ungrateful because I'd already worshiped every fiery inch of her.

No list can describe the woman I'm looking for, the woman who can fulfill my every desire. If there were a list, there'd be a single name.

Maia.

CHAPTER NINE
MAIA

On the morning of my twenty-fourth birthday, Daisy wakes me up by licking my face. It jolts me from my deep sleep; my happy girl doesn't care.

"*Dai-sy,*" I whine, hiding under my pillow. She nudges her big head under my arm. Her intense sniffing makes me laugh, but I jolt away once she licks my armpit. I flip onto my back and she instantly plops her head on my chest. Anyone unaccustomed to her weight would crack a rib from her.

"Okay, I'm up. I'm up. Hi, pretty girl."

Poppy watches the debacle from the foot of the bed, uninterested in joining the cuddle fest. She deprives me of so much love that I nearly yelp in joy when she rests her head on my leg. My eyes flutter shut and I wrap my arms around Daisy. If I look to my right, I'll see the mountains through the double doors leading to my patio. Waking up here, in my own home, with my dogs beside me and my other animals elsewhere on my twenty-fourth birthday is a gift.

When I graduated from college two years ago, I never

imagined I would be here as the princess of a country and richer than I thought I'd ever be. When I told Esme and Lyla that I don't want any gifts, I meant it. Perhaps gift-giving just isn't my love language, but I'd rather they help me clean an animal shelter.

Okay, that's not the best idea, because there's zero chance I would leave without another dog.

But hey, I'm rich, right? I can afford another pet.

Maybe *that's* my birthday gift.

"All right, time to get up before I turn our home into a zoo without even having coffee yet," I say to Poppy and Daisy. Even though I pay her well, I feel like I'd have to ask Esme first.

My dogs leap right from the bed, and Daisy steps on my stomach in the meantime, pulling a groan from me. "*Oof.* Daisy girl, you really gotta know your size."

I swing my legs over the edge of my bed and stretch the kinks out of my back and neck. I wince as I turn. The twinge in my upper back may be familiar, but it wasn't this bad yesterday.

I spent thousands of euros on specialized pillows and mattresses and I *still* wake up in pain. Apprehension gathers in my stomach. There's a chance Lyla will want to take me out tonight. If the pain persists, I won't be in the mood.

My phone has a dozen happy birthday texts, and half of them are from Nina. I spend the morning on FaceTime with her as I feed the animals and get ready for my short day at the garden.

"Did you have anything set up today?" Nina asks. "I really wanted to plan something, but morning sickness has been kicking my ass the last couple weeks."

I frown. "How do you feel now?"

She shrugs. "Not that bad. Wesley's making me break-fast right now. I just hope I can keep it down."

"I can have Esme drop off Daisy for some cuddles."

Nina grins. "That's okay. But you're avoiding my question. Do you have anything planned?"

"Nah, just time with the pets today. Lyla will probably come over."

"You don't go out as much as you used to."

It's my turn to shrug. "Unfulfilling I guess."

Because I'm tired of waking up the next morning feeling like I had a full-body workout. A night out on the town doesn't always make me think of endless laughs and good music. It's making sure I'll have somewhere to sit. It's wearing shoes that won't hurt my feet three times faster and more intensely than anyone in the group.

I don't tell her that I'm tired of fighting my own body.

I spent much of yesterday crouching or bending over in the garden, both at work and at home. But Lyla was with me all day and I doubt her back is punishing her like mine is.

Nina eyes me through the phone, but I lean out of frame and pretend to do more of my makeup. She's good at sniffing out secrets. Wesley arrives with her breakfast, saving me from interrogation. One of the biggest reasons I love Wesley for my sister is because I trust him with her. Keeping her calm and happy is his full-time job, one he takes more seriously than ever now that she's pregnant.

"I'm gonna eat, but I'll stop by later, okay?"

"Sounds good. Love you."

"Love you too, birthday girl."

My sister talked me through the morning before I could have a chance to realize how lonely I am. My animals keep me company, but I'm an extrovert. I enjoy being around people in spite of my issues with the media and public. It feels weird to not be going out tonight—whether it's my favorite club or playing board games at Lyla's.

I might just be going to the garden for a few hours to wander, not to work, but I still get dressed up. My floral dress exposes my shoulders and hugs my upper body. The sleeves flare out by my elbow and are almost as long as the uneven hem. I top it off with a simple vest and knee-high boots and as many rings and earrings as I can stack on.

In the break room, Lyla has balloons and a mini cake waiting for me. The birthday card is bigger than the cake itself. But every employee at Felicity Gardens, including the gift shop staff, signed the card along with cute messages. I'll have to remember to thank everyone.

"Oh, it's perfect," I weep, pulling her into a hug. "Thank you so much." Beside the cake with twenty-four written in icing, there's a vibrant bouquet of flowers. "And oh my god the flowers are *stunning*!"

Blossoming pink lilies, eucalyptus, baby's breath, sage, foxglove, fern, purple tulips, and others. It's the most beautiful bouquet I've ever seen. I inhale the sweet aroma of the lilies, a smile pulling at my lips.

Lyla shakes her head with a smirk. "I didn't get those."

"What? Then who did?" I search for a card. The only person I can think of is Dr. Pagoda, but she's not the flower-giving type.

My friend points behind me, and I deflate at the sight of Tristan in the doorway, looking solemn and sexy at the same time. Does he wear anything other than a button-up and slacks? He somehow makes it freshly attractive every time.

"Happy birthday," he says, and I really want to reach out and twist his nipple for daring to sound that hot with his British accent. It's flustering. It's frustrating. And it's not fair.

"What are you doing here? It's not Tuesday."

He glances at the bouquet.

"These are from you?" I ask.

He nods.

"Why?"

"I believe I just indicated why."

Aaaaand there goes my attraction toward him. "Don't get smart," I bite. "It's well established I don't like you."

"Just say thank you."

I cock a hip. "Don't tell me what to do."

I'm not being the irrational one. If he's extending an olive branch by giving me flowers on my birthday, he should extend the whole branch, not just a twig. Don't essentially throw flowers in my face and go *"here, now we're cool."* No matter how beautiful they are.

Tristan clenches his jaw, suppressing a huff as he saunters over. He places an envelope on the other end of the table without breaking my gaze. His deep, accented voice penetrates me when he repeats, "Happy birthday, Maia."

I don't move until he leaves the room—mostly because I'd likely fall to pieces if I shifted a muscle. No man has ever angered and aroused me the way Tristan does, and I'm not even sure he intends to do the latter.

"Only you two can argue over a gift exchange," Lyla mutters, then nods to the envelope. "What is it?"

I ignore her remark, open up the paper, and nearly drop it right away. You've got to be *fucking* kidding me. I look at my friend. "A receipt of an anonymous *five-million-dollar* donation to clear student loans of my alma mater's graduating class this year."

Lyla snatches it to see for herself. "What the shit?"

"The great thing about being a billionaire is I could do both."

I didn't think he would actually do it. There are so many things I want to say—to ask. Most of all: *why?* Like Lyla said, only Tristan and I can argue over a gift exchange. And like I said, it's well established that I don't like him. So why would he do this? Money really isn't an object to him.

Despite my hesitations, I owe him a thank-you. I'm not *that* bad. But by the time I rush to the lobby, then to the courtyard, I find his Maserati long gone.

CHAPTER TEN
MAIA

"**S**URPRISE!"

Nina, Wesley, Esme, her husband Sergio, and my cousins Vanessa and Jace stand in my backyard with kazoos and party hats. I'm surprised Nina got Wesley to put on a cone hat; it belies his Mr. Grumpy attitude. My sister, on the other hand, grins wildly and skips over to me.

"You didn't have to do this," I say, though I'm still smiling.

She wraps me in a hug. "Of course I did."

I hug her tightly. I still haven't heard from Dad today, but my sister gives me enough love. She always does.

"Thank you," I mumble into her hair. "I love you."

"I love you too."

I finally give Poppy and Daisy my attention after they've been circling my feet and pawing at me since I arrived. I hug each person and animal here and cackle when my duck Olivia nips at Wesley's ankles.

He nearly jumps out of his skin and tries to tiptoe away without stepping on her. "Whoa, Maia, get the duck, get the duck."

I watch the scene unfold with mischievous pleasure. "She's just playing!"

Olivia chases my brother-in-law around my big ginkgo tree with her wings outstretched as she quacks. I nearly fall over laughing as I scoop her up and away from him.

"That's not funny," he says, eyeing my duck and taking a step back.

"It's kinda funny," Nina says.

I move closer and hold Olivia up to him, her caramel wings flapping hard enough for a feather to break free. "Are you scared of a little duck?"

Wesley dodges a wing and snatches a patio chair, lifting the heavy item with ease and extending it between us. "Stay back."

Nina and I bust out laughing. "Don't make her angry," I warn. "Elliot might come fight you."

"Why are their names Elliot and Olivia again?" He fails keeping the judgment off his face.

"From *Law and Order: Special Victims Unit*."

"That's not weird at all."

I cradle Olivia to my chest. "Don't judge what you can't understand!"

My sister plants a birthday crown on my head and shows me the vegetarian charcuterie spread she made for everyone. She can't cook for shit, but she makes a mean charcuterie. Birthday festivities include a few rounds of Cards Against Humanity and drinks around the fire pit. Well, for the group, yes, but Wesley spends the time playing fetch and roughhousing with Daisy. I keep telling Nina she needs to get that man a dog before he steals mine.

By the time three o'clock rolls around, I start compulsively checking my phone. Dad may live in another time-zone, but he should be awake by now. A few texts from distant friends and—*barf*—Diego chimes in. I delete his message immediately. Even Aunt Beverly called me this morning and we chatted for nearly twenty minutes.

It doesn't help that I've been suppressing my back pain throughout the day. I've been upright for hours and I can feel my body crumbling.

"You okay?" Nina asks, the bonfire amplifying her concerned stare.

I immediately sober and shake my head. "I'm good."

"Are you sure?"

"Yes, Nina. I'm fine." I huff out a breath and rise to my feet. "I'm gonna get another drink." By the time I reach the kitchen, I slump at the table from the stabbing pain in my shoulder blade.

I don't like to take painkillers because of my anxiety over becoming reliant. I have an addictive personality and I've been told by old friends that they could see me becoming an addict. Not to mention Dad and his previous dependence on alcohol. I'm scared, but I'm hurting. And I'm miserable. I squeeze my eyes shut.

"Hey," Esme says, her gentle voice pulling me from my thoughts. Her Maldanian accent makes everything she says so melodic. "How do you feel?"

"Hey, yeah, I'm just—I hurt a little bit, that's all."

She sees directly through my false words. *A little bit* doesn't cover the pain I'm in. Instead of calling me out, she suggests, "Medicine?"

I bite back frustrated tears as I nod.

On one hand, I'm convincing myself to listen to my body and rest. On the other, I refuse to let this pain control my life. I am at war with my own body, and I never thought I would be particularly grateful for the ability to walk.

That's a blessing you start counting when you're eighty-four, not twenty-four.

Fear and grief inundate me at the idea that this will always be my life. No amount of doctor's visits, specialists, and physical therapy will change it. It's never enough. I could exercise morning and night and eat clean every day and it still won't matter. The aches will always come.

After I toss back the painkillers with a glass of water, I head to my closet to change. Each movement is slow and stiff but it's a relief to get out of my bra and these heeled boots.

"Maia?" Esme calls.

"In here!" I lower onto the tufted couch in my closet.

"I came to see if you needed help changing. Can I come in?"

"Yeah, come in. I'm all right, though. It's not that bad right now."

My friend lowers beside me on the couch. Honestly, Esme has the best job in the world. My office pays her six figures to take care of my animals when I'm at work and assist me when my chronic pain is too much to handle. She only lives up the road of our mountain village and is one of three people who have the code to my gate—Esme, Nina, and Mason. My three most trusted people.

I swallow a sigh and lean back, grateful for the relieved pressure on my back. I wipe the tears from my eyes before they can reach my chin.

"Can I ask you something?" my friend says quietly.

"Of course."

"Why do you hide your pain from your sister?"

Jeez, where do I begin?

"I, uh... Well, she knows I have chronic pain. It's just

that Nina lost a lot of her childhood because of my dad's drinking. I did, too, but she shielded me from so much."

"And you don't want her to worry about you?"

I shake my head. "She spent her whole life worrying about me. And she has more on her plate now than ever before. I'm a big girl. I'll be okay."

Esme takes my hand. "But you're not right now."

"It's my birthday. I'll cry if I want to," I joke softly, and my friend grins.

It's hard to keep up appearances sometimes, but I don't know what else to do when I'm in this much pain. I'm tired of being the screw-up. I'm tired of being the person that others feel they need to be hyperaware of.

I can't lie; I love my life. I like being privileged. I like feeling special. My sudden new life as a royal and a socialite hit fast—and I gobbled it up at first. But the public's prying, relentless eyes ruined me physically and emotionally.

Magazines like *Kosita Daily* love to write about my flaws. How I'm a hypocrite for riding a jet ski. Fake scandals that I mistreat staff—the evidence based on someone pretending to be me. I've been used and inspected and received threatening "love" letters and several inappropriate packages. Some with blood and other bodily fluids. I'm popular with adolescents. Not so much anyone else.

My home is my safest haven possible. I love having company and sharing my comfortable space with my loved ones, but that list of people is small.

"Maia? Ez? Where you at?" Lyla wanders until finding us, but yelps at the sight of my tears and dashes away. Less than thirty seconds later, she returns with a tub of Oreo ice cream and three spoons.

"Tears instantly mean ice cream," Lyla says, plopping

on the other side of me and passing out the utensils. My heart swells. I already had three slices of cake, but fuck it.

The three of us eat ice cream in comfortable silence. When I turned twenty years old, I never thought that in four years I would be inside a house that I own, let alone famous and the princess of a country. I have everything I could ever want and need; my friends and family threw me a surprise birthday party.

I should be grateful—not crying in my closet because I can't saddle up a little longer or feeling sorry for myself because my parents haven't wished me a happy birthday.

"Tristan donated a lot of money for you today," Lyla mentions.

I roll my eyes over a scoop of ice cream. And then there's *that*. "Oh, god. Don't even."

"Who?" asks Esme.

"The billionaire who talked his way into working at Felicity."

"Oh, *right*. What did he donate?"

"Five *million* dollars to wipe out student debt at the college Maia went to in America."

Esme's jaw drops. "Five million? Are you serious?"

"He *likes* you," Lyla sings.

"No, he doesn't. He feels guilty."

"For what?"

I shrug. "I don't know. Being a natural asshat."

Lyla leans over me to look at Esme. "You should hear them argue. It's like their foreplay."

"Is not!"

"You'd definitely fuck him, stop playing."

I groan. "I wouldn't. Let's not go there."

"I want to know what he looks like," Esme says with a grin, and Lyla immediately digs out her phone. Within a couple of seconds, she hands it over with a picture of Tristan I haven't seen before.

"Whoa, let me see, too." I lean over onto Esme, resting my chin on her shoulder. It's a paparazzi shot of him at the beach, shirtless with shorts just a little too short, but reveals his strong thighs. He has a few more tattoos and the mere sight of him makes my ears warm. He's so fine it's not fair, and his lack of interaction with the media only makes him hotter.

Esme zooms in on his chest. "Oh, my."

"It's just not *fair*," I whine. "How could someone that hot be so—*urgh*." I stab at the thick ice cream. "It doesn't even matter. He's a billionaire who hoards his money and I'm not some starry-eyed gold digger."

Tristan has only been at the garden for a month. In between our arguing, we fall into moments of comfortable silence. He'll mutter questions about what I'm doing and when he decides not to make some remark regarding its functionality, it's quite pleasant.

My temper is so much harder to maintain when he's around. Dr. Pagoda was right that it could teach me to control myself, but I'm not sure I should be. He's one of the richest people in the world and he inherently gets under my skin. He knows exactly what to say—and I mean *exactly*. The nonchalant tone, skirting around my point, only to turn it around on me. It's almost gaslighting.

Okay, yes, I may have been calling him a greedy, selfish twat in the meantime, but that's beside the point. It's a dangerous game, poking each other to see how far we'll go.

He thinks I'm a hypocrite, but it's also not his business that I cap my income at 500,000 euros a year—which is more than enough even for an average family. Everything else, I donate and redistribute.

Esme hands back the phone and sighs. "Imagine the things you could do with that much money."

"Okay, yeah, that sucks," Lyla agrees, "but if you don't want to ride him 'til the wheels fall off, you can just send him my way."

I snort. Before I can reply, both Daisy and Poppy barrel their way into my closet. Daisy might be coming to cuddle my troubles away, but Poppy is definitely here for the ice cream.

"Hi, my babies!" I squeak. My Rottweiler settles at my feet while my Shiba Inu hops on the couch to sit between Esme and me.

If I didn't have Daisy and Sage to fill my well of animal love, I might feel envious of Poppy's inclination toward Esme. I don't have favorites, but Poppy would get ten times the amount of love and affection if she would only let me. I can't count the number of times this bitch dodged my kisses.

Nonetheless, I wrap my arm around her and scrub her fur until she's deemed it's enough and puts distance between us.

Nina appears in the doorway of my closet, her hands planted on her hips. "Hiding out in here while you have guests is *rude*, Maia."

"Wha—they *are* my guests!"

She gives me a pointed look, though I know she's right. One of her perfectly manicured eyebrows lifts as she eyes the tub in my hand. "At least share the ice cream."

Nina—and Wesley—hang back once everyone leaves. While Wesley hangs out somewhere inside, my sister helps me garden. The sun is finding its way to the horizon and sparrows sing as they flitter from tree to tree. My painkiller has kicked in and I'm giddy to feel the earth between my fingers. We're transplanting some flowers I had been growing in my greenhouse as Daisy and Poppy chase each other around the stone path.

Usually, they're not allowed in the fenced-in garden because both of them have a tendency to dig. Within ten minutes, they're panting and lying under the shade of my apple tree. My swinging bench looks cozy right about now.

"Did you tell Dad about the baby yet?" I ask as I pat soil around a recently transplanted marigold.

A shadow falls over Nina's face. "I don't want to tell him over the phone. I've been trying to get him to fly out, but he keeps coming up with excuses."

Dad and Ruby, my stepmom, moved back to America when Ruby's mom Etta was diagnosed with cancer. Neither Nina nor I is upset about them moving, but Dad rejects all our efforts to be there for him and help. He went from relying on us—mostly Nina—to fix everything to barely wanting to talk to us.

"Well, he still hasn't called me today, so... I don't think he's in the mood to put in effort."

"*What?* Are you serious?"

"Please don't say anything," I beg. My sister isn't afraid to tell Dad to step up for me. She's always willing to defend me before herself.

I haven't seen either of my parents since Christmas and have only spoken to Dad sporadically. It's because I got into an argument with my stepmother after she made some snide comment about Nina and Wesley flying back to Maldana before the new year for work. I defended my sister. Ruby doubled down. Dad defended his wife and got angry at me in the meantime. Nothing is ever simple with him, and our lives as royals are complicated enough.

"Maybe Etta took a turn for the worse," Nina suggests as she leans over the garden bed to drop another plant into a dug hole.

I whistle for Daisy to stop digging up freshly placed mulch. Unlike Poppy, Daisy is a better listener. "I wouldn't know," I tell my sister. "He doesn't tell us anything. You know when he does find out about the baby, he's gonna complain you didn't tell him sooner."

She huffs. "I know. Wesley's been trying to make me feel better. He even offered to fly home to convince Dad to come back with him."

I pout in awe. "That's so cute. Sadly, I think he's the last person Dad would wanna see."

She makes a noise of disgust. "Yeah, I know." She wipes the sweat from her head with her forearm. "No more of this sad talk. It's your birthday and this is probably the only time I can garden for the next month."

CHAPTER ELEVEN
TRISTAN

I should have expected Maia to react as such. There's constant tension between us and I can't lift it no matter how hard I try. My growing attraction toward her doesn't help. We can't stay civil for shit; we're constantly at each other's necks. More so her than me, but sometimes I can't help poking her in places I know bother her. Seeing her frustrated turns me on even more.

The elevator doors open, revealing the top floor of my building. Augustus is already waiting for me except he's distracted by whatever is on his phone. Without lifting his head, he hands me the scheduling tablet with the screen pulled up on the day's calendar.

"The meeting with Ingram is in thirty minutes," he says, trailing behind me.

"Who's Ingram?"

"The new Head Operations Officer for the UK."

Ah, right. I try to meet with the directors of each division for the sense of community and respect; I find myself less interested in doing that with each meeting.

"Oh, and Ms. Farrugia is in your office."

I freeze before reaching my door. Celine? I look at Augustus over my shoulder. "Why?"

He shrugs. "She wouldn't say."

I drop my head back. It must be important enough to bypass our assistants. I find her on the couch, typing away on her phone. She hardly looks up as I step inside and close the door behind me.

"You're late," she says.

"I'm the boss," I bite. "I decide what's late. Why are you here and not in your own office?"

I cross the distance toward my desk and set down the tablet. After dealing with Maia's attitude yesterday, the last thing I feel like doing is being anywhere near my mother.

She rises, her expression tight. "I need to make sure we've got this mess with Felicity Gardens under control."

"There's no mess."

"You are *one* more failed donation away from slinging mashed potatoes at the shelter—and that can't be kept out of the press."

"Then what are you here for?"

"You said the princess still didn't trust you. Has that changed?"

I release a gritted sigh. I lied. Being near Celine is not the last thing I feel like doing—it's being near her *and* discussing my turbulent relationship with Maia. Celine is a stranger to my inner thoughts and that won't be changing anytime soon.

"I'm working on it."

That doesn't pacify her. "You're straddling the line here. We have to keep two parties in the dark and *you* tend to lose focus."

"When have I lost focus?" I snap.

She blanches as if I should know. "When you nearly

missed that meeting with the shareholder that ended up making us meet our yearly goal in the first quarter."

That was my first year on the job and a mere month after Grandfather had passed. I was partying my grief away the night before, and after I almost screwed up the meeting, I hired Augustus. I haven't had a misstep since then.

"I was grieving," I say, my voice quiet. "Not that you know anything of the sort."

Celine scowls. "Grow up, Tristan. If you're not fit for the job, you need to step aside."

My irritation flares into anger. That's exactly what she wants—the company. All my mother does is take. She took my family away and she's fighting tooth and nail to take Space Tech.

"You'd like that, wouldn't you? It's been your goal all along."

She crosses her arms. "There's no shame in realizing this is more work than you can handle. You can put all your focus in getting these volunteer hours in and then you can take the inheritance and retire early. I am giving you an option *not* to work. Do you know how many thirty-year-olds would jump at the chance to get five hundred million euros and never work another day in their life?"

I'm not thirty yet, but that doesn't matter to her. Grandfather didn't raise me to drop out of the company— especially not to end up relinquishing it to Celine. He didn't trust her, but he kept her close out of love for his daughter. I lost any maternal love I had before I turned sixteen. By the time I turned twenty, she stopped being Mum and became Celine.

Grandfather managed to keep the noses of Space Technologies clean. Maia doesn't realize that I'm not the true definition of evil and corporate greed. Celine would, without a doubt, sacrifice integrity to cut corners.

"I am *not* giving you my job," I seethe, slowly advancing. "You can trick the board into thinking you're important, but I know who you are. You're a snake. A liar. A manipulator—"

"I'm still your mother and you will not speak to me that way," she barks, her brows cinching.

"*You're a nuisance!* Do not talk to me about family when you are the reason it broke in the first place." I march to the other side of my desk, rearranging some files to distract my anger before I throw something across the room.

She follows, the fabric of her bell-bottom pantsuit swishing. "Are you seriously bringing this up? Ten, fifteen—"

"Twenty fucking years, Celine! You sent my sister away twenty years ago and haven't spoken to me about it once." I remember listening from around the corner as she and my father spoke in the living room.

"Dani has to go," my mother said. "She won't stop. We both know it."

"Are you sure? What about Tristan?"

A pause. "Nothing will happen to him. He will be fine, but you have to take her. Leave in the morning."

The following morning, they were gone before I woke up. I cried the entire day, although Celine kept telling me they had only gone on a trip. I knew the truth. My mother had never been affectionate. I had Estelle, my nanny and practically a hired mum. But I withdrew from everyone once Dani and my father left. The only person who could get me out of my shell was Grandfather.

"Oh, for god's sake," Celine huffs, tossing her hands in the air. She stops in front of my desk, her voice dripping in acid. "*You. Have. Everything!* You have a life that most of the world dreams of and all you can do is whinge about mummy not giving you a hug when you were a child. Get over it—"

"Where is Danica?"

"It's done, Tristan. Move on. It was not just me. Your grandfather was the one who suggested it, and it was the only solution available."

Does she hear herself? This answers nothing and gives me a ton more questions.

"Solution to *what*?"

Celine tries to gather herself. She sniffs, tossing her brown hair from her face. "Believe it or not, I'm trying to protect you. Drop it."

I don't understand why she's not grasping the severity of it. This is not about a pet who died prematurely and I'm trying to grasp the concept of death. We're talking about a person. A human being. There's no scenario where sending away Danica is a reasonable solution.

"She was your daughter."

"She was a monster," Celine counters. "She would have ruined everything."

"You are—" *Horrible. Repulsive.* How could I have a mother who speaks of her daughter as a monster? "Just get out."

"I'm—"

"Get the fuck out of my office!"

She deflates from my severe tone and face. If she doesn't leave in the next ten seconds, I may force her out. She lingers in the tense silence. When she slithers out the door, I flop into my chair.

CHAPTER TWELVE
TRISTAN

A few hours later, I'm on a jet to Sicily.

Romèo's finally available, but is bound to his home island. I meet him at a private rooftop lounge overlooking the sea. There are a few other patrons and a live musician playing an acoustic guitar softly. The spring weather is exceedingly warm, taking my normal medium brown skin into a russet shade.

I turn to Romèo. "What took you offline for a while?"

He lifts a shoulder, evading my eyes. "Work."

"Everything good in the restaurant world?"

"Nothing crazy," he admits. "Sometimes we have to keep our competition in check."

I snort. "And how do you do that?"

"My father is a good businessman."

Romèo's family is huge. I've met one or two of his relatives, but I couldn't pick them out of a lineup if asked.

A waiter arrives with a plate of calamari and my stomach rumbles. After yesterday and this morning, authentic Italian food and a good drink are perfect. A view of the sunset over the Mediterranean Sea doesn't hurt, either.

"I'm guessing things on your side aren't good?" my friend asks, hinting at the fact this is the second time I've hit him up within a couple weeks.

"I've been working with the princess." *Working* is more so *being berated on a weekly basis.*

"The princess? Of Maldana?" He almost looks impressed. "Fuck, mate. That's a new one for you."

"It's not like that. I need community service hours to meet the inheritance terms from my grandfather."

"How are you working for the princess? And for free?" Romèo laughs. Like me, he was born rich.

"At some research facility in a botanical garden."

"So, you're watering plants and then what? How much?"

"Five hundred mil."

He lets out a low whistle. "Should be easy motivation then, no?"

I shake my head. "I *thought* it would be easy. Flirt. Get what I need. Leave. But the princess is a fucking pain in my arse who spends the entire time whinging about how rich people are ruining the world."

He holds out a hand, an incredulous look on his face. "She's a princess."

"That's what *I* said!" I don't tell him that I'm not exactly against what she's saying. She delivers it in the worst way possible, but I never come out and tell her that she's wrong because she's not. And that's the most frustrating part. Perhaps it's the stubbornness that Grandfather instilled in me. I don't like change. And the things Maia demands of people like me include a whole lot of it.

"Mate, all she does is yell at me," I say. "Nothing more. It drives me fucking mad."

Romèo has a wicked grin. By wicked, I mean he's a damn Cheshire Cat. "You like her, don't you?"

I release a breath through gritted teeth. The desire for her came on strong and quick and I'm not entirely convinced she's not a siren or doing witchy spells at night. I wouldn't put that above her.

"Any man with a brain would want her. Thank god we live in a stupid world." I toss back the last gulp of alcohol. "She still makes me want to put my head into a shredder."

He cackles and leans back in his seat, swishing the wine around in his glass. "You hate her because she's above you."

I recoil. "What?"

"She's a princess, man. Women fawn over you because of what you can do for them. There isn't anything you can offer her that she doesn't already have—or can get."

I grunt, staring out at the vibrant orange sunset. It reminds me of the dress she wore on her birthday yesterday. The flowers were orange and she wore a sun necklace. I don't respond; there's nothing to say to prove him wrong, because he's right. For the first time, it's embarrassing to admit that the women in my life were essentially bought. Money can't buy Maia.

If I want her, I have to work for it.

I feel a bit more like myself the next day.

Before, I would have gone to Grandfather. But I haven't had him in nearly three years. Even though I miss the days of lounging with him, discussing things from business strategies to books, it was nice to feel like I had a friend again.

By midday, Augustus and I are heading back to my office after a meeting. I stop when I realize he's not paying attention to any of my requests, only to see him staring ahead, eyes wide and mouth agape.

"Augustus."

He blinks himself into reality. "Sir, I don't ask for much. But will you please introduce me?"

I follow his gaze and almost have the same reaction. Out of all the people to show up at my building, she's the last person I'd expect.

"Maia."

She stands by the elevator wearing a blue halter top and tight, high-waist jeans. Her caramel brown curls puff around her face and cascade below her ribcage.

"Hi," she says, her kissable lips glistening with lip gloss.

I can damn near feel Augustus tense as she makes her way over to us and I withhold from elbowing him. He's not making either of us look good right now. She smiles at my assistant and extends a hand.

"Hi, I'm Maia."

He scrambles to free his right hand before taking hold. But instead of shaking it the way she tries to, he merely holds her hand and bows. Kill me now. "Your Majesty. I-it's an honor. I'm—"

"Augustus, fetch my lunch," I say, eager to put both of us out of misery. It seems to reorient him, for he steels his shoulders and clears his throat. Yet he doesn't stop staring at her. I don't miss the way his eyes roam over her every feature.

"He's not a dog," Maia argues.

"He's my assistant and is paid to do as I ask."

"You *didn't* ask. You demanded like he was your pet."

I inhale deeply, chiding myself for thinking we could ever have a civil conversation. "Is there a reason you're here?"

"At the very least, you could say please."

Biting back my retorts, I turn to my assistant. "Augustus, will you *please* fetch my lunch?"

"Yes, sir," he says, eyes remaining on the princess. "Would you like anything as well, Your Majesty?"

"No, I'm all right. Thank you, though." When he leaves, she turns a glare on me. "Is it that hard?"

I want to gouge out Augustus's eyes for watching her too long. If I knew exactly what he was thinking, I'd probably follow through. He couldn't handle Maia; she'd eat him alive.

Maia is a lot of woman. And I don't mean chest or bum wise. Her femininity soothes you and her wits cut you. It's a high that few men can handle.

I still don't like how he was drooling all over her.

"Now that you've embarrassed me in front of my assistant," I say, "what can I do for you?"

"Oh, please. He was so giddy you could've dropped dead and he wouldn't notice." She flips her hair over her shoulder and strides ahead. "This is your office?"

I follow her into my own office. Her gaze brazenly wanders the space as she tosses her purse onto an armchair. She surveys the near-empty bookshelves, a few sculptures, and a picture of Grandfather and me. She lingers on the last one.

I fear what it'd look like with Grandfather and Maia in a debate. He'd likely call her a talkative bitch behind her back and I'd rather not know what she'd call him. He preferred the women in his life to be docile and quiet.

"I didn't say you could make yourself comfortable," I tell her.

Maia cuts toward me, her narrowed expression fading into nonchalance. "Oh, am I invading your workspace?"

She lowers herself into the big chair behind my desk, and I sit on the edge of the surface beside her. I don't expect to enjoy the sight of her in my seat. But goddamn, she wiggles her arse to get comfortable and I have a sudden desire to be a chair. One long leg crosses over the other and she clears her throat. I find her waiting glare, and I know she caught me staring. It's getting harder and harder to pretend I don't want to bend her over a table and spank her attitude right out of her.

I cross my arms. "What are you doing here?"

She watches me earnestly. "I wanted to thank you in person. For my birthday gift."

"You're welcome."

"I also want to know why you did it."

"Some say it's rude to question a gift."

She tilts her head and sends me yet another glare. "We both know I don't care if I'm rude to you."

"Right. Why is that again?"

"You should be a politician with all this deflecting."

"Because I knew it would make you happy," I say without thinking. My heart thunders.

"And why do you care about my happiness if I'm so rude to you?"

I open my mouth, then close it. "I have no obligation to match your attitude."

Rather than relief or resignation, her face twists as if in

pain. She shakes her head. "Why are you like this?" she mutters. Her body tenses as frustration builds. "Why don't you—give more of a shit? Just tell me, because I really don't get it."

"Get what, exactly?"

"Empathy!" She hops to her feet without breaking our gaze. "I don't understand how someone with so much wealth doesn't do even a fraction of the good they can reach. How do you just *ignore* it? Why does it take my birthday for you to do something like this? Why don't you care about how much pollution your company creates? Why don't you care that some of your employees around the world can't afford to feed their families? Why don't you care enough to use all of the resources you're *lucky* to have to help people? *Why don't you care, Tristan?*"

For the first time, Maia watches me with sincerity, openness. My chest tightens.

The company was quite literally handed to me. There isn't a time in my life when I wasn't rich. Millionaire, billionaire, I'm not sure it matters to me. Grandfather taught me to seek power, but he didn't teach me the responsibility that comes with it. He didn't teach me about the consequences.

I like to argue with Maia and I'm never left speechless—until now. She doesn't toss me an insult that lets me skirt her questions or points. She studies me with her big, vulnerable brown eyes and if she touched me, I'd turn to putty in her hands.

I wish I had an answer. I wish I had something to say beyond, *"I do. I care."* But I say nothing because she wouldn't accept that. We haven't known each other long, but I understand that much.

I believe actions, not words, pretty boy.

At last, I break our stare, the intensity gutting me from the inside out.

A knock echoes at the door with Augustus's timid voice on the other side. "Sir, I have your lunch ready."

CHAPTER THIRTEEN
MAIA

Diego has been texting me all weekend.

Yesterday, I responded and told him to leave me alone. Now it's Tuesday afternoon and my phone chimes on my way to the Rainmore Greenhouse.

"Are you fucking—" I mumble at my phone.

> DIEGO
>
> Hey, how'd you sleep?

As if my previous text didn't say: *Take a hint. My answer is no. Leave me alone.*

"Everything okay?"

I jump at Tristan's voice behind me. Sometimes I forget he's there; he either watches me work silently or we're at each other's throats. "It's fine. Just—nothing."

I step into the greenhouse as I swipe to Diego's contact and hit block. I should have done this the other day.

"Doesn't seem like nothing," Tristan presses.

I clench my jaw, crushing my rising temper. Why are men so goddamn pushy?

"Men keep bothering me—and you're Exhibit B."

"Same guy as before?"

"Yep. I just blocked him, so it should be smooth-sailing from here on out."

He hums, his lips pursed as I stop at the potting section of the greenhouse. I have to make reports and check up on a few plants that had pests. But Tristan's reaction gives me pause—and I better not spot any judgment on his otherwise perfect face.

"What?" I press.

"Nothing."

"Don't act like you've never had a woman trying to come back for more after you've said no."

He looks offended. "My women have better sense than to reach out."

I grimace, taking out a single gardening glove from the cupboard. "Ew, I'm *definitely* adding misogynistic prick to your list."

"Every woman I'm with is a fully grown, consenting adult."

"How sad you feel the need to mention that. Are you one of those creeps who wants ten wives?"

"No." He shakes his head vehemently. "Not into sharing of any kind."

I scoff. "You manage to make something good sound so selfish."

"Good?" He quirks a brow.

"What?"

"Me being a one-woman man. Why do you find it good?"

Damn. Busted. I stand up straighter, grabbing the correct clipboard and fleeing the area. "I don't."

He still follows. "You said I manage to make something good sound so selfish. Something good meaning—"

"I know what I said," I interrupt, but don't add anything else as I walk down the curved path of the greenhouse. I dodge the gigantic elephant ear leaves.

"Jealousy is not a good look on you," Tristan teases from behind me.

I halt dead in my tracks and whirl toward him with all the attitude I can muster. *Hell no.* He will not think he won. "One, I look good in everything. Two, I'm not jealous."

He hums, his expression smug. "Of course, Your Majesty."

Spring is the best season.

And I'm not just saying that because of my birthday.

It's a relief when autumn hits after a long, sweltering summer. But the world coming alive again on the heels of a dark winter is invigorating. The budding trees and flowers offer hope, another chance of growth. May is Felicity Gardens' busiest month—it's the perfect in-between weather before it gets too miserably hot here in Southern Europe.

The garden doesn't open until eleven on weekdays, so I take advantage of it by visiting the most popular section. I sit under a weeping willow on the riverbank, listening to the water trickle downstream. A few Mallard ducks float by, and if this were my own property, I'd feed them. But we don't need them coming back.

Slivers of sunlight peek through the willow's swaying tendrils and glitters on the water. I close my eyes and inhale the scent of mulch and fresh-cut grass as sparrow birds sing in the tree above me.

All at once, stress drains from my body.

"What are you doing?"

I gasp, a hand to my chest as my heart leaps into my throat. I see Tristan behind me, waiting. It wasn't a *oh-ha-ha-you-scared-me* type of thing. It was a full blown *holy-shit-I-almost-pissed-my-pants* type of scare.

Just like that, any tranquility I garnered is tossed into the river.

"Jesus Christ, the fuck is wrong with you?" I snap, reorienting myself.

"All I did was ask what you're doing."

"You snuck up on me!"

He crinkles his nose. "It's not my fault you didn't hear me coming."

"Right, because nothing is *ever* your fault."

"I repeat my question: what are you doing—besides your favorite pastime of yelling at me?"

I bite back a groan. "Meditating."

"Meditating? You're this brutal even when you *meditate*?" He huffs. "Well, fuck me."

If I weren't so damn pissed he ruined my peaceful morning, I might have chuckled. Or even full-belly laughed. "What do you want?"

"Dr. Pagoda is looking for you."

I snatch my bag and swipe the dirt off my butt. Tristan watches me, but I refuse to shrink under his stare. This is my territory. My garden. He doesn't say anything as we head down the sunny path. Daisies, purple coneflowers, and black-eyed susans flank us on either side as fig trees scatter beyond. I notice him staring at the biggest tree as we near it.

"It's beautiful, isn't it?" I say, unable to stop myself.

"Hm?"

"The tree." I walk over to the gigantic roots. They grow

directly vertical as if creating little walls, but the tallest one reaches my knee.

"What kind is it?" he asks.

"Ficus aurea, or strangler fig, or just fig." His gaze is locked on the massive growth on one of the branches. I point to them and say, "Those are called aerial roots. They'll grow straight into ground and actually help the tree get stronger by becoming another route to transfer nutrients. We're debating on whether we should let them grow or trim them back because strangler figs can be invasive."

"Invasive how?"

I pause to gather the easiest way to say it. "Well—they're strong, obviously." I gesture to the roots below my feet and winding around my ankles. "And like it says in their name, they strangle. Which isn't much different than the ivy you saw me remove on your first day here. They can overgrow the other plants here. On the other hand, they can be really good for the ecosystem. It provides protection and food for birds and squirrels." I shrug. "It might not even matter in the end; this tree will be here hundreds if not thousands of years after me."

"Wait—*thousands*? Of years?"

I nod eagerly. "Absolutely! The oldest living tree is almost five thousand years old. It was germinated some-time between—oh, what was it?" I mutter to myself. "I think three thousand BC? Two thousand BC? Something like that."

Tristan looks like I'm telling him I invented gravity. While I'm surprised he doesn't know the potential lifespan of a tree, I don't say anything. I don't want him to get discouraged.

"Wait, how do you—why—*what*?"

I chuckle and pull my ringing phone from my pocket. "Shit, it's Dr. Pagoda. We better go."

Reluctantly, he rips his wonder-filled gaze from the tree to follow.

My boss is waiting eagerly as I meet her where the pasture meets the forest.

"Te Maégla, stara protí?" she asks in Maldanian.

Your Majesty, are you ready?

"Ready?" I echo. "For what?"

"To be in charge."

I pause mid-step. Dr. Pagoda watches me with bright eyes and a smirk. She knows how long I've been waiting to be in charge of a project. After nearly a year under her training, she finally thinks I'm ready!

I tamper my giddiness as she explains the issue at hand. Lymantria dispars—or spongy moths—have destroyed this part of the forest. We were lucky enough to build Felicity Gardens around an old-growth forest which would help us protect five-hundred-plus-year-old trees, but these pesky little moths managed to fell a section of them. We—I— have to work quickly so they don't ruin any more. To start, I need a trunk slice of the oldest felled tree, and I have cut it off with a chainsaw.

There are only a few in the field with us. Aside from Lyla and Dr. Pagoda, Colin and Stephen from the care team are here, too. Tristan stands off to the side, watching the scene unfold. I label the appropriate tree before Colin helps me put on the protective chaps and clasps the buckles behind my legs. I slide on gloves and accept the offered helmet. It's not my first time with a chainsaw; I've cut things in practice during safety training. However, this is the first time doing it in the field. I bite the inside of my cheek to keep from smiling as I tie my hair into a low knot.

I love my job.

"What are you doing?" Tristan asks with a slightly panicked look as I pick up the chainsaw.

"Working."

"There's—you can't get someone else to do it? I can—"

"Do I scare you?" I ask, purposely settling the machine on my crotch.

Tristan stares at the chainsaw, which conveniently looks like a dick. "The idea of you holding a chainsaw does not instill comfort in me, no."

A wicked smile spreads across my lips. I tip my head so the protective mask falls over my face. "Either put a mask on or get back. It's gonna get messy, pretty boy." Before he can reply, I yank the cord to start the machine.

His interest in the trees earlier surprised me. I thought that everyone knew that trees could live for thousands of years. Who knows how long with the proper care? I still feel rage just thinking about the woman who'd burned down one of the world's oldest trees in Florida. We need more people who give a shit.

Maybe I shouldn't be too quick to push Tristan away. The goal is for him to understand more about the earth, right?

After slicing off a section of the tree, Stephen and Colin transport it to the research building for me. I wander the area with my notebook, jotting down ideas and observations. It will be good to know what species frequent this section. I find a dead moth—the very one that's invasive—and pick it up with the tweezers from my field kit. I use a leaf as a makeshift plate as I beckon Tristan over.

"Lymantria disbar," I say, angling the insect in his direction. They're usually a shade of brown, but this one is mostly white.

He examines the lightly patterned wings. "This tiny thing destroyed huge trees?"

His awe reminds me of when I first started learning about nature. There's so much wonder all around us I couldn't possibly understand how anyone could be fascinated with much else. Nature—the earth—is the other half of human life. We can't exist without it. The discoveries and the community that comes along with Felicity Gardens are what make me whole. Anyone who spends time here is touched by its magic, and it was only a matter of time before Tristan felt it.

"Lymantria means destroyer in Latin. So yes. This tiny, fragile little thing chipped away at a mighty, two-hundred-year-old oak tree until it crumbled." *Over seasons*, I want to add. It couldn't be done within a single growing season, so they've been here for years.

"Reminds me of you."

I snort. "I can't tell if that's a compliment."

"Me neither."

I don't know if today has slipped into a dimension where down means up and left means right, but I chuckle, and so does Tristan. We chuckle *together*—and it's not as exhausting as arguing all of the time. It doesn't mean I'll stop, but it's a nice break.

CHAPTER FOURTEEN

TRISTAN

"This is what you lot do every day?" I ask as we head back to the research building.

Maia shrugs. "It varies, but more or less, yes."

I'm finding a deeper appreciation for nature as long as she's the one explaining it to me. When she does, she has the brightest light in her eyes as if she needs to share it or else it would blind her. I lie to myself by saying I stay quiet so she doesn't yell at me. That's partly true, but I just like watching her work.

Her brows crease, not unlike how she looks when annoyed, this time with focus. She double-checks reports, surveys the plants for any pests. I'm sure the handiwork is reserved for the time I'm here, and the rest such as meetings and teamwork for the rest.

I've also noticed just how clumsy she is. In the month and a half I've been here, I can't count the number of times she's knocked into tables, chairs, dropped pens, clipboards, and plants. It never bothers her, either. She'll mutter *"ouch"* and move on like it's nothing, only for her to whine about a bruise she has no idea how she got. And she stretches a lot. She'll roll her shoulders after watering plants and extend her neck after writing reports. It's why I wanted someone else to use the chainsaw. The mere thought of her getting hurt makes me panic.

There's no one inside lab #3, which is where I follow Maia. It's silent as I sit at the center island to jot down more notes. In a normal scenario, I would have declined Dr. Pagoda's suggestion to start writing things down. But I need this to go as smoothly as possible.

"Come here," Maia says. "I want to show you something." When I rise, she asks, "Do you know about the fires of 1913?"

"In Maldana? Of course. I'm shocked you do, too."

She cocks a brow. "And why is my knowledge surprising?"

"You weren't educated here."

"Neither were you."

I cross my arms and suppress the urge to smirk. "Were you researching me, Your Majesty?"

"Don't make me regret being nice to you."

"You have *never* been nice to me."

"Just—shut up and come here." She gestures for me to come closer. The circular tree stump she'd sawed off earlier sits under a bright white light.

"It's a tree," I say.

She gently elbows me. "Here." She brushes her fingers over the tree rings, specifically over a darkened scar. "This is from the fires of 1913."

I lean closer. "Really?"

Maia beams with a nod. "Here, feel it." She takes my hand and presses the pads of my fingers to the same scar. I feel the ridges in the wood, the hardened mark scraping against my skin.

"It's like you're traveling back in time," she says softly. "Fascinating, huh?"

My heartbeat slows. An outdoor smell lingers from our time in the woods, but her usual rosy scent punches through. From up here, I have a full view of her long lashes. Her hair is still knotted at the base of her neck to reveal her bronzed face. She was paler when we first met, but her light honey skin has darkened to a tawny brown. Her round cheeks and pouty lips look so fucking kissable and I don't know how much more torture I can take.

"Completely."

Maia looks up at me and I'm hard instantly. Thankfully, she doesn't notice, but she still withdraws. "Okay, enough of that." She clears her throat, pointedly avoiding my gaze. "I have to work, go away."

I find my seat again before she can spot the bulge in my pants. What would I even do? Ask her on a date? She would spend the entire time insulting me and judging me for whatever I did or did not do. I want to know what she tastes like. I crave the sounds she would make if I pleased her and I need to make her laugh again like I did earlier today. I'm not a funny bloke, but I'd enroll in clown college if it meant she would laugh.

We work in easy silence for another fifteen minutes until footsteps slow around the corner. I glance up in time for Augustus to pop up.

"Mr. Farrugia," he says as if relieved. He's been searching for me. He flinches when seeing Maia. "Your Majesty." He bows, his tablet clutched at his side.

"It's nice to see you again, Augustus."

He smiles. "And I, you."

"What are you doing here?" I ask a little too harshly.

"I—you weren't answering your phone."

"I shut it off. Celine kept bothering me." She wasn't; I didn't want to be interrupted during my time with Maia.

"Yes, well, it's about the conference on Friday. Another representative from Apple just RSVP'd."

A hint of panic begins to rise. I have more than profits riding on this deal being closed. "Dammit." I pull my phone out of my pocket to turn it on.

"I wasn't sure if you wanted to increase—"

"We'll talk about this at the office."

"What's the conference for?" Maia asks, stopping on the other side of the island.

"Nothing," I say.

"I can find out on my own, so you may as well tell me."

"It's not important." I turn to my assistant. "We'll head back now—"

"Augustus, would you mind telling me what the conference is about?"

I send a glare her way. She's butting in and knows it. She smirks. "You know about *my* job. I can't know about yours?"

He looks between the two of us before responding. "Uh, it's a conference with company representatives, Your Majesty."

"What kind of companies?"

"Augustus, don't." There's no good way this ends. I'm not sure he realizes just how feisty and direct the princess is.

"Mining and technology."

"Mining." She perks, a hesitant expression pulling at her features. "Mining where?"

"Uh—the—the Congo."

"And how many acres?"

He bristles and looks at me, unsure whether to reveal that information. It doesn't matter at this point; none of it should have been shared.

"A million," I answer.

Maia doesn't hide her surprise, glancing to Augustus as if seeking confirmation. She shakes her head, attitude building. "Let me get this straight—"

"Maia—"

"You come here with your whole *show me your ways* attitude, acting like you're ready to be humbled and shit only to turn around and bid on ripping up a million acres of land for profit when you and your company are already billionaires?"

Shame bubbles inside of me. I can't tell her she's wrong. "It's not as—"

She sees right through my weak argument and goes right for the jugular.

"*Fuck you*, Tristan. Stay the hell away from me." She storms out of the room, past an utterly stunned Augustus. It only irritates me more.

It doesn't hurt that she said *"fuck you"* with her whole chest. What guts me is the disgusted look on her face.

And the troubling emotions that follow.

My guilt isn't from feeling as though I led her on, but the hypocrisy of it all. I had been so focused on my goal of getting in these volunteer hours to get my inheritance faster that I didn't consider the irony. Not attending the conference wasn't on my radar. It's business. My absence would be a topic, an issue.

Either way, any ground I covered with Maia was just completely scorched.

Thanks to my assistant.

I scowl at Augustus, who shrinks as I step closer. "I don't care if the bloody pope is begging for you to answer a question. You work for *me*. If I tell you to keep your mouth shut, you do it."

CHAPTER FIFTEEN
MAIA

In spite of finding out Tristan is the heartless asshole I always assumed he was, I still have work to do. I'm leading the project to eradicate the lymantria dispar from our forests. These moths hurt the ecosystems in many ways, and the last thing I want to do is spray pesticides. The forest would bounce back eventually, but it's already vulnerable. There's no one-size-fits-all for getting rid of them; I have to factor in the climate and other local species.

Curled on the couch in the break room, I brush up on the history of these moths and common ways to get rid of them. They managed to take down a large, old oak tree. That's no easy feat. It means they've spent multiple growing seasons attacking this region. It doesn't help that they're native to our current region, meaning it will be a lot harder to get rid of them. Dr. Pagoda is trusting me with a huge task; I can't let her down.

Their feeding months are just beginning, so it's the perfect time to put in the work. I spend a solid four hours gathering mountains of research from our own department and the internet. Other responsibilities pull me away at some point, but I hop right back to it until the sun starts to set.

Playing fetch with my dogs and cuddling Sage and my ducks is the perfect way to unwind after a long day. Esme had dropped by midday to let Elliot and Olivia have some freedom in the yard instead of being locked in their coop to avoid predators, so I don't feel bad about putting them to bed after twenty minutes of roaming time.

It's not until after I make myself dinner that I think about Tristan for the first time today. The day was filled to the brim with research, but I yank out my laptop to look up the conference Augustus was referring to.

It doesn't take long to find articles describing the negotiations. The conference isn't mentioned, but many companies—Apple, Android, Space Tech, Samsung, Google, and a whole lot more—are competing for the handful of mining companies that contain the rights and permits to land in the Democratic Republic of Congo.

According to the article, many of the tech companies have been feeling pressure from their shareholders to expand. What baffles me is the way this article is written, as if the biggest concern is which company can pull through with the best deal.

I seek out another source depicting the humanitarian concerns and—dreadfully—find myself on social media. I log in with my burner accounts to get on-the-ground information. People share their stories straight to the camera, unfiltered. Everything must be taken with a grain of salt, but the proof is there, clear as day. Part of this deal includes expansion into occupied territory: the town of Lukinda.

They make videos and posts about their local government cooperating with the mining industry. They're protesting. They're marching. People are sharing and spreading the word on social media, but it's not on any major news network.

There has to be something I can do. I don't have social media anymore, but I'm not a fan of hitting repost and then moving on entirely. I'm too angry for that.

But when I'm angry about an injustice and ready to do something, my first step is Nina. She helps me act out of logic, which has proven time and time again that it gets me just a tad further in my goals.

I'm pacing in front of my kitchen table as the phone rings. Finally, after *hours* (ten minutes), Nina answers my FaceTime.

"Hey," she sings.

I huff, already exasperated. "I need help."

She looks at the camera, her expression sobering. "What's up?"

I explain everything I found out, leaving out the fact that I felt mildly duped by Tristan after thinking he began to actually care about things. In between asking questions and making gasps of horror at the dilemma, she sets the phone down and extends her body across a yoga mat in a downward dog pose before the cobra pose. Except she places it at the top which gives me a full view of her boobs in a sports bra.

"Can you flaunt your big tits another day?" I ask, my face twisted in envy.

"Oops! Sorry." She moves the phone to the side, then giving me a view of her little baby bump in tights. It's still so weird to see my big sister pregnant.

"Anyway, I don't know what to do," I continue. "But I can't sit around."

"Well, Maia..." Her voice takes on that sympathetic tone. "I'm not sure what we *could* do other than make a public statement." She shrugs, tossing one arm overhead to stretch. "Unless you can convince a bunch of greedy people to be *less* greedy..."

"I'll do that, then." I consider for a moment. We have no ties to this conference or deal. But this is why I accepted the crown, right? To get me into places that others can't.

Nina snorts. "How are you going to do that?"

"I'll go to the conference," I say, thinking out loud. "Maybe I can try to convince them to give a shit."

Nina sits cross-legged in front of the camera. "You're serious?"

"It's the best choice. I can find out where it is and—" I lift a hand, searching for the word. "Buy a ticket, I guess. Find a way to be someone's plus-one if I have to."

She studies me for a few moments, taking in my sincerity and the logistics of it. Eventually, she gives a slow nod. "They might have you sign an NDA about attending."

"Perfect. I don't want the public to know." Considering my luck, they would twist it and say I was there in support of the mining. I can get a seat at the table; I won't squander it.

My sister opens her mouth as though to speak. "I, um— you could..." She laughs, her face flushing. "Sorry, Wesley's staring at me."

Off-screen, he says, "You've been doing yoga in front of me for the past ten minutes and you expect me not to stare?"

"Well, I..." Her face still red, she looks at me through the camera. "I gotta go, Maia. We'll talk about this tomorrow."

I crinkle my nose at the thought of what's about to ensue. "Ew, bye."

I send an email labeled *urgent* to my office so their first task tomorrow is getting me a ticket to this conference. I take a sick day to anticipate my access and prepare all of my facts.

Mining destroys habitats, causes erosion, and can contaminate soil and water. Based on the accounts of Congolese citizens and activists, there are no restrictions in effect to ensure safety. I'm well aware of the fact that the laptop I'm using for research is made up of these harvested materials. But mass production is often unnecessary and tramples on the rights of other forms of life. It's not right. Reaping the benefits of a practice doesn't mean it's exempt from evil.

Then there's the displacement. It's said to be voluntary, but nothing says *it's your choice* like a group of corporate men who have as many mistresses as they do cars. They're powerful, amoral, and dominant.

I don't know if I can stop them. I don't think I can. But I wouldn't be able to live with myself if I didn't try.

After some negotiations and a hefty transfer from my savings account, I have a ticket to the conference. The afternoon is filled with various meetings: Nico from the Lord Chamberlain's office coordinates my transportation and accommodations, George from communications prepares a safety net story if I'm spotted by paparazzi, Mason rehashes security measures, Nina and our team of advisors, Stella, Dan, Alina, and Jordan, go over my diplomatic approach.

I'll be a fish out of water and need to integrate myself. Rather than nudging my way in by cozying up to a single person and exploring their connections, I'll lean into the path of least resistance to start. I have to be comfortable standing on my own and making my way around the room.

Eventually, I'll talk my way to the most powerful executive in the room, but not before I've spread the ideas of environmental and humanitarian impact among my previous conversations.

Jordan, the most brutal of them all, flat-out says it won't work. He thinks I'll be disrupting them like a tick.

"I think you underestimate her charm," Nina says. She's taking the video call in her home office; I can spot her lamp made of stacked rocks in the background—the very one I vow to steal every time I see it. "She knows how to work people."

I crinkle my nose. "I don't like saying it like that."

"Then you have to be careful so you don't sound like you are lecturing," Jordan says, his Maldanian accent heavy. He's never been the best at speaking English and I always feel left out when he and Nina are chatting away in another language. Yeah, it's been years, but I'm barely conversational. My sister was fluent by the time she was crowned queen. Languages come easily to her. Not me.

"Get personal," Alina suggests. "It will make them feel important."

"Not too much," Stella argues. "Wealthy people like their privacy."

"You can do this," Nina tells me. "You're passionate. If you use your knowledge and passion in a way that invites people in instead of teaching them, you'll get it done. At worst, you'll cause a delay. It's still a step forward."

I nod, ready to repeat those words over and over for the next forty-eight hours. This is my chance to make a bigger difference than ever before. I won't mess it up.

CHAPTER SIXTEEN

MAIA

I wear a fitted black dress that reaches the very top of my knees. A simple silver necklace adorns the square neckline and my defined curls spill down my back. My dress is long enough to be professional and tight enough to be scandalous. Unlike Nina, I have no problem with flirting my way through. My height alone makes me stand out and my goal is to garner attention. If I catch their eyes, I may catch their ears.

It's raining in London tonight, and quite a bit colder than Maldana. I shiver as I step through the back entrance, Mason in tow. Usually, Zeke would accompany me at an event like this where I can easily be spotted and recognized. He might be shorter than me and built like a house, but there were a few rumors about the two of us. He's known to my fans. And tonight, I need discretion.

Mason waits in the decadent lobby as I step into the ballroom. It's the length of a football field as three glimmering, lavish chandeliers dangle at equal distance from the ceiling. The dais along the wall is lit up and the walls are a soft shade of gold. There's assigned seating at the dozen or so circular tables, and half of them are abandoned in favor of congregating at random pockets. It seems more of a party than a conference.

I dive right in, starting with the person whose seat is assigned beside me. He's a young executive assistant with one of the mining companies, and he completely agrees with all of my ideas. Like me, he wants there to be better safety and ecological regulations and for the mining zone to exclude Lukinda. However, in fear of losing his job, he's reluctant to speak up. I keep this in mind as I move on to speak with someone else. There are a lot of people here tonight and I need to speak with as many as I can.

It's easy to strike up a conversation with one of the wives at the open bar. Her name is Alice and she's here with Eddie, her husband and CEO of an England-based computer company I've never heard of.

"—and we've just returned from Switzerland and here we are," Alice says, finishing her story with a sip of champagne.

"How was Switzerland? I've never been."

Just as my question sends her into a fit of Swiss praises, a man I'm assuming to be her husband steps up to her. "Found someone to talk the ear off of, dear?"

She taps his arm. "Oh, stop it. I'm making friends."

I grin at already being called her friend. Alice winks at me over her champagne glass. Before long, Eddie and I start chatting, too. I use the opportunity to bring up the ethical concerns of these deals and even though he's receptive, I have no way of hinting whether he plans to do anything about it. It sends him into his own rehashing of his vacation in the Congo. I feign interest.

I've been scanning the room habitually since I walked

in, seeking out Tristan. He's taller than most of the people here, but I have yet to see him.

Until now.

He and I meet gazes at the same time from halfway across the room. He startles, blinking repeatedly as though I'm a figment of his imagination. My stomach clenches when he savors me from head to toe, and I admit he looks entirely delicious in his dark blue slacks and white button-up. His thin silver necklace matches the tiny diamond studs in his ears.

Before Eddie can realize I've stopped listening to his story, I rip my eyes from Tristan's just as he deciphers the real reason I'm here. I smile at the short man in front of me with a smug sense of pride. Tristan's stare burns through me.

"Eddie, I'm sorry," I interject, a soft hand on his forearm. I glance at Alice. "If you'll excuse me, I have to find the ladies' room."

"Oh, of course!"

I slip away from the two of them and stride toward Tristan. The room is big and crowded enough that Alice and Eddie likely won't notice it was just an excuse to break away from the conversation.

Tristan stands chatting with a middle-aged white man with golden hair, a thick midsection, and hanging jowls. The man notices my approach, giving me a full view of his sparkly blue eyes. I bet he was handsome in his youth.

"Fancy seeing you here," I say to Tristan, who can hardly manage a pleasantry. "Aren't you going to introduce me?" I turn to his company.

"Joseph Stratford," he says, his accent American. He watches me with a hint of familiarity.

I shake his extended hand with a warm smile. "Maia."

His face broadens with recognition. "The American princess of Maldana. It's an honor, Your Majesty." The shift in his body language tells me he was open to my presence, but my title piques his genuine interest. "How do you know Mr. Farrugia?"

"We've crossed paths once or twice." I lean closer. "If you don't mind me asking, where are you from? Don't get me wrong, I love living in Maldana, but it can feel so much like home to hear an American accent sometimes."

Joseph grins. "I know exactly what you mean. I'm from Georgia. You?"

"A Southerner," I drawl, a flirtatious glint in my eyes. "I'm from Massachusetts. A Yankee through and through."

"As long as you're not an actual Yankees fan, we're good."

I laugh a little too hard.

"Now, if you don't mind *me* asking," he continues, "do you have any stock in the companies here tonight? I'm just a little surprised to see someone like you here."

Ninety percent of the women here are either plus-ones or staff, and I have no doubt I'm the youngest attendee. I shake my head. "Not financial stock, no."

Joseph tilts his head slightly. "I don't follow."

"I'm here to discuss what we can do to improve the ethical efforts of the deals made tonight."

"The... ethical efforts." The look on his face tells me he's truly lost.

"Well, the goal is to make everyone involved happy, right? That can happen, but there should be adjustments made to achieve that unanimous goal."

"Like what?"

I start my speech in the way I practiced a dozen times. I'm fully aware that Joseph and I have all but pushed

Tristan out of this conversation. He stands at my side, simmering quietly with anger.

He can back me up. He can care about the people of Lukinda who were betrayed by their government. He has the chance to do some good, and he won't.

It only encourages me.

"You've been quiet, Mr. Farrugia," Joseph eventually says. "What are your thoughts?"

Tristan looks down at the empty glass in his hand. "I think I'm out of whisky."

It's as if a blade slices my stomach when Joseph laughs. In just a few words, Tristan managed to diminish everything I just said.

"I am, too. Allow me to refill for us."

Tristan nods at Joseph with a smile, which only turns to a frown when he leaves. "We need to talk."

"Yeah, no shit," I snap, ready to tear into him for belittling me like that. Before I can, he takes my elbow and guides me from the crowd. I glance around to see if anyone notices; no one does. His grip tightens and my anger rises. If he squeezes any more, I'll make a scene.

I dispose of my glass on a waiter's serving tray as we head—*I'm dragged*—to the hallway on the far side of the room that leads to the bathrooms. Sconces with low, warm light are dotted down the hallway on archways.

As soon as we're in the dim lighting, far from people, I shove him off me. "Grab me like that again and I will slice off your testicles and shove them down your throat."

Tristan is unfazed by my threat, but he does back off with his hands up in surrender. "You here to get back at me?"

"Excuse me?"

"Because you were angry at me the other day? This isn't funny. This is my work."

Would it be a cherry on top to make him angry? Absolutely. But it's not the reason I'm here. I don't chase men.

"You think I'm that petty? That I'd fucking chase you? I'm here because you and all these men are about to commit a humanitarian and an environmental disaster."

Tristan releases a quick, sardonic laugh. "And you thought you were going to stop deals worth billions?"

"I had to do something. It's better than bending over for money the way you do."

He grimaces. "Spare me the self-righteous speech, all right? I've been working on this agreement for months—"

"An agreement that displaces hundreds of families—"

"Each of whom is receiving a very generous package with more than enough money and resources to start fresh—"

"You're bribing them into giving up their ancestral lands *so you can rip it up*! You'll be ruining ecosystems and biodiversity!"

"This is *business*, Maia!"

"*And this is life!* Why is it so fucking important for you to put profit over having a fucking soul?" I step back, releasing a huff. My frustration definitely includes anger toward him. If I didn't want to speak with him, I wouldn't have let him drag me away. I could have stood my ground; a small part of me hoped he'd actually agree. I was foolish. "Men like you hate it when people, especially women, make you face what your *business* deals do."

"No," he snaps, invading my space until I'm backed against the wall. "Not *women*. Just one. One *royal* pain in my ass. One maddening, aggravating, and outrageously beautiful woman who disagrees with every step I take."

We're roughly the same height when I'm in heels, but his broad shoulders nearly trap me. The tension between our bodies thickens and I can't rip my eyes from his, the intensity burning me from the inside out.

I swallow. "If you took the right steps, I wouldn't have to disagree with you."

Tristan leans in dangerously close, close enough for me to smell the alcohol on his breath, close enough for me to feel the heat from his body. He's clean-shaven, his facial hair trimmed perfectly as it always is, and his pine and musk scent is inviting when I should be slamming and locking the door. But I can't. I don't just leave the door open, I take half of a step inside by tilting toward him ever so slightly.

"And what about this?" he whispers, his accent sending sparks down my spine. "Is this the right step?"

He shifts closer, and I let out a tiny but audible gasp. My hands fly to the V-neck of his button-down, my fingers curling over the edge. Whether it's to pull him close or push him off is debatable.

"I... I don't know," I admit.

Though he leans in first, our lips find each other like magnets in a flash of heat and longing. My trembling hands travel to his face as if to ground myself in this reality: *I'm kissing Tristan. Tristan is kissing* me.

His tongue prods my lips and I don't hesitate deepening the kiss. He groans, pinning me flush against the wall as he tugs my dress up just enough to nestle his leg between my thighs, gently rubbing the perfect spot. Lust pools deep in my stomach and the whisky lingering on his tongue sends sparks through my mouth, its spice melting me. Without my permission, a moan pulls from my throat as his hands take a strong hold of my hips.

I slip my fingers through his collar just to feel more of his warm skin. He moans when I tug his bottom lip with my teeth, and the sound ignites something deep inside of me. Our tongues clash as both of our defenses melt together. His lips leave wet kisses on my neck and I drop my head against the wall, squeezing my eyes shut to keep from falling into him entirely.

Three words echo in my mind: *I want him, I want him, I want him.*

I can't stop my whimper when his tongue drags from my jaw to my collarbone. Goosebumps douse my body and my nipples tighten. My legs tighten around his thigh at the feel of his rock-hard erection. If I don't stop this, I'll fuck him right here and now.

"Let me go," I whisper, hoping he doesn't sense my desperation. His hands fall from my hips instantly, braced on the wall behind me. I ache for him as soon as he pulls his thigh from between my legs. Ripping myself from the most delicious kiss I've ever had is torture, but I have to. This is wrong and *not* why I came here tonight.

He steps back as I fix my dress.

"We can't do this," I say, my voice hoarse. "I—I can't..." I shake my head and, without another word, I push past him and don't look back.

CHAPTER SEVENTEEN
TRISTAN

Maia nearly ruined everything.

I've been working on this deal for the last two months, but to tell the truth, I don't care anymore. The accomplishment of closing the deal would have paled in comparison to finally kissing the princess of Maldana.

An unexpected giddiness runs up my spine at knowing what she tastes like at last. What her moans sound like. How she feels pressed up against me. It's nowhere near enough; I need more of her, and it's the one time I'll admit I'm greedy.

Part of me is regretful because I want to take things slow with Maia—and I don't understand why. I wouldn't have objected to sleeping with her last night, but I essentially pounced on her out in the open. I feel as though I disrespected her, even though she broke my shirt button and I had to return to the conference with my chest exposed until Augustus brought me a replacement.

Kissing has never done much for me, yet I couldn't stop staring at her mouth last night. All I kept thinking about was how soft it would be, how her bottom lip would feel tugged between my teeth, how it would look wrapped around—

I drag my hands down my face. *Pull yourself together.* I'm working through Saturday so we can close this deal once and for all and I can't let these thoughts distract me.

I doubt Maia knows that Joseph was simply being kind. While I was on a flight back to Kosita, he faxed over his final version of the contract. She hadn't swayed him or anyone else—except for me.

This deal would have gotten Celine off my back and kept the board satisfied. They're not happy with Space Tech's profit momentum stalling and they're depending on my ability to wrap up this contract so we can push more products.

I hadn't drafted the plan; my role is to advocate for it and broker the deal. The Human Resources department approved it on ethical grounds, so I paid no mind to the community impact. After reviewing it, I was appalled at the potential aftermath. And my own company approved this? I can't pretend to be completely ignorant. Perhaps I gave no more thought because no one else had. It's a shite excuse, but I'm paying attention now.

I waffle back and forth for ten minutes, not wanting to make changes just because of a woman. Though I know she's not wrong. I can't deny it. I've never taken a stand such as this. Is there a right time? A wrong time?

I finally hit the intercom button to summon my assistant. Within seconds, Augustus appears at the door.

"Before we sign this contract," I begin, "I need you to research a potential shift in the mining zones in Lukinda. See if it's possible to avoid the most populated areas or cut the town out of the mining map altogether. And to avoid any sacred lands."

He doesn't look up as he jots this down in his little note-book. "Yes, sir."

"Can you have it done in an hour? If not, I can push back the meeting."

Augustus shakes his head, his face contorting as if I insulted him. "No, this is easy. It'll be done."

Without saying anything further, he turns on his heel and returns to his desk. Augustus is a damn good employee and if he asked, I'd gladly increase his salary. One of the pillars of knowledge from Grandfather included only giving raises to those who ask. Those who ask have more drive, and we want driven employees to stay.

My assistant wasn't lying when he said it would be done efficiently. Ten minutes before my requested time, there's a printed and stapled contract amendment in front of me. With his own copy, he sits in the chair before me and rehashes the content section by section.

"—and even with the improvements in every other area, there *will* be a decrease in the estimated profit," he finishes. "We're punching up."

I sigh, rubbing a hand down the back of my head. Although both of our companies bring in billions, Joseph won't be happy with a decrease in profit. "We have to try. This is brilliant work, Augustus."

He beams in pride before modestly schooling his reaction into a nod. "Thank you, sir."

"You'll sit in on the meeting?"

"Yes," he says, his modesty slipping again as his eyes widen and he sits up straighter. "That would be—yes."

Joseph rejects the amendment.

The meeting lasts a little more than two hours and consists of our respective lawyer teams and assistants. Augustus and I defend the amendment from beginning to end, but Joseph refuses to consider even an extension. My diplomacy manages to keep our relationship professional, but as soon as we're on our way back to my office, I lean toward Augustus.

"Find a zoning attorney and have him call me. The best one you can find. No budget. One with a specialty in cultural lands, if you can," I add.

He nods, already pulling up his phone and typing away. A knot of apprehension seizes me. Or is it guilt? This is my assistant's job—and I have no problem with assigning him tasks.

Having him work without giving him recognition until he asks doesn't sit right with me. Grandfather's former assistant, Roberto, had worked for him for nearly a decade, and I don't ever remember seeing Roberto in anything but a foul mood. My grandfather isn't here anymore. Perhaps I don't have to do everything the same way he did.

As Augustus gets to work behind his desk, I try to focus on reports until I get a call from Celine an hour later. She and the board must have heard about the botched deal. I know I need to deal with them eventually; I was hoping that wouldn't happen until at least Monday.

"What's this I'm hearing about us backing out of the deal?" Celine asks.

I bite back a huff. "I can't go through with it in good faith."

"Why not?"

"We'll talk about it at the Monday meeting." Honestly, I need more time to gather my thoughts and prepare a defense. My plans of sculpting tonight have flown out of the window. Hopefully I can at least send Augustus home before dinnertime.

"There's no reason not to go through with Stratford!" Celine argues. "What the bloody hell has gotten into you?" Ah, the real reason she called me. She can't be as blunt in front of the board. "The inheritance is getting straightened away and I admit the investment in Mexico locations worked out. Aside from the dip in China, all is fine. It's not just me you need to convince, you have to convince the board this is a good idea."

"I will see you at the Monday meeting, Celine. I'm hanging up."

"Tristan—"

I set the phone on the receiver, grateful for the silence encompassing my office.

CHAPTER EIGHTEEN
MAIA

Shit shit shit shit *shit*.

I made a mistake. A huge fucking mistake. I never should have let him get that close to me. But my god, he smelled so good and seeing him angry set something alight inside of me. If I hold my dress from last night up to my nose, I can still smell his cologne—musk and pine. I may have sniffed this a few times.

Or ten.

I had begun melting as soon as he'd pinned me against the wall; the moment his lips touched mine, both of us dissolved into each other. It's all I could think about for hours until I fell asleep. The good. The bad. Maybe it would be worth a one-time thing. We could get it out of our systems and move on with our lives. Obviously, nothing could happen between us. Our morals don't align. I could never be with someone who is content doing nothing with untapped resources that could change the lives of millions, maybe billions.

It just doesn't make any sense. Underneath our bickering, Tristan is *kind*. He can be surprisingly funny and he's curious and witty and was incredibly thoughtful on my birthday. But how genuine was it? The donation did amazing things and I'm grateful he did it, except I don't want to be the reason he's charitable.

Maybe that's being dramatic. It's good to inspire others, right? Isn't that what my status is all about?

I toss and turn for hours in my hotel bed. After Tristan and I kissed, I dove back into the conference and spoke with over a dozen more people. All of them were kind, but some were passive-aggressive enough to tell me this was none of my business. A lot happened tonight, but all I can think about is Tristan.

My thoughts spiral overnight, and it doesn't get better the time Sunday morning rolls around when I'm back in the comfort of my own home. I stare at the article blazed across my phone screen.

An anonymous party has hired Karl Bastel from Bastel Associates, a German law firm specializing in zoning, to represent Lukinda in the following implications. There's no official statement on who hired one of the most successful firms in the field, but representatives speculate that Space Technologies is behind it. The tech company was rumored to have outbid Apple in negotiations, but Stratford Inc. announced their deal with Apple this morning.

Space Technologies is run by one of the world's youngest CEOs. Tristan Farrugia inherited his grandfather's company only two years ago at age 27. The company increased profit by—

I shut my phone off. It was Tristan who hired them. It has to be.

I compulsively invite Lyla, Esme, and Nina over under

the impression of having a simple dinner tonight and I spend the afternoon cooking to distract my tumultuous thoughts. I need to talk to someone about what happened with Tristan. Nina's been asking what happened at the conference and I honestly don't know what to say.

Was the kiss a one-time thing? In the heat of the moment? Or is it the start of something? I'm not sure what I want the answer to be.

I mumble curse words when the scent of over-cooked peppers burns my nostrils. From my seat in front of the stove, I reach over for the spatula and push around the vegetables before lowering the heat. The chair might offer relief for my aching legs, yet it doesn't help what feels like my crumbling back. I've been upright for about four hours straight and my need for food is the only thing keeping me from keeling over.

The doorbell echoes through the house, making Daisy and Poppy erupt into fits of barking. Daisy's dense bark rumbles my bones.

"Yoo-hoo!" calls Esme's sweet voice.

Relief fills me that it's her instead of Lyla. I need to lie down. "In the kitchen!"

"It smells good in here!"

Thankfully, the red peppers are the last thing that has to be cooked for my famous homemade tacos. They're Nina's favorite and I made extra for her.

Esme's happy face appears in the kitchen, her dark gold hair glowing in the late-afternoon sun.

"It's almost done," I say as she peeks under the lids of finished dishes.

"I'm so hungry. I can't wait to try it!"

"I hate to ask, but can you finish cooking the peppers

for me? They're just about done, but I need to lie down. My back—"

"Yes, go, go." She shoos me away, reaching for the spatula. "This is what you pay me for."

"Thank you so much." I grab an ice pack from the freezer on my way to my bedroom. The muscles in my back huff in relief as they're put to rest. My body so often likes to give up on supporting me, not unlike an ailing grandmother. I give myself the fifteen minutes I need to recharge before Nina and Lyla arrive.

My sister wears a baggy sweater, and it hints enough that she's still keeping the baby a secret.

We eat dinner in my gazebo. Early spring gives the evening air just enough nip for us to need a blanket when the breeze shifts. Fairy lights blend in with the pink-orange sunset glowing behind the mountains. The four of us laugh at swapped stories and clink our glasses at each other's recent work achievements. Esme's achievement is that she woke up before noon.

We're drinking sparkling apple cider because I stopped keeping alcohol at home and Lyla forgot to bring any. Even without alcohol, it's a serene night. I relish the scent of my lawn and freshly-mulched garden around us and I adore the sight of Poppy and Daisy playing off in the distance as Elliot and Olivia wander. I can't wait until it's warm enough to swim at the private lake.

I'm not a quiet, mysterious person. For most of my life, I've been the loudest one in the room. Although I can keep a secret, it's unlike me to hold some things in when I don't know what to do.

"I need your opinions on something," I say to the group.

"Oh, how was the conference!" Nina bursts, recalling the last time I asked for her help.

"That's what this is about."

"What conference?" asks Lyla. After I stormed off last Tuesday, Lyla was the first person I told about the mining deal. She doesn't know I went to the conference.

I clear my throat. "You know that conference Tristan and his assistant were talking about?"

She nods.

"I went."

Her eyes widen. "You *went*? Why?"

"What conference?" Esme asks, and I explain the whole situation, leaving out certain details the same way I did with Nina. But Lyla eyes me.

"After I did some research, I saw it's a huge issue. They were arguing over who gets to displace thousands of families and rip up the earth."

"Then why did you go?" Esme questions. The good thing about having a round table is that no one feels left out of the conversation. Esme is a housewife and my overpaid helper, but she's incredibly smart and emotionally intelligent.

"I wanted to do something. That's why I'm the princess —to do what others can't in the name of good. I wanted to convince someone to actually give a shit."

"Well, you're the princess because of your mom, but I get it," Lyla says.

Before I can react, Nina presses, "Well, how did it go? Did it work?"

My shoulders droop at the potential of disappointing my sister. She's always talking about my skill and how my hot-tempered attitude limits me.

"No," I admit, "I don't... think so."

The three of them give me their own confused look. I shrink under their stares.

"I—" Instead, I pull out my phone and show each of them the article. "I think this was Tristan."

It takes a few moments for the three of them to skim the article. Esme takes a little longer since English is her second language.

"Why do you think it was him?" Lyla asks.

"Well, we started yelling at each other in the hallway."

I pause to clear my throat, but Lyla adds, "Nothing new."

"And then we kissed."

Nina gawks. "You *kissed*?"

Esme gasps dramatically, a goofy grin on her face. Lyla, however, is rendered speechless with a dropped jaw and wide eyes.

"We just kissed, though," I add. "That was it."

Even though I wanted so much more.

Esme sobers when realizing the other two aren't as gleeful. "Wait, that's a good thing, right? We were talking about you hooking up with him on your birthday."

"I didn't think she'd actually do it," Lyla admits, and my chest caves. I look at Nina, hoping she'll say something better.

My sister lifts her shoulders. "From the way you spoke about him, it seemed like you two had a thing."

"Why didn't you say anything?"

She hesitates, reading the hopeful nature on my face. Nina has always been perceptive—and honest. So, even with remorse written on her face, she says, "I didn't want to encourage it."

In a way, I *did* make a difference. There are actions being taken against the deal, but it might be hinged on some rich asshole wanting to get into my pants. And the last thing I feel like dealing with is my sister's slight judgment in my romantic decisions on top of the threat to my—our —career.

"Right," I mutter. "I know it was dumb, but something's being done. That was the goal, right?"

"The very fact that he was *at* that conference in the first place tells you—"

"Yes, I know, Lyla, thank you."

"He's not going to change for you."

I stare at my friend incredulously, hoping she realizes the boundaries she's pushing. I'm not stupid.

She only continues. "It wouldn't last, and *your* career would be one in shambles while he's—"

"Back off," Nina bites, her eyes flaring with anger. "She's a grown woman who can make her own choices and guilt-tripping her isn't helping anything."

Lyla's mouth snaps shut. Even Esme leans a little further away. I fight the prick in the back of my eyes. The only time I hate confrontation is when it's with people I care about. Those can cost relationships, but I almost weep at my sister defending me.

"What I *also* wanted to say," Nina continues, turning toward me, "is that while I didn't encourage it, I wasn't going to stop you. You're smart. You won't get yourself into a situation you don't think is worth being in."

Nina is the only person who's had complete faith in me. The Higher Court—the leaders of the royal institution— was ecstatic to have her as their queen. Me, as the princess? I was their gamble. But my sister has fought for me every step of the way and secures our freedom in a historically oppressive environment. I just don't want to take advantage of that by engaging in a PR nightmare that is Tristan Farrugia. I can see the headlines now.

The Princess Is A Hypocrite—Again

Princess Maia Seen Kissing Tech Billionaire Despite Her Environmentalism Speech

Princess Maia's Latest Romance Is The Juiciest One Yet!

I gulp the last bit of sparkling cider in my glass, wishing it were wine.

CHAPTER NINETEEN
MAIA

The curiosity gets the best of me.

I enlist Mason's help to get Augustus's cell phone number on Monday afternoon. I worked at the garden for the first half of the day, and now I'm "working" remotely doing research. In reality, I pace my bedroom as my phone call to Augustus rings on speaker.

"Hello?" he says.

"Augustus?"

"Who's this?"

"It's Maia!"

He hesitates. "Is this a joke?"

"No," I say with a chuckle. "We met at the Space Tech building and Felicity Gardens." Again, there's hesitation. It goes on long enough that I check if the call is still connected. "Hello?"

"Your Majesty!" he exclaims. "How—how are you? My apologies. I wasn't expecting your call."

"I know, I'm sorry to call you out of the blue—"

"No worries! How can I help?"

I bite the inside of my cheek as I plop on the edge of my

bed, twirling the tassel on the corner of a pillow. "Is Tristan in the office?"

"Uh, no, he went home for the day."

"And would you happen to know where that home is?"

Augustus laughs nervously. "Um—I'm not sure Mr. Farrugia is okay with me sharing his home address."

"I just need to talk to him, and it really shouldn't be over the phone. Please?"

"Well—I... He—I don't believe he's actually home, Your Majesty. Have you tried calling him?"

I doubt he knows what happened between Tristan and me. It's not my place to tell him and frankly, I don't want him to know. But I *need* to speak with Tristan somewhere other than either of our workplaces, and our final interaction didn't exactly end on a satisfactory note—I awkwardly walked away.

"If he's not home, then you don't have to give me his home address! Do you know where he is?"

Augustus doesn't respond. I feel guilty for putting him in this position, but to find out where Tristan is, I'd have to go through official channels. Official channels have leaks and untrustworthy people. And I'd die of embarrassment if I were to text him first. I'm not sure my current method is any better, but I can't shake the growing need to see Tristan in person and face this head-on.

I can't cower. That's not who I am.

"Okay, listen," I continue. "I'm sorry for making you uncomfortable by asking you this, but I can find out by asking around, which will probably leak to the press, and that won't be good for either of us. I just need to talk to him in person—in private. And if this *does* leak to the media, the volunteer agreement will be broken. Tristan wouldn't be happy."

After a moment, he says, "You'll tell him you black-mailed me into doing this," and his matter-of-fact tone makes me straighten. My phone dings with the address, and a grin spreads onto my face.

"You are the *best*, Augustus! I owe you one. He won't even know it came from you!" I make a kissy sound at the phone before we hang up.

Before I can stew in my guilt of manipulating him, I hop up and get ready.

I slip into a cream-colored cotton dress that falls to the middle of my thighs and pair it with strappy sandals and a crocheted purse. My dress has yellow flowers and suns stitched around the edges. I try not to look *too* done-up, so I leave my hair out and curly and opt for basic makeup. I'm not going there to seduce him, but I'll be damned if I don't show up looking good.

And at least the outside can look put together whereas on the inside, I'm utter chaos.

My mind races the entire thirty-minute drive, including the wild fact that I'm driving thirty minutes just to talk to him in spite of everyone I know warning me to stay away from him. It wasn't just me in that hallway. Tristan kissed me just as passionately.

The chemistry between us is palpable, but the under-lying curiosity is why he's doing this and why he won't come out and say it. How much of his generosity is genuine? How much of it is simply to win me over?

I knock heavily on his door after parking on a side street. This seems like an industrial building turned into apartments, and at least it's a more residential area of Kosita. People here are more likely to mind their business.

My heart nearly beats out of my chest when Tristan opens the door. He flinches at the sight of me, and my stomach roils at the sight of *him*. He wears a white tank top and gray fucking sweatpants as if I didn't already have a loose sense of control of myself.

"Maia?" He looks down the hallway on either side of me to see if I'm alone. "How did you—why—?"

I wait for him to finish stuttering, my arms crossed. "Are you going to invite me inside?"

Tristan shifts aside, and though I'm not sure what I was expecting, it certainly wasn't *this*. Past the overhang, the ceiling lifts another twenty feet with windows just as tall. On the left side of the room is an array of sculptures of humans, animals, nature, and more. To the right—work tables, supplies, and a kiln in the far corner. I find myself drifting to the sculptures. Some are as tall as I am and some are the size of a fist.

But they're incredible.

I gawk at a detailed sculpture of an owl, the dips and curves creating the perfect shadows to capture the feathers.

"If you're done," Tristan says, startling me, "I'd like to know why you're here."

"Did you make these?" I ask.

He nods slowly. "I did."

Like my home, this is Tristan's oasis. There's soft jazz music playing and an open window replenishes the room with fresh air.

"They're beautiful," I mumble. He doesn't reply, and I inhale deeply, gathering myself. "You blew the deal with Joseph Stratford."

His tense shoulders sag, making a knot of concern twist in my stomach. "Your speech moved him, remember?"

I cross my arms again, partly out of embarrassment for what I'm about to admit. "He was playing me. I know he signed with Apple. Instead of you."

Tristan shrugs and heads toward one of the work tables. "Dunno what you mean." He starts cleaning art supplies with a rag.

"And you hired Karl Bastel," I add. "Why?"

"How did you know to find me here?"

I clear my throat. "A little birdie told me."

He squints. "It was Augustus, wasn't it?"

"He's an innocent party and I blackmailed him. So leave the poor man alone." I give him a subtle puppy dog look in the hopes of sealing the deal. He rolls his eyes in response, but I doubt he's angry enough to punish his assistant. I make a mental note to check in with Augustus in a few days.

"You could've called me," Tristan says. "Or texted."

I ignore his statement, not ready to verbally admit I wanted to see him. "Why did you hire Karl Bastel?"

"Or even waited until tomorrow at the garden."

"Tristan."

He tilts his head. *"Maia."*

I watch him clean the tools, the way the muscles in his hands flex as he scrubs clay from them. "You're not answering my question."

"You're not answering mine," he counters.

"I asked first."

A sardonic smile pulls at his lips, and I ache at the memory of tasting them just days ago, of tugging his bottom lip between my teeth. He sets down the tools and rag before stalking over to me. My five-eleven height means I take up space, and I often naturally garner the attention of whatever room I'm in. But Tristan's presence humbles me, his thick brows dented and his eyes narrowed into slits. His harsh expression belies the charming smile I know he possesses.

"You could have called," he repeats, still advancing toward me, "or texted, or waited. I'll be at the garden *tomorrow*. Instead, you harassed my assistant to give you this address because yes, although Augustus is rather weak in the knees for you, he wouldn't roll over just like that. That alone means you'll answer *my* questions first."

He stops when there's a foot between us. I bristle under his heavy stare. In nearly every encounter, I've been in control of the conversation. I'm not as controlling as my sister, but I'm confident. I know what I want. That's always been the kind of person I am, and I almost don't recognize this meek version of myself.

"I... I wanted to understand," I admit, forcing my arms to stay at my side.

"Understand what, exactly?"

Why you changed your mind. Why you hired the law firm anonymously. Why you donated millions of dollars as my birthday gift. Why you kissed me. Why I haven't been able to stop thinking about said kiss.

And why I want more—so much more.

"If—if you really care." I sober quickly, clearing my throat. "Or if you're just trying to win points with me."

Tristan scoffs. "I know this might be inconceivable to you, but I *am* capable of empathy and I'm *not* as in charge as you think I am. If I piss off too many people, the board can vote me out of my own company. I wasn't lying when I said change takes time."

"You're open to it, then? Change."

He hesitates. "I thought you said you believed actions, not words."

Warmth flutters through my chest. He hasn't explicitly said it, but it was he who hired Karl Bastel. The list of reasons *not* to lean into what we have is dwindling until my vision is too blurry with desire to read anything.

My voice is soft, fragile. "I did say that, yeah—"

He barely lets me finish before he's humming in agreement, seemingly eager for me to admit defeat. To admit that I might have been wrong about him and that I want him as badly as he wants me. His gloating nature agitates and arouses me all at once. When he notices my stare lingering on his mouth, his tongue drags across his lower lip. The movement is subtle and more than enough to stir my lust for him. I glare at him for knowingly teasing me. He chuckles, the sound heavy in his chest.

"You piss me *off*," I groan, closing the distance and capturing his mouth with mine.

CHAPTER TWENTY

MAIA

Tristan devours my mouth like a man starving.

He doesn't hesitate to kiss me back, his arms caging me instantly. Our lips dance and our tongues collide as we battle over who dominates.

His ferocity feeds my own; I grip his shirt tight enough to hear a couple threads pop.

Closer.

I need him closer. I arch into him as he leans into me and we stagger backward until I hit one of the tables. I hear items clattering to the ground, but he doesn't let me break the kiss to check. He scoops beneath my thighs and plops me on the surface, his hands massaging where he grabbed me.

I gasp into his mouth, marveling at the feeling of his touch. He yanks me to the edge of the table, which is the perfect height to slam his bulge between my legs.

Tristan starts kissing along my jaw until he reaches my earlobe and gently nibbles. By some random strike of luck, it doesn't tickle.

"I need to taste you," he says, his hoarse tone and

accent making my nipples tighten. His arms hook under my knees to scoot my hips up. "Lie back." He tries to push me flat.

I stop him, startled by the command. "Don't tell me what to do."

He sends me a glare as he hikes my ankle over his shoulder, hooking a finger in my panties to shift them aside as if it's an everyday thing. "You even argue during sex?"

"I wouldn't have to argue if—"

My body tenses when his finger dips inside of me. I gasp, withholding my moan the best I can.

"Does it make you wet to fight with me?" he asks, and it's hard as hell not to lose myself to the pleasure rippling down my legs. His finger curls relentlessly. "You're completely soaked."

I snatch his arm, my chest heaving. He takes the back of my neck with his free hand and dips his head to kiss along my jaw again. "I'll bet you were this wet when you were scolding me in front of everyone, hm?"

I manage a scoff. "You wish."

Without warning or teasing, he slides in a second finger. My legs tremble in ecstasy, the moans spilling from my mouth as I stretch around him. His fingers reach part of me I didn't know existed, and I collapse onto my back, writhing from the pleasure. The table shifts and I hear a crash behind me. I sit up fully, gasping at an unfinished bird sculpture now shattered into a dozen pieces.

"Oh my god! I'm so sorry!"

"Leave it," he says, using the break as an opportunity to pull my dress aside to reveal my breasts. He closes his mouth around one of my nipples, his tongue swirling as his finger curls.

"But"—I pause to release the moan his touches demand —"I broke your sculpture."

He kisses between my ribs. "I'm working on a better masterpiece."

His long fingers curl and massage inside of me, almost similar to how he might work on a sculpture. Sparks shoot down my legs, all the way to my toes.

"Oh, my god."

When I'm stretched wide enough, he fingers harder, faster. The pleasure ripples through my hips so intensely that I feel one of them *crack*. I don't even think Tristan heard it over the sound of my arousal on his working fingers. The lust in my lower belly only grows; I've never been this wet before. The pressure builds and builds until he yanks his fingers from me, but my body still trembles.

"Fuck, you're squirting," he grits out.

He doesn't wait to slide back inside and work me even harder. My brain can hardly manage a coherent thought. All I can think is, *I've never, I've never, I've never...*

I claw at his shoulder, praying he doesn't think of it as a sign to stop, as my moans echo through his studio. Tristan lowers and adds his mouth to the mix, his tongue lapping and fingers curling to turn me into a gushing, whimpering mess. His warm, heavy tongue lands on my clit and his groan at my taste sends vibrations through me. The last thing I expected to see today was Tristan's head between my thighs as he latches onto me hungrily.

My body shudders and my legs tighten around his head as I shatter around him with an embarrassing swiftness. When I collapse against the table, breathless, he leans over and scoops me up with ease. I wrap my legs around him as he carries me across the room.

"What are you doing?"

He kisses my chest. "Taking you to the bedroom so I can fuck you properly."

I try to shake off the haze. I'm sixty percent positive my legs would collapse under me if he were to set me down, but I need to think clearly.

"You have a bedroom in your studio?" I ask as he sets me at the end of the bed. It's a luxurious albeit boring room with a window to my right and a closet and bathroom to my left.

"I'm here most nights," he says into my neck, his hands roaming my thighs, but I keep glancing around the room, my gaze landing on the nightstand beside the bed. A memory hits me hard. *"My women have better sense than to reach out."*

My women.

Reality sets in quickly—I need to be smart.

"And how many women have you brought here?" I ask, biting my cheek as I regret the words instantly. Maybe I shouldn't have said *that.*

Tristan freezes, his teeth grazing my neck as he scowls and pulls away. He lifts his gaze as if composing himself before tightening his hold on the back of my neck. He looks me in the eyes. "None."

I lean back on my wrists, looking up at him. "I'm not crazy to be concerned. You all but gloated about having your own harem."

"Listen to me." His deep voice turns raspy. "I've *tried* wanting other women since the day I met you. But my thoughts, my desires, my *body*—it only wants you, love, and it's agony."

I lift a brow. His body only wants me? As in...?

A sly grin spills onto my face. "Are you saying you couldn't get it up?"

He slumps, his forehead touching mine. "Agony. Complete agony."

Part of me is skeptical and wants to ask questions. The other part is too horny to care. I pull him down to me for a kiss, my hands wandering to his sweatpants. When I tug his pants and boxers down, I stop.

"Are you fucking kidding me?" I snap. I sensed he had impressive girth, but his length and curve are the cherries on top. Tristan smirks, leaning in to kiss my neck without replying. His dick is heavy in my hand as I slowly stroke him, eager to know what he feels like inside of me.

"No wonder you're such a dick. You've gotta put it somewhere."

He laughs into our kiss and guides me onto my back, climbing on top of me. He rips off the condom wrapper and slides it on before thrusting into me without tease.

My back arches instinctively, and I do my best to tamper my reaction—his ego *and* his dick are big enough. But Tristan doesn't hold back. Ecstasy clouds his features as he pushes in inch by inch, nearly splitting me in two. His voice is a strained grunt. "Holy fucking—*fuck*, Maia."

I feel myself quiver around him. My mouth opens, but I don't respond. I can't. This new feeling, not just his size, but his body, his smell, his taste—it's intoxicating and unleashing a new fucking dimension. We should have done this the first day we met.

I clamp down on my lip to withhold a moan, but he notices and chuckles lowly in my ear.

"It's so cute how you're holding back."

Tristan leaves wet kisses on my neck before tossing my legs over his shoulders and folding me in half like a lawn chair. I force myself to let go of my stubbornness. I'm dominant, but his increased pace is too good to do anything other than take it.

"Oh god," I whimper, reaching up to cage his jaw between my thumb and index finger. I tighten my hold in warning, but my voice is nothing but a plea. *"Don't fucking stop."*

His thrusts send me higher, higher, higher until he yanks out of me, followed by a fountain. My cheeks warm. I feel a *little* bad about ruining his sheets. But he doesn't seem to mind. He lets out a long groan, not unlike a growl.

"You're gonna make me come if you keep doing that."

I laugh. "Don't tell me you're a minute man."

Tristan moves my legs to brace an elbow beside my head. While keeping eye contact, he grabs my hips to keep me still, making him go impossibly deeper with each stroke. My body clenches around every inch of him, and he grins when my eyes roll back. He's doing this to be cocky, but even he can't contain his pleasure as a small grunt escapes him.

"I've been dying to fuck the attitude right out of you."

Just as I open my mouth to argue, he fucks faster. The words vanish, replaced by gasps and whimpers. I hate him and I don't want him to stop.

"You drive me *fucking* mad," he whispers, his large hand wrapping around the base of my neck to both control and steady me. He thrusts almost painfully, dancing on the edge of too much. "You ruined everything. I had it all figured out and you and your—" He moans, pushing deeper into me as his lips hover mine. "*Shit.* You and your smart mouth will be the death of me."

I close the distance and clamp my teeth around his bottom lip. "You can handle it."

Tristan grabs me and flips us over in a single, fluid motion so I'm on top. "Ride me."

"You're lucky I want to," I spit, "or else I'd smack you for being so goddamn bossy."

"You're one to talk."

"Shut up." I push him on his back and plant my feet flat under me on either side of his ribs. With him inside of me, I lean back with my wrists holding me up. He watches himself slide in and out of me as I ride him, his moaning as loud as my own.

"God, you're so fucking hot," he grits out, a faraway look glazing over his eyes as his head falls back against the pillow. I could ask him to buy me a spaceship right now and he would offer to build it himself.

"Not God. *Mai-a*." I say my name slowly, annunciating both syllables.

"Same thing."

A smile pulls at my lips. It invigorates me that he can't control himself because of me. "You better not come yet," I warn.

He sobers, a fierce look in his eyes. "You're not in charge here."

As I reach behind me, I slide down harder on his dick to the hilt and stop the same moment I grab his balls. His jaw clenches tightly, making the veins in his neck pop.

I smirk, clenching as he hits my G-spot. "Wanna bet on it?"

Tristan's face is a mix of pleasure and anger as he lifts his hips to destabilize me and pull me closer so my chest is against his. His large hands cover my ass, holding me in place as he fucks from beneath me. I claw at his chest, my thoughts blending from the pleasure. It's not until I'm coming down from another orgasm that I realize he came, too. I squeeze my eyes shut, head dropped on his shoulder.

I'll be damned if I ever admit that we came together the first time we had sex. If he doesn't know, I won't be the one to tell him.

We lie together, catching our breath and realizing what the fuck we'd just done. I thought once would be enough to get it out of our system, but the floodgates have opened. No pun intended. The last thing I want is a relationship with him, but I'm already planning the next time we can do that again.

My body is still tingling as he discards the condom and crawls back into the bed. I have to lie with bent knees to avoid the wet spot.

Another fact that couldn't be tortured out of me: Tristan's the only man who's made me squirt. I didn't know I could do that.

It's still silent between us, a newfound truce lingering in the air. He kisses my shoulder with a tenderness that surprises me.

A phone on the nightstand to my left starts ringing, the vibrations and melody echoing through the room.

"Pardon me, love," he says, and I hate that British accent for making him sound so enticing. He reaches over me to the nightstand and I peek the name Valentina across the top. My stomach tightens. I don't want a relationship with him. I stand by that. But I also won't be another notch on his bedpost. I've been enough notches in my lifetime.

"Who's Valentina?" I ask once he ignores the call and slinks back to his side.

"No one important," he dismisses, hesitating at my skepticism. "A friend."

"I'd hate for my friend to say I'm no one important."

"Maia..."

"What? And what happened to *my women know better than to reach out*? Which is pretty messed up to say, by the way."

"I was joking. I wanted to get a rise out of you."

I can't help myself. Maybe I'm looking for reasons to be mad. For a reason to never do this again. Kissing him was already a mistake. Now I'm literally lying naked in bed with him. Reality crashes into me. The tingling numbness is gone and the strain from stress comes in full force. It had hurt when Tristan wrapped his hand around my collarbone, but I didn't want to say anything. Now I'm paying the price.

"I have to go," I mumble, tossing aside the sheet.

"What? Hang on—what just happened?"

"What happened is that I came to my senses."

"Valentina isn't my girlfriend. She's just someone I know."

"I don't care about *Valentina*." Partly a lie. On one hand, I want to rip out the extensions I just *know* this bitch has. On the other hand, I don't fight over men. A sudden fear grips me over what would happen if the media thought I was fighting someone over a man. I step into my dress. "This was a mistake."

"Maia—"

"Do you know what would happen if other people found out?" I snap, my voice cracking as I spot my shoes. "My career would be over. My reputation is threatened enough and the last thing I need is to be another notch on a man's belt."

"You are *not*—are you hurt?"

I scoff at the audacity. "No. I'm fine."

He wasn't referring to my feelings, but to the way I

winced when I put my sandal on, the way I keep my right shoulder in place as much as I can. Fuck. A flare-up is coming on quick.

"That's not what I—Maia, wait!" he yells as I leave the bedroom. I hear him fumble out of bed. *"Shit."*

I snatch my purse from one of the many tables.

Tristan pads behind me. "Love, can you just wait?"

I let out a resounding "No," over my good shoulder before slamming the door behind me.

Tears of pain, regret, and frustration rush to the surface as I head to the elevator. It's not that I regret the sex, and that's the worst part. It was phenomenal, but all I can hear are the warning voices of Nina, Lyla, and my entire PR team. I'm pushing him away, but it's impossible not to. There are dozens of reasons why this was a horrible idea.

What the fuck was I thinking?

I'm here in broad fucking daylight! Anyone can see me. The elevator could stop on a floor and pick someone up. They can recognize me—and I'm in tears and stiff as a board and absolutely have sex hair. *And I can't even lift my arms high enough to fix it.*

Kill me now.

CHAPTER TWENTY-ONE

TRISTAN

I've died and gone to heaven. Or whatever afterlife there is.

I've slept with a lot of women in my twenty-nine years, as many as four at the same time. It wasn't my first time being with a woman who squirts, either. But there isn't a single one of my sexual experiences that can compare to Maia. It's not a certain thing she does—it's just *her*. Her soft skin, her plump lips, everything. I want to bottle up the sight and feeling of her coming on me so I can relive it over and over. Sex with Maia is like dipping into heaven, a paradise that ensnares you. She's a vixen whose every move is that much more erotic.

She was angry when she'd left, but I was hoping to smooth everything over at the garden today. Valentina doesn't mean anything to me.

I find Lyla in the break room, who smiles at me from behind her laptop. "Good morning!"

I glance around, hoping Maia is getting something from the closet. Nothing. "Uh, g'morning. Where's Maia?"

"She's staying home today," Lyla says, closing her

computer and scooping up a clipboard and empty mug. "She said her back hurt."

"Oh."

Her back? She's twenty-four. The only reason I can think of for a twenty-something-year-old having a back injury is if there was an accident.

Panic washes over me.

Fuck, fuck, fuck. Did I hurt her? Was I too rough? She said she was fine when she winced yesterday. I rifle through my memories, and it's possible I wasn't as gentle as I usually am, but she wasn't soft, either. I have scratches on my back to prove it.

I need to make sure she's okay. My hands tremble as I take out my phone to text her as Lyla washes her mug at the sink.

How are you?

Lyla said you weren't feeling well.

I stare at the screen, waiting for her response to chime in. Nothing.

"Are you ready?" Lyla's voice makes me jump.

I lock my phone. "Yeah. All good."

She smiles. "You can follow me. I'm taking over for her today."

I simply nod, following her out of the break room and into the greenhouse. Not only am I spiraling over wanting to speak with Maia and make sure she's all right, but I don't want to be at Felicity Gardens if she's not here. Without her, it doesn't feel important.

Lyla senses my discomfort. "She told me you guys kissed, so you don't need to act weird or anything."

I flinch. "I, uh—okay."

I'm not sure what I'm supposed to say to that. I hadn't mentioned Maia since I asked where she was. It's clear Lyla doesn't know we did more than that, and I won't be the one to update her.

Maia and Lyla are best friends, but I've never paid much mind to the latter. She's American, like Maia. Her dark, wavy hair falls to the middle of her back and she has a long face and big mouth, making her every smile and word demand attention.

"So, we'll be doing a bit of the hands-on stuff today," she says, transferring a tray of seedlings onto a cart.

I take the next one from her hands and place it on the lower shelf.

"Thank you, you're so sweet."

I roll the cart behind her. It may be her typical affect, but she walks with a particular pep I hadn't noticed before. But even as she explains that we'll be transferring these seedlings outside and have to label them properly, I only think of Maia.

Is she okay? How bad is the pain? Did I leave any bruises? Lyla is her best friend and she doesn't seem too worried, so I'm likely overreacting. I still check my phone at any available moment but I haven't received a text back.

I don't say much as Lyla and I kneel in front of an in-ground garden bed. In spite of the turmoil in my mind, the sky is cloudless and the heat is quickly climbing. Lawn mowers rumble a few hundred feet away, smothering any birdsong I heard earlier.

"So," begins Lyla, "do you know why this part is so fickle?"

"Why what part is?"

She gestures around us, at the unplanted seedlings. "Transferring."

I blink myself back into the present. "Oh, uh. No. No, I don't."

She looks surprised. She puts on a pair of gardening gloves with a Felicity Gardens logo on the wrist. "Seedlings are delicate. We put them through training to try and build strength. Maia didn't teach you this? She's usually the one taking reports on our seedlings."

"She taught me about a few."

She hums. "Well, I'm going to have you write down the labels as I handle the plants, if you're all right with that."

"Oh—yeah. Of course." For the next few minutes, she shows me how to take the proper notes and double-check that the right seedling is in its assigned spot. I write down the conditions of the day planted and any discoloration or split leaves.

I admit that Lyla's approach is way more hands-on than Maia's. But I like watching Maia work—and she'd made it clear she didn't want me there.

I prefer our method. She'll break our silence or stubborn stand-off when she cares enough about a plant or fact. That's how I know it's truly important. I'm here for volunteer work under the guise of learning, and while they seem to go hand-in-hand, I miss Maia's method. It was more authentic.

After a couple of seedlings are planted, Lyla swishes her hair out of her face. "Crap, I forgot to tie my hair back." She holds up her gloved hands. "Can you do me a favor and take this hair tie and tie my hair back? Just a low ponytail—I'm low maintenance."

I don't understand why she can't take off the gloves to do so, but I comply, anyway. More than anything, I want to leave the garden entirely and go find Maia. I need to make sure she's okay, but I don't think she wants to see me. Not after how she left yesterday.

"Uh, yeah, sure." I gently take the hair tie from her wrist and she scoots toward me, leaning her head back.

"Don't look at my tattoo," she warns teasingly. "It was a drunk dare a few years ago."

I offer a fake chuckle, though I couldn't give two shits if I tried. As I tentatively tie her hair, I notice the 'live, laugh, love' tattoo written in script on the back of her neck.

"I've been meaning to get it covered," she continues, then turns back around and takes the next seedling to plant. She glances at my forearm. "Something like that would be ideal."

From my rolled-up sleeves, my snake tattoo is the only visible one. "Oh, yeah. I got this a long time ago." I don't have many, but this was one of my firsts.

"I've been trying to brainstorm, but I can't think of anything. Any ideas?"

Before I can think of an excuse to get me out of giving Lyla tattoo recommendations, my phone vibrates in my pocket. I nearly drop the clipboard trying to retrieve it.

AUGUSTUS

McCloskey requested to push the meeting by an hour. Permission?

I grit my teeth before typing back a quick *yes*.

"Everything okay?" Lyla asks at the anguish on my face. I school my features into neutrality.

"Yes, all good." I clear my throat. "Have you heard from Maia? Is she okay?"

While subtle, I don't miss the deflation in her eyes. "Yeah, she's fine. It's always something with her."

My chest flares with agitation. I may not have many,

but shouldn't friends care when the other is hurt? It doesn't take a psychiatrist to see that Maia is fiercely independent and capable. I watched her cut a tree with a chainsaw and look happy doing it.

More importantly, I wonder if Maia knows that Lyla has been subtly trash-talking her while aware of the fact that we kissed. I bite my tongue, all too aware of how vicious women can be and not wanting to insert myself between two friends.

Lyla can make intonations all she wants; she's not Maia.

Back at my office in the city, Augustus briefs me on what I missed. The board wasn't pleased during our Monday meeting about the deal falling through. It helped that I hired Bastel & Associates with my own money rather than the company's. It barely affects me either way.

Through chatter between assistants, Augustus tells me McCloskey and Barnes met privately this morning—without the presence of the other board members. It raises a red flag, particularly after yesterday; I want to avoid any collusion.

"I'll speak with them," I assure Augustus.

"Do you want me to set up a meeting?"

I shake my head. "I want to keep it informal. I'll have to draw it back to the good it can do for us down the line."

He nods, closing the cover on his tablet.

"One more thing," I say as he turns toward the exit. He's not the first person I'd prefer to ask about this, but I don't know what else to do. I can't stop worrying about Maia. "Are you in a relationship?"

Augustus blushes. "I'm flattered, sir—" He stops at my

glare. "No." He clears his throat. "I used to be engaged, but presently, I'm single."

"Why did your engagement end?"

He hesitates, and I fear I've offended him, though he knows more about myself and my family than I'd care to let on. "Uh, his infidelity."

"I'm sorry to hear that."

To my surprise, he snorts. "I'm not. I dodged a bullet. He was crazy." Then he squints. "Why do you ask, sir?"

I shake my head, rubbing the back of my neck. "Nothing. I just—I think I messed up. And I'm not sure I know what I did."

"Not sure you know?" He lifts his brows. "Have you asked her?"

"I've called. And texted. No response."

Of all people, I can't believe it's Augustus I'm speaking to. I could talk to Romèo, but it feels weird to call him up and ask for advice on situationships. I'm not sure men do that sort of thing. Perhaps they do—I simply haven't had enough friends to know. But Augustus is right there, and I can trust him to be discreet.

He hums in consideration. "You don't want to be creepy."

"Creepy?"

"How many times have you called her?"

I huff, exasperated. "I don't know. I'm just trying to figure out what else to do."

"Then go back to the garden and talk to her. Was she not there today?"

I stare at him. "I never said who it was."

My assistant glares at me, something I never thought he had the balls to do, but I suppose I respect his candor. "I'm not daft."

Ah, right. Maia hounded him for my studio address.

I'm too embarrassed to tell him I might have physically hurt her during sex. The shame and guilt are too much to bear, and I'm not sure how much longer I can go without speaking to her about it.

"If you really cared about the princess," Augustus says, "you'd find her and talk to her."

CHAPTER TWENTY-TWO
MAIA

My flare-up kept me in bed most of Tuesday.

A nerve around my upper spine rendered me so stiff I could barely turn my head to the left and not at all to the right. The pain ran from around my shoulder blade and all the way up to the base of my skull. Esme was over most of the day to take care of the animals and tidy the house.

I was stubborn enough to change my pants by myself, but she helped me with my shirt. Esme manages to do her job without making it seem as though she's my servant and it's my favorite part about having her around.

I'm too embarrassed to respond to Tristan's texts. I stormed out of his studio like a childish coward. Sure, he pulled an asshole move, but I may have overreacted from already being in pain. He called me a few times, each going unanswered. Truth be told, my flare-up couldn't have come at a better time. It's distracting me from spiraling over what happened with us and just how much of a mistake it was.

But I can't think of him right now. I need to manage this flare-up so I can refocus on work.

After half-assing work on Monday and staying home on Tuesday, I'm itching to return by Wednesday. I'm still hurting quite a bit, but doing a few small tasks will assuage my under-productivity guilt. I avoid the paths of Lyla and Dr. Pagoda, since they would no doubt demand I leave and go home. Esme isn't coming over until noon, so I have only a little time before Mason drives me home.

Watering a few of the seedlings should be easy enough. I rise onto the stepladder and sway the watering can over the shelves of plants. The twinge in my back warns me, but I only need to extend another inch... just *one* more.

I wince from a sharp, sudden stab in my neck. The pain overwhelms my senses, making me forget I'm standing high on a stepladder as I shift back. The watering can clatters to the ground as I flail for a grip to keep me upright. My hand lands on a tray of seedlings, which only falls with me.

I cry out as I hit the floor and dirt rains over me. At least the tray is only flimsy plastic and doesn't hurt when it lands on my head. The embarrassment is painful enough.

Agony lances across my upper back, yanking tears from my eyes instantly.

All I wanted to do was water some plants.

I used to be the best player on my volleyball team. I could hold a plank for nearly five minutes and could out-sprint most of the team.

I feel as though I've been reduced—*diminished*.

Covered in wet dirt, I hunch over the toppled stepladder and sob for the life I've lost. It's not fair. I love my life in Tropoli, but I didn't *choose* it. A simple night out on the town left my body sore for days. Traveling across the country—across the continent—meant factoring in enough time for rest. I can no longer hit the ground running and I don't know what I did to be this way. I'm constantly stuck between wanting to give my body enough recovery time and refusing to let this pain control me.

"Maia!"

I tense at the new voice, blinking in the hopes that my eyes are lying to me because there's no reason for Tristan to be standing in front of me.

"What are you doing h—"

I stop at the panic in his eyes. He covers the distance in two strides and drops beside me. "Are you okay? Where does it hurt?" He reaches into his pocket. "I'll call an ambulance."

"No." I snatch his wrist, fighting a sob of pain at the movement. "No ambulance. I'm fine."

Tristan scans his gaze over my crumpled, state covered in wet dirt. His thick brows knit in fear as he caresses my shoulders. "Love, you're crying in pain."

I sniffle and shake my head gently. "I just—I need to lie on the couch."

I look toward the door to the break room behind him. He huffs in protest, but locks his arms under me without warning and stands like I weigh nothing.

"What are you—?" I groan at his absurdity. "Oh jeez, Tristan. I can walk."

"Don't care," he says, adjusting me with a grunt. The sound stabs my gut with lust, and my throat tightens.

I wipe the tears from my face before I cradle my hands against my chest because the alternative is to hold him, and I damn sure don't trust myself around him anymore. It was a mistake. Fucking him was a horrible, mind-blowing mistake that felt so good that I have little strength to stop myself if the opportunity is presented again.

My weight tugs his black T-shirt aside to reveal his collarbone tattoo. I drag my gaze over the ink, over his

Adam's apple, his stubble, his sharp jawline. Fuck, I could just lick from top to—

"You're drooling," he taunts.

I shut my eyes, internally slapping sense into myself. Pull it *together*. I just acknowledged it was a mistake and I'm already thinking about how it might feel to rip his stupidly expensive shirt right off him. Worse yet, I touch the corner of my lips, smothering the relief that I wasn't actually drooling.

Tristan catches me and laughs. I'd pinch his nipple if he weren't carrying me. He lowers me onto the chaise of the sunset yellow couch. "Where does it hurt?"

"My upper back," I say quietly, wincing as I adjust a pillow between my head and the wall. He tries to help, but I shoo him away. "Can you just get the ice pack in the freezer? Then I'll be fine. You don't have to worry."

Never mind there's still wet dirt covering me—and staining my brand new tracksuit—but I don't need him here longer than necessary. He doesn't respond, only retrieves the ice pack and settle sit behind me.

"Thanks," I mumble.

Still silent, he moves toward the door. I don't expect hand-and-foot treatment, but at least say *something*. I open my mouth to tell him as such until he takes out a roll of paper towels from the closet by the exit. What the hell is he doing? After dampening a few in the sink, he sits in front of me, his hip against my thigh.

The ice pack tingles as tension starts melting away and I send a quick thank-you to my past self for deciding to bring an ice pack to work.

I flinch when Tristan reaches up with the damp towel and starts wiping dirt from my forehead. He notices my reaction, and though I recoiled out of mere surprise, his face breaks apart with regret.

He clenches his jaw, ripping his eyes from mine. "I'm sorry."

"For what?"

"I should've been more thoughtful, more—more gentle. Yeah, you drive me mad, but I wasn't trying to hurt you. I would never—"

"Tristan," I break in, trying to catch his eye. "What the hell are you talking about?"

"Your back. I was too rough the other day."

I clamp my mouth shut to keep my jaw from dropping. It makes sense now—the texts, calls, showing up here.

"This wasn't you. You didn't hurt me," I assure him, touching his arm. "This is my chronic pain. It's a flare-up. That's all."

"Really?"

An amused smile threatens my lips and I barely smother it. But I keep my voice soft. I like taunting him, though I can't stop the warmth fluttering through my chest. Tristan looks so frightened, so terrified at the possibility of hurting me. He was a little rough, but he looks racked with guilt already. I was surprised he'd been calling and texting so often. He's not the type of man who chases a woman.

"Really," I confirm.

Relief washes over his features, his concerned brows relaxing. *"Christ, Maia,"* he grumbles, dropping his head into his hand before scraping it down his face. "I've been going mad thinking I hurt you! You looked like you were in pain when you left and then you ignored me!"

"Well, yes, I was. It started to build up on Sunday and

it's just at its worst. I should've stayed in bed. That's my fault."

"How often does this happen?"

"The pain?"

He nods.

I shrug. "Every day."

"Every day?" he echoes, horror etched onto his face.

"Not this bad. I'm bedridden only a few times a year. But I'm in some type of pain every day, yes."

Tristan watches me in disbelief.

I don't typically like going over my medical history. I've repeated it so many times I've practically memorized it the way I memorized the *Law and Order: SVU* intro.

I huff. "I had a bad dive in a volleyball game in high school," I begin. "I shattered my knee and had to get surgery. It's fully healed now, but ever since then, I've always had some kind of pain. I break down faster. Some days, it's my hips. Others, my knees. Most often, it's my back or neck. Which is ironic, because it's not even the spot I injured in the first place."

"What kind of pain?"

"Uh, aches. Aches and a lot of almost-dislocations."

Not enough dislocations for Ehlers-Danlos Syndrome, not enough sleep distress for Fibromyalgia. Normal blood-work results. Normal x-ray results. My medical history is filled with *almost*s, leaving me largely undiagnosed and miserable. As if I didn't have to fight the validity of chronic pain enough. But Tristan doesn't need to know any more of the specifics of my battles. If it were up to me, he wouldn't know at all. I can't hide much from Nina; she witnessed my downfall. Dad still thinks I'm faking it and that I just need to hit the gym. He didn't really give a shit when I needed knee surgery, anyway. He only asked if I could take my recovery to my bedroom so he could nap on the couch when he was buzzed.

"It makes so much sense now," Tristan says, shaking his head as if he should've known. He continues wiping dirt from my temple, brow line, and hair.

"What does?"

"Why you're always stretching and why it never seems to faze you when you bump into things."

How does he know these things? Was he watching me?

I thought it would feel awkward seeing him again after we hooked up. I told myself we were a mistake, but I can't stop staring at his lips.

My phone starts buzzing from my bag on the table. Tristan rises before I can ask him to retrieve it for me.

"That's probably Esme," I say quietly as he hands me the bag. "I'm supposed to be home resting."

"You're okay, then?"

I nod. "My security is outside to drive me home. I'm okay. Thank you for your help."

He doesn't look too pleased to be leaving, but I answer Esme's call before it goes to voicemail. As he heads toward the door, it dawns on me that he never revealed why he came here in the first place.

CHAPTER TWENTY-THREE
TRISTAN

Relief is too short and too simple a word to describe what I feel.

Knowing I didn't hurt her lets me rest easy, but I still struggle to focus and often find myself itching to text Maia and check in—even though I saw her yesterday.

After a morning of dreadfully slow meetings, Augustus peeks his head into my office around one o'clock to tell me McCloskey is getting lunch in the cafeteria, per his assistant. It's the perfect time to casually bump into him and squash any potential collusion between him and Barnes. I've only entered the cafeteria myself once; I hope my arrival won't be too obvious.

I straighten out my dress shirt before making my way downstairs. Grandfather took a lot of pride in being from Maldana, and he openly admitted that he stayed in London because of me. When I moved here with him, he poured as many resources into the Kosita office as necessary. There are nap rooms, gyms—plus a personal trainer for any employee who requests one—a gallery dedicated to Maldana's history and lore, and even free courses for anyone who wants to learn Maldanian. The cafeteria is more of a restaurant than anything, and I find Brian McCloskey sitting by a large window that overlooks a modest courtyard garden.

My gaze lingers on the tall shrub at the center of the circle, waiting for Maia to pop out from the other side. I see a garden and I instantly think of her.

I shake it off and wade through the tables. The amber and mahogany decor add a somber contrast to the bright day outside.

"Brian," I greet.

He looks up from his phone. There's an untouched burger on the plate in front of him. "Tristan! I don't think I've ever seen you down here," he says in Maldanian. Despite his Irish name, he was born and raised in Kosita. He and Grandfather had been particularly close—and I have to use that. I have to reinforce that I'm his grandson and I know what's best for the company. It's infuriating enough that I alone am not respected enough as CEO, but there are only a few people I can't strong-arm into getting what I need.

I lift a shoulder and respond in Maldanian. "Grandfather spent a lot of money on making the building what it is. I figured I should enjoy it more."

There's some truth to that. I usually eat alone.

Brian smiles. "I'm glad to hear that."

I gesture to the open seat across from him. "Can I sit?"

His pale face brightens in surprise, but he doesn't deny me. At the end of the day, I'm his boss. "Yes, sure. Of course."

I lower into the chair, noticing the bumblebee on the other side of the window. It buzzes near a purple flower—which I can only describe as a sad-looking daisy. Maia would know what kind it is. The bee bumps into the glass a couple of times, pulling Brian's attention. He notices my staring and likely assumes I'm watching the bug, too, but my only thought is Maia and the next time I get to see her.

I clear my throat. *Who the bloody hell am I?* I don't fucking marvel at flowers and dream about a girl. I turn my attention to the task at hand.

"How are you? How's the family?" My eyes dart to his left hand, hoping I didn't miss the news of a divorce. But a simple gold band is in the same place as it has been for the last twenty years.

"Good, Shannon and Jonah are starting university soon."

I pause, remembering the annoying little kids who would always follow me around as a teen whenever at a gathering with Grandfather. "University?" I echo in disbelief. "My god, it's truly been ages since I've seen them. What are they going for?"

"Shan is studying fashion and Jonah"—he rolls his eyes—"is studying *literature* of all things."

A smile tugs at my lips, but only because I know Maia would have something to say about it—and would likely be snarky.

"I have no doubt they will both do well in their fields," I offer, truly not giving a shit.

"I'm sure," Brian agrees.

"Grandfather always made sure I was on top of my studies. My business classes were easy, but the information tech ones could be difficult. Even so, most of what I know comes from him."

He watches me steadily as though realizing the true nature of my visit. His dark, greasy hair is slicked back from his forehead to give an open view of his wrinkled yet sour face. "Right... He was a good man."

I nod. "He was. Smart, too." Underneath the table, I tap my fingers along my knee. "With every large decision *I* make, I heavily consider what he would have done. And I know you would never undermine *him*."

Brian looks away, reaching for his glass of water. After taking a sip, he says, "No, I wouldn't. I understand."

I smile. "Good." I scoot back from the table, the scraping chair echoing. "I won't disturb you further, Brian. I'll let you get back to your meal."

By Friday, the urge to talk to Maia is killing me.

There's nothing particular to talk about, although I do want to know how she's feeling. I know I could just text her, but then again, I could simply go to her house. Like some celebrities, her address is public knowledge and a passing destination for tourists. According to the internet, her perimeter is under 24/7 surveillance and an alarm will go off if anyone stands at her front gate longer than ten minutes.

After having Augustus find me the name of the highest-rated ice cream parlor in the city, I call them to see if they have cinnamon bun ice cream. I remember seeing pints of it in the freezer at the garden with Maia's name written on them. And everyone knows that Maia loves ice cream.

With a hefty bribe, I have a parlor put together a custom-made pint and pick it up on my way out of the city and toward Tropoli. She doesn't know I'm coming and I can only hope she won't shun me.

Surprisingly, she buzzes me through her gate without a fight.

I park beside her electric Porsche that sits under a canopy of solar panels. Of *course* she drives a car that's powered by the sun.

As I get out of my car, a sudden wave of anxiety floods my stomach at the sight of Maia standing on her porch, barefoot and with her arms crossed over her chest. Her long hair puffs around her bronzed, sun-kissed face. Her cheeks glow as if she spent most of the day outside. Something twists in my chest.

"What are you doing here?" she asks.

I shrug. "I was just in the neighborhood."

Her large shorts threaten to slip over her hip and her mile-long legs shiver from the breeze as the sun behind the house casts a cooling shadow.

"Don't lie to me."

Her argumentative tone makes me hard. I remove my sunglasses and stride up the path, stopping just before her. The porch step makes us the same height, and I stare straight into her earthy brown eyes before noticing a couple freckles have popped up on the slope of her nose. I fight the urge to kiss every single one.

"I wanted to see if you were all right," I admit, then hold up the paper bag. "And I brought ice cream."

Maia lights up as she focuses on the bag. But she quickly furrows her brows. "What kind?"

"Cinnamon bun."

"*No way,*" she gasps, snatching it right from my hand. "How? It's so hard to find!"

"I asked a parlor to make it."

She squints. "Asked?"

"Paid."

I missed her, and I'm tired of telling myself I didn't. I'm not in love with her or anything and there's no saying how far this thing between us will go. I still run Space Technologies; that won't change.

It doesn't mean I don't think of her at every available moment, that I'm not thinking of ways to spoil her. But she already has everything she could ever want. It's not like I could buy her a country to rule—which I can—because she already fucking has one. Romèo was right. Maia is above me. There's nothing I can offer her.

I just want to soak up every moment I can before she realizes that.

I'm here to make sure she's all right and if her pain is any better. She didn't specify whatever condition she might have—therefore I can't research it and find what would help. But massages help aches, right? Maybe I can give her a massage. I'm used to fixing things and I don't like that I can't take away her pain.

She eyes me. "Fine. You've bought yourself temporary entrance."

Inside, two barking dogs bombard me with sniffs and nuzzles. The bigger dog, the Rottweiler, nearly knocks me over from excitement.

She whistles once. "Girls!"

Only the Rottweiler listens; the smaller dog continues her sniff-fest, but dodges my pets in favor of curiosity. I follow Maia to the right, down a small hallway until reaching the dining room. Vines drape from the walls to a chandelier dangling over the large wood table. Farther back is an arched doorway that leads to a kitchen. The sloped glass ceiling reminds me of a greenhouse, especially with the plants lined atop the cupboards.

"Blood Sage!" Maia yells. "Get your butt off the counter!"

She puts the ice cream in the freezer and scoops a reddish cat off the island.

"Your cat's name is Blood?" I ask.

"Blood Sage." She totes the creature like a prize. "It's a plant. The color matches her fur. I usually call her Sage, though." She takes a paw and waves it at me, but the cat doesn't look impressed. And I suddenly notice its missing leg.

"Three legs?"

Maia nods, cradling Sage against her chest as she hums soft tunes. "A shelter in Kosita found her after she was hit by a car. I got her before Poppy and Daisy."

I reach down to pet the smaller dog, the one with tan fur. Unlike before, she leans into my touch as I scratch behind her ear. "Which one is this? Daisy?"

"No, that's Poppy. My sass queen. Daisy is my big, beautiful doofus. She's always tripping and running into stuff." Daisy, the Rottweiler, nudges my other hand, begging for the same affection as her sister.

"Any more animals I should know about?"

I expect Maia to laugh and shake her head. Instead, she lights up. "My ducks! I'll introduce you."

She speeds off down another hall, her animal army in tow. I do my best to keep up and look around at the same time. The walls are painted a soft yellow with dangling plants strewn everywhere. The vines, in combination with the wall art, would seem cluttered, but it all flows together. Just like Maia. Aligned. Comforting. Perfect.

My gaze drifts over the professional portraits of her dogs and cat, of her friends and family, including her mother, Queen Ophelia.

Maia guides me through a greenhouse that leads to the backyard, which is just as pristine and teeming with plant life as inside. Two light brown ducks ruffle their feathers and dive into the feed that she tosses out.

"This is Elliot and this is Olivia."

I recognize the names instantly. "Like from *Law and Order*?"

She lights up again. "Exactly! If the writers won't finally put them together, I'll do it myself."

"They don't mate?" I ask, gesturing to the ducks.

She leans in with a hand as if telling me a secret. "Elliot's a girl."

I follow her back into the kitchen where she grabs a spoon and digs into the ice cream I brought her. As soon as she takes the first bite, she visibly melts from the flavor, her eyes rolling into the back of her head. "Bro, this is so fucking good, I'm not even gonna lie to you right now."

I laugh at the Maia-ness of it all. She *almost* manages to turn crass into a charm of its own. She's honest in a way that expects the best version of everyone she meets. It took me longer to learn that it wasn't in arrogance, albeit her vitriol getting the best of her quite often, but from the potential she sees.

"So you came to check on me," she says, leaning against the counter. "I'm alive. Now what?"

Her dogs come bouncing in, clearly energetic. Truthfully, I didn't know what would be next. I want her. I always want her. But I also need to know she's all right. Even though I'm here, and even though she already saw my fear over possibly hurting her, I'm nervous. My heart pounds in my chest and I'm grateful that her pets offer an escape.

"Now I play fetch with your dogs."

"It rained yesterday. You might get your sneakers wet."

From her pointed look, I know she's referring to the fact that I don't like to get dirty. Not in that way. I inhale deeply and glance down at my suede Armani sneakers. What do I care about more—messing up replaceable shoes or seeing Maia smile?

I shrug. "I'll just get new ones."

She rolls her eyes, but the corner of her lips lifts. And that alone is worth it.

CHAPTER TWENTY-FOUR
MAIA

I didn't think the sight of Tristan playing fetch with my dogs would do anything to me. But I like it. He's unaffected by Daisy's barreling head and Poppy constantly leaving the ball exactly where she fetched it from.

Even though I'm nearly a hundred percent back to normal, I'm not stupid enough to risk throwing a ball and re-agitating my neck. So I sit at the patio right outside of my bedroom and watch Tristan play with my animals.

"You're smiling at me," he says, snapping me back to reality.

"What? No I wasn't." I pull the corners of my lips downward and cross my arms. He doesn't hide his amused grin, and it only makes my stomach tingle with butterflies. I'm not sure there's much he could do that wouldn't be sexy in some magical way. He can scratch his ass and I'd find it attractive.

His thin gold chains dangle as he wrestles Daisy for the ball. I send a prayer of gratitude to my past self for getting a large dog that makes Tristan put in an effort—meaning I get to see his muscles bulge. I bite the inside of my cheek.

Am I ovulating or something? He wrenches the ball and throws it across the yard, which makes the hem of his shirt reveal his abdomen briefly.

Good god, woman. Get a grip.

Wishing the glass of water beside me was a shot of vodka, I throw back the last sip. I instantly hiss in pain and bunch my shoulders together. The nerve in my neck flares up, and a sudden resentment fills me for getting distracted and not being mindful of what I'm doing. I shut my eyes and wait for the pain to subside; it doesn't.

Tristan notices. "You all right?"

He crosses the distance between us swiftly, placing a gentle hand on my shoulder.

"I'm fine, I'm fine," I say hurriedly. I don't need him to get too concerned. This, like every other ache and flare, will pass.

"You don't look fine, love." His soft voice cuts into my agitation. "C'mon. Let's get you inside."

I want to argue and insist that I'm fine. As sexually frustrated as watching Tristan... *exist* makes me, I need to lie down. I let him help me to my feet, but insist on space as I head inside. I need to be able to walk inside myself, able to get myself to a safer space without any help. I have to give up so many liberties because of my pain. After fucking up at the garden, I need this.

I do, however, let him grab one of my ice packs from the freezer.

"Do you want me to bring you the ice cream?" he asks once I settle down. I smother an amused chuckle. This caretaker side of him is adorable.

"No, that's okay."

Tristan settles onto the couch beside me, moving my feet onto his lap. "Have you been tested?"

I blink. "Have I what?"

His eyes widen. "No, not that way! I mean your back. I did some research and it may be an autoimmune disorder."

A tiny smile tugs at my lips. The man in front of me is so unlike the one I've known at the garden. "Of course I've been tested. I've been poked, scanned, felt up, interrogated, you name it."

"And nothing?"

"They say everything is normal."

"Clearly it's not."

The muscles behind my neck tighten. I clench my jaw. "Can we not talk about this right now? I'm not in the mood to be a medical mystery today."

"Okay." Tristan pauses. "My apologies."

I gently shake my head, his endearing accent dulling any irritation. "It's not your fault."

"Nor yours."

Those two words make tears prick my eyes instantly. It's *not* my fault. I gently tilt my head back, eyes squeezing shut as I gather myself. I refuse to cry in front of him again.

"Now is usually when I read or watch TV to distract me from the pain," I say.

"I'm not much of a reader."

I sniffle. "TV it is, then."

Tristan gets up to grab the remote. "What are you in the mood to watch?"

I'm not sure when it became known that he'd stay and continue spending time with me, but I'm not complaining. I don't want him to leave.

"Well, what kind of movies do you like?" If I didn't have an ice pack, I'd lean forward in interest. A person's preferred movies say a lot about them.

He shrugs. "I don't really watch movies. Or TV."

"You have to have at least a favorite."

He tosses an arm over the back of the couch as he considers. "*Training Day.*"

"With Denzel?"

"Yes."

"Not *Wolf of Wall Street*?"

Tristan scowls at me. "I'm just a stereotype to you, aren't I?"

I giggle. "I'm just teasing."

"I like early 2000s movies. Mostly because it's the only time I really watched movies at all."

I wonder what he was like as a child. Has he always been pompous and charming? The kid who sweet-talked his way into anything? He's been rich his whole life, so I don't doubt he was a spoiled brat.

"What other 2000s movies? Rom-coms? Early 2000s rom-coms are top tier."

He shrugs. "Not really any of those. *Love & Basketball*, I guess."

I smother more of my surprise. From what I know, his father wasn't in his life, and his mother and grandfather are both white. I highly doubt a rich white guy was concerned with keeping his grandson in touch with his Black side.

"I did watch a lot of the show *Girlfriends*, though," Tristan admits.

I bark out a laugh. "No freaking way. Who was your favorite character? It was Toni, wasn't it?"

He cringes and shakes his head. "No, she was awful. I had a crush on Joan growing up."

"Toni could be cool, though."

"She was a horrible friend."

"So was Joan."

"No," he insists. "All of them were lucky to have a friend like Joan Clayton."

I laugh again. I like this side of Tristan. "Mya was the best of all of them, though."

He shrugs. "I don't remember her. It's been a long time."

"Let's watch it!" With a few remote clicks, I pull up the first episode on whatever streaming service I can find. A pro of not having to worry about bills.

"You watched a lot of American shows and movies," I point out.

He doesn't move his gaze from the TV, nor does he budge. "My dad was American. I watched it with him."

It's definitely too soon in *whatever* this is between us to ask anything further. Instead, I brush my leg against his thigh, hoping it resembles a sort of comfort.

We watch the first few episodes in relative silence, save for when he points out Toni's flaws. It seems that Tristan will always be her number one hater.

"What do you have against Toni?" I ask at one point. "She's rich like you."

"And you."

"Okay, fair."

"Having money doesn't give you the freedom to act like an asshole."

I snort. "Actually, it does. We both know any rich person can get away with shit by paying for whatever they fucked up."

He hesitates. "It shouldn't be that way."

I roll my eyes. There's plenty I could say that proves it matches him, down to the very fact that he tried to buy his favor at Felicity. Regardless of how well I bite my tongue, he senses the stilted quiet.

"What?" he presses.

"Nothing."

"You want to say something," he says. "Spit it out."

"I don't feel like arguing with you."

"It doesn't have to be an argument."

I roll my eyes again. "Maybe you think of Toni as a cautionary tale. You don't want to be a rich asshole like her. But need I remind you that it's the basis of every single argument we've had?"

Tristan doesn't reply. He stares at the TV, his jaw clenched. Since we started watching the show, he's slumped down enough that he could rest his cheek against my knee if I bent my leg.

"Maybe it's why I'm here," he says eventually, his voice almost quiet. "I like that you hold me accountable."

Ah, fuck. Why did he have to go and say something like that? On one hand, it makes my heart melt and on the other, I'm not his coach nor is it my job to teach him how to be a better person. But maybe it's presumptuous to assume he wants me to teach him compared to wanting to be a reflection of a person's company.

I smile. "And because I'm good in bed."

He grins. "That, too."

CHAPTER TWENTY-FIVE
MAIA

After a few more episodes and icing my upper spine for far too long, I sit up to stretch. Angling my neck sends a series of cracks and pops that catch Tristan's attention.

"*Jesus,*" he huffs as I crank out a firework show. Each shift reveals absent tightness, taking away the majority of the pain.

I release a breath when I'm done. "That felt so good."

"That sounded scary."

With my newfound range of motion, I fluff up my hair and situate my tank top. I can feel his eyes on me, and I'm tired of pretending I haven't been wetter than Niagara Falls since he got here. I pause the TV before climbing on top of him. He startles, pressing himself up against the cushion but has no apparent interest in stopping me. I straddle him, lowering right onto his crotch.

He inhales sharply, but says, "Are you sure? If you're still in pain—"

"Do I look like someone who does something she doesn't want to do?"

Tristan gulps. "No."

"Then shut up and kiss me."

His eyes fall to my lips, and I feel him getting harder beneath me. My stomach roils when he captures my mouth with his. An involuntary moan vibrates my throat and he tenses when I grind my hips.

"I've been thinking about you," he mumbles.

"You have?"

"All the time. I'm dying to feel you again." His breathy voice conveys desperation, something I'm happy to sate. He kisses me roughly but touches me softly, his hands savoring every inch of my skin. His tongue dips into my mouth, giving me a taste of what I've been missing all week.

We kiss and I grind and my head is getting dizzy from how badly I crave his body. I *need* him to do what he did last time. It was a feeling I've never experienced before and I'll be chasing that high the rest of my life, even after he's long gone.

"Let's go to the bedroom," he says.

I hum. "Not a fan of couch sex?"

"Love, I'd fuck you just about anywhere, but right now, I have plans for you."

I bite the inside of my cheek to hide my giddiness. He follows me to my room and snoops around as I lock my patio doors and close the blinds. I retrieve the remote from my nightstand, dimming the lights into a warm hue with a tint of red.

Tristan tugs me to him. "If you're in pain or discomfort at all, please tell me."

"I will." I smile, endeared by his concern—but he takes it as sarcasm.

He grasps my chin. "I'm serious."

I match his stern look and deep voice. "Me too."

I can tell he wants to be annoyed, but he can't hide his amused smile. He kisses me again, his tongue sweeping into my mouth. I want this. I want *him*. He frustrates me beyond reason and I don't understand why he won't do even a fraction of the good his wealth allows him, but he sates my desire better than anyone I've ever been with. I can only hope the second time is just as good.

He slips his hand between my legs, snaking into my shorts and inhaling sharply. "You've been soaked this entire time?"

I nod, and he slips my tank top over my head before kissing down my chest.

"Turn around and bend over for me," he says, intensifying the ache in my lower belly and erupting sparks along my skin.

And even though I comply by stretching my top half across the bed, a sense of disappointment twists through me at the lack of intimacy. Our first time was heated and vigorous—it left both of us with marks afterward. I was hoping this time would—

Well, fuck me, never mind.

Tristan's oiled hands slide up my back, his thumbs putting pressure on either side of my spine. *Where the hell did he get oil from?* Glancing to my left, I spot the bottle of lotion I always keep on my nightstand.

"Feel good?" he asks.

Fuck. Why does he have to sound so goddamn sensual in everything he says? I only manage to hum a *yes* in response as he digs into the perfect sore spots between my shoulder blades. Chills swarm my skin as a wave of pleasure washes through my body. His touch drags down to my lower back again, massaging my dimples. Perhaps it's all of those sculptures that make him so skilled with his hands.

He kneads my muscles like he's molding clay and I dig my face in the blanket as euphoric bliss shudders through me. I hate that he can break me apart like this; no man I've been with has taken such care of my body this way. I don't care how good it feels; it's too vulnerable and I can't take it. His erection presses against my ass, and I wiggle my hips impatiently. He chuckles.

"Relax. We'll get there."

"There's condoms in the drawer."

"Like those'll fit," he says, amusement lacing his tone once he checks the drawer. "I brought one."

"Just one?"

I hear him chuckle again as he opens the condom. "Trust me. Once will be enough. And I can always get more." He grabs one of the small pillows on my bed. "Lift your hips for me, love—there you go." He stuffs the pillow under me. I wiggle my hips yet again when he stops just at my entrance, teasing me with the tip. *Motherfucker*. This is all I've been thinking about all week.

"If you don't fuck me in the next ten seconds I'm getting out my vibrator."

His thumb digs into my lower back. "I just massaged you and you're tense again."

"Because you're taking your sweet ass time."

"If you'd shut your mouth, I'd already be fucking you by now."

My eyes widen as I lift onto my elbows to look back at him. "Who the *fuck* are you talking—" I break off with a staggering moan as he fills me to the hilt. I drop back onto my chest, melting into the mattress from the pleasure.

"If I'd known this would shut you up, I would've fucked you a lot sooner."

I release a moan and manage to say, "Don't be a dick."

"Ah, but that's your favorite part about me."

Tristan starts slinging his hips back and forth and I clamp my teeth around the blanket to stifle my whimpers. The muscles in my body dissolve into ecstasy, any previous stress vanishing entirely. My climaxes come on quick and hard until I feel weightless. He doesn't stop thrusting the pain from me until he thrusts a tad too hard. I cry out, a hand behind me against his hip.

"Fuck, did I hurt you?" he asks, his movements stalling as he leans over me.

"I'm fine—it's just too deep."

"Then let's switch. Lie on your back."

I pull him with me and we climb under the blankets. He tucks another pillow beneath my hips before dipping inside of me once more. My legs wrapped around his waist, Tristan resumes thrusting with each one sending me deeper into a haze. But it's not enough.

"Harder," I press.

I brace for more, but his eyes flutter shut and he shakes his head. His pace slows. "I don't want to hurt you."

I touch his face, my thumb brushing his lower lip. "You won't."

My heart weeps when he opens his eyes. I've seen him agitated, cocky, lustful—never frightened. He looks down at me with a mixture of fear and longing and it's the most vulnerable I've ever seen him.

"You won't," I repeat, my voice a mere whisper. "I promise."

I pull him to me and connect our lips. I feel him hesitate, until his hold on me tightens as he picks up pace and force. Pleasure instantly builds, yanking any coherent thought from my mind. Tristan unleashes something feral inside me. Desire claws its way out of my skin just to touch him. My fingers drag down the ridges of his body, making him release a shuddering breath onto my neck.

His thrusts turn sloppy, and the tension pulling at his neck tells me he's about to finish. I arch into him without thinking as our orgasms crash together.

We lay tangled, catching our breaths. He kisses my forehead and the reality sinks in that I was a fool for ever thinking this could have been a one-time thing. We're too good together.

It's weird to see him in my bedroom—naked, of all things. Out of the men I've dated since becoming princess, technically Roman was the only one I've ever invited over, although he came over with Jace and my family. I may not have invited Tristan over, but I'd be sad if he left.

Daisy scratches at my bedroom door, her whines echoing. "I should take her and Poppy outside."

"Yeah, it's getting late."

My stomach tightens as he rises, sliding on his boxers.

"You're leaving?"

"I'm not arrogant enough to assume you want me staying in your house."

I slip into one of my T-shirts at the end of the bed as I muster what to say next. I don't want to admit it, but I want him to spend the night.

"Well, do you want to stay?"

"Do *you* want me to stay?" he counters, and I suppose I can't blame him for asking. I'd do the same.

"I mean... I wouldn't mind it..."

"Being minded and being wanted are two separate things."

Dammit. He's really going to make me work for it. I slump, rolling my eyes. "Okay *fine*. I want you here."

"You don't have to sound so mad about it."

He starts laughing when I throw my hands in the air with exaggerated frustration.

"Well, maybe I *am* mad about it!" I exclaim. "You still piss me off."

Tristan reaches across the bed to pull me closer by my waist. "It's okay. I like pissing you off."

It makes me want to shove him away for being condescending yet pull him closer because I like it when he kisses me. I hate this.

CHAPTER TWENTY-SIX
MAIA

Tristan and I manage to act normal at the garden even though Lyla knowing that the two of us kissed. I haven't told her that we slept together and I'm not sure I want to. It would make it too real. She'd ask questions I haven't even asked myself yet.

Friday rolls around, and while it's usually us two watching movies for hours, Esme joins us. The credits for *Clueless* have been rolling as Esme and Lyla debate over the next film: action or romance. Esme wants to watch *Notting Hill*. Lyla wants to watch *John Wick*. It reminds me of when I was hanging out with Nina last year. We'd only gotten halfway through the movie before she made me turn it off because it reminded her too much of Wesley—of his past.

Every now and again, I forget that my brother-in-law used to hunt and kill people for a living. The only Wesley I know is scared of my pet ducks and loves waiting on my sister hand-and-foot. It's annoying, honestly. Romance as a whole doesn't interest me. Nina and Wesley are so wrapped up in each other it's a wonder they get any work done. I can't fathom a world where I put that much love into someone. Soft and cuddly are the last words anyone would use to describe me. I'm all teeth.

Well—with people, yes. I'm soft and cuddly with animals, but let's be honest: anyone who isn't kind to animals cannot be trusted. Even Wesley, a former hitman, spends an impressive amount of time playing with my dogs every time he's here.

But other than that, I'm sharp edges, outspoken, and too much for men. Romance isn't in my cards. In spite of all this attention I get from the media and fans, it's nothing personal. They're looking for something to take from me— a hug, a picture, an autograph, a statement. I feel like a statue. I'd just like to be *me* sometimes. And though I wouldn't trade my life for anything, it's time I accept that my love life is limited to a few weeks or months of sex and adventures. I suppose that's not the worst thing in the world.

"Earth to Maia," Lyla says.

I blink my thoughts away. "What?"

"*Notting Hill* or *John Wick*?"

I hum. If I'm being honest, Anna in *Notting Hill* bothered me sometimes. I'm in the mood for unlikable women.

"*Notting Hill.*"

Esme squeals as Lyla huffs, flopping back onto the couch. Blood Sage hops onto my lap, curling into a fuzzy little ball.

As the movie starts, my phone vibrates with a text. I have to force the grin off my face.

TRISTAN

I'm struggling to come up with an excuse to come over.

Do you need dog food?

> Have you considered just asking?

No, because then you would know I like you.

What do you need?

I bite the inside of my cheek, contemplating if I should be dirty or reply with something completely unsexy. *Yeah, I need an outdoor broom to sweep up duck shit.* Or *Yeah, I need you to bend me over the couch and fuck me until I can't feel my legs.*

But that might be too much.

I look down at the feline purring against me and send a quick message before I can reconsider.

> Cat litter.

Cat litter? That's the best I can come up with?

> I have company, though. Deliveries can't be made until after five.

Company?

Oh shit. That could definitely be seen as though I have another guy here.

> Lyla and Esme. Movie Friday.

Be there at 5.

And at five p.m. on the dot, not long after my friends have gone home, Tristan is at my gate, holding up the cat litter at the security camera. I'm already laughing by the time he's at my front door. He doesn't waste time saying, "Delivery," before dropping the bag at my feet and capturing me in a kiss.

Over the next month, it becomes our ruse.

Next Friday, he delivers that outdoor broom and dutifully drops it at my feet. He barely gets out the word *delivery* before I bunch his black button-up shirt in my fist and yank him into a kiss.

He hums as he stumbles back into the house. "Love, this shirt costs ten thousand."

"That's fucking stupid," I mumble against his lips, slamming the door behind him so the dogs don't disturb us. The front courtyard is as secure as the backyard, so I'm not worried about them.

Without breaking the kiss, Tristan presses me against the wall with a hand behind my head. "But I like this shirt."

I brush his nose with mine, my hands sliding up his chest. My fingers brush the tattoo on his collarbone before curling around the black fabric.

"Me, too."

In one movement, I rip the shirt in two, buttons popping off and clattering in different directions.

Tristan slams his mouth on mine, our tongues lashing. If he's annoyed about the buttons, he doesn't show it. His hand pushes its way between my thighs and snakes into my shorts. I moan into his mouth at his fingers swirling my clit.

"You were this fucking wet waiting for me?" he purrs.

"Yes," I admit in a weak breath, "even though you were pissing me off this week."

He laughs, his tongue dragging down the side of my neck to douse my body in shivers. "It's hard to keep my hands off you, love."

I roll my eyes in both annoyance and pleasure—which basically sums up our entire situationship.

The next weekend, we're in the same position.

This time, he delivered a toy for Daisy, and she and Poppy are wrestling over it outside. I'm pinned against the wall again, and instead of fucking me against it like before, he hauls me up. I wrap my legs around his waist as his hands slip beneath the skirt of my sundress.

He groans deeply. "You answered the door without panties? *Fuck*, Maia."

I release a smug chuckle as he staggers toward the open sitting room around the corner. He drops us onto the tufted couch without breaking the kiss. His tongue sweeps into my mouth once more, sending a wave of lust rolling through my stomach. I jump at his fingers swiping up my slit.

"You're ready for me every time," he mumbles, rolling on the condom. His pants are just barely beneath his ass, but both of us are too needy to wait.

The next weekend, we end up in the dining room.

He delivered a toy for Poppy this time, and the two of them are outside wrestling over it. Tristan has me splayed out at the edge of the table like I'm his meal. While propped on my elbows, I watch him standing between my legs, a sight I've been craving all week.

His fingers grip the back of my neck as his thumb pushes up my chin so I meet his eyes. "I know what you were doing on Tuesday," he says, his voice husky. "Bending over in front of me. Flirting with the mail carrier."

I smirk. "I can flirt with whoever I want. You're not my boyfriend."

Tristan's gaze hardens, his sexual frustration oozing out

of him in waves to feed my own desire. He starts sliding into me inch by agonizing inch, stretching me out.

"Say it again," he taunts.

"You're not my—"

He pushes in all the way in, stealing my words. Any control I had over myself vanishes—and he knows it. "I love shutting you up with my dick."

"Fuck you."

He smiles and brushes his thumb across my lips. "The amount of curse words that fall out of this pretty mouth should be illegal."

I lick his thumb before gently clamping it between my teeth. "You liked my filthy mouth last weekend."

He inhales sharply and picks up pace, our synchronous moans filling the vacant dining room.

Very few people know the code to my gate, but we're in plain view for them to see should they enter. No one knows Tristan is here with me. We're untainted. Hidden. Private. And all at once—free.

By mid-June, I'm struggling to adjust to Maldana's extreme summers. New England was manageable, but ninety-plus degrees each day feels like a crime. I'm searching for every excuse to stay inside and I almost feel guilty until finding Dr. Pagoda in the break room sitting in front of a fan.

I laugh. "Your office got too hot?"

She snickers, her accent strong as she gestures in search of the right word. "The—the air conditioning break."

My boss is hardly ever in the break room since she not-so-humbly has a kitchenette in her office. I pout on her behalf. It's Tuesday, meaning Tristan trails in behind me.

His job was to hold the jumbo umbrella over us as I did a quick round of pest-checking before opening time.

Dr. Pagoda watches as Tristan strolls to the other end of the table. He hardly looks affected by the weather in his linen pants and collared white shirt. It's the epitome of business casual.

"You look like a cool cucumber," she says in broken English.

I smile at my boss's misuse of *as cool as a cucumber*.

"The heat doesn't bother me," Tristan replies.

Her lips turn down as if impressed. She angles her face toward the fan, giving me a profile of her beak nose and small mouth. Her eyes close as she relishes the cool air. The sight reminds me of a marble statue from antiquity.

"How is the project I gave you?" she asks suddenly, eyes still closed.

I clear my throat before sitting across from her, rifling through the paperwork on my clipboard filled with data I have to upload into the system. "Good. We've definitely noticed a decrease in the moth activity. We've increased bird predation and placed raised beds in close proximity to attract tachinid flies. According to reports, it seems to be working, just a little slower than we need."

"Why raised beds?" she asks, her eyes slitted in the way they always do when she's focused. It makes her look mean, and anyone who doesn't truly know her would believe she is.

"The oak trees are old and the soil is too acidic. It would require a lot more resources and it's too far into the growing season, anyway. Raised beds were the best and cheapest option."

She pushes the fan aside. "Did you select an insecticide in case?"

"Methoxyfenozide. It has the lowest risk."

"And I trust you've been working with the entomologists?"

It's interesting how she struggles with English words such as air conditioning, but doesn't stutter over entomologists.

I nod. "Dr. Thomas has been weighing in. He says it can't be solved in a single season, but he would reach out to his contacts for their input since the affected region is so large."

Dr. Pagoda tsks. "It's a matter of time before they reach the orchard."

"I know, but we're trying everything we can."

These moths are attracted to fruit-bearing trees, and we have an orchard in the public sector that visitors can pluck from. The last thing we need is for those trees to become infected.

She leans over and places her hand over mine. "You're doing good, Maia. Don't worry."

I give her the most confident smile I can muster. Even though I don't have a master's or doctorate degree like all of the scientists here, I've been working diligently and passionately under their guidance. I need to prove that I can keep up and earn my spot here outside of my royal title and status.

Until dealing with complete assholes in the royal institution, I'm eternally grateful for Dr. Pagoda. She's wise and collected and unintentionally funny.

"Maia has gotten better, no?" she says, turning to Tristan. "Not as mean?"

"Hey!" I squawk. "I'm *right* here!"

"Hush, child."

An amused smile spreads across his face. "Maia is just fine."

I'm more than fine. But I keep my mouth shut.

"Are we helping?" my boss asks.

Tristan tilts his head. "I'm sorry?"

"You are here to learn about plants, yes?"

"Oh." He sits up straighter, clearing his throat. "Yes. I can honestly say that volunteering here has helped me find a deeper appreciation for nature. It's inspired me to hire an attorney to represent a town under threat of mining."

Any of my unserious thoughts vanish. I cross my arms, my stare heavy.

What in the fuck?

That's not what happened, nor is his reason. Dr. Pagoda, on the other hand, is fooled. She places a hand to her heart and looks at me.

"You hear that, Maia? And you wanted to kick him out." She rises from her seat as her phone rings. "That's what happens when you give people a chance."

Yeah, they lie.

Dr. Pagoda answers the phone and starts speaking Maldanian. As she departs, the warning bells in my head get louder.

"Why did you lie to her?" I ask once we're alone. I force myself to look at him, hoping I can stay strong in the face of —well, his handsome face. "You know that's not what happened."

"I couldn't tell her the real reason."

My chest tightens. I fear the answer, but I have to ask. "Why are you here, Tristan?"

He doesn't remove his gaze from mine when he says, "You."

"Bullshit."

"Seriously? Even now?"

"*Especially* now," I argue.

He scoffs gently. "I like you, Maia. I've always liked you. Is that so hard to believe?"

Part of me doesn't believe him. Sure, we've been drawn to each other since he got here, and our underlying attraction only recently came to the surface, but my taste in men has never ended well.

"You tried donating money here because of me?" I ask.

"Yes."

"And now that you're here. Now that we've slept together, why are you still a volunteer?"

"I made a promise of three hundred hours. I intend to see it through."

I break our stare, unable to let it sink in. Is that it? Seeing me and wanting me are the believable parts. But going so far as to pledge three hundred hours of volunteering—just to talk to me? I don't buy it, and it doesn't change the fact that he's still CEO of a massive company and a hoarding billionaire.

"I'm not easily won," I tell him.

Tristan smirks. "I know."

"Sleeping together doesn't make you my boyfriend. Especially if you still run a wasteful company."

He clenches his jaw, leaning his elbows on the table in front of him. "I know you care about the earth and all, but I run a business. Our goal is to make money."

I force out an answer before I lose my temper and call him a condescending dick. I still grimace. "For what?"

He tilts his head. "I don't—"

"Making more money for *what*?" I press. "It's not like your employees are paid enough, so constantly increasing profit only means you and your buddies get richer." I match his pose, my elbows on the table. "So yes, Tristan. I'm asking what you're trying to make more money for. What could you *possibly* need that you don't already have within reach?"

His throat bobs as he swallows and fumbles for a response. I scoff, rising to my feet. "As you think of an excuse, I'll get back to work *caring* about the earth and all, you condescending dick."

CHAPTER TWENTY-SEVEN
MAIA

On Friday, I wake up to a text from Tristan. He doesn't attach a message, only a link to an article.

CEO of Space Technologies Gives Nearly A Billion In Bonuses to Staff

My heart thuds heavily in my chest as I skim the article. He doesn't give a direct statement, but every in-store staff member—both part-time and full-time—in Maldana is receiving a bonus of twenty thousand euros, followed by a promise to raise wages for every direct Space Tech employee around the world.

It's a good thing he's not here right now because he would get the best blowjob of his life.

I have to remind myself that this is the bare minimum. This is what someone with his wealth *should* have been doing from the start; it doesn't mean I'm not touched by the effort and I'm not clamping my bottom lip between my teeth to keep from grinning. An odd sense of pride in myself swells in my chest.

I don't respond to the text message, unsure of how to

make it seem like he's not doing this for me. He should do it for him, and I shouldn't be presumptuous.

Another text chimes in before I can move on from thoughts of him.

TRISTAN

Almost forgot to ask. What do you need delivered today?

My stomach twists, and not necessarily in a good way.

We're always at my place.

You are more than welcome to come to my studio tonight.

Are you inviting me?

Yes.

…

I'm waiting.

For what?

For you to invite me. I want to hear you say it.

Even if it's over text

I want you to come over to my studio tonight. I'd like to spend the evening with you.

I bite the inside of my cheek to keep from smiling. For some reason, his formality only adds to my fluster.

What time should I be there?

I don't know why, but tonight sort of feels like a date.

Our first date.

Usually, people have sex on the third or fourth, so we're a little out of whack. Is there a *we* to begin with? I shake my head, my hands tightening around the steering wheel. I'm ten minutes away and my heart is pounding and my pits are sweating. We've spent weekends together, but this isn't like lounging around my house, never wearing a complete outfit and playing the Law and Order board game for hours.

My red dress has bell sleeves that flare out at the elbow and is short enough to be on the revealing side, yet long enough to be comfortable. The folds flow like drapes as they tie into a knot at the bottom of the V-neck, and the snug fit is suddenly suffocating.

"Why the fuck am I so nervous?" I yell out loud before turning up the volume to Lauryn Hill's *Doo Wop (That Thing)*. It's literally just hanging out with Tristan. I've had his dick in my mouth but I'm panicking at spending the evening with him. I don't do this. I don't know what it is about him that makes this so different, but this feels like *more*.

There's no reason I shouldn't treat this like any other time we've spent together. Shit, was I supposed to bring something and say *delivery* when he opens the door? Fuck it. Fucking *fuck it*. Okay, Tristan might have been right about me cursing too much.

City driving distracts me as I make my way to his neighborhood. I don't miss the honking, sudden stops, and the endless number of moped drivers. I'm still envious of Nina for taking advantage of riding through Kosita on a moped before it became much too dangerous for us to do now. Too many people know our faces, and no one wants to be the person who ran into the princess or queen on a moped.

Once I pull into his building's parking garage, I spot Tristan up ahead in loose slacks and a short-sleeved button-up. He tucks his phone away at the sight of my car and I bite the inside of my cheek. He got a haircut. I can spot his thin gold chains and the tattoo around his collarbone. Just about everyone I know would tell me this is a bad idea, but one look at him and I know I made the right choice.

"You were waiting for me?" I ask as I step out of my car.

He only nods, closing my door behind me. "How was the traffic?"

I gulp my nerves down. "Traffic was fine."

Tristan takes my hand in his, surveying my outfit before pressing a kiss to my knuckles. "You look beautiful."

Jesus Christ on a stick. He's not supposed to compliment me so earnestly. Heat rushes to my face and ears as I mutter a *thank you.*

Compliment him back.

What do I say? You look pretty? I'd jump your bones in an instant? Before I can speak, he tugs me toward the elevator.

As soon as the elevator doors close behind us, he pulls me flush against him and captures my lips in a kiss. A moan escapes me as my arms find their way around his neck. A mere kiss soothes my anxiety and makes me wonder why I was so nervous in the first place. Just last weekend, we were laughing to tears after seeing Sage's reaction to the tin foil on my kitchen counter to keep her from jumping up on them. I snorted; Tristan wheezed. Both only made us laugh harder.

I pull from the kiss, grinning sheepishly. "Hi."

"Hi," he whispers. He gives my hip a squeeze before the elevator doors open and he leads me into his studio.

The evening sun bathes the room in orange light, but it didn't stop him from lighting candles on one of his work tables. Sure, perhaps we were going to sculpt together, and in retrospect, my dress wasn't the right choice, but I hadn't expected *this*. Jazz music plays softly from an unseen speaker and the candlelit table has a spread of food waiting for us.

"You did this?" I ask, my voice soft. As sad and corny as it sounds, no one has ever been so thoughtful for me before.

"I figured we could eat before I teach you how to sculpt."

"And how do you know I can't sculpt already?"

The words are out of my mouth before I can stop them. I can't help that I'm naturally combative. Tristan must notice the regretful discomfort on my face; he doesn't reply, only takes my hand and guides me toward the food. I curl my free hand into a fist, hoping to squash my awkwardness.

For some reason, it's so difficult for me to say *this is beautiful, thank you for doing this*. Sure, men have offered me luxury cars, rides on their private jet, and expensive jewelry, but this feels thoughtful—and all he did was order some food and light a few candles.

There's a large Margherita pizza, hummus and pita bread, and two glasses of red wine. A Maldanian stereotype, but I'm not complaining.

"This is—" I swallow, gesturing to the food and set up. "It's really nice. Thank you."

I'm not used to such treatment, but it's Tristan. We're

just having fun. As we eat, my gaze wanders to the dozens of sculptures around the studio. I gesture to his work. "How did you get into this?"

Tristan shrugs. "Dunno. I took a class in primary school and it just stuck."

I lift my brows. "So you've been doing it for a while."

I never would have pegged him for the artistic type. There's no denying the insane talent that goes into work like this, but I'm surprised at how... subtle he is about it.

"My grandfather didn't encourage it. He thought it was a waste of time, so I stopped for a while." He doesn't look at me as he speaks, and I note the hunch in his shoulders.

"Well, what about now?" I press. "Have you thought of sharing them?"

He shrugs again—and I almost like the sight of a sheepish Tristan. "I've always thought of my work as something to hide. If I did share them, it'd probably be anonymous."

I pout. He's talented. I don't like that he feels ashamed of it. "They're beautiful. I think the world should see what you're capable of."

He meets my eyes, finally, and my throat catches at the vulnerability. The corner of his lips lifts. "Thanks. You ever think you'll get into drawing again?"

Ah, I almost forgot he found my old sketchbook last weekend. "Maybe. I kind of stopped completely after moving to Maldana."

"Why?"

I hum, racking my brain. Pencil and paper used to be my favorite pastime. I loved sketching nature—trees, leaves, plants, flowers. It helps my field notes for work now. Other than that, it's a memory.

"I don't know. Maybe being princess ruined my creativity."

I offer a sardonic chuckle, but Tristan doesn't find it amusing. Like I did with him, he pouts. "Hopefully it'll come back."

And like he did with me, the corner of my lips lifts. My voice remains soft. "Hopefully."

ROY LANE

CHAPTER TWENTY-EIGHT
MAIA

If not for the calming weekend I had with Tristan, I would be fuming at what I discover at work on Monday.

Instead, I'm just really pissed.

My tree traps have been emptied and the zones of egg masses have been cleared. After another attempt at encouraging predation, I was going to shift gears this week—until someone beat me to it.

I head toward the research building in search of the assailant. The sweltering sun only worsens my agitation, but the air conditioned building soothes me slightly. The first person I run into is Lyla, who's headed in the direction I came from.

"You okay?" she asks, stopping in her tracks at my expression.

"No, I—someone cleared the zone I was working in." I jam a thumb over my shoulder. Dr. Pagoda wouldn't assign someone else to the project, so I'm at a loss as to who would do it.

I expect surprise from my best friend, but she relaxes and waves a hand. "Oh, I had a few interns clear it out."

I flinch in surprise. All the data I planned to gather is gone. "What—why would you do that?"

She tucks her dark hair behind her ear. "We had to take a step sooner or later. The breeding season is just about over and something needed to be done."

"I had a team going out this week!" I argue. "They were gonna gather data for the egg masses."

The worry in her face eases at my explanation. "That's unnecessary information, anyway. You would've wasted your time."

I step in her path before she can walk away. There's so much to unpack—starting with the fact that it's my project. She knows that it's my first one, and my chance to prove myself to Dr. Pagoda.

"That wasn't your call to make."

"What's the big deal?" she wails, exasperated. "We all work for the same company. Everyone here is a team and we share projects all the time. You don't get to shut everyone out because you're the princess."

Bullshit. It's not about being princess. She's getting her doctorate. I'm one of the very few scientists without education beyond a bachelor's degree. She knows I have to work twice as hard.

"Lyla. You know how much this project means to me."

"It's *one* tiny thing. It's not going to change the outcome and you're still in charge of it. Relax."

I bite my tongue, forcing myself to walk away. There's no inching around the fact that my status as princess is the reason Felicity Gardens exists. Yes, in a way, this garden feels like it's mine. But I'm not the one in control. Felicity's board is filled with exceptionally smart scientists who have as many years of experience as I am old. One of the board members straight-up told me my choice of school is one of the worst in our field. I have to prove myself time and time again. And though I wouldn't have it any other way, this is my chance to show what I can do.

An entire football field's worth of data has been cleared and I was going to use that information to determine the next step. I needed every bit of information I could gather so I could avoid signaling the "I need help" sign, showing I'm not ready to tackle this.

Lyla is supposed to be my best friend; we've *been* best friends since the first day we met. Our energies ping-ponged off one another and it was relieving to find someone as bold as I am. Part of why I love our friendship is that she doesn't treat me differently because of my royal title—and I'm starting to wonder if it's because she resents it.

While my title might be affecting my friendship with Lyla, my advisor team informs me about an opportunity hosted by the UN in a couple of weeks.

A member of the British Royal Family cancelled their attendance at a charity gala and the UN wants me to replace them—*and* host it in Kosita, too. It's an auction to win a lunch with me to discuss the expansion of their own charitable cause, and the bids on the lunch are donated to a charity of my choosing. It feels a little demeaning to dress up and have people bid on time with me specifically, but the thought of funding schools—specifically in Black communities—back home in America eases the feeling instantly.

Tristan is pleased when I tell him about it, but I sense his hesitation. He comes to my house after work on Tuesday to help me pick out a dress.

I've been stewing over what happened with Lyla; we hadn't spoken since the confrontation and according to Nina, she's a backstabbing bitch. I couldn't bring myself to defend Lyla even if I wouldn't go so far as to call her that. She's the first true friend I've made post-princess.

I'd never admit this aloud, but I'm grateful Tristan is here, strewn across the couch in my closet as I rifle through clothes. He's helping me keep my mind off it even if he's still working and typing away on his phone.

Sage curls up beside him and he distractedly pets her. I hate how much my animals have taken to him. Daisy and Poppy are a few feet away either chewing a bone or ripping up yet another toy.

The silky fabric of the floor-length dress swishes around my legs as I step in front of the mirror. "What about this one?"

When Tristan looks up, I see his breath hitch in his chest. Though his jaw is slack and erection is growing, he shakes his head.

"Too revealing."

I frown and look at the way the V-neck connects at my sternum. Despite the revealing chest, everything else is covered—not even a slit to show my leg. I smooth down the orange sunset fabric. It was handmade in a tiny Sicilian shop by a woman named Imelda.

"For a charity event or in general?" I ask.

"Both."

I glare at him. "Don't pull that controlling shit on me. It won't work."

He locks his phone and slides it into his pocket. "You're

auctioning yourself off and I've said nothing," he blurts. "In my world, I've already failed."

"I'm not *auctioning* myself off. It's a bid for a lunch—"

"A date."

"A *meeting*," I correct, "to discuss a project for their charity of choice. It's a way to get rich people to hand over their money and do some good."

I can't let him know there's a tiny, tiny part of me that agrees. I'll never hear the end of it.

"I had Augustus pull the guest list," he says. "Most of them are men."

I roll my eyes, though my stomach stirs from his interest in the event. "If I have to let a few men think they have a shot in order to do some good, then so be it."

His eyes trace my figure again, his jaw clenching as uncertainty crosses his face.

If I want to wear a revealing dress, I will.

If I, as a single woman, want to lead on a few rich men for a good cause, I will.

Tristan isn't here with me because I follow a man's rules. I step over to him, placing my finger under his chin to raise his head. My voice is gentle, but my words aren't.

"You don't have a say in this."

"I will murder any man who touches you," he says quietly, apprehension still written across his features.

"You won't," I reply, "because we're not together."

"We're not."

Not a question, but a statement.

"I haven't forgotten you're a greedy corporate bastard."

He bristles. "What if I told you I donated ten million to animal shelters across the world this morning?"

I shake my head. He still doesn't get it. "I'd say no one should be able to donate that much money over coffee."

He huffs. "I can't win with you."

I turn away. "If you think this is about winning, then our relationship will be shorter than you think."

I rifle through more dresses. Although he's being possessive, he's right: it's too revealing for a charity event.

"I'm not as bad as you think I am," Tristan eventually says.

I pause. I'm not trying to make him feel like a bad person. Not anymore, at least. But I can't let up on the fact that he has more money and power than ninety-nine percent of the world. He's not the one percent. He's the point-five percent.

"Just because there are people worse than you doesn't mean you can't do better."

After a brief, heavy silence, I hear him rise behind me. He turns me around, taking my hands in his. Even though I'm slightly—only slightly—peeved with him, I love seeing both the contrast and similarities of our skin—his sepia tone and my tawny shade. Darker and lighter, but undeniably brown.

"What would you do?" he asks. "If you had my money, my assets, company, stocks, everything."

I look up at him in surprise before snorting. "You don't want to know."

He nods, an earnest look crossing his face. "I do. I want to know everything you'd do."

"Really?" A giddy thrill drums up my spine. "This is exciting. There's so much! Okay, big picture-wise, end famine where I can and invest in restoring the agriculture of those countries or whatever it is that will help stop the spread in the future. And then if I ran Space Tech, obviously everything would be made with renewable sources and recycled material. I'd even offer discounts for everyone who turned in their old stuff for recycling. Then I'd stop that bullshit money-grab you do by having a million-and-one different chargers and make *everything* compatible. And then I'd stop charging an arm and a leg for headphones. I'd make regular investments to end climate change and fund efforts for renewable energy sources around the world. And then obviously there's education funding in *every* aspect. Public schools, community colleges, sex education. My god, there's so much..." I shake my head, overwhelmed by the ideas. "These are things you could do every day. Not all of them might be your problems, but you're blessed with more power than it seems you even realize. And it just—it saddens me that you ignore it."

Tristan nods again. "Okay."

"Okay, what?"

"I'll see what I can do."

I lift a brow. "About which part?"

"All of it."

I snort, partially to cover my uncomfortable disbelief. He's so sure in every word he says. "I'll believe it when I see it, rich boy."

He smirks, leaning down to kiss my cheek. "What happened to pretty boy? I liked that one better."

CHAPTER TWENTY-NINE
TRISTAN

The third anniversary of Grandfather's death hits harder than it should.

It's Thursday and I've been running reports and drafting proposals for hours. With a few of our international locations going under, I need to pull in new methods.

My mind keeps drifting to Maia.

I told her I would see what I could do about her ideas. A year ago, I would have scoffed. The world is changing and Grandfather isn't here anymore. I'm the one in charge. The decisions are mostly up to me.

He and Maia would have hated each other. I have no doubt he would have called her a bitch behind her back—until Maia would start an argument with him. Then he would say it to her face. He always taught me to be respectful toward women, but always preferred that they were submissive. Maia is nothing like that and I wonder if that's why I'm so drawn to her. She's different from what I was raised to want.

She would make a hell of a businesswoman, but I can't

imagine her working somewhere like Space Tech. She has a big heart and a lot of hope in spite of all she's been through with the public and media.

Grandfather's deep, raspy voice—ruined from decades of cigar smoking—cuts into my head about how much of a mistake I'm making. For considering Maia as a partner and especially considering her ideas for the company.

I started mourning him the moment we learned his cancer was terminal, and I know he made sure to give me all of the advice he had pent up inside. He believed in me. He took pride in me when no one else had. Not my father and surely not my mother.

Space Technologies thrives because of how Grandfather prepared me. I thought I had everything I needed to know, but I've never felt more lost. The weight of this job hits harder than ever and I don't know where to look. It's the first time I'm embarrassed by the company—something that would have been beyond my comprehension a year ago. A world of untapped decisions came into full view, things that have sustenance and legacies.

While I have knowledge in information technology—it was my university concentration—it's not my focus. The CEO role at my level is management. I steer the ship. I keep us on top. It has less to do with IT work, and I'm okay with that. It gives me peace of mind when things run smoothly, and I'm good at keeping everything under wraps. The free moments outside of work, I sculpt. In a way, it's the ultimate form of management. It's up to me to build a good statue out of material. It's meticulous.

The company's name is about physical space, not outer space. Grandfather wasn't ashamed to exist. *Stagnant men go nowhere,* he would say. He wanted me to grow the company, but I just have different ideas on how.

As much as I don't want to include Celine, if I want to make our company greener, it would help to have her on board. Around noon, after tossing back a protein shake, I head to Celine's office with a knot of dread sitting in my stomach.

"Enter," she says once I knock on the door. She types away behind her desk, wearing a navy pantsuit with her hair tied back to show off her warm tan.

"Tristan." She speaks my name like I'm a lost ghost searching for the correct place to be. Sadly, I'm not lost.

I clear my throat, hands stuffed into my pockets. "I have to speak with you about something. D'you have a minute?"

My mother glances at her computer screen, clicks the mouse a few times, then folds her hands in the center of the desk. "I'm listening."

"I'm thinking of making a shift in the company, and it would help if you were on board."

Her thin brows lift in curiosity. She removes her reading glasses and leans back in her chair, arms crossed. It creates an air of confidence and shows she has the upper hand. That's all she's ever wanted. Dominance. Control.

"What kind of shift?"

"Going green. Sustainability."

She hesitates. "In what capacity?

"As much as we can handle."

"If it's going to cost us money, you can forget about it."

My patience thins. I force my gaze to the ground, gathering my composure. "I'm not asking your permission. I'm asking for your support."

She sneers. "Then the answer is no."

"Why?"

"With our numbers tanking in Australia and the manufacturing issues in Asia, a costly project is an idiotic move."

Celine knows she's the only one in the entire company who can speak to me this way, and she takes advantage of it whenever she gets—often in front of other people.

"I have no doubt we would attract consumers with more sustainable practices. It's a hot issue."

"Exactly! So we can switch to eco-friendly packaging and call it a day. McCloskey and Barnes already think you're too young for the role. Don't rock the boat by adding this new-age rubbish to the mix."

Hm. I didn't know Barnes and McCloskey thought that, but it's good information to save. "Then I repeat my earlier statement, I'm not asking your permission."

She narrows her eyes at me. "Today, of all days, you bring this to me. Why?"

A tiny nip of fearful realization hits me. Did I subconsciously come here because it's Grandfather's death anniversary? That door slams shut immediately.

If anything, I'd rather go to his house—his mansion outside the city that I can't bring myself to sell just yet. I spent a few years of my childhood and most of my summers there.

"It has nothing to do with that," I say, my voice firm.

"He hated the idea of going green," Celine reminds me. It's true. He thought it was a waste of resources, that the rubbish industry needed products. Everything was a business to him. "There were a lot of things he hated," she adds.

"At the very least, let's save his criticisms for tomorrow."

She rolls her eyes. "The only reason he left me the European division was because you had no kids when he was on his deathbed—and he wanted the company to stay in the family. He made it clear he didn't want me to have it."

"Because you're a snake."

"Because I'm a woman."

Grandfather was misogynistic. I cannot argue that. It doesn't change the number of lies Celine has told. Perhaps she became this treacherous because of the way he raised her, but neither was my fault. I've been stuck between an ugly dispute that hasn't ended despite one of them being dead.

I know the real reason Grandfather gave her the European division. It wasn't just because I'm childless; it's to keep his enemies close. He gave me insurance—proof of her betrayal that could have her removed, even arrested. I'd rather not use it, but it's there.

"Grandfather didn't force you to give away Danica," I blurt.

"For Christ's sake," she huffs, rising from her seat. "This again?" She wanders to the window as if trying to ease out of the conversation.

It pisses me off.

How can she be so nonchalant about it?

Perhaps I'm sentimental today and reflecting on the past. My sister's disappearance has lingered over me for years and I fear my memories of her will diminish the way Grandfather's will in time.

"She was my sister."

"And *my* daughter," she snaps. "You don't know half the things that have happened in this family."

My anger surfaces with a vengeance. She has no right to stand there and pull rank. "What family, Celine? You're my mother and I call you by your first name!"

"I'm sparing you. If it weren't for me, God only knows what she would've done."

I scoff. "A seven-year-old. You were afraid of a seven-year-old girl?"

She starts rearranging the files on her desk, her hands trembling. "All you need to be concerned about is that out of everyone in this family, *you're* the one who came out on top."

"And I did nothing for it," I say, echoing a phrase she's so often spewed over the course of my life.

"Exactly. If you were born a girl, we wouldn't be having this conversation."

"None of this changes that I still don't know anything about why Dani was taken away. And *where*. I deserve those answers."

Celine glowers at me. "I'm telling you now, stop asking questions."

"*No.*"

She hesitates, ripping her gaze from me. Her profile is sharp, all edges. There are rare moments I see her as more than a venomous thorn in my side. Moments where I see her as my mother, as Grandfather's daughter. As much as he loved family, he didn't take women seriously. It must have been frustrating as his daughter.

But what about Dani?

Her daughter?

"My father," Celine stumbles, "is... *was*... not the man you thought he was."

"That's not enough," I grit.

She lets out a shaky sigh. "We sent your sister away because she kept trying to hurt your grandfather. She was violent and uncontrollable."

"The fuck does that even mean?"

"I mean trying to plunge a *knife* into him in the middle of the night. *That* kind of violent."

I flinch, unable to digest the words spewing from her mouth. This happened when Danica was seven. Celine is talking about a seven-year-old committing attempted murder.

"You're lying."

"I'm not lying."

"She was a child," is all I can manage to say.

My mother shakes her head with a tiny sardonic grin. "You were off in Maldana for the summer, you don't know how bad it was. Something snapped and she became a nightmare. Whether it was with a pencil or a fork, she was trying to jab it into your grandfather's neck. She had to go."

I must have an unknown second sister because there's no way we're referring to the same person.

"We are talking about *Danica*," I say, annunciating each word. "The girl who never grew out of bringing her stuffed bunny wherever she went. The girl who cried for days when she realized her chicken nuggets were made of actual chickens. A child doesn't turn into a killer overnight. Do you hear how ridiculous you sound? Something *happened*. I'm hoping you at least asked her why."

Celine opens her mouth, but no words come out. "I— she... she was looking for attention."

"Attention for what?"

But she doesn't need to reply for the realization to sink in. Claws rip across my memories, my trust, my *life*.

Celine looks away as shame clouds her eyes.

Grandfather did god-knows-what to his granddaughter. My sister. Chills shudder through my entire body; my mind spins.

Danica must have been petrified. For an innocent child to be so frightened that she fought to protect herself because no one else would.

The words fall from my mouth. "How could you do that?"

She blanches. "*I* didn't touch her!"

Fury curls in my gut. Celine learned her daughter was being abused and decided to send the child away. Grandfather lived a luxurious life. He was happy. He *raised* me.

"Listen to me," she insists with a trembling voice, "I did what had to be done. Space Tech was just taking off and a scandal—"

I snatch the computer monitor off the desk, yanking the cords as rage sears through me. Celine flinching is nothing but encouragement.

"*SHE'S YOUR CHILD!*" I scream, launching the monitor into the bookshelves. "*And you abandoned her like a fucking coward!*"

How could she do this?

How could *Grandfather* do this?

My hands tremble in fury, but Celine is too frightened, too cowardly, to do anything but shake like a leaf behind her desk. I wouldn't hurt my own mother—but I certainly wish Grandfather were alive only so I could be the one to put him in a grave.

CHAPTER THIRTY

TRISTAN

The man who raised me was a monster.

He was the pinnacle, the patriarch, of this family. Celine and I have battled in his footsteps to be the best and reach the top. What would I have done if I had found out earlier? What would my life look like now?

After I storm out of Celine's office, I pace my own. There's no hope of getting work done, and the harrowing combination of shame and frustration sends me to the studio.

I try to sculpt. I spend an hour detailing and re-detailing because I can't get it right no matter how many sections I switch to. I clench the shaping tool in my fist to keep from destroying the sculpture.

I remember that summer.

Romèo and I spent it lounging by the pool and doing nothing important. Dani usually came with us to Maldana, along with the slew of nannies and house staff to watch over her. I don't remember why she didn't come, but I know I was grateful. I was happy not to deal with a nagging little sister for the whole summer.

Meanwhile, the very man I idolized had been hurting her.

How could I be so stupid?

I'm her older brother. It was my job to protect her and I failed spectacularly.

Two people were gone from our family overnight. I don't know where my father took her, or why he was complicit in all of this. He'd never been particularly present.

From the start, it's been Grandfather.

A monster.

My mind shuts off and I find myself climbing into my car and driving. I consider stopping at a park just to wander, but that won't help anything. I don't want to be alone with my thoughts, and a public place would be the loneliest.

I've spent years alone. Even before Grandfather's death, I spent most of my time with my own thoughts. And for the first time, I hate the silence. I hate the creaking emptiness of my studio and my penthouse.

So I keep driving.

I drive out of the city and through the countryside until I reach a familiar divot in the mountains.

Rather than asking why I'm here right away, Maia opens the gate for me to pull in.

Apprehension seizes my chest; she's made it clear what she thinks about Space Tech—and therefore my grandfather. I'm not sure what I'll do if she says "I told you so" as a way of proving billionaires aren't trustworthy.

I'm crossing a line by being here. It's far more intimate than we agreed, though I can't bear being anywhere else. If sculpting isn't working out, if it's not soothing me, I have nothing left. It's been my haven for years and it's not working tonight.

Maia rotated in my mind because there's never a time she's a faraway thought, and she became my instinct. Nothing could have convinced me to turn around on the drive here, but I'm almost frightened as I knock against the mahogany wood door.

I lean against the threshold, fighting to hold back tears.

Monster.

That single word keeps turning over in my mind. The man I idolized growing up was a monster. I couldn't look at either of my parents for role models. Grandfather stepped in when they didn't. No matter what, I was fucked either way.

What does that say about me?

The humid night air gathers on the back of my neck. I shut my eyes to keep myself together as I wait for her.

Even now, even when I'm falling apart, Maia's beauty takes me aback. She has no makeup; her hair is pulled into a bun at the crown of her head; she wears a shirt big enough to hide whether she wears pants or not. She watches me with her doe eyes, and they only widen when she realize my disheveled state.

"Tristan—"

"I don't want your judgment," I say. "I just—I didn't know where else to go. I didn't know what else to do." My voice cracks at the end, and she still doesn't say a word. Only watches with genuine concern. Fear, even.

I inhale a shaky breath. "I... My grandfather—" I sniff and look away. I have to say it aloud. It's the least I can do after the turmoil Dani went through. "He raped my sister when we were kids."

Maia gasps, her expression breaking which, in turn, breaks me. The tears rush to the surface as she gathers me in her arms instantly.

"Oh my god," she whispers. "I'm so sorry."

She pulls me inside and shuts the door behind me. Despite the sadness, Daisy and Poppy sniff and wiggle excitedly.

Her soft, rosy scent fills my nose and the familiar air of Maia's house eases the tension yanking in my chest. All that's left behind is the raw ache of frustration.

We stand there for a while as her hand glides up and down my back. Although I still have to lean down, I love the fact that she's tall, too. It's another thing we have in common. Being compatible with this woman, even in the tiniest of ways, gives me hope that I'm not a bad person after all.

She leads me to the living room where she'd set up camp. It looks somewhat tidy. Considering how messy she can be, it tells me that she took so long to open the door because she was cleaning.

"Let Daisy give you cuddles," she says, urging me to the dog end of the couch. She whistles to the Rottweiler. "Daisy Baby. Up."

Daisy hauls herself on the cushion—and Sage follows not long after. Instead of following suit, Poppy settles herself at my feet, wanting to be close by, but not touched. I love all of the nicknames Maia gives her animals even if she usually says them in an irritating squeaky voice. *Daisy Baby. Poppy Poo. Sagey Pie.*

But that's Maia. She might be more honest than she needs to be and have major trust issues, but she's more affectionate and loyal than she gives herself credit for. Being near her feels like home.

"Wanna tell me what happened?" she asks. Her gentle voice sends warmth tumbling through my body. My stomach caves with the daunting yet comforting fact that I feel better with her near.

With my head in my hands, I relay everything I learned today, followed by tidbits of memories when Dani was sent away. She doesn't say anything, only runs her hand up and down my back.

"I just—I hate that I can't kill him for hurting Danica," I admit. "All these years, I blamed Celine for ruining our family. She's done horrible things, but..." I grimace. "Grandfather takes the cake."

"I'm so sorry," she whispers again, and I nearly shiver at her nails raking across the base of my neck. "What about your dad?"

I shrug, feigning nonchalance. "I don't give a damn about him. He went along with it like a coward. Growing up, he was always off gambling, anyway."

Until Grandfather's death, he was the only constant person. Dad left, Dani was taken, I never counted on Celine, and Romèo disappeared. I won't admit it aloud, but losing my best friend—my *only* friend—hurt. The only person who stuck by me was my grandfather. And he turned out to be the worst of them all. Had he abused anyone other than my sister? It rattles me that I'm so close to something so horrific. It's something that happens to families you see on the news, on TV. Not in your own family.

I panic at the thought of failing Danica. It's a slap in her face that I gave him a good grandson after what he did.

Nico Farrugia raped my sister.

I want to deny it, but is it truly so hard to believe? He wasn't the type to harass women.

Because he had his sights set lower.

My stomach lurches in disgust as a wave of nausea hits me. I tense and fight the urge to vomit onto Maia's living room floor. I wish I had a baseball bat. I wish I were at his house.

That's where I should have gone. I should be at the mansion destroying everything he owned. How could he do this? To our family? To a *child*?

"Breathe," Maia says, her sudden voice slicing right through me. She kneads my shoulders apart. "Just take deep breaths."

I do. I lean back on the couch, giving Daisy a chance to settle her heavy head on my lap.

"I want to kill him," I say. The words sound so little when said aloud.

He's dead. I can't do anything. I expect Maia to say as such, but I simply feel her nod and say, "I know."

"I have to get rid of his house," I blurt. "I didn't want to sell it before—it's where he died. But now... maybe I can find something about Dani. Anything of hers. Don't pedophiles do that? Keep... *fuck*." A rush of tears surfaces and I lean forward again, snapping my eyes shut. "He was a fucking pedo, Maia. The man who raised me. What does that say about the person I've become?"

"Look at me." She takes my face in her hands, forcing my gaze to hers. "He broke your trust and hurt your family. You were a child—there's nothing you could've done differently. And the person you've become? That's *your* choice. He doesn't get that power over you."

I drop my head against her chest. I wish I could believe her. She's smart, and I know she's right. But every voice in my head is warning me that my shot at being a decent person is ruined.

CHAPTER THIRTY-ONE
MAIA

Since Tristan has been spending just about every weekend at my house since June, he doesn't have to worry about packing clothes here.

I don't know how that happened—how hooking up has turned into him having a drawer and turning to me when he's sad. I'm glad he came to me, though, and I was almost hurt that he thought I would judge him. Neither of us has to voice the fact that I wouldn't have liked his grandfather even before finding out what he'd done. Tristan was betrayed by one of the few people he thought he could trust. I'd never judge him for that.

It was a more somber weekend; he helped me garden, we walked the dogs on my private trail, and went swimming in the lake. I got distracted by the wildflowers along the path and before he could kill a bee for harassing him, I stopped him and explain their importance. Like months ago at the garden, he was amazed.

After he leaves on Sunday evening, I respond to a few emails about donation projects and possible volunteering. My time helping residents in Kosita either fix or build their homes has imprinted on me forever, but I had to leave. I haven't done as much community work since I moved out here.

I've been chased, stalked, assaulted, and invaded. I couldn't sleep. I triple-checked my locked doors and covered my one-way windows because I didn't trust them.

I'm no doctor, but it was easy to connect stress to my worsening chronic pain. I had to leave the city. It was killing me slowly, brutally.

I tie my curls into a low bun before slipping on my pink gardening apron. The work I did in the city was remarkable, but I can't help anyone if I'm crumbling. Now, as my dogs run circles around me and my ducks splash in their pond, serenity fills my chest. It doesn't matter that it's cloudy; I can see the mountains from my backyard and hear my trickling fountain. This is perfect.

I get an alert on my phone for the front gate and find my sister sticking her hand outside of her white car, waving at the camera.

It's not like her to drop by unannounced—and I don't have any missed calls or texts. I mostly need time to clean up so she doesn't judge my mess. I shed my apron and head inside for the front door. Once I open it, I find her hobbling up the front steps in a long, flowing sundress that looks comfortable as hell, to be honest. Her curls look moisturized and full, but they're falling out of the messy bun atop her head. Leave it to Nina to look so elegantly messy.

"What are you doing here?"

Without saying hello or giving me a hug, she brushes past me inside toward my eager pets and says, "I'm escaping my mother-in-law." The fresh summer evening air whooshes inside. Although it's sunny, it's far too hot to keep the windows open.

A manic laugh escapes me. "That's funny. But Miss Olive seems so nice. What happened?"

"Nothing," she cries as I close the door behind me. "That's the worst part. She's so freaking sweet and helpful and she's done absolutely nothing wrong and my husband is beyond perfect but I swear to god if another person asks me if there's anything I need I'm going to punch them in their teeth, but how *awful* is that when they're just being—"

"Breathe, Nina." My sister is the second person I've instructed to breathe this weekend. Next thing I know, one of my dogs will be choking.

"I wanted chips, right? I said that I wanted chips, and Miss Olive pulled up a recipe to make *homemade* ones. Like —from *scratch*."

I place a hand on my chest. "*Awww*, that's the sweetest thing I've ever heard."

Nina closes her eyes and shakes her head as she caresses her baby bump. "I just wanted chips, Maia. From a bag. Salty, unhealthy chips that will make my tongue swell."

My poor overstimulated sister. I wrap my arm around her and guide her into the living room. "I've got chips, okay? Let's get you on the couch."

"The worst part is I don't even want chips anymore. Do you have french fries?"

"I will get you french fries."

She nods vigorously, her fuzzy slippers shuffling against the ground. "Not the waffle ones. I'm not in the mood for those today."

"Got it, no waffle fries."

The moment I settle her on the reclining couch, I whip

out my phone and text the first person I can think of. Mason.

I shoo Poppy and Daisy away from my sister as I hand her the remote. She extends her arms. "I want Poppy."

"She won't cuddle with you," I say, though I still pick up my dog and hand her over. As expected, Poppy immediately jumps back down and shakes out her fluffy gold fur before trotting away like a diva. Nina pouts.

"I'll get Sage. She'll cuddle up." I gather my cat in my arms and she meows at being pulled away from her comfortable tree. "I know, Sagey Pie," I squeak. "But your rent is due and I only take payment in snuggles."

At her heart, Blood Sage is a snuggle monster. She'll lie on or near me as if it's what she was born to do, and is completely unbothered by Poppy and Daisy's chaos. She finds a spot cuddled up against Nina's boobs and my sister hums in content.

"Can you get me another pillow?"

I snicker. "Yes, my queen."

I bring her the body pillow from my bed. I know she has a big fancy one shaped like a worm at home, but for now she gets Gerry the Giraffe. It may be hot outside, but my air conditioning makes it chilly in here, so I grab a knitted blanket and settle it over her.

"You're the best," she mumbles as I sit beside her.

"Are you having any other symptoms?"

"Other than feeling like a bitch-nado twenty-four-seven? I'm peachy."

I laugh, imagining her testing the world's most patient man. Wesley is a saint for putting up with it. I might be the sassy sister, but when Nina's in a foul mood, she can out-bitch me in a heartbeat.

She rubs a hand over her swollen belly. "I feel a lot closer to Mom, though."

"Really?"

"I barely have any memories of her, but... the baby helps me feel closer. It's like I get to share this experience with her... even though she's not here."

"Because she went through the same thing." It's half a question, half a statement.

"It's exactly what she felt when she was pregnant with us." Nina smiles. "The baby being a girl only makes the bond stronger."

I lift my head, a gasp escaping my lips. *"It's a girl?"*

Her eyes grow wide. "Oops."

I clamp my hands to my mouth and fight the tears. *We're having a girl!* 'We' might be a strong word in this sense, but my sister and I mothered ourselves and each other growing up. Now we get the chance to give our family what we longed for: a chance to heal.

"Just don't tell Wesley I told you," she adds. "We wanted to keep it a surprise."

I sniffle and touch her bump. "I'm getting a niece. Did you pick out a name?"

"We're still going back and forth on a few."

"'Maia' is a *great* middle name, by the way."

Nina chuckles. "I'll think about it."

She's lying, but I don't press it since Mason knocks on my front door. It's either him or Esme because no one else knows the code. Daisy and Poppy bark and I hush them on my way to the foyer. I find my head of security's mildly annoyed face as he harbors secrets behind his back.

"I am not a deliveryman," he says slowly.

I scrunch my nose. "But you brought it anyway."

His shoulders droop, his gray beard masking his frown as he reveals the bag of food from behind him. But he suddenly pulls his other hand and presents a double cupholder of two vanilla milkshakes.

I grin. "You're the best! You know I text *you* because of trust and love, Macey Mace. I can't get a regular delivery-man. There are some real weirdos out there."

Which is true. I genuinely don't trust any man more than him, not even Dad. The only person who has every bit of my trust is Nina. Irritatingly so, my mind flicks to Tristan. I want to trust him. I wonder what it would feel like to have him so close to my life. As trustworthy as Nina, Mason, and Esme. I'm not sure about Lyla anymore.

But I'm not a fool.

I can't trust Tristan yet. Technically, we're still just a hookup.

"Well, Wesley called me while I was picking up the food," Mason explains.

"For what?"

"He's worried. He guessed she would come here and asked if I would bring her a milkshake, too."

I grimace as I gather the fries and shakes. "She's fine."

As Mason departs, I realize it sounded like I was annoyed at Nina's sudden drop-in with a plea for fries. But no, I was uncomfortable on her behalf at being smothered. I head back into the living room where my sister sits up, waiting eagerly. She perks up at the extra goodies.

"Milkshakes?"

"Wesley guessed you'd come here and took it upon himself to call Mason and have this delivered, too."

I expect her to roll her eyes and scoff about this being exactly what she was getting away from. Instead, her eyes light up. "Really? That's so thoughtful. He knows I've been on a milkshake kick this week." She scoots closer to accept the drink and bag of fries.

"You don't find that overbearing? He literally called Mason to check on you after he *knew* you were feeling smothered."

My sister glares at me as though I'm a child. "No, it doesn't bother me."

"Why?"

"Because I love him," she says simply. "He's just concerned, Maia. That's all." Then, an eager smile pulls at her mouth. "You'll understand when you're in love."

I grimace for the second time. And again, I hate that I instinctively think of Tristan. I don't trust him, so I certainly don't love him.

I slurp my milkshake as I plop on the other end of the couch. "Don't threaten me."

"You're so cute when you think you're immune to love."

"I don't think I'm immune. I'm just... *uninterested*."

"Liar."

When I gape, she continues. "You forget I've known you your whole life. You haven't gone a year without dating or hooking up with someone since, like, sophomore year of high school. Maybe earlier."

"One, you make me sound like a slut and two, *hooking up* and *love* are very, very different."

Nina rolls her eyes and plops a fry into her mouth. "Three, we as a society have moved past slut-shaming and *four*, underneath your denial is a girl who just wants to be taken care of."

"I can take care of myself."

Even though Esme's literal job is to help me take care of myself.

My sister stares at me long enough for me to shift uncomfortably. Another sly grin spills onto her face. "You think I haven't noticed that's not your shirt?"

Lo and behold, I completely forgot to change out of Tristan's T-shirt. It's plain and gray but the size and fit are obvious signs it's not mine. I draw my knees to my chest, but the damage is already done. "Shut up," I mumble, to which she laughs.

"When you're ready to tell me about him, I'll be eager to listen."

The best thing about my relationship with my sister is that we don't push each other. We don't pry secrets from one another because we know we'll share everything eventually. There comes a time when we prod and overstep, only because one of us is genuinely worried we're driving ourselves into the ground. I respect her space and she respects mine.

"Do you know who it is?" I ask.

"Of course I do. But that's not the point." She slurps the last remnants of her milkshake while I'm not even finished half. After setting the empty bag on the table, subjecting it to an inspection by Poppy and Daisy, she lies back down with both Sage and my stuffed giraffe.

"That hit the spot," she huffs, wrapping herself in the blanket and releasing a long breath. She's asleep within minutes after turning on the TV—and I can tell from her light snores.

I use it as a chance to clean up my messy house because

I *know* she wants to say something about it. I search for all signs of Tristan and realize just how threaded he is in my home. He doesn't have clothes lying around, but he helped me pick out the plant stand for my monstera. He helped me hang my fern in the corner.

I went from having no men in my house to having the same one over constantly. We have to slow down. This isn't the type of relationship we agreed on, nor am I adapted to this. I'm glad he came to me about his grandfather, but we're starting to mimic a couple. It's too much for me to handle.

By seven p.m., Nina is old-man snoring so loud that Daisy stares and tilts her head. I pull out my phone to text Wesley.

> Your wife is snoring on my couch.

> On my way.

He shows up less than ten minutes later.

And I don't know if I'm simply noticing for the first time or if he's been working out, but Wesley is broader than I remember. He takes up more of my threshold than before.

"Everything's okay?" he asks, slipping inside.

"Yeah, I just think she felt a little smothered."

Daisy is happiest to see him, but he only spares her a second of affection before finding my sister on the couch. He crouches to her level and gently shakes her awake.

"Hey."

Nina's eyes flutter open, and a tired smile spreads across her face. She reaches out and touches his cheek. "Hi."

"Ready to come home?"

She sleepily nods. He chuckles, presses a kiss to her forehead, and rather than helping her sit up, he slides his arms under her and lifts. Nina nuzzles her face into his neck.

In the two short years they've been together, I already predict they'll last forever. Nina and Wesley just *fit*. My sister has always been my role model, and now I envy her relationship. I didn't at first. Their overly affectionate natures almost disgusted me and made me realize that I've never truly been in love. If real love is Nina and Wesley, then it's a more foreign feeling than I thought.

"I'll come check on you tomorrow," I call to her.

She nods, peeking over his shoulder like a child. "Love you."

"Love you, too."

Her gaze darts around the room. "Good job cleaning up, by the way."

I snort. "Thanks, mom."

CHAPTER THIRTY-TWO
MAIA

Lyla and I haven't had Movie Friday since our confrontation at work.

One week, she'd bailed for a date. And we haven't spoken of it since.

Things are still awkward between us, but we've had enough civil conversation at the garden where I told her about the auction coming up this weekend. She mentions she'll be in the city, too, as her new fling has a yacht and they'll be heading to Kosita Bay. I feel like I should say something about our confrontation, but the truth is that we haven't been the same and I'm not sure we will be.

"You don't get to push people out because you're the princess."

Is that what she thinks I do?

This distance between us makes me look at our friendship differently. I'd latched onto her the day we met and had no reason to question the authenticity. She's always defended me. I've always defended her. I don't know if there was a shift at one point or if I've missed signs along the way.

The charity auction tonight is private, save for the red carpet with photographers. I have to pretend I wouldn't rather be home watching TV, but tonight is for a good cause. Just before I give Alina my phone to step in front of the cameras, I get a text from Lyla.

Good luck at the auction tonight!

My chest warms. I don't know if things will be the same, but I have to try.

Thank you!

I hand back my phone before stepping in front of the flashes, and it doesn't take long for a sheen of sweat to layer my skin under the warm lights. The praise and demands of the photographers fill my ears but I've long since learned how to tune them out.

If I wore this dress in the Massachusetts winter, I'd blend with the fabric. But my summer skin complements the sunshine shade well. The halter neckline loops around my throat modestly, but the silk wraps around my chest like Saran Wrap and spills loosely at the high waistline. My updo is adorned with plenty of loose curls to frame my face and I'll have to send an extra thank-you to my makeup artist because the sixties-themed eyelashes match perfectly with the color of my dress. I'm excited to see how the pictures will turn out.

Caroline, my stylist, had found this dress from a Maldanian seamstress and designer. She honors my request of never dressing me in high fashion designers and keeping to small businesses. We've managed to boost the sales of nearly a dozen mom-and-pop designers. After such a feeling, I could never use my platform for haute couture.

I glance to the end of the red carpet, hoping for one of the staff members to usher me along for the other attendees to get their picture taken. Amidst the distracted staff, security, and attendees, I spot the tallest of them all.

Even though I specifically told him *not* to come.

I excuse myself from the cameras, relishing the relief from the hot lights and flashes. Goddammit. It's difficult to be mad that Tristan ignored my instructions when he looks impeccable in his bowtie tuxedo.

"What the hell are you doing here?" I hiss once he follows me farther from the cameras. But they're everywhere. And it will be impossible to keep my hands off him. I naturally gravitate toward him and I'll stare at him too long without even realizing.

"To make some donations," he says in an obvious tone. The realization hits that he's not here to support me; he wants to see who bids the highest.

"No, you're here to assert dominance over me."

Tristan starts to smirk, but deflates at my deadpanned expression. It's not his place to have any input on what I'm doing tonight. Sure, debates could be made if we were a couple. But we're not. And I made that very clear.

His gaze rakes over my figure. Not out of hunger or lust —a sight I'm used to seeing from him—but... *awe*. Pride, even. He extends his palm and I stare at it, confused, until he flicks his gaze to my hand. My stomach tingles.

What if someone sees? There's no use—someone *will* see. I set my hand in his, and he presses a soft kiss to the back of my knuckles. Kissing my hand is a typical greeting of a princess. It's just up to me to act normal.

"You look breathtaking, Your Majesty."

Butterflies break free in my chest as he roves his eyes over me once more. It doesn't change the fact that he's here for some possessive reason. I pull my hand back and clear my throat.

"Just don't make a scene."

Public speaking has never been my thing.

I have no problem talking in front of a crowd of people; it's the self-control that gets me. Delivering a speech is too orderly for me and I don't trust my focus enough to remember everything.

Regardless, it's part of my job as the princess.

The United Nations changed venues at the last minute since a British prince had cancelled. The management team was stressed yet grateful for our open arms. It was a lot to pull off in a short time and the least I can do is thank them publicly.

I knot my hands together on the podium surface as the faceless crowd watches me. Dehumanizing the audience helped me with my initial fears. People judge the little things. Creatures don't.

My voice echoes. "Thank you to the U.N. for having me and hosting this incredible event. On behalf of Maldana, we're honored to have you here. The Maldanian Common-wealth is committed to using our resources in strictly altru-istic manners that reflect our values, and events like this help us reach that goal. Therefore, we will use this opportu-nity to match the donation of the final bid for our royalty package. By bidding on this package, you could win an overnight stay in Kosita's palace and a behind-the-scenes visit to our oldest archives. The Commonwealth will sponsor a charity of your choosing and this determination will be made over a meeting with a member of the royal family—yours truly. Together, we'll discuss strategies to improve philanthropic causes and create a plan to move forward. With our matched donation, we can reach our vision of a just world." I pause to catch my breath and shift gears. "By bidding tonight, you can walk home with a four-hundred-year-old book of Arthurian legends in Great Britain, a three-day vacation in a luxurious villa in the Brazilian rainforest, or even a piece of artwork completed by Van Gogh. Most importantly, you'll go home knowing that, without a doubt, you made the world better."

Applause thunders in the room, though my stomach sinks in dread. I already know that people will criticize the way I spoke.

She sounds like a robot.

She looks so uncomfortable up there.

She's been Maldanian for five minutes. She's not one of us.

She can't even speak Maldanian!

Every royal advisor has warned me to never falter in my use of *us* and *we*. It would be more comforting if their insistence were from a kinship standpoint rather than a PR one.

I dine with the U.N. team that planned the event tonight. We have pleasant conversations, but none that will stick with me. I keep seeking out Tristan to no avail. Did he leave? I don't think he would without saying goodbye first. I wish I had my phone on me so I could text him.

Just last week, I told myself that we needed to slow down. Yes, I'm peeved he ignored my request not to attend tonight, but he's here now. And I want to be near him.

After appetizers, the auctioneer takes bids on a historical artifact that should surely be in a museum rather than private hands. Nonetheless, it sells for fifty thousand euros.

And once dinner is over, the rest of the items and packages are auctioned off. The royalty package is saved until the end, and my heart is thundering.

The team instructs my advisor, Alina, and me to sit aside from the stage as the package is being bid on, and it finally gives me a view of Tristan. He sits at one of the round tables between two couples in the back of the room. He doesn't look menacing, but certainly not happy.

"We'll start the bidding at ten thousand euros," the auctioneer begins, a pale, balding man with a hint of a Maldanian accent. "I see ten, fifteen? Fifteen it is, twenty over here, twenty-five, thirty, thirty-five over there..."

My heart starts to sink. The higher the bids, the deeper it falls. Even with everything included in the package, people only care about the lunch with me.

And it shows by the fact that it's only men bidding. Not a single woman.

I thought it would feel empowering to encourage millionaires to donate their money, but I feel used.

I search for Tristan, who doesn't lift his paddle once. I don't know who I'm more disappointed in: him for not bidding on me or myself for expecting him to.

One man has been consistently bidding—one I've never met or seen before. He's white and though he looks at least a decade or two older, he's attractive with a clean-shaven face and slicked dark hair that's definitely dyed. His gaze is trained on me.

"Seventy thousand!" the auctioneer calls, gesturing to said man. "Going once..."

My chest eases at the thought of this finally being over.

"Going twice... Eighty thousand to this gentleman over here!"

I watch the crowd silently tense almost in unison. In the back, there's a red paddle raised. Held by Tristan.

"Going once—ninety thousand!"

The man whose name I don't know holds up his paddle with a tight jaw.

Before the auctioneer can count down, Tristan holds his up once more.

"One hundred thousand, ladies and gentlemen! A new record of the night!"

Gasps erupt across the audience. I inhale deeply, glancing at Alina beside me who is just as intrigued and confused.

"Going once, going twice—hundred-ten from the gentleman over here."

And it goes on.

And on.

My stomach caves as dread creeps over me. The undertones are bright and clear; they're bidding over me. I'm nothing but an object up here. Not human. An item whose worth is determined by these two men.

Tristan patiently waits his turn to lift his paddle. He even sets his ankle across his knee and sips his drink as if at a lounge. We've reached 150,000 and the crowd is vibrant with chatter. They whisper to one another and exchange looks between me and the two men. My heart hammers in my chest. I have been trying to pry myself from the narrative of being boy-crazy.

This was a horrible idea.

Tristan raises his arm in another bid, this one 170,000 euros.

A small part of me wants this other man to bid, for Tristan to cave because he doesn't get to win after crashing my night. This was to expand humanitarian efforts. To make the institution look better.

Now, if I'm lucky, this won't be a tabloid since it's a private event, but it'll definitely be the talk amongst the rich folks—the very people whose respect I'm trying to earn.

"...Going twice... *sold!* The royalty package is granted to the gentleman in the back!"

I sag with bittersweet relief. The audience erupts in thundering applause at the largest donation of the night.

The institution will *not* be happy that they have to donate 170,000 euros.

CHAPTER THIRTY-THREE
MAIA

"I suppose we should congratulate him," Alina says as we head backstage.

I shake my head, watching Tristan advance toward us. "I'll deal with it."

"Are you sure?"

"Positive."

Once I send Alina away, I gesture for Tristan to follow me. I'm too annoyed to have this conversation where people can hear us. Not only did I ask him not to come, but my next request was not to make a scene. His donation is all people can talk about and I'm far too traumatized from past scandals to be associated with a man in any type of gossip.

"Maia," Tristan sings, his voice a warning as he trails behind me.

"Oh, don't you dare," I snap. There's not a chance in hell he sounds like *I* did something wrong.

Zeke, my bodyguard who accompanies me in public, appears at the other end of the hallway like a ghost. He's quiet and good at his job and I never felt the need to get to know him the way I did Mason.

"Make sure no one else comes in," I order.

He nods without a word as Tristan follows me into the women's restroom. Rich people restrooms are more of lounges; there's an elegant chair and a large mirror with a ledge for reapplying makeup.

"Do you realize how embarrassing that was for me?" I snap, watching him remove his suit jacket through the mirror.

"It takes two in this one, love. That man wanted you."

"Who cares!" I whirl toward him. "Someone wanting me does *not* mean they get me! This was a night to make a ginormous change in a charity and instead it was like watching two dogs fight over the last bone."

He drapes his jacket over the chair. "Then take your pick of a charity! I'll follow through with the donation; you know that."

"This isn't about me!" I shout. "It was about encouraging other millionaires to take an interest in giving back! And you—you and that other asshole turned it into a pissing contest. Both of you should've just whipped it out and measured!"

"Well, there's no competition with that one, innit?"

If I weren't already offended by his possessiveness, I may laugh at that. But I don't.

"Seriously? Tristan, this was an important night for me."

His amusement fades. He tries to close the distance between us, but I back up until I hit the ledge. "I'm sorry that it took away from the purpose of the night. Truly."

I don't stop him as he brushes a loose curl from my face.

"If he won, more fools would think they have a chance with you."

I groan, pushing him off and sliding my butt onto the

small surface. My legs instantly relax from the removed pressure of standing. "That possessive bullshit is not cute. He doesn't determine my worth, and screw you for thinking he would."

"Fine. But in every scenario, he doesn't deserve you."

"And you do?"

"No." Tristan gives me a sad smile. "I'm one of those fools, love. I'm just more selfish than the rest of them."

I roll my eyes. After last weekend, I don't like hearing him talk badly about himself. He's not perfect, but he's nowhere near the type of person his grandfather was. The man in front of me has a good heart. I can't deny that.

"You're not a fool," I say quietly, rolling my swollen ankles around until one of them cracks. Even though I'm sitting, my heavy heels weigh them down.

Tristan notices my discomfort and pulls the chair closer for me to rest my legs on the back. He runs a hand up my leg. "Do you forgive me?"

"No, but you're not a fool."

He tugs my dress aside and presses a kiss to my exposed knee. "Allow me to make it up to you, Your Majesty." He squeezes my right ankle, digging in his fingers as he massages up my calf. "How do your legs feel? Your back?"

I shrug. "Nothing new."

"That's not what I asked."

"My knees and lower back hurt a bit. But I can manage."

Tristan hums, focusing on massaging my other leg. No man has ever cared for my illness the way he has before.

Correction—no man has cared for my illness at *all*.

I'm more than a lot of men bargain for. Not only am I hotheaded and loud, but I'm always in some type of pain. I can't remember the last time my pain levels were naturally at a zero, where I could twist and jump and bend within the normal range of my age and strength.

"I liked your speech, by the way," he says.

I scoff. "I felt like a robot."

"You were perfect."

I have to suppress another roll of my eyes. I'm not used to this. Men don't care this much about me and I've long accepted that. This type of attention is more than I can handle.

He pulls away and heads toward the sink. He rolls up his sleeves before washing his hands.

"What are you doing?"

"Washing my hands."

"No shit, but why?"

He dries them off before returning to me. "Did I not say I would make it up to you?" Tristan hikes up my dress over both knees before depositing my ankles on his shoulders.

"What—*here*—"

He cuts me off with a kiss. My breath hitches at his touch between my legs as if his fingertips are electric. I feel him melt against me as he rubs in circles. My defenses crumble. Sure, I was pissed at him moments ago. He practically marked me as his—as if I'm something to be marked at all.

On the other hand, he showed everyone that there's no price worth more than me. He would have bid as much as the auctioneer would let him just to show that.

"I wasn't letting any man outbid me," he says against my lips. "He looked at you the way I do."

"What way would that be?"

The knot in my belly intensifies when he gently sucks on my lower lip while tugging my panties aside. "Like he was locked in darkness and you're the only sunlight."

God, I fucking hate it when he says stuff like this. It makes us feel real. Like we're more than our hidden affair.

I bite back a moan when he slips a finger inside of me.

"You think you can stay quiet for me, love?"

I nod, but quickly fall apart as his finger pumps relentlessly. No matter how hard I try, I can't get enough air in my lungs as pleasure shudders down—*up*—my legs that are still hiked over his shoulders. He destroys me with ease, intently watching my every twitch, my every attempt to withhold my moans.

"Fuck," I whimper, tightening my hold on the ledge to keep from squirming.

My dress tightens around my chest and I would do anything to not be here right now. I wish we were at my house, completely naked and free to be as loud as we want.

The filthy sounds tell me that I'll make a mess within seconds if he doesn't stop. I reach for his belt and fumble with it.

"Fuck, Tristan—*please*."

His eyes flash, his focus narrowing. "Please what?"

I yank his belt from the buckle, still tugging desperately. But Tristan ignores it by inserting a second finger inside of me.

"Please *what*?"

I fall slack against the mirror behind me, my chest heaving as the wet sounds multiply. I feel myself tighten around his fingers. "Please fuck me—*please*."

As if struck, Tristan pulls out and unzips his pants with a speed so quick that I'd laugh if I weren't so horny. He miraculously takes a condom out of his wallet, and I make a note to mention it later.

He doesn't hesitate sliding into me with a single thrust. It feels too good for either of us to smother our moans. He leans onto me, my legs hooked over his elbows.

"You okay?" I ask when his head falls against my neck.

"Yeah, you make me dizzy."

We silence any sounds we make with a kiss as he thrusts and thrusts and takes me to a higher ecstasy than before. It's more intimate than I ever could have thought possible.

The pleasure rippling through my body snatches any discomfort from the evening. My illness plagues my body and brings me pain every single day. Tristan is a catalyst for pleasure. He takes my pain and flips it into ecstasy, unlocking an entirely new piece of my soul. With him, I'm in control and unleashed at the same time.

He gives me a few orgasms before he finishes, and I'm not sure he knows how much *his* climax turns me on. It makes me feel like we're threaded together.

I keep waiting for us to fizzle out. All of my relationships do, and we're nearing my usual expiration date. But the sex just gets better and I dread every day he's not part of.

Tristan slumps against me, breathing heavily. Something's *different* now. Whatever we have—this thing between us is not the same as it was yesterday. It's more than that. And I think he knows it, too.

Still inside of me, he kisses my jaw, my cheek. "You are mine and no one else's."

My head is telling me to deny him—to say no. My heart doesn't tell me yes; it simply knows there's no stopping from falling into him. I don't say yes. I seal it with a kiss.

CHAPTER THIRTY-FOUR
MAIA

In the end, it didn't matter what Tristan did at the auction.

This is worse.

Much worse.

Princess Maia slammed for her attitude toward men: "They had a good thing going, but she hung up on him—literally," says insider.

I stare at Esme. "Is this a joke? Like, you're fucking with me, right?"

She glances at Lyla. The two of them showed up on my doorstep this morning unannounced and invited themselves in. Because of this.

"No. I'm sorry."

I hand her back the cell phone and get to my feet. "Can you read it to me? I might break your phone in a blind rage."

Esme hesitates, but reads it anyway. *"It's reported that the princess's latest conquest, Diego Montero, the son of Spanish politician Diego Montero Senior, is another of the many broken hearts she's left behind. Her Majesty the Princess and Mr. Montero met at Prince Jason's birthday party last summer.*

According to inside sources, they hit it off right away, but 'wanted to take it slow'."

"Lies. All we did was fuck and he showed me his annoying video games."

"You shouldn't hear this," Lyla says, her expression full of sorrow as I pace in front of the TV. At least I know that, when a crisis happens, she'll put aside our differences and show up for me.

"Where are they even getting this information? It's fake. It's all fake."

My heart pounds. My communications team is going to *kill* me. Aunt Beverly is going to kill me. I promised her this year would be different and I've kept my word. Until now.

Esme keeps reading. "*Montero was spotted with his on-and-off girlfriend, fitness influencer Justine Scott, and some timelines aren't adding up. Days before Prince Jason's party, Scott—*" She stops, her eyes skimming ahead before finding mine. "They're accusing you of wrecking his relationship."

I reach for her phone again, curious about this damn timeline. I gasp. "That fucking cheater! How was I supposed to know he was sneaking off to her house when we were fooling around? All this means is I should probably get tested. It's such bullshit! He's the one who lied, and *I'm* getting blamed. Most of this shit isn't even true!" I hand back the phone with an echoing groan and continue pacing. "I never met this girl and I never hooked up with anyone else when I was with Diego. We always hung out alone. They're saying he cried and begged me to take him back— that shit never happened! They missed the part where he told me not to gain weight, where he ignored me the entire week Daisy had to get surgery. He's a piece of shit and I wouldn't fight a cold over him."

"You don't have to convince us," Esme says with the

same pitiful expression as Lyla. While the latter is wearing shorts and a T-shirt on this sweltering August morning, Ez is dressed in a pretty pink dress because she's about to go to a cousin's birthday brunch.

I made the mistake of confiding in Diego about needing to gain weight and muscle for my chronic pain. He told me I shouldn't, that I was *fine* the way I was.

My phone on the coffee table buzzes, and George's name pops up. Great. My communications team heard about it.

"Hi, George."

His scolding is instant. "This is what you call a better year?"

"Oh, come on! This is the first super bad tabloid this year."

"Yeah, and it's one of your top ten worst."

I squeeze my eyes shut. "Look, this isn't my fault. It's all lies anyway."

"It will *always* be lies!" he yells. "How many times do I have to say it? It's never about the truth or how clean you are. It's about who you surround yourself with. *That's* the part you keep messing up."

"I tried! I told him to leave me alone!"

He hums sardonically. "Ah, that part is true, then. You hung up on him... Look, *you* might not look at what people are saying about you online, but it's our job. And people aren't happy. There's speculation that you've always been a snake."

My blood runs cold with dread at the thought of the cruel words they're reading. I turn my gaze to the ceiling and fight to keep the tears at bay. My jaw clenches and I feel my friends' eyes burning into me. Yet I only feel one of them is judging me.

"How do I fix this?" I say quietly.

George doesn't hesitate. "You do nothing. You talk to no one. Let us handle this; we're professionals by now."

"I'm sorry."

"Don't be sorry, be better."

He hangs up, and the tears break free. Esme scoots closer, wrapping me in her arms as I sob. Days like today are when I miss my old life—where the number of people who knew me was in the thousands, not the millions. This was always meant to be my life: plants, people, and pets. I used to be a full extrovert. Over the years, the articles, the comments, and the paparazzi chipped away at me until I faded.

"This just doesn't feel fair," I mumble. Daisy plops her head on my lap, her chocolate eyes staring up at me with fear and hope. My love bug is always worried about me. I scratch behind her ears.

Lyla watches me from the other side of the coffee table, pacing slightly. "The good thing is you're not new to this. You know how to fix it."

I sniffle, pushing the hair back from my face. "I don't even know how to respond to that, Lyla. Hanging up on a man doesn't give him the right to talk shit about me to the press."

"I'm saying this is a chance to learn from your mistakes. Roman, Kareem, Jay, Roman again, now Diego. The media knew about *all* of them. What are they gonna say when they find out about Tristan?"

My stomach caves. *She knows?*

Lyla must notice my disbelief because she rolls her eyes. "I'm not stupid. I see how he is around you at the garden. And yeah, people online are being sexist, but that's always gonna happen. How will Dr. Pagoda and the board see you now? You don't realize it, but I was helping you on that project because they still see you as immature and un—"

"That's enough, Lyla!"

Both our eyes snap to Esme, our gentle-mannered friend. She glares at Lyla, her voice dripping with discontent. "If you're not here to help our friend feel better, then maybe you should leave."

She blanches. "I'm just trying to tell the truth. I'm not being a good friend if I don't call her out on it."

"That doesn't mean you have to talk to her like she's stupid!"

"I never said she's stupid!" she argues, then looks down at me. "Maia, you know I don't think that." In my silence, she presses, *"Maia."*

Is she right? Have I brought all of this on myself?

But Diego was harassing me. What else was I supposed to do?

It suddenly feels like Lyla is working against me. She says she's trying to be my friend by telling the truth. Maybe I understand that on some level, but she's never been mean before.

"I think you should go," I say, the words surprising both of us.

Lyla stares at me in disbelief. She waits for me to elaborate, but I don't have the bandwidth to have the discussion about our friendship right now. With an irritated scoff, she storms out. The front door slams shut.

"What if she's right, though? I keep making the same mistakes."

Esme shakes her head. "Friends don't kick you when you're down. No matter what."

"Thank you," I mumble, fighting an onslaught of tears —grateful ones this time. She wraps me in her arms and I lean my head against her shoulder. I love how she always smells the same—Gucci Bloom. It's been her obsession since I bought it as one of her many Christmas gifts.

Her phone dings in her lap. "Sergio is here. Are you sure you don't want me to stay? I can tell him to go without me."

"No, I'm fine. I promise. I actually want some time alone."

She hesitates, but slowly nods. She gives me another tight hug and even kisses me on the cheek. Cheek-kissing is the one Maldanian habit I haven't come to like. I don't say anything, though.

"Call me if you need me," she says.

"I will. Please, go have fun." Like clockwork, *my* phone starts buzzing with another phone call. My sister's name and face flash across the screen again. "Besides, Nina's calling and I have to update her."

Esme concedes, likely because she knows Nina won't hesitate to barge through my door if she hints I need someone.

"He—"

"Who do I need to fight?"

CHAPTER THIRTY-FIVE
MAIA

With Nina pacified, I climb back into bed.

Sage, Daisy, and Poppy all join me for my 90s-2000s movie marathon. It's not the Saturday I had in mind, but it's far too hot outside and I'm far too depressed to do anything but stay in bed. Esme took care of Elliot and Olivia before she left, so I'm not worried about my ducks. Besides, their coop is air-conditioned.

I've been getting *are you okay?* texts from my cousins, Vanessa and Jace, and Aunt Beverly even called me. She had stopped checking in after about the fourth or fifth *Kosita Daily* or *Maldana Press* article about me being a spoiled party girl or a difficult person to work with. Just in the past two years, we must be on scandal number twenty.

The first movie I watch is *13 Going On 30*, then *10 Things I Hate About You*, and I'm just about to start *Uptown Girls* when Tristan texts me.

TRISTAN

How's your Saturday?

I snort. How can I answer that? Because it's pretty fucking horrible if I'm being honest.

I've been in bed all day.

Are you sick?

I chuckle at his bluntness.

No.

I attach a link to the article from *Kosita Daily*.

It's a disaster.

My communications team is pissed at me again.

I'm coming over.

You don't have to.

I'm fine

This happens a lot. I'm just being dramatic.

I don't care. See you soon.

I don't have to let you through the gate.

Then I'll be out there all day until you do. I'll be sitting with my air conditioning on and I know you don't want me to burn unnecessary gas.

Dammit. He's right.

Fine.

But fair warning, it isn't pretty over here

He doesn't answer.

I hop out of bed to freshen up; I brush my teeth again, wash my face, put on more deodorant, and tackle my matted curls. It's been wrapped up in a bonnet most of the day so I spritz a little water and add leave-in conditioner to spruce it up.

I climb back into bed and debate whether I want to start *Uptown Girls* or wait so Tristan can watch it with me. He secretly loves my chick-flicks even if he won't admit it. He gets far too invested in the story to claim otherwise. Just a few weeks ago, I'd put on *The Prince & Me* for background noise as I cleaned the house, and I found him and Daisy watching intently. He was furious that Paige broke off the engagement with Eddie.

Daisy is the only one I hold back as Sage and Poppy rush to the front door as it opens. My Rottie could do damage if she thinks Tristan is a burglar, but her docked tail wags in excitement once he appears in the threshold. For the umpteenth time since I adopted her, I send a quiet curse to Daisy's first owners who docked her tail at all.

Tristan crosses my room without glancing at me and heads straight for the curtains. He sloshes them aside one by one to let the sun douse the room in light. I slam my eyes shut, but it's too late. He could have at least warned me—or even said hi. Daisy barrels into him in excitement, forcing his acknowledgement.

"Um, hel-*lo*," I sing, waving a hand. "I'm over here."

Tristan leaves the dogs and cat behind and sits on the edge of my bed, his hip against my thigh. "Are you in pain? How's your back?" he asks, sliding his hands gently up my waist.

I shrug. "Some neck pain. But that's from stress."

Poppy jumps up behind him and continues her sniffing

fest across his back. He ignores her, leaning down to press kisses from my collarbone up to my ear. My eyes flutter shut as I sink into the feeling. Shit, how does he do that? A few touches, a few kisses, and the day seems more manageable than before. I bite back a sigh. I don't want him to know how much he eases me, but I might be far past that.

"I brought some ice cream," he says—as if he couldn't be any more perfect in this moment.

"Cinnamon bun?"

"Cinnamon bun."

My joy falls away as I remember the reason he brought it in the first place. He pulls back, and I watch his face for any reaction as I ask, "Did you read the article?"

"No."

"It's okay if you did."

"I didn't read the article." His gaze on mine doesn't falter, and it makes me want to cry in gratitude. "Anything I want to know, I can ask you personally."

"It's all lies, anyway. I never knew Diego was messing around with his ex while we were hooking up." I feel the stress in my neck bunching as I inhale shakily, frustrated tears pricking my eyes. "*He's* the bad one here—and everyone's seeing him as the victim and apparently I'm some home-wrecking snake. My publicist team is trying to come up with a plan, but what's the point? There are a *dozen* more stories like this to come. It's what always happens, I make some slip-up and—"

"Take a breath, love," he whispers.

At this point, tears are streaming down my face. Tristan reaches behind me, digging his fingers into the back of my neck. I hadn't realized how pinched together I was, how close my shoulders were to my ears. I ease under his touch, releasing a tearful sigh.

"It's fucked up," I mumble.

"I know."

"And Lyla thinks it's my fault."

"How would it be your fault?"

I pull back with a sniffle, avoiding his eyes.

"I mean, I get it. I really never should have been with Diego in the first place; he acts so happy-go-lucky but at the end of the day he's a big gaping asshole—"

"Love—"

"Like a nasty one," I add, to which he nods. "He could be real mean. I don't understand why I ever put up with it when—on a *good* day—he's a six out of ten and I swear to god if I ever see him again I'm going to rip off his subpar dick and shove it—"

Tristan cuts me off by pressing his lips against mine. I melt under his soft kiss, not realizing how much I missed him even though we had sex just last night. I like waking up with him here—and it was just me this morning.

"It was the safest way I knew to get you to stop talking," Tristan says.

"Smart move." I brush my nose against his. "Can you bring the ice cream here? Pretty please?"

"The point was to get you out of bed."

"Baby steps."

"And what step has been taken other than *me* opening the curtains?"

I hesitate, toying with the sheets. "You." I can't bring my voice above a mumble. "I feel... better—now that you're here."

Tristan always calls me beautiful, he admits to thinking of me often, and he insists we're good together. In terms of *my* average affection toward men, I practically just proposed to him. And all I really said was *you're cool.*

I tilt my head, flashing him my best puppy dog pout. "Please?"

He inhales through his teeth and I don't miss the hint of desire as he glances at my lips. It brings me back to last night, how it was the first time I ever begged Tristan during sex or otherwise.

"Fine," he grumbles, and I perk in satisfaction.

Little victories.

Esme must be reading headlines and social media comments because she makes a shared folder and uploads screenshots of the most positive posts she comes across. Nothing makes you want to focus on kindness like seeing the most vile, misogynistic statements from people protected by a screen.

One image is of me and highly edited—my eyes are not blue—with the caption *'telling my grandkids this was the queen'*. Another screenshot says *'the European tabloids have had it out for her from the get—I don't believe a word they say'*. Another: *'Princess Maia is living her best life while a bunch of racist misogynists try to drag her name through the mud. She's unbothered by these lies'*. It's attached with a series of photos of me, social media pictures that were snatched before the royal institution scrubbed my accounts.

The internet has turned images of me into memes: me at twenty with heart-shaped sunglasses at a festival, looking relaxed and unconcerned, me throwing up the peace sign with friends when we were camping as teens, Nina and me in our preadolescence during a Throwback Thursday. I noticed the final picture is often being used in social debates regarding our Blackness. These memories of my life have become fodder for both jokes and arguments and it's an unexpected form of invasion.

I'm a person. Not a talking point.

Beside me in bed, Tristan is scrolling on his phone. He doesn't use social media at all, but I learned that he's a history buff. I like that he's not heavy into war and imperialism like a lot of male history buffs; he learns about cultural revolutions and enlightenments.

"Pictures of you have gone viral," he says suddenly, and my heart drops. He notices my panic and adds, "Good ones! This is a good thing."

He slouches down to my level and shows me an article praising my outfit from last night. Only a few images had been taken and I'm so grateful I decided to dress more modestly. It was bad timing for Diego's story, though; my attendance at a charity gala in a dress by a local designer does nothing but wonders for my image, especially today. It's not why I do it, but it comes in handy.

"See?" he says, and I feel his eyes on me. "It's already looking up."

I lean my head against his shoulder, grateful he's here. It's not just the sex. I *want* him here. Everything is calmer with him around. I can stop being so tough and cautious because he knows me. He understands me almost as much as Nina does. The worst part?

That doesn't frighten me.

CHAPTER THIRTY-SIX
TRISTAN

I'm falling in love with Maia.

To be quite honest, that's putting it mildly. I am astronomically and monumentally in love with her. I love the way her eyes squint when she laughs. I love the way she wants to be a mama bear to every critter and creature she meets—even the spiders. I love the way she'll go from using a baby voice on her pets to cursing someone out within seconds. *It's called multitasking*, she would say. And that's another thing I love. Her rambling passion for the things that matter to her, which is *a lot*. She cares about other people so much. It's inspiring.

I'm furious that no one is taking the steps to look after Maia after this scandal. They're all standing by and *letting* it happen. There's no real initiative to stop the bad press against her, resulting in almost monthly scandals about her love life and vulnerable moments caught by the paparazzi that have been plastered on the front page. It's happened multiple times, and though a lot of people are online defending her, it breaks my heart that she's at the center of so much criticism.

By Monday afternoon, Augustus has the documents I requested.

It's hardly past the morning, but I throw back a tequila shot to calm my nerves. I'm not anxious about the world finding out the threats I'm about to make; I have enough power and resources to either suppress or rise above it. A tiny part of me says this is a bad idea solely because Grandfather would be proud of me for stooping so low. I don't want to align myself with him anymore.

The other option is to let Maia suffer—and that's not a true option at all.

Is this wrong? Yes. I do feel bad about that, but no one will find out.

I rise from behind my desk as Augustus leads the guest into my office. I give my assistant a grateful nod as he closes the door behind him.

"Mr. Montero, thank you for meeting me," I say, extending a hand.

"Thanks for inviting me."

Diego signed an NDA and relinquished his phone and all other electronics. We're completely alone.

I told Augustus to hint that there would be a possible brand ambassadorship, considering he has five million followers on Instagram.

I gesture for him to sit on the couch of the sitting area as I lower into the chair across the coffee table. It takes all of my willpower not to crack his head against the glass surface. I don't know what Maia ever saw in him; his obnoxiously patterned Gucci shirt, his over-gelled hair.

"I promise I won't take up too much of your time," I say, lining up three folders in a row between us. "I'd like for you to take a look at the options I've laid out for you."

"Options for what?"

I open the first folder. "This one is about the three women you sexually assaulted in—"

He holds his hands up, blanching. "*Whoa*, I never raped anyone."

"Oh, I know that. But that's not what this story says."

"But—"

"*Sh*," I interject sharply. "This will be best if you save questions for the end. This article goes into great detail about the assaults, and each will release within a few weeks of one another to establish a pattern of character. The second is rather genius." I open the second file. "This is a murder. Should this be your choice, evidence will be planted so that you are on the hook for this poor woman's death. The real killer will be in the clear. All of this is morally wrong, I know. But if you'd prefer to keep both of us on God's good side, go with the third."

Fuck that idea of going high when they go low. When it comes to Maia, I don't care how low I have to stoop.

Diego struggles desperately to keep his fear hidden. Although he's a spoiled, arrogant prick, his money can't save him. His father is a politician. The first two stories would reflect poorly on Mr. Montero Senior, and Diego would be cut off.

He gulps. "What's the third?"

I open the third folder to reveal the PR plan. "You admit you were lying about Maia."

His eyes snap to mine, his relief quickly replaced by anger. "All of this is really for—"

"*Careful*," I grit. "I advise you to think very carefully about the words about to come out of your mouth. Be grateful I'm giving you a choice at all because I *will* take it away."

He glares at me, his caterpillar eyebrows cinching

almost comically. His nostrils flare as he snatches the folder with the PR plan and reads it over.

"I wasn't lying. She hung up on me."

"I was there," I admit. "You were harassing her."

"Why were you there?"

I lean back in my chair, irritated that he thinks we're friendly enough for him to ask me a question. "When you're ready, sign the third page and we can both be on our way."

Diego stares. "You're serious about this?"

I don't respond to such a daft question. I let him come to his own conclusion and realize that we're not friends. This is not a practical joke. And that I will take him down by any means necessary.

After a hesitant moment, he signs.

"Pleasure doing business with you," I say, rising to my full height—at least half a foot above him. "There's a copy of the NDA on the last page, should you forget the consequences of speaking about this meeting to anyone."

He gives me one last glare before stomping out like a petulant child. No matter how much I try to convince myself to feel regret, all I feel is pride and comfort. Maia will be okay. It's a gamble as to whether she would be furious or not, but I'll cross that bridge once the PR plan is in motion.

Augustus appears in the threshold after Diego's departure. "Was it a success?"

"He'll make a retraction and won't bother her anymore."

"Good."

Just before he walks out, I think of Maia and how she scolded me for my treatment of him months ago. "Augustus," I call, and wait until he turns around. "Thank you. I know that working over the weekend is not ideal."

He lifts a shoulder. "I'm glad to help. I never thought she was treated fairly by the press."

"Still. It was your day off. How does a bonus of fifty thousand sound?"

He flinches in surprise, but it's quickly replaced by joy. "It sounds like you're spending a lot more time with the princess." He grins, and I can't bring myself to be annoyed at his statement. "Thank you, sir."

On a late Tuesday morning in August, Maia is nowhere to be found. I head into the break room and see Lyla hunched over the dining table on a laptop. She looks up and smiles.

"Good morning."

"Morning. Where's Maia?"

Lyla closes the computer. "She's in the field working on *her* project. So you're with me today."

I double-take, noting the emphasis. I wonder if Lyla's aware of just how much I know; that she threw Maia under the bus on the invasive moth assignment and how she faults Maia for a man's poor decisions.

It wouldn't be the first time I've joined Maia in the field. In fact, we're hardly in the same spot the entire time I'm here.

"Uh, I can't just go join her?"

Lyla gives me a sympathetic look. "No, Dr. Pagoda says you're with me today. Boss's orders."

That's a first. Part of me wants to send Maia a text to confirm; hopefully I'll see her at some point today.

"Uh, all right. What's on the agenda?"

Lyla smiles again. "Today, we're recapping. We'll put Maia's teaching skills to the test."

There's a voice in the back of my head saying this isn't right. I haven't been alone with Lyla in the time I've known her, and there's something off with her demeanor. She and Maia have been on the outs as far as I know, and the last thing I want is to be dragged into the middle of it. Women can be vicious.

Lyla guides me around the garden for an hour asking me questions about my knowledge on certain plants and practices. It seems innocent enough; she jots down a few notes without saying a word. All the while, I keep my eyes peeled at our surroundings, hoping for a sight of Maia.

We see each other constantly, but she's my favorite part of the week. I look forward to every moment spent with her, and I don't like that this time was ripped away. I want to be near her.

By the time Lyla and I reach one of the many greenhouses, she asks what I know about barbaricina columbine. A smile tugs at my lips as I recall one of the arguments Maia and I had. I relay the information I learned while omitting that part, but Lyla stares at me.

"Do you think you've learned a lot while volunteering here?" she asks.

"Absolutely. Maia's a great instructor." *When she's not yelling at me.* I keep that to myself lest I get her in trouble.

"What would you say is your favorite part about her?"

"I beg your pardon?"

"As an instructor," she adds quickly. "What would you say are her strengths and weaknesses?"

"What does that matter?"

It's not like Maia is going to teach a course. She told me herself she could never be a teacher.

Lyla shakes her head as if it would make all of my

apprehensions vanish. "I'm just trying to gauge how you feel about her."

"Why?"

She chuckles. "Relax. It's so Dr. Pagoda can see how much she's grown. For example, if you say her weakness is impatience, then we know she hasn't changed much."

The underlying tone makes my blood boil. "You don't need me to figure that out."

"Well, it's not like the media is helping. I'm assuming you saw the article about her and Diego?"

I swallow uncomfortably. I don't understand what Lyla's game here is.

"Um, yeah. Yes, I saw it."

She tsks and shakes her head, rifling through the papers on her clipboard. "I keep telling her to be careful who she messes with. A politician's son is a big no-no."

"People make mistakes."

Lyla snorts distractedly as she scribbles something down on the clipboard. "Some make mistakes, some *live* in them, you know what I mean?"

"Is there something you're hinting at?" I do my best to keep the annoyance out of my voice. I already spent yesterday threatening someone away from hurting Maia, and I'd rather not have to do the same with a woman. "If you have a question, please ask it."

She lifts her head slowly and places a hand on my arm as if to emphasize her pitiful concern. "It's not a question that *I* ask you. It's one you ask yourself. Before you two blow up—and you will—just make sure it's really worth it."

I wait for her to elaborate, but she doesn't. A cryptic response like that answers nothing. Make sure *what* is worth it? The money? For a moment, I fear she knows about the inheritance, but that would be impossible. She must be referring to Maia, but despite their arguments, the last thing I would expect Lyla to ask me is if Maia is worth it.

If so, I may truly question my hesitation toward threatening women.

I step back from her touch, breaking the moment of expectation—of her expecting a response, me expecting an elaboration. I draw up to my full height, clenching my jaw to gather myself.

"I hope you have a good day, Lyla. I'm going to head out," I declare. *Before I say something I regret.*

CHAPTER THIRTY-SEVEN
TRISTAN

I decide to check the break room one last time before heading out—and I'm grateful I do.

Maia stands at the coffee maker and tosses a look over her shoulder. She smiles at the sight of me. "Hey. I was looking for you."

"Apparently, Dr. Pagoda paired me with Lyla. I wanted to text you."

She turns around wearing her typical outfit of high-waist jean shorts and a Felicity Gardens T-shirt. She crosses her mile-long legs at the ankle, and though her skin has specks of dirt from her outside tasks, I'd love to run my tongue up each leg.

There's a curious furrow in her brows. "Yeah, I saw you two. Why was she touching you?"

I smirk, my hands sliding onto her hips. "Are you jealous?"

While I expect the glower she sends my way, I don't expect her demeanor to remain stoic and unflinching.

"If you saw that," I continue, "then you also would have seen me walk away."

"Did she hit on you?"

"I don't want to get between you two."

Maia folds her arms across her chest. "You didn't answer the question."

"She didn't hit on me. But she… advised me to reconsider my priorities."

"Priorities like what?"

"You."

"*What?*" she screeches, dropping her crossed arms. "That bitch. Why would she do that?"

"I think she's jealous of you."

Maia snorts. "Trust me, she's not jealous. She pities me."

"Pity is often a mask of envy."

Lyla is certainly jealous. Why else would she be dead set on pointing out her friend's flaws?

Not wanting to let it spoil my limited alone time with Maia, I shake my head and gather her cheek in my palm, leaning down to kiss her.

"She can't take me, love. You're my priority."

I press kisses to her reddening cheeks. I love making her blush because of how much she fights it. She wears her heart on her face without meaning to.

I haven't told her the reason I spend the night at her house as often as she'll let me. It's to see her at a particular point in time: between six and eleven a.m. I like seeing her at all times, but during these hours, she's her purest self. She romps around her backyard in her short shorts and tank tops that always match because of her unnecessary collection of pajama sets. Whether it's her blue, pink, green, or patterned set, she always pairs it with her pink rain boots with yellow flowers on them. Her hair is either braided, in a bun, or in a ponytail, but messy every time.

She'll spend this time with the ducks and dogs while the cat is usually curled up near me on the patio. She'll bring me a flower from her abundant garden and sometimes a pepper or tomato to go along with it.

I don't give a fuck about Lyla.

I don't even know her last name.

I drag my lips down Maia's neck, feeling her shiver under me.

"*Tristan*," she admonishes lightly, glancing toward the door. She arches into me. "Someone could see us."

Before I can give her space, she bunches my shirt in her fists. I brush a stray curl from her eyes.

"So come over tonight," I say.

"What?"

"Come. Over. Tonight."

She lifts a brow. "Your home or your studio?"

"My home. I want to cook dinner for you."

She hums. "I can't tonight. I have plans with Nina. And meetings with advisors this week. Maybe Friday?"

"Done." I peck her lips once more. "It's a date."

Just a couple months ago, we were in this same room, ready to rip each other's heads off. Now, we want to rip off something entirely different.

I still feel guilty about what happened at the auction and want to make it up to her. I'd followed through with the donation and passed off the palace visit to the front desk secretary in my office building, which pacified Maia in the end. My possessiveness got the best of me; I wasn't lying when I said I don't like to share. I'm not keen on any man working with her, but out of respect for Maia, there's a line I shouldn't cross.

When I filled Grandfather's role at Space Tech, the board was hesitant for a number of reasons. A lack of ethical dedication was one of them. The truth is: I wouldn't have done that for the company. I wouldn't pin a murder on an innocent albeit shitty man to save Space Tech.

But for Maia?

In a heartbeat.

The inheritance dilemma is heavy on my mind today. My conscience begins gnawing at me slowly, painfully. It's been hours and it hasn't let up. I fear it's not going to.

The inheritance isn't more important to me than Maia. I would rather lose five hundred million euros than her. There isn't anything that's worth that.

I haven't answered Maia's text, but she knows I'm sculpting and how focused I get. Aside from my workout earlier, it's helping me get out my frustration at what my life has become.

I slide the shaping tool through the clay, adding more definition to the tentacle of the octopus draped over the sculpted rock. I pause from working on the tentacle to move to the octopus's eye. I turn on the jazz music that Maia hates because she finds it too slow.

Grandfather never encouraged this hobby of mine. He didn't hate it, but he made it clear there were better things I could have been doing with my time whether it was golf, basketball, or partying my way through women. I've indulged the last one for years, and it's only now striking me as odd that my grandfather encouraged me to sleep with as many women as I could.

I enjoy the idea that he wouldn't approve of her. It's the start of unraveling everything he's ever taught me, and though it's a painful process, there's no one better to be at my side than her. I quickly realized the allure of charitable work when it really matters. It's easy to sign a check, to tell Augustus to send a donation through. Seeing the way it affects people only gives me the drive to do it again. I was never exposed to life beyond riches growing up. It was always something on TV or something relayed to me. Hearing Space Tech employees express gratitude for the raises did not make me happy. All I felt was embarrassment, shame, and anger. It was something I should have done years ago.

I didn't want to say *you're welcome*. I wanted to say *I'm sorry*.

"I can't believe he apologized," Nina says from her seat under the umbrella.

I shake my head. "I know. I almost don't believe it."

My sister slurps the last drops of her virgin piña colada before whipping out her phone and typing away. She points to the other side of the plant I'm kneeling in front of. "Don't miss the one in the back."

I send a grimace her way. We might be celebrating the fact that Diego suddenly retracted his statement and admitted he lied, but I'm the one bent over in the blazing sun doing my sister's gardening because she's six months pregnant. Whatever. At least *my* drink beside me has alcohol.

I drop a few ripe cucumbers into the basket as Wesley approaches with a glass in hand. He trades Nina's empty drink for a new one, paid for with a kiss.

"Thank you," she muses, to which he hums a response and plants one last kiss on her head before leaving. I grimace at the mushiness of it all, but something clicks into place.

"Wait—did you text him to bring you another one?"

She nods, swirling around the ice in her new drink and settling deeper into her reclining chair. Even though she has a big ass pool twenty feet away, there's a tiny inflatable one under her feet. Her adorable maternity bathing suit is pink and flows over her bump. Her curls are piled on top of her head with a few tendrils framing her face. "I'm carrying his child. The least he can do is bring me a new drink."

I pull my lips down in consideration. True.

Nina notices my reaction and smirks. "Are you ready to talk about him yet?"

"No." I bristle. "Especially because Lyla told him to make sure I'm worth it."

My sister freezes, her jaw slack. "Shut the fuck up. No she didn't."

I nod, my heart still aching from the betrayal. I don't know if Lyla and I are friends anymore. Friends don't let friends be shitty people. I get that. But I don't think that's what's happening here. Tristan said it was because she's jealous; I have a hard time believing that.

"Oh, that *bitch*!" Nina scolds. "Wesley'll take her out."

"*Nina.*"

It's a different type of threat because Wesley actually could and would. And I've never heard my big sister curse so much. Usually that's my thing.

"I never trusted her," my sister continues.

"I know."

"She's always trying to one-up you. What did Tristan say?"

I bristle again. It's weird to be talking about Tristan with anyone. It makes us seem like we're in a real relationship, and I don't have a good track record with those. I lift a shoulder.

"He walked away from her."

There's nothing average about our situation. We're not normal. I'm a princess. He's one of the wealthiest people in the world. Maybe it's the thrill that lured me in—the threat of damnation. Isn't that what I'm known for? Messing up? It might not be that big of a scandal. Half the world expects me to have some devious plot to upend everything Nina's worked for and take her place on the throne. That's the last thing I want to do.

The reminder floods me with dread. It's been known that my mishaps hurt her, and I can't keep doing it. I'm trying to convince myself that the fallout wouldn't be as bad, but the reality is, it would be catastrophic.

But the thought of losing Tristan rips me in two. I don't know if he'll ever change or stop the damage that Space Tech does. I'm not sure I could fully love him if he doesn't. He's done admirable—dare I say basic—things since we met, but is it enough? Being in limbo like this is killing me. I'm holding back, and I'm not one to do things halfway. I want to love him with everything I have. I want to wake up beside him every morning. I want to always find him sculpting in the middle of the night because of he always has trouble sleeping and then fall asleep on the couch as he works because I can't keep my eyes open.

And the most frightening part is that I can imagine building a life with him. Tristan would be a phenomenal father—and the fact that I'm even thinking about it shows how head over heels I am.

Nina has always been the more approachable one. She has a charm that can disarm an entire army. Me? I turn men off with my energy and forceful nature. I'd be lying if I said it upset me; I have way fewer horror stories than my sister and friends. I'm the attack dog. I'm the first to tell a man to fuck off and eat shit.

"What are my girls doing out here in this heat?"

Both Nina and I startle from the new yet familiar voice. We turn to the back door to see—

"Dad?" we exclaim in unison.

He walks toward us, a grin on his face, as Wesley stands in the threshold with an impassive expression. I hate that I can never tell what he's thinking.

Nina struggles to get to her feet as we wrap our dad in a hug. His familiar scent inundates me, and I realize how much I actually missed him.

"What are you doing here?" my sister asks.

I glance behind him. "And where's Ruby?"

"She stayed behind. Couldn't get days off work." He touches Nina's swollen belly. "And a man finds out he's going to be a grandfather for the first time—he has to come!"

Nina, tired of trying to get him to visit to tell him in person, caved and told him over the phone last week.

"Why didn't you tell us you were coming?" I ask.

"I tried calling! *You* specifically, young lady."

I clamp my mouth shut. Not because he's right, but because there's no point in arguing. He called me once in the middle of the night.

"Well, you're here now," Nina says, "so let's get you something to eat. I'm sure you're hungry after that long flight. We should have something in the fridge I could whip up."

Dad releases an exhausted sigh. "Sounds good to me. I'm starving."

Before I can protest that my sister one: hates cooking

and two: says her feet get swollen if she stands longer than five minutes, Wesley buts in.

"I'll cook," he says, looking at her, "you rest."

She doesn't argue. We go inside, and the air conditioning sends welcomed chills over my body. Between the two of us, we like to keep our homes nice and freezing in the summer. It's a good thing we use solar in a sunny climate.

"How's Ruby?" I ask.

He plops onto the plush couch with a huff. "She's okay."

"What about Etta? How's she?"

Ruby's mom has been dying for the last year after being a chain smoker for decades. Dad falls silent as my sister and I sit. He toys with the corner of a pillow before saying, "She passed. A couple months ago."

"*What?*" we echo.

"Months ago?" I add.

"Why didn't you tell us?"

Not calling on my birthday is one thing, but I'd at least expect a notification about my step-grandmother dying. Even though we weren't close, Ruby is grieving her mother —and I care about her.

"It's complicated," Dad says with a shake of his head. "She didn't want to disturb you girls."

"How is it complicated?" Nina asks, her face twisted in concern.

He tries to wave it off. "It's—Ruby just... she needed time to herself to grieve... When you visit home there's security hovering in the neighborhood and over here there's"—he gestures to the entirety of Nina's expansive open floor plan—"this. And it's a lot."

"She's still family. You could have at least let us know."

He purses his lips. "Don't make this a big deal. This is what Ruby wanted, and she gets to grieve how she wants."

Nina and I lock gazes. The betrayal gripping my heart is reminiscent of when we discovered our heritage as royals. Dad hid it from us, claiming we deserved a normal childhood, but a childhood with an alcohol-dependent and emotionally absent father was anything but normal.

"Well, how's she doing?"

"She... puts on a brave face, but she's struggling."

My heart twinges. I wish she trusted us enough to respect her decisions. At the very least, we could talk to her so she knows she's not alone.

"Should I put my stuff in the same room as last time?" Dad asks suddenly.

Panic grips me at the thought of him being around Nina constantly. His presence is stressful and Wesley said work overwhelms her more easily now.

"Dad, why don't you stay with me at my house?" I suggest.

"Nonsense, there's, what? Five bedrooms in this house?" He reaches across the couch cushion to take Nina's hand. "I missed six months already." He looks back at me. "Maia, see what's taking Wesley so long. Tell him not to worry about making me anything fancy."

I glance at my sister, debating whether I should argue more about him staying with me. She gives me a small nod of approval before I get up and head to the kitchen.

Wesley stands behind the counter, preparing a sandwich.

"Did you know he was coming?" I hiss at him, sliding onto a stool at the breakfast bar.

His face twists. "Of course not."

"He says he's staying here."

Wesley shakes his head, holding his hands up in surrender. "It's up to Nina."

"Nina would let a truck run her over and then apologize for being in the way. Help me convince him to stay with me. She doesn't need him making these remarks all the time."

"What do you want me to do? Start an argument with my father-in-law when my pregnant wife is already stressed?" He releases a sigh as if he's struggling with what to do, too. "If she tells me she doesn't want him here, I'll ask him to leave. If it gets bad, I'll ask him to leave." He levels a glare at me. "You said you trusted me with her, so do it."

I scowl, knowing he's right. Years ago, I told him I would break his neck if he hurt her and I still mean it.

"Etta died," I blurt.

"Ruby's mother?"

I blink, surprised that he remembered. If I remember correctly, he's met her twice. "Yeah. Months ago."

Wesley flinches, the same as I did when finding out. He shakes his head without needing additional clarification that yes, Dad just now told us. "I'll give him two days. If it doesn't go well, I'll send him to you."

I nod before hopping off the stool and heading to the freezer. I pout. The ice cream isn't in the typical spot. "Where's the ice cream?"

"Top left," he says without pause—as if he was expecting my question.

I push aside the bag of peas. "I don't see it."

"Top left."

I roll my eyes. "I heard you the first time, doofus. I still don't see it." I suddenly feel a big, heavy hand on top of my head and angling me to the object in question.

"Top. Left," he deadpans.

"Don't touch my hair!" I swat his hand before sending a punch flying at his chest behind me.

Wesley barely reacts to my hit and he flicks my ear hard—just to piss me off. I whirl around and even though his hands are up in defense, I manage a *smack* on the back of his head.

"Don't fuck with me," I say, though my voice is playful. "I'm a scrapper."

He barely dodges my next attack as he scoops up the plate of food and a glass of ice water. Thank god I didn't grow up with boys.

CHAPTER THIRTY-NINE
MAIA

Instead of Movie Friday with Lyla, I go to Tristan's apartment for an early dinner.

Our disintegrating friendship hurts more than I care to admit. While I don't imagine myself getting married any time soon, I always pictured her as my bridesmaid. She was supposed to be my person.

But any possibility of rekindling vanished when she advised Tristan to reconsider our relationship rather than taking care not to hurt me. The latter is what I would have done. If she were happy with someone, I wouldn't sow seeds of doubt in such a manner.

Tristan's apartment building is even more secure than his studio, so I'm not worried about being seen anywhere in the city. It's my first time here and I'm weirdly nervous; I've never been inside his home before.

He hasn't mentioned anything about the ideas I gave him for humanitarian work, and I refuse to pester him to do the right thing.

If he wanted to, he would.

It's that simple.

Once Tristan greets me at the building's back entrance, he punches in a code in the elevator. The doors shut and I find myself gently pinned against the wall, his pine scent filling the space between us.

"Hi," he says against my lips.

I can't fight my smile. My chest constricts at the joy curling around it. "Hi."

He kisses my cheek, my jaw, then my lips and I don't know when we got so affectionate with each other.

I really gotta talk to Nina. I need sisterly advice.

"What are we having for dinner?" I ask.

"It's a surprise. I want to show you something else first."

The doors open straight into the penthouse and I nearly gasp at the view. The open floor plan makes it possible to look out of the glass walls from any spot. The evening sun casts a soft apricot hue over Kosita; the ancient city is etched into a small mountain and far to the left is the sparkling blue Mediterranean Sea. The old architecture is mixed with a few modern skyscrapers and if I squint, I can spot the soccer—or football, I should say—stadium. Milagro, my old neighborhood, is a few blocks away.

Tristan tugs me forward, making me realize I'd been admiring the view without even leaving the elevator. My loft in the city was by all means luxurious, but I had opted for a lower level so my acrophobic sister could visit me without being unnecessarily petrified she would fall over the balcony.

The penthouse has mahogany tones and enough statues, probably made by Tristan, that they're more stored here than displayed. The elevator in the center of the apartment opens up on either side. The kitchen is to the right and the living room is to the left. Farther, hallways lead deeper into the apartment. Each room Tristan shows me is as luxurious as the last, but there's a sheen of dust on almost every surface.

"It looks..." I pause, finding the right word.

"Overpriced?" he guesses.

"I was gonna say abandoned."

He shrugs. "I'm either at the office, the studio, or your house. Today's the first time I've been here in... months."

"Do you want to spend more time here?"

Tristan hesitates, then snakes a hand around my waist. "I want to be where you are."

I roll my eyes despite the smile pulling at my lips. "All right, lover boy," I tease.

He hums. "Rich boy, pretty boy, and now lover boy. I think that one's my favorite."

"Can you tell me what we're having for dinner now? I'm starving."

"Just one more thing." As he leads me to the living room, he says, "I want to take you on a trip."

"No, no trip," I whine, slumping behind him. "Just dinner. I haven't eaten."

He chuckles before depositing me on the couch. "Not today. Next week. The week after. Whenever you want."

"What kind of trip?"

"A private beach in the Maldives."

I hesitate. Are we ready for something like that? A weekend getaway is one thing, but the Maldives is a whole ass vacation.

Tristan notices.

"Stop thinking of reasons to say no—and listen." He clicks a remote and the TV flicks on to reveal graphs and numbers. "I had my office calculate expenses and carbon emissions. To offset the emissions of the private jet, I'd have to donate that much. So I doubled it." He clicks a button and the screen flips to a collage of pictures of a house surrounded by jungle on three sides. The fourth side is steps to the ocean water. "We'd be staying in a villa on our own private beach. All of the waitstaff are paid handsomely *and* treated well. I spoke with them myself." He clicks the remote again to reveal a few logos of non-profits. "And we could spend a day—or a few—volunteering to help stray animals or cleaning rubbish from the ocean. Or both. Your choice."

My heart melts, spilling through my ribcage and flooding my body.

He made a fucking presentation to convince me and it's the most thoughtful thing anyone has ever done for me. I don't know how we got here—when we stopped being a hookup and started becoming *us*. Tristan and Maia, The Couple.

"And I know you don't like leaving the animals," he continues, and I startle, realizing how silent I am. "You could bring the dogs. The villa is huge and I could hire a dog sitter when we go out. Just say yes, my love. I can fix any issue. Just say yes."

A hookup wouldn't look at me the way Tristan is now, vulnerable and hopeful, his joy hanging onto whether I utter the single word he's looking for. I've never been teth- ered like this or have someone so wrapped up in me that their happiness is linked to mine.

Fuck, is this what Nina was talking about? Is this what being in love is like? I thought I would hate being respon- sible for a person's joy. It's too much pressure. But mine is his and his is mine, feeding off one another.

"Yes."

His face breaks apart with relief, and the distance

between us is closed before I can say another word. Only when he's kissing me do I realize something different. He calls me *love* all the time. Today is the first time he said *my love*.

Just say yes, my love.

My feelings for him punch through my body. Fear nips at me, threatening to take over and rip me from this moment.

Finally, I let myself dive headfirst into us.

I don't hold back with my kisses and touch. The only time I'm physically affectionate with him is during sex. Kissing just to kiss—that's new to me. I'm too far gone.

Tristan made boshi mashuni for dinner, a Maldivian salad with pita bread on the side. The curry and coconut flavors are to die for and I can't wait to eat this very dish on a tropical beach.

We spend the evening talking about what we could do and where we could volunteer. His hesitant expressions make it painfully obvious he's volunteering for my benefit.

After the surprisingly filling meal, we sit on the balcony to watch the sunset. The sky-rise building means no one is above us and there's enough of a barrier to hide us from view. No peeping Toms—one of the big reasons I had to leave the city.

I hate feeling like I have to hide Tristan. Both of us are okay with keeping this a secret, but I can't stop the remorse that comes along with it. The more time passes, the more I struggle to imagine my life without him. He's not perfect; I don't want him to be. But I love the efforts he makes and the way he inspires me to do more of my own inventory.

The way he gives me the space to be myself helps me feel more understood than ever before.

Nina has my back no matter what, but she's married now. She has a baby on the way. She's creating her own little family and I won't always be part of that. And that's okay.

When I'm with Tristan, I feel whole. Not in the sense of completing me—in having everything I need outside of myself. He's my Saturdays spent alone. My late-night ice cream cravings. My laughter. My best friend.

My love.

Three words echo in my mind: *I love him, I love him, I love him.*

I love Tristan so much I don't know how I can build a life without him.

"What's wrong?" Tristan asks, pulling me out of my reverie.

My chest tightens. I purse my lips and clear my throat to buy time. "Uh, nothing."

He squints. "You're lying."

"I also don't want to talk about it."

He frowns and tightens his arm around me from our spot on the lounge chair. "Are you having second thoughts about the Maldives?"

"No! No, it's just—my dad's in town. And it's stressing me out." It may not be what I was thinking of seconds ago, but it's not a lie, either. If not for Nina, I'd want to leave for the Maldives tomorrow. I know she has Wesley, but still.

"Your dad?" echoes Tristan.

"Yep. He's here and he didn't wait to start judging everything me and Nina are doing." I snuggle against his chest. "I don't want to talk about it right now. Please."

Tristan pauses. It's unfair, considering he's opened up

to me so much about his grandfather. I do want to tell him about it. But the evening has been so peaceful and I don't want to ruin it. One thing will lead to the other and there's still so much we need to talk about.

So I'm thankful as hell when he kisses the top of my head and doesn't say anything further.

CHAPTER FORTY
MAIA

S aturday evening, Tristan is in my garden with me harvesting some vegetables.

We've already gathered two large baskets, both of which will be given to the closest food bank because we're barely halfway through harvesting.

Tristan hands me the basket and crouches under vines. After a few tugs, he reaches back and drops four ripe tomatoes in the basket. I bite the inside of my cheek as his shirt stretches taut across his shoulders. Why is everything he does hot as hell?

"Is this one ready?"

I blink. "What?"

He angles a zucchini toward me. "Can I pluck this one?"

"Uh, yeah. It's good."

We pluck most of the ripe vegetables and have to stop both Poppy and Daisy from digging up the garden bed.

All at once, my peaceful little world expands a tiny bit, yet it looks so different. I can't wait to cook with the harvest; homegrown food tastes sweeter when it's shared.

I let him take over all of the picking because it hurts my

back, and it's easier for me to sweep the coop. Through the window, I spot Sage lounging by the trickling fountain under the shade of the apple trees. Poppy lies splayed out under the sun like a baked potato while Daisy tries to get Elliot and Olivia to play with her. Elliot flaps her wings with a loud shrill when my Rottweiler nudges her with a heavy paw. Golden hour turns Tristan into a bronze beacon in the shroud of green. My heart warms at how handsome he is. Over the past month or so, we've created small habits and routines around my house, and I love how he fits in so well at my home.

When he notices I'm staring, he grabs one of the abnormally large cucumbers he plucked and totes it in the air with a grin. He's too far to hear my praise, so I give him a thumbs-up, endeared by his excitement. However, he ruins the moment when he places it on his crotch like a penis with a mischievous glint in his eyes.

My shoulders droop in disappointment in spite of the smile threatening my lips. Why are men like this? I resume the sweeping until he eventually joins me to help replace the hay.

"That cucumber is huge, no?" He laughs.

I hum. "The biggest I've ever seen."

My phone buzzes in my back pocket, and I gasp when I see the notification.

"Fuck."

Tristan's head pops up. "What is it?"

My stomach sinks. No, no. This is too soon, but there's nothing I can do—I won't hide him in my closet, but the last thing I need is for one of the most judgmental people I know to be up-to-date on my love life. Through my security system, I watch his waiting car.

"My dad. He's here."

His eyes widen. "Like, out front?"

Not to mention that Tristan would likely rather eat glass than meet my father. It's not like I've painted him in the best manner.

"Is this okay?" I ask, hitting approve to open the gate since Dad started waving at the camera impatiently.

Tristan shrugs. "It's fine. I don't mind."

"Are you sure? I can sneak you out the back."

He gives me a playful glare, setting down the shovel and walking with me. "We're not teenagers."

I swallow the nerves bubbling in my throat. Out of the plenty of men I've dated, I haven't brought a single one home. It's not as if I needed to find anyone worthy; I wanted to keep those two parts of my life separate. Dad is a stressor more often than not and I always vowed to dump any man who feels aligned with him. I refuse to end up with someone like him.

I latch the gate to leave the animals in the backyard, crossing the courtyard in front of my house. My heart thunders in my chest as Tristan follows.

"Hey, Dad," I say, then notice him pull a duffel bag from the passenger seat. "What happened?"

I swear to god if he got into an argument with my pregnant sister—

"Ah, you were right. Nina needs—oh." He freezes at the sight of Tristan. "I wasn't aware you had company."

Before I can introduce anyone, he steps up and shakes Dad's hand firmly. "Hi, I'm Tristan Farrugia. It's a pleasure to meet you, sir."

Dad doesn't hide the way he sizes him up, but gives him an impressed nod. "Pierce Laffley. Pleasure as well."

"What happened at Nina's?" I ask.

He shakes his head. "You were right. I was a bother there, and I didn't want to stress her out."

"I didn't say you were a bother. But you're welcome to stay here. Let me get you set up in the guest room."

Inside, Poppy and Daisy are waiting by the back door barking and scratching at the glass. They come crashing in and pepper Dad with sniffs and hugs.

After asking Tristan to put the ducks in the coop and I set up Dad in the guest room, the three of us end up in the kitchen.

"What do you do for work, Tristan?" Dad asks.

"I own a tech company, sir."

"His granddad invented Space Technologies," I say as I pull Poppy, Daisy, and Sage's dinners from the fridge.

Dad blanches. "Shit, seriously?"

Tristan dons a modest smile. "Yes. But I didn't have the technological skills he had. I stay on the business side of things."

"Still. That's impressive, son." He lets out a whistle. "You're the big boss." Then he snorts and gestures toward me. "You gotta be if you're dealing with this one."

I grit my teeth. "Thanks."

"You didn't tell me you were seeing anyone," he says, and I know he's hinting at the fact that I never let anyone inside my house. Similar to being the first man to meet my dad, Tristan is the first man I've let inside my home.

"We're just friends," I reply, hoping that Tristan knows I don't mean it.

"Maia," Dad warns with a tsk. "Don't string him along."

Tristan flinches in surprise. "She's not, sir."

I bite back my frustration and set down my pets' dinners. "Why would I do that, Dad?"

More importantly, I want to ask why he would say that

in front of Tristan. Sure, my romantic pursuits could fill a book, but I never take advantage of anyone, and Dad always thinks I am.

"I know how you get."

"How do I get?"

He narrows his eyes at my serious tone and tosses an elbow over the back of his chair. "Stop. I'm teasing. I'm just glad this one's Black."

"*Dad!*" I look at Tristan with an apologetic expression, but he only dips his chin as if telling me it's all right.

"Hey, I got two daughters, and one is with a white guy." He points at Tristan. "You're my last hope."

Before Tristan can reply—because what could he even say?—I interject. "My mom, *your* first wife, was white so I don't understand why you'd say that. And not that it matters, I've dated Black men before. Can we please stop having this conversation?"

"Come on, Maia. Out of all the things you get up in arms about, I would've thought you'd be the loudest about this."

I shake my head, not wanting to dive into the reasons I'd rather not have this conversation with him. Nina has someone who takes better care of her than I could have imagined. She always had a tendency to date men who were beneath her in life—and now she's with someone worthy of her. I'd never diminish their relationship over something like race and I'm disappointed Dad would.

"Fine," Dad concedes, "I'm headed to the bathroom and then we can see what's for dinner."

The moment he's gone down the hall and I hear the door *click*, I turn to Tristan. "I'm *so* sorry. I don't know why he says stuff like that."

He rises to his feet and crosses the kitchen. "It's fine; I know you're not stringing me along."

"He always does this!" I say in a harsh whisper, leaning against the counter. "He finds little flaws, these little preconceived ideas about me and it becomes everything he knows me as! To him, I'm still the same stupid girl in high school. He doesn't even ask how work is going at the garden! He likes to use my accomplishments to brag to other people but *noooo*," I sing, drawing out the word, "he doesn't want to be there for me when I'm actually doing the work."

I have yet to call Ruby about her mom; I don't know how to even approach it, considering she didn't want Nina and me at the funeral. Not attending the funeral is one thing; not telling us about Etta's death is something else entirely. But the last thing I want to do is make Ruby's grief about me.

Tristan places a comforting hand on my waist, pulling me to him. "I know, love. You deserve better."

I release a huff and drop my head on his chest. His pine scent comforts me, and I lean into it, nuzzling my nose in his shirt.

"Are you wiping your nose on me?" he asks with a laugh.

"No, you smell good."

He wraps his arms around me, only solidifying my sense of peace. "Take as many sniffs as you need."

I chuckle as he presses a kiss to my temple. I forgot how good it feels to be truly, genuinely supported.

CHAPTER FORTY-ONE
TRISTAN

One of the many things I love about Maia is that she's used to luxury.

I haven't taken many women on my private jet, but the few I have had were over-the-top. I spent the better part of the ride taking pictures of them. We ascend the steps into the plane and instead of her jaw dropping at the inside, she smiles and greets the crew.

The stewardess, Josephine, is on most of my flights. She's remained polite enough just to avoid conversation, but her pale face shows more emotion than on any previous trips. She half curtsies and half bows as if she changed her mind mid-curtsy.

"Your Majesty," she says in a loose breath. "It's an honor to meet you."

Maia shakes Josephine's hand, eyeing the name tag. "It's nice to meet you, Josephine."

I'm so used to being the star in the relationship—the one people brag about because of my status and money. The power imbalance wasn't always stated, but it was obvious enough. Now, I get to be in the shadows. I get to show off who I'm with and feel special because of it. I'm with the fucking princess and I would live in her shadow forever if it meant I could be at her side.

Maia greets the rest of the small crew before we settle into our seats for takeoff. She barely reacted to the luxury of the jet, and I think I love her more for it.

My stomach tightens when I see her frowning at her phone.

"What's wrong?"

She angles the screen toward me to reveal her background: a rare picture of Daisy, Poppy, and Sage calm enough to sit still together. "My babies."

I run my hand along her arm. With her dad going back home to the States days ago, she's finally able to take a holiday with me. I don't want her worrying about the animals, too.

"They're home safe with Esme."

"I know, it's just..."

"They're your babies," I finish for her.

She chuckles as if embarrassed by the fact. She tucks her phone away and snuggles at my side as Josephine relays the safety procedures.

We'll be the few inhabitants on the island and since we'll technically be in their hurricane season, I'm in close contact with the weather team in case it gets too dangerous. Not to mention, Maia's security team had followed a list of protocols before we could leave. We have over two dozen people ensuring our safety, so I'm not worried.

Once we're in the air, Josephine brings us bread and oil as an appetizer for the eight-hour flight. In between movies, Maia and I talk more about our childhoods and lives before each other. I notice she avoids the glaring topic between us: *us*.

I haven't forgotten about what she'd do with my wealth. She said she wouldn't believe me until I showed her results, so I've been working quietly.

There have been bumps in the road—like finding out that my grandfather was a monster. But it encourages me to continue working on these changes. The fact that Grandfather would hate everything I'm doing with the wealth he passed down only makes it sweeter. He doesn't deserve an untainted legacy.

One of the many proposals Augustus and I created is to discontinue various forms of chargers in lieu of one that's compatible across all devices for Space Tech products. I have ultimatums disguised as suggestions for companies I have a large amount of stock in to make big strides toward sustainable practices.

I'm working on everything Maia suggested and she doesn't know a single thing about it. I just hope it will soften the blow when I tell her the real reason I came to Felicity Gardens in the first place.

Maia's face is glued to the window during landing and all the way to the villa.

A man named Omar will be our butler for the week. He's a middle-aged man with thinning hair and a round belly and of course Maia ended up chatting away with him.

She gathered that he's a widower with three daughters abroad in university. I already know that she'll bring up the idea at some point for me to increase his pay to cover their tuition. And I will—because I can't say no to her and it *does* feel good to help people.

The expansive villa sits over the water, an infinity pool

blending with the cerulean tones. A jungle courtyard out back bleeds onto the beach. I booked the surrounding houses so they would all be vacant.

I watch Maia drink in the sight of the open floor plan, from the sparkling sea to the courtyard. A breeze flows through the house, brushing her curls across her grinning face.

An incredulous chuckle releases from her chest before she flies across the marble floors and into my arms. I've never felt happiness such as this—so much was missing from my life and I find all of it in a sassy, foul-mouthed five-eleven woman. My body vibrates with an influx of joy as I spin her around.

"Do you like it?"

"I love it," she hums, capturing my mouth in a kiss.

I love *you*.

The words press against my tongue, begging to be said. But I won't tell her before I come clean about the inheritance.

Omar is long gone and we're finally alone. No flight crew. No drivers. No staff. Just us. Maia feels it, too. Lust snakes through my stomach when she clamps her teeth around my bottom lip. Months ago, I'd guessed she was a biter.

Thank heavens I was right.

Within two days, we create an almost domestic routine. She's always awake before I am and puts the coffee on. As it brews, she'll climb on top of me and pepper me with kisses until I wake up. I'll give her a few orgasms before making breakfast as she does yoga overlooking the water. I'll get hard again at the sight of her arse up in the air, but I with-hold pursuing her again until after breakfast at least.

It's not too much different than what we do every weekend at her house. But we're so far from everyone and everything we know that it's easy to let our guards down completely. We've fucked in the ocean and in the pool and overlooking both as the sun set in shades of purple and pink.

Today, the sun blazes against the waters. Clouds are sparse and the breeze is just enough to bring a bit of relief. Maia and I had walked to the tiny market up the road for produce this morning before taking a dip in the ocean. I settle into the kitchen to cut up the papaya, watermelon, and bananas—all of which taste different than the ones I've had before.

Celine's name pops up on my phone and it's almost enough to sour my mood for the day. I hit decline and hope Augustus will be her next stop.

The counter gives me a view of the courtyard where Maia is, clad in a knitted bikini that shows off her lengthy, lithe body. She investigates the flora of the backyard, completely lost in her element.

The words *I love you* sit on the tip of my tongue, begging to be said. But I can't tell her—not before I come clean. She deserves that much. Dread crawls up my throat at the idea of her hating me, and I know she will. My girl is fierce. Loyal. She takes it as seriously as breathing.

As if I'm not plagued enough, Celine's name flashes across the top of my screen again. I'm seconds away from launching my phone into the ocean.

"Why are you calling me and not my assistant?" I ask without greeting my mother. Augustus is taking all of my calls while I'm away.

She doesn't miss a beat. "Because he's useless."

Because she couldn't get what she wanted.

"I'm hanging up."

"You've been difficult to reach and I'm trying to wrap up your grandfather's will," she says hurriedly. "You can pause whatever you're doing and give me the respect of an update after all I've done to help the company."

Rage burns inside of me. Celine believes she saved Space Tech by upgrading a few locations in London, but it's something anyone in her position would do.

"What do you want?" I grit, turning my gaze to Maia in the yard. She's oblivious to my conversation as she snips a pink flower from a bush.

"It's been almost two weeks since you've reached your required hours. I've done my part; it's time you do yours."

Talking to Celine while looking at Maia paints a distinction between old and new. I was raised to be greedy and power-hungry, and Celine and Nico are clear examples of who I don't want to become.

"That reminds me," I say, "I'm taking your part of the inheritance."

"I beg your pardon?"

"The lying, the cheating, I'm done with it. So your portion will be donated to help childhood sexual abuse victims."

Celine pauses. "What makes you think I'll give it to you?"

I recall the conclusion that Augustus and I had drafted. "If you fail to comply, I'll hire a Supervisor of Northern Hemisphere Affairs. Which is, essentially, a fancy word for snitch. They'll oversee your division in *excruciating* detail."

"Oh, Christ, Tristan," she scoffs. "You can't take my money."

"Then I will personally fund your new boss whose sole job is to ruin your day. I'm done with the competition you started against your own son. I can't make Nico pay, but you will."

"While you walk away with *everything* and I have nothing of the money *my* father left for us? How is that fair?"

I loathe that she dares to talk of fairness when she abandoned her children for power. She chose Space Tech over her daughter. I'll never forgive her for that.

"You have your portion of the company—be grateful I'm not contesting it," I hiss. "Don't call me again."

I hang up on Celine and continue slicing the fruit with more vigor than before. Maia is still outside and thankfully unaware of the conversation. I don't want her to see me frustrated.

She's tucked the pink flower behind her ear and my gaze roves her body, stopping at the sheer wrap tied around her waist.

Her beauty only multiplies when I remember how kind she is—when she's not hungry or overstimulated. She likes helping most people and every animal and always has hope that others can make better decisions.

Maia smirks once she notices that I'm staring, swaying into the kitchen. She's so fucking beautiful it makes me tense with need.

"Stop staring at me."

"No."

She glowers. "Pay attention to what you're doing so you don't cut yourself," she warns, gesturing at the knife in my hand. I may as well plunge it into my chest to carve out my heart for her.

I slice up the rest of the fruit before we lounge in the

hammock together. I can hear the waves crashing against the shore as leaves rustle in the wind around us.

"What kind of tree is that?" I ask, pointing at the spindly yet sturdy tree that's barely tall enough to loom over us. Its fruit reminds me of a pineapple.

Maia shifts her head on my chest. "That's a screw pine, but here they call it maakashikeyo. The yellow drink we had at the market earlier is from those fruits."

"So we could pluck those and eat them right now?"

She chuckles. "If we wanted to, yes."

It's embarrassing to admit that, before Maia, I was disconnected from where my food comes from. It was either in a store or placed in front of me.

"Did you do research before we came here?" I ask, and she looks up at me with an innocent smile.

"Maybe. I like to know the places I'm visiting."

The hammock sways and jerks as she struggles to sit up and face me. She manages to look like a beautiful yet clumsy fawn as she fumbles, huffing a curl out of her face. Maybe I'm just a little obsessed with her.

She turns her gaze onto mine. "Can I ask you something?"

"Anything."

"Why did you bring me here?"

Because I love you and wanted you all to myself.

I could tell her now. I could come clean and reveal everything about the inheritance and the reason I came to the garden in the first place. But there's nothing but serenity between us right now. This would ruin it. My stomach twists in fear.

What if, after this, she believes everything I give her is conditional? That I'll drop bad news with every gift?

"Because I knew you'd like it." Truth.

She glances off, slightly peeved.

"And I wanted you all to myself," I add. More truth.

Her expression calms as if pacified by my answer. I reach up and adjust the flower behind her ear.

"What kind is this?"

"Pink Rose," she says. "It's their national flower."

To my surprise, she removes the rose from behind her ear and places it on mine. My gaze roves over her glowing cheeks and sparkling eyes. A year ago, I was convinced I'd be alone forever.

Now, my forever is sitting right in front of me.

CHAPTER FORTY-TWO
MAIA

This place is paradise.

If you don't count the fact that it's been raining on and off for the past four days. It doesn't bother me; it's an excuse to hang around the villa.

For the longest time, I was never the one to stay indoors. I was the friend who wanted to sneak out. I was the friend who had a party on my calendar every weekend. I sought conversations with every person and found adventure at every turn.

Then the adventures started to hurt.

Hanging out with friends on a yacht all day was followed by a days-long recovery. A night out at the Lynx Room left me sore for a week. More blisters. More injuries.

I became *fragile*. And I refuse to admit that to anyone, even Nina.

It took until last night to finally find a sleeping position that didn't hurt my hips, neck, or back. Everywhere on this island is walkable, and it's small enough that I would look pretentious driving. So I'm content to be with Tristan and spend hours in the sun, swimming and reading, then hours inside when it's raining, fucking and still reading. I'm not a huge bookworm, but it's nice to get out of my reality.

We're headed to a neighboring island today to clean up trash at the beach, and my hair is *not* cooperating. I let out a frustrated groan, my tired arms dropping to my sides.

Tristan steps into the bathroom behind me. "What's wrong?"

"My hair," I pout. "The humidity is making it so frizzy." I lift some of the long strands because at this point, frizz replaced my curls.

He comes up behind me and brushes it away from my face, a tiny smile playing at his lips when my frown is exposed. "Leave it out."

I flinch in surprise. "Leave it out," I echo, "and frizzy?"

"It's beautiful," he says, gathering my mane and moving it aside to kiss my cheek.

I shake my head. This isn't adding up. "You think I should wear this mess when we'll be out volunteering all day? Where other people will see us? *Together*?"

He rolls his eyes playfully, toying with the strands. "I like your natural hair."

I turn to look at him fully rather than through the mirror. I love my curls—mostly. Enough not to straighten it all the time, but that doesn't mean I'm not self-conscious about it when it's a mess. What he says is still not clicking with me.

"You like it when my hair is like this?" I ask. I need to hear it. Explicitly.

Tristan sighs, tightening his arms around me and dipping his chin to stare into my eyes. "Love, you could shave your head and I'll still find you the most beautiful woman in any room you're in. But your natural hair is beautiful and I'll fight anyone who says otherwise."

I chuckle at the dramatics of it all; my heart still warms and I kiss him in response. I reach up to gently brush my long nails on top of his head. His hair is usually shaved enough for waves, but now it's grown just long enough to see curls.

"You have curly hair, too."

He smiles, flashing his stupidly perfect smile. "See? We're more alike than you give us credit for."

Beaming, I lean forward to peck his lips. The only person who knows I'm here with Tristan is my sister. Esme thinks I'm here with extended family and I hate that I'm still lying to her.

After this trip, I have to come clean with the people in my life because I don't know how I can think of Tristan and me as anything but permanent.

Two hours and five trash bags later, my back is screaming at me. I pull my shoulders back with a wince.

"We're done," Tristan says with a finality that, even amidst the pain, arouses me. He takes the trash picker from my hands and peels off our gloves. "You've been selfless enough today."

I'm too tired to argue. When we return to the villa, I finally tell Tristan he can shower with me. He's as giddy as can be as he rushes into the bathroom to turn on the water. I smile to myself. Yes, his giddiness makes me happy, but I plan on him giving me a massage under the steaming hot water.

"Oh—I forgot to give this to you," he says, pulling something from his pocket. "I found it on the side of the road before we left."

He reveals a faded orange rock where one half is crystallized and the other is bumpy and dull. It's the size of an avocado pit and glistens under the bathroom light.

"Oh, it's so pretty!" I muse.

"It's yours."

My heart softens at his grin. I didn't know rock-giving was my love language, but I've learned a lot of new things about myself because of him. I lean in and steal a couple of kisses.

"I love it. Thank you."

In the end, I didn't have to ask Tristan for a back massage. He saw my reaction when the scorching water hit my aching back. He pulls me closer and kneads his fingers into the tight muscles, coaxing out the tension. I let out an involuntary moan.

"Have you been practicing or something?" I mumble as he hits the perfect spot.

"I researched some techniques for back pain."

I huff. "Stop being so romantic and thoughtful. It's nauseating."

He laughs, dipping his head to kiss my shoulder. "As soon as you stop liking it so much."

I run my fingers through the ends of my knotty hair. It would take a lot of effort to wash it today, effort I don't have in stock. But Tristan has been noticing every aspect of my actions and if I wasn't so exhausted and in love with him, I would feel smothered.

"Do you need to wash your hair?" he asks.

I groan. "I should, but I don't know if I can stand much longer."

He hums in thought, squeezing my hips. "Wait here." Without further explanation, he steps out of the shower butt ass naked and strides from the bathroom.

"What—you're getting water everywhere!"

"It'll dry!"

I never thought I would want someone as attentive as him. Clingy men have been the bane of my existence and I rejected romance so much I thought I hated it. It turns out I hated every man but him.

A few seconds later, Tristan returns with a kitchen stool in hand and I shamelessly stare at his sculpted body. All that is *mine*.

He places the seat directly under the water and gestures for me to sit. "I'll wash your hair."

I scrutinize the stool. It's marble, so it should be fine under the water. I lower onto the seat and instantly pull him to me for a kiss. I want to tell him I love him. I want him to tell me he loves me more.

"Thank you," I say against his lips as the hot water sprays against my back. "For everything. Bringing me here. Renting this incredible home and for setting up volunteer days and donating all of that money—for everything. This was the most thoughtful thing anyone has ever done for me."

Tristan's eyes soften, his thumb grazing my cheek. For a split second, his smile falters before he kisses me again to rid any chance of questioning it.

CHAPTER FORTY-THREE
TRISTAN

I want to tell her so bad.

There's an insatiable desire inside of me to say *I love you* over and over until the words run together and I can't think straight. We have two more days here—and even though I want to tell her the truth first, I don't want to pop this bubble. It doesn't matter that it's been raining half the time; this is the most perfect vacation I've ever been on.

For our last full day, we're volunteering at an animal shelter on a neighboring island. It's embarrassing to admit that I've never done volunteer work I wasn't forced to do, be it a class or the inheritance requirement. Money has filled the gap between my connection with humanity. Donating money instead of volunteering. Paying for silence or services when there could be conversations and connections. Paying to enter elite circles with people I don't truly care about.

Neelam, the owner and only employee of the clinic, gives us a quick tour of the two-room building. Even though she's the only one who works here, three other people are neutering an unconscious cat. They must be volunteer animal doctors.

One of the mutts in the many crates barks incessantly at us. The sound echoes, disturbing the cats and a few dogs who were resting. The stench of dirty, sick animals burns my nostrils, and I can tell from Maia's smothered reaction that she hates it, too. But she's a lot more graceful than I am. The humidity makes the smell a hundred times worse. The wall paint is peeling and I'm sure those holes are from bullets.

I grew up rich. The only "poverty" I've experienced was being drunk in the middle of the night in Peckham back in London. I hardly remember that night, regardless.

"How long have you been working here?" Maia asks.

"About three years," Neelam replies, her accent strong. "But, it's getting difficult. People bring street cats here every day, and we have to say no to most of them."

"How come? Space? Staff?"

"Yes. We do CNR," Neelam explains, hands tucked into the pockets of her white doctor's coat. Her rich brown skin glows with sweat. "Catch, neuter, release. We don't have a lot of resources to do much more."

"You're funded by donations?"

She nods, and Maia, ever so talkative, manages to turn the conversation personal and chats about Neelam's educational background and childhood. I slink from the discussion to survey the cats, both wandering and recovering in crates. My chest twinges with pity.

Neelam deposits us at our first task outside so she and the volunteers can focus on the more important work.

Debris from the storm last night scatters across the webbed concrete of the front porch. Before we start sweeping, Maia bounces over and pulls me in for a much-too-quick kiss.

"Thank you," she says, smoothing a few wrinkles out of my T-shirt. "I know you'd rather do other things on vacation, but this means a lot to me."

My discomfort about the day begins to dissipate. We're doing some good. We're vacationing in this country, and even though we're helping their economy by it, there's always more we can do.

"If it's important to you, it's important to me."

She smiles and the words *I love you* keep fucking haunting me.

After sweeping, we clean and refill the outdoor litter boxes, food bowls, and water bowls. At least a dozen stray cats circle us as we dish out the food. A few of them take to Maia, purring and brushing against her legs.

When we move inside to clean, one of the incontinent dogs pooped herself without realizing it. Maia can't hold her laughter when I gag at the barely-solid shit I have to clean up.

"You pick up Poppy and Daisy's poop all the time," she argues.

"That's different." I wince at the foul smell, dropping the bag into the bin. I scrub my hands with soap for a solid three minutes.

In three hours, we've made the place as spotless as it can be. We sit at an island chatting, and one of the wandering cats climbs its way to the surface. He has gray-and-black stripes and is abnormally small compared to the others.

Maia whimpers as she reaches out with wiggling fingers. Suddenly, I'm unsure whether coming here was the right idea; she's going to turn her home into a zoo. The cat—who I admit is extremely cute—nudges his head into her outstretched palms.

Neelam grins. "This is Poe. He's feral, but he spends a lot of time here so we ended up naming him."

"He knows where the food's at," I say as Maia feeds him one of the cat treats. She's oblivious to what I'm saying as she makes baby sounds and scratches Poe's exposed belly as he stretches. I reach out to pet him, too, but he suddenly latches onto my hand. Maia tries to grab him, but he's not being feral; he's being playful. A smile pulls at my lips as Poe nibbles on my fingers before licking them and nuzzling his face in them.

Neelam scratches behind his ear. "He likes you. He's very antisocial and doesn't like to interact with others."

Maia snorts and looks at me. "Sort of like you."

Months ago, I might have leaned into that and tried to have a better comeback. But I can't argue with her. That's definitely like me.

Poe purrs as he cuddles up in my large hand. I scoop him up to cradle him against my chest. I keep my free hand hovering near his paws in case he decides not to trust me. All he does is snuggle up. I've never been a cat person—or an animal person, really—but I would throw myself in front of a train for Poe.

"How old is he?" I ask.

Neelam shrugs. "Two, maybe? Three?"

"Really?" Maia quips. "He's so small."

"It might be his mixed breed. I don't know. The other cats steal his food because he's so small."

Maia whimpers again, this time from sadness. She pouts and reaches across the island to pet Poe.

"How much for him?" I ask Neelam.

She shrugs again. Not out of indifference, but sincerity. "We're a clinic. He's not ours."

"You want to keep him?" Maia asks, her face lighting up in surprise.

I look at Poe as he tucks his tiny paws under him and closes his eyes. His immediate trust bundled up in such cuteness makes my heart fall out of my chest. I see how Maia is with her pets, and I love them, but I want my own. And Poe seems to understand me right off the bat.

I lift my finger, and Poe nudges his furry little face into it, his body vibrating with a purr. "Yeah. I do."

"Good." Maia suddenly bends down, disappearing behind the counter before returning with an orange cat and plopping it on the surface. "Because I want this one."

"Wait—"

She runs a hand down the curving spine of the cat. "Her name is Calendula. Callie for short."

"Calen-what?"

"Calendula. It's a flower. And I needed to even it out, anyway. Two ducks, two dogs, two cats."

"You're serious."

Maia doesn't reply; she grins. "Look, they like each other."

Perfectly enough, Callie is licking Poe behind the ears. I did *not* think a vacation in the Maldives would result in coming home with two more animals to take care of.

"They'll need to be examined by customs first," Neelam points out. "They may need to, uh,"—she rubs her fingers together as she searches for the right English word—"quarantine them."

"Would you be able to give them vaccinations?" asks Maia.

"Yes, we will give you everything you need for the government, but we ask for payment."

"Oh, of course! We'll pay whatever you need."

I clench my jaw. Maia will pay whatever it takes to bring these cats to a better life without second thought of the price, but her eagerness to help leaves her open to scams. Not that Neelam would scam her, though she might certainly overcharge on the account of Maia offering whatever they need.

She glances at me, the corners of her mouth falling. I fix my expression even though it's too late; she saw my hesitation.

"What else would I need to give them?" Maia asks, and they fall into a discussion about a plan.

I slip my phone out and text Augustus, swatting at one of the many flies bugging me today.

Draft a donation agreement for an animal clinic in Malé run by Neelam Hassan. They need building repairs, more space, and new equipment.

Ten million.

Please.

Neelam is kind enough to keep Poe and Callie in crates overnight as we wait for the supplies to be delivered. Maia and I head back around dinnertime, and I feel her attitude the entire time. When we step off the boat and into a car, she keeps sneaking glances at me and eventually crosses her arms and legs, one foot incessantly bouncing.

It could end here. I could tell her that Augustus is

working on a donation as we speak. But a smile pulls at my lips at her attitude, her little impatient huffs.

She strolls into the villa, her hips swaying. "Funding the clinic wouldn't be skin off your nose. Why didn't you offer?"

"Because I didn't want to make any promises before getting Augustus to draft the donation agreement. It should be done right, not in the heat of the moment."

Maia whirls toward me, her mouth falling open. She studies me, my amusement, my hands in my pockets. She expected an argument, not a conversation. Then, realization dawns on her beautiful face.

"You knew I was mad and didn't say anything!" she wails.

My laughter only confirms it. I scoop her over my shoulder before she can whack me on the arm. She lets out a yelp as my shoulder digs into her hips. "If you didn't assume the worst, you wouldn't have been mad."

I regret the words as soon as I speak them. She's not wrong. She assumed the worst of me the day I walked into Felicity Gardens—and she was right. It's different now, and I'm more in love than I thought possible, but there's still a lot I'm hiding from her. The fear of her reaction is paralyzing. I don't know what to do.

"No, you're right," she says, still dangling over my shoulder as I head into the bedroom. She gives my left arse cheek an apologetic squeeze. "I should've known."

"No matter, love." I gently bring her down on the bed and pull her closer to me by her hips. Her shirt rides up to reveal her skin, and I run my thumbs along her stomach. Desire curls inside of me. I lean down to capture her lips with mine.

Maia brushes our noses together. "It does," she says,

her voice soft and caressing. "Let me make it up to you." Her hand brushes my thin gold chain dangling over her as she reaches down to gather my dick in her palm, the warmth making me twitch.

She hums against my mouth. "Hmm, wait, no. Food first. I'm hungry." Her gaze wanders as she gathers her thoughts. "Both of us stink so I wanna shower before we have sex but that's too long until we eat but I don't want to eat too much so maybe we can have a snack and then have sex—maybe even *in* the shower if I'm feeling up to it."

I smile at the sparkle in her eyes, simply happy to be part of her thought process. "Sounds like a plan."

Although we get to fly back to Maldana with Callie and Poe, the Department of Agriculture takes them for further testing and potential quarantine. We spent most of the flight online shopping for cat collars and toys. I already have a personalized blue collar picked out for him. I'm excited to go back to work for the sole reason that Poe will have his own cat tree in my office.

But my first day back at work is Maia-less and cat-less and I hate it.

Even with the post-vacation high, I know I have to tell her about the inheritance. Ideally, tonight. I should have told her sometime this past week, but I couldn't dare puncture the pure joy it was. Should I start by telling her I love her? Or say it afterward?

After, definitely.

No—before.

Fuck. I won't sugarcoat it. *The real reason I volunteered at Felicity Gardens was to meet terms of my inheritance, but I fell in love with you.* But that's not the problem. It's the money. It's always been the money.

The real reason I volunteered at Felicity Gardens was to meet the terms in order to inherit five hundred million euros.

That's the truth. I should have told her months ago, but beating myself up over that won't change anything. This is where I'm at and I need to deal with it.

I take a break from my whirlwind thoughts to review quarterly reports for North America. Until a 3:30 meeting request pops up in the corner of my screen.

Attendees: Celine Farrugia, Declan Stone, Nina, Her Royal Majesty The Queen, Maia, Her Royal Majesty The Princess.

"Augustus," I call, my stomach caving.

"Just saw it," he yells through my cracked door. "I wasn't told anything about it."

3:30 is one hour away. Celine scheduled this on purpose. She knew I hadn't told Maia about the inheritance and wanted to beat me to it.

I check my phone to see no new messages from Maia; this must be as last-minute to her as it is to me.

That's not fair.

Celine's words from our last discussion ring through my mind. She can't stand when I'm happy or successful. My wins mean one thing: her loss.

I pick up the phone to call our lawyer, Declan, in the hopes that he can't make the meeting and will need to reschedule. It may be my only chance to get ahead of this.

CHAPTER FORTY-FOUR

MAIA

Even though I got home from vacation last night, I'm taking off work for the day.

Travel and flights have gotten significantly better with money. I no longer have to worry about stiff commercial airplane seats and sitting in one spot for hours upon hours. While I don't instantly think of pain every time I travel anymore, there's still debilitating exhaustion. Brain fog. Headaches.

I spend the morning dozing and lounging, doing whatever I need to refuel myself. Around noon, Nina's assistant Stella calls me about a 3:30 meeting in the city with Tristan and his mother about his volunteering. Since I was excluded the first time, I'm happy to join. I send a text to Nina on my way out the door.

Leaving for the meeting now. Want me to pick you up?

Already on my way.

Okay

> My head is killing me right now

> I threw up three times this morning.

> You win.

> Want to cancel?

> No, I'm already halfway there and I'm going stir crazy in the house.

I bite the inside of my cheek. The public knows about her pregnancy by now, and even though it's been met with praise and excitement, I still want to keep her away from cameras.

> Is Wesley with you?

She attaches a picture of her leaning her head on Wesley's shoulder. Her eyes are closed but she has a pleased smile and rosy cheeks. The photo only reveals the lower half of her husband's bearded face.

> Stopping for milkshakes. Want one?

> No, I'm good. Thanks.

> See you soon.

The meeting will be a good chance to hear Tristan's intentions and new knowledge from working at the garden. It's about time he tells me whether he's making any of those changes I suggested. I hope he doesn't think I forgot since we went on vacation.

After that, maybe we can talk about making us real. And public.

I hate lying to people about us. I hate the idea of their judgment more. My previous hatred for Tristan was deep-seated and loud. It's almost embarrassing to be this different, this in love with him—especially if he keeps unethical practices with his company.

Not only that, I *need* to know he feels the same way about me. Only then will I feel safe enough to fall. I can handle anything else—as long as he loves me back.

It's a good thing the meeting is at the palace, a place where Nina is comfortable enough to wear slippers. She waddles across the courtyard.

"I hate this," she mumbles.

"I doubt it will take more than ten minutes."

"Not the meeting." She points to her belly. "This. I hate being pregnant. I'm so over it."

I link our arms together. "Just a few more weeks."

"With my luck, she'll be late."

Wesley is steps behind us. Nina told me that even though he's better about giving her space, he won't leave her side. My guess is that he's more paranoid than ever that someone might try to hurt her. Even though he tracked down and dismantled Lo Revinastí, the Maldanian militia that wanted to overthrow the monarchy by killing Nina, he knows exactly the kind of threats that we receive. He's in charge of the monarch's foreign intelligence.

My heart leaps at the sight of Tristan waiting outside the conference room, but crumbles with concern; he's arguing in hushed tones with a woman—his mother. I've never met Celine Farrugia, but I saw her picture when doing a deep dive online about Tristan.

She has dull brown hair and blue eyes and if I didn't know she was a terrible mom, I might admire her as a powerful woman.

Their arguing ceases when we're spotted, but I keep an eye on Tristan, his knotted shoulders and frantic expression. He tries to school his features and fails miserably.

"Your Majesties," Celine says, slapping a fake smile on her face as she curtsies. Tristan echoes his mother with much less enthusiasm.

"I promise this won't take up much of your time," she adds.

I nudge my sister. "You go ahead. I'll be there in a second."

Both Celine and Nina head into the room with Wesley not far behind. I place a hand on Tristan's arm to hold him back.

"Are you okay? You look stressed." Considering we returned from vacation just last night, he shouldn't be this upset so quickly about whatever it is.

"I'm fine," he says quickly, shaking his head. He takes one of my hands and kisses my knuckles. "We have to talk. I have to tell you something."

My stomach tightens. No one ever wants to hear those words, but he's kissing my hand, so it can't be *that* bad. Before I can respond, Wesley reappears outside the room to take station by the threshold as if he's still Nina's bodyguard. It reminds me that she's not feeling well—and I want to get her out of here and back home as soon as possible.

"Let's get this meeting over with first," I say to Tristan, my voice soft. I brush his cheek. "Then you'll have all of my attention."

Fear flickers through his eyes. "Maia, it can't wait."

"Nina's not feeling well. I want to get her out of here so she can rest."

I take his hand to bring us inside. I wouldn't be able to

focus on what he's saying with all of them waiting for us. I know I made the right decision at the sight of my queasy sister at the far end of the rectangular table. She sits across from Celine and another man I don't recognize. He's perhaps fifty-something years old with gray hair and a slim build.

He stands from his seat and bows. "Your Majesty. Thank you for joining us."

"This is Declan Stone, our family lawyer," Celine says, her firm tone demanding the attention of the room.

The skin along the back of my neck prickles. There's something about Tristan's distress that puts me on edge.

"We simply need confirmation that Mr. Farrugia has completed three hundred hours of volunteer work," Declan says.

I shift in my seat. "Can I ask why this needed to be a meeting?"

This could've been an email. But I've learned to keep that to myself. Both Tristan and Felicity Gardens needed NDAs for his volunteer hours—us to protect our reputation and him to protect his company.

Declan Stone slides a stapled contract and a pen across the table. He opens his mouth to speak, but Celine beats him to it with a nonchalant wave.

"We need witnesses for the signature." She looks at my sister. "The second and third page, Your Majesty."

"Have you learned a lot at the garden, then?" Nina asks with a glance at Tristan, though I can tell she's fighting to pretend to give a damn.

Tristan gulps before nodding. "Yes, it was—an amazing experience working at Felicity Gardens this year."

I want to ask about the plans for changes within his company, but his distress is enough to give me pause.

Perhaps I can talk to him about it tomorrow or sometime this week. Whatever he's stressing about is written all over his face.

"Then perhaps another time we can have a meeting about sustainable practices for Space Technologies?" Nina continues.

"Of course," he replies, dipping his head.

"See?" Declan adds, finally able to get a word in. He smiles. "I told you two volunteering wouldn't be so bad. Everyone comes out on top and Nico can finally rest."

"Nico?" I echo. Tristan's grandfather? "What does this have to do with him?"

Nina is too distracted searching for the signature line to listen, so I place a hand over hers to stop her from signing.

"I'll tell you later," Tristan says, and his urgency gives me pause. Is this what he's worried about today?

I look at Declan. I wouldn't count on Celine to tell me the truth and it's clear Tristan missed a detail. "What does this have to do with him?"

"Well, this is Nico Farrugia's will. His inheritance terms for his grandson."

"My father's dying wishes," Celine adds, giving Tristan a pointed look. "He wanted his grandson to stay humble and remember what it feels like to get his hands dirty."

"You didn't mention this at the first meeting," Nina says, flipping to the first page of the contract without signing anything.

My heart is thundering in my chest, but everything clicks together. When they said family lawyer, I thought it meant the same one they've used for years. Not a literal family lawyer, an executor of a will.

"Wait—" I cut myself off, my thoughts turning.

His inheritance terms for his grandson.

Realization crumbles through me, piece by piece, memory by memory. My mind flies back to one of the first conversations I had with him.

"You might have convinced my sister and the board that you actually give a shit about the environment, but not me. I don't trust a damn thing you say."

I was right. I was right about him and his intentions the entire time.

When I look at Tristan, the despair on his face confirms it. He was there for his inheritance. For fucking *money*.

"How much?" I ask. With every second that ticks by, my anger builds. The more I wait for his reply, to admit it, the deeper I slip into rage.

Celine flinches. "Your Majesty, I'm afraid that's a personal—"

"How much fucking money, Tristan?"

My echoing voice is the last sound in the room for a heavy pause. *How much was I worth? How much were we worth?*

He doesn't meet my eyes—like a fucking coward. "Five hundred million."

My heart fractures, carving a deep crack. He needed to meet the terms of inheritance, and he used Felicity Gardens to get it. All while knowing we were trying to make a difference. He played us. I was the one who suspected him the most. I made it perfectly clear I didn't trust him. So he had to silence me. He had to curb my suspicion and did so by leaning into our attraction.

Hatred burns its way through my skin. I reach in front of Nina and snatch the contract, ripping it in half twice before throwing it at him.

"Go straight to fucking hell."

I rise, knowing that I need to be as far from him as possible so I don't do something I regret. Like kill him.

"Maia—"

"You fucking played me."

His past words come back to me. *"I like you, Maia. I've always liked you. Is that so hard to believe?"* But he was lying. He wasn't there because of me.

"I didn't know how to tell you." Tristan rounds the table to meet me at the door.

"Bullshit! You were only at my house every weekend for five fucking months!"

"I didn't want you to find out like this. Please, if you'd let me explain—"

"I don't want your explanation," I snap as I rip open the door. "I want you to stay away from me."

I try to ignore Wesley, who perks when I storm out of the room. This is humiliating enough and I'm grateful no one from work is here, too. Like Dr. Pagoda.

"Maia, *please*. Let's just—"

The sound of Tristan begging sets my chest on fire. He doesn't get to do that. He doesn't get to act helpless. I whirl around on him, shoving at his chest.

"Don't play the fucking victim," I seethe, and his distressed expression doesn't worry me anymore. It only feeds my anger. "*You* made the decision to lie to me every fucking time. I betrayed *everything* because of you. I lied to myself, my friends, my sister—and for what? *For you to get over five hundred million dollars?*"

I don't realize I've grabbed a vase to throw until my brother-in-law is behind me, wrenching it from my hand and pinning my arms against me. I thrash against him, but it's useless. Everything is useless. I can't overpower Wesley the way I can't overpower the tears blurring my vision.

Every kiss, every laugh, every moment spent together was a means to an end. The tears burn my eyes, but I refuse to let him see me cry.

He played me for five hundred million.

Nina is at my side in seconds. She blocks Tristan from my sight, muttering soothing words as she and Wesley guide me in the opposite direction. Shame and humiliation claw their way through my chest.

What have I done?

CHAPTER FORTY-FIVE
TRISTAN

Congratulations! Poe has been medically cleared and is ready to be taken to his new home!

I stare at the email. Fuck. How could I have forgotten about Poe so easily? I was so sure I wanted him; it seemed like the obvious decision. Now I realize I only wanted a cat because of Maia. And now that I lost her...

I have Poe delivered to my studio anyway.

I expect an influx of memories from the Maldives, followed by a bout of sadness. But I owe it to him to try.

I spend an hour cleaning my studio—mostly broken shards. I destroyed half of my sculptures after Maia broke up with me.

It's humbling to clean up years of hard work and dedication, but this loss is nothing compared to her.

I was furious at Celine for always trying to undermine and humble me. I was furious at Grandfather for ruining this family, hurting my sister, and raising me the way he did. Most of all, I'm furious at myself for not giving Maia the respect of honesty months ago. I should have told her before the banquet, at least.

Without the full truth, I had no right to claim ownership over her. Not that night and not any time after.

Once my cat arrives in a carrier and I tip the courier, I take Poe to the couch that Maia would doze off on when she spent hours at a time here. I've had it for years, but she's left her mark on everything. It's like my world hardly existed before her.

"Hang on," I mumble, unlatching the crate and scooting back to give him room. Hopefully his feral side doesn't come out and make me realize it was a colossal mistake to adopt a stray from another country.

Poe inches his way to the front, sniffing and creeping along the cushion. My chest warms ever so slightly. When he reaches my leg and sniffs, he starts clawing his way up my torso.

"Whoa, chill." I grab his body, but don't pull him off. His clawing isn't angry—it's frightened.

Any thought of giving him up flees my mind, and I chide myself for even considering it. He wraps himself around my neck and I lean back, sinking into his cuddles and scrubbing his fur. I wince at the smell. He needs a bath.

"Sorry, mate. I know that was a lot of change for you."

He purrs in response, nuzzling his face into me. There are dark clouds both outside and around my shoulders, but Poe makes it a little less unbearable.

"You bought a cat?"

"*Rescued,*" I correct, my mind instantly drifting to Maia and her constant corrections. She refuses to admit she has a savior complex.

Augustus stands in front of my desk, staring down at

Poe, who's curled up on my closed laptop. My assistant is failing to hide his judgment.

"Uh... *why?*"

I give him a pointed look. No matter how soft rescuing an abnormally small cat makes me look, I'm still his boss. Augustus sobers, his features fading into indifference.

"It's cute, sir."

"He," I correct, petting between Poe's ears. "His name is Poe."

"Like the poet?"

I shrug. "If you'd prefer. It was the name he already had."

Over the past day, I've realized Poe is the chillest animal to exist. He likes to relax, play with the feather toy I bought him, and nap on or near me. He eats like he's never met food before and stretches the most adorable stretch to ever exist.

I despise that I can't share this with Maia. I have dozens of pictures of him already and need to stop myself from sending her each one.

If not for Poe being a constant reminder, I'm afraid my anger and hatred for Celine would overpower me until I did something irrational in retaliation. While I needed to tell Maia the truth, my mother knowingly sabotaged us.

Nico and Celine betrayed me and hurt Danica much worse. They don't deserve peace.

Poe can only heal so much. I'm plagued by memories of Maia's laugh, smile, and kiss at every waking moment. And I still can't fucking sleep at night. I sculpt because it's the only thing I can truly focus on.

It's been four days since I fucked up and I've barely slept the amount of a single night's rest.

I made the mistake of trying to call her again today.

Yesterday, I swore I would give her time. But I wanted her to know that I brought Poe home and I wanted to ask how Callie is settling in. If she gets along with Sage and the others.

I had everything I could ever want. As long as she was in my life, I was content. It doesn't matter where on this earth I am. If Maia is there, there is nothing more I need. She insists I'm the best version of myself and will accept nothing less. Before that, I hadn't realized what I could accomplish. I owe it to her.

Later, throughout the night, I make progress on my tree sculpture. I didn't sculpt nature pieces as often as I did before I met Maia. I'm not sure if I have less interest in other people or increased interest in nature—probably both.

I take Poe to the office with me at the crack of dawn. No one other than security fills the building, which gives me time to pull myself together. With hardly any sleep and attention to myself, I look as awful as I feel. I haven't shaved. I haven't showered. My motivation for just about anything is obliterated. I hadn't realized just how threaded Maia is in my life until she was gone. Every instinct and thought drift to her, and the hole she left behind is so wide and painful that all I see is darkness. All I feel is agony.

I try to lounge on the couch in my office and review reports and memos for the shareholder meeting later today. It takes exactly ten minutes for me to break out the bourbon. I'm not dumb enough to drink on an empty stomach, so I grab something resembling breakfast from the cafeteria.

Poe is scratching away at his cardboard wall, content as can be. He's still mad at me for giving him a bath last night by refusing to cuddle or sleep near me. It's okay, though, because I'm mad at him for the scratches on my wrist.

I find myself taking shots whenever a memory of Maia hits me. On the dark side, it's often. On the bright side, I finally get some rest.

Before I know it, a ringing phone down the hall startles me from a slumber on the couch. My crusty eyes rip open to find my office still shrouded in darkness, but sunlight fights through the curtain edges. Poe is curled by my head, seemingly over his foul mood. The blanket over me and my vanished plate from breakfast tell me someone was in here —and if it was anyone other than my assistant, I'm going to be furious.

"Augustus," I call, though my windpipe feels as crusty as my eyes. I clear my throat. "Fuck... *Augustus!*"

"I'm coming, I'm coming," he grumbles, appearing in the threshold of my office. "There's water beside you."

"What time is it?"

"Three p.m."

"*What?* Shit—"

"I canceled the shareholder meeting," he says, his irritation on full display. "You would have embarrassed yourself and the company."

"Yeah." My head is pounding and I'm far too groggy to be annoyed at his attitude. He's right.

"Just rest. Next meeting is at five."

Still flat on my back, my gaze is stuck on the ceiling. Despite the much-needed rest, I'm somehow much worse than before I went to sleep.

"I miss her," I admit, hating the way my voice cracks. "I loved—I love her."

Augustus pauses. "I know, sir... Get some rest."

He closes the door when he leaves. What else could he say? *Yeah, but you fucked up. Get over it.*

I shut my eyes and pray this hell will be over soon.

"There's something on your face."

The strange but familiar voice pulls me from yet another slumber. My eyes aren't crusty this time, but something still must be wrong because I refuse to believe that Romèo is standing in front of me.

"What the hell are you doing here?" I ask, hoping I don't come across as angry. I'm more confused than anything.

He shrugs, his motorcycle helmet dangling from one hand. "I called your office when you weren't answering your phone, and your assistant told me you were sleeping. Then I knew something had to be wrong." He points to Poe curled up beside my head. "Now I definitely know something's wrong."

Romèo has seen my sleeping habits since we were children. Playing video games into the night during sleepovers said enough; he was always the one to fall asleep first. A few times, I would still be awake when he would rise in the morning. And never before in my life did I show an interest in pets or animals.

"It's a long story," I grumble, though it isn't. I just don't want to talk about it.

"You told her, then?"

Without disturbing Poe, I sit up and swing my legs over the edge of the couch. "Worse. Celine ambushed me. Then she found out."

Romèo lifts a brow. "I can't say I'm surprised."

It's a relief I don't have to explain to him what makes my mother so awful; he knows. He's seen it. "You flew here to check on me?"

He drops into one of the armchairs. "Is that so bad?"

"You didn't before."

"You weren't in love before."

I snicker. "Like you know anything about love."

His lack of reaction is a reaction enough. I tilt my head. "Tell me about her," I press.

Romèo shakes his head, a lock of his dark hair swaying with the movement. "Nah."

I roll my eyes. "It'll get my mind off Maia."

Fuck, just saying her name makes my heart twinge. She's more than embedded into my life, she's entwined in my very soul and I don't know how much longer I can do this. I need her back.

Poe stirs awake, eyeing Romèo. My friend is even less of a cat person than I am, so I hold my son to my chest to keep him from finding his way over to our guest.

After a moment, Romèo clears his throat and leans forward on his knees. "D'you remember Andrea from primary school?"

I rack my brain briefly to no avail. "Doesn't ring a bell."

"Andrea Cortez. Andie. She was American and only attended for a year. Big, curly hair. Quiet."

"She was Black?" Our school was mostly white, so I imagine I would remember her, but I don't recall any quiet, curly-haired girls named Andie. Quiet girls aren't my type.

"Yeah."

"I don't remember. You had a crush on her?"

He lifts a shoulder, neither denying nor confirming. "I think about her a lot."

I wanted him to help me get my mind off Maia, and it's

surely working because I have a dozen questions. "Why'd she leave? Do you still talk to her?"

"No, not since she left."

"Have you tried to find her?"

"No," he says, but the hesitation on his face is clear as day.

"If you tell me what happened, we can find her."

My curiosity doesn't matter; Romèo does what he usually does when the topic gets personal: he shuts down. He falls back in the seat and looks at Poe curled up against my chest. I can only imagine how pitiful I look; unshowered, unshaved, and with an abnormally small cat in my hands.

"I'll tell you if you tell me why you got a damn cat."

Touché.

CHAPTER FORTY-SIX
MAIA

I spend most of my time crying. Daisy hasn't left my side since I came home from finding out Tristan is a liar. Poppy, ever so detached, proceeds with business as usual.

Even though Nina had driven home with me and held me as I sobbed, I didn't tell her everything. I didn't tell her just how in love with him I am.

It's not the first or even the fifth time I've cried to her about a boy I liked, but I'm not sure she understands just how different this is. And I'm far too humiliated to update her on it.

The feeling of defeat makes it so much worse. It's the reality of knowing I hadn't proved Lyla wrong. I'd rather choke than tell her she was right; I'm not sure we could ever be friends again and the loss of two important people sends me into yet another fit of tears.

I was convinced that all Lyla and Nina had to do was get to know Tristan. But I fell for his lie.

I prided myself on being confident enough to see through the bullshit that so many men pull. It's what kept my heart mostly protected, especially over the last few years. I haven't cried over a boy since before college. For years, I wasn't the heartbroken one. Not the one in tears.

I wanted to fall in love with Tristan without losing myself, but the old Maia is nowhere in sight. I have no idea who I've become. I was never supposed to be the one to give up anything for a man, especially not my morals. Men like Tristan, obscenely wealthy and selfish, have always been red flags. But I made an exception and suffered the consequences.

Never again.

It was stupid to ever think I could hide it from Esme. The moment she comes over to help me with Callie, my new cat, she notices something off.

She looks at me as she pets Callie. "What happened?"

Dammit. Just those two words. Those two simple words break open another dam of tears. She sets the cat aside and wraps me in a hug.

I tell her everything.

In the end, Esme wipes at a tear on my cheek. "You didn't have to hide it from me," she says. "I wouldn't have judged you. I'm not Lyla."

I sniffle, shaking my head. "I just feel so stupid."

She gives me a lopsided smile. "Love does that to you."

The only consolation of the past few days is Callie's arrival. I'm lucky enough that she gets along with everyone, and even manages to pull Sage out of her shell. I've never seen her so playful before and chide myself for not getting her a friend sooner. I keep fucking everything up.

"You're so lucky," I mumble to Esme. "You've been with Sergio forever."

She tucks her legs under her, one arm slung over the back of the patio couch. "It wasn't always easy."

"But you've always loved him."

She nods, unable to argue.

"And you know he's always loved you."

She nods again. "It sounds like Tristan loved you, though. Everything he's done before that—he has to love you."

I curl the blanket tighter around me. October in Maldana are much warmer than Massachusetts, making it the perfect weather. It's much more manageable and I feel as though I can function in transition seasons. Extreme heat or cold does a number on my body and energy, rendering me practically useless.

"He never said he loved me," I say, "and I don't trust myself anymore. I just... never thought he would lie about something like that."

Esme frowns, squeezing my shoulder. Daisy is curled up at my feet while the rest of my pets, Callie included, play together and roam in the yard to my right. I have a tracking collar on Callie in case she gets too adventurous and hops the fence.

Comfortable silence falls between us and my eyes flutter shut. Sadness and anger have consumed me for the past few days. Tristan calls me every afternoon, which rips the wound open again. I decline every single one.

After I had answered his question of what I'd do with his wealth, we never spoke of it again. Sure, it's "his" money, but he told me he would make a change. He would implement *something*.

The thought sobers me.

Fuck it. Fuck *this*.

I can't sit around feeling sorry for myself. *Waiting on a man to be better*.

The thought rips a laugh straight from my chest. I don't wait for men.

"What's funny?" Esme asks, her glass of rosé still in hand.

"The fact that I'm still crying over him." I push the blanket off me and stride to the french doors leading into my bedroom. Within five minutes, I gather Tristan's belongings in a box—T-shirts, dress shirts, sweatpants, boxers, even his toothbrush. In my nightstand drawer, I grab one of my pre-rolled weed joints and a box of matches. In the shed, I grab the lighter fluid.

And because I'm not stupid, I grab the fire extinguisher.

Esme's eyes grow wide when she sees all that I'm holding. "Uh oh."

"Feel like having a bonfire?"

I dump the contents of the box into the fire pit before squirting lighter fluid on top.

Esme sets her wine glass aside and sits up. Per usual, she's the epitome of tranquility with her golden hair, mom jeans that barely reach her ankle, and a blue button-up that she somehow mastered the perfect waist-tuck for.

"Are you sure about this?"

"Completely." I stick the joint in my mouth and scrape one end of the match along the side of the box. I haven't smoked weed in months and I'm not even sure how strong this will be, but I need some kind of relief that doesn't involve crying or violence. The flame roars to life, lighting one end of the joint before being tossed into the fire pit.

A steady fire grows within seconds. Then I toss some more lighter fluid, taking puffs at the same time. To my surprise, Esme smiles.

"I hope you plan on mailing him the ashes."

My eyes widen. "Oh, that's *genius*."

She tosses her hair over her shoulder. "See? I can be mean."

The corner of my lips lifts. As much as I love her level-headed nature, I'd also love to see what would happen if someone double-crossed her. The quietest ones can be the most feral.

"Never be anything but yourself, Esme Livanos."

I return to my seat beside her and pick up my own glass of rosé. She reaches for the joint before offering her glass to mine.

"To his reckoning."

I laugh for the first time in days, clinking my glass with hers as the flames engulf Tristan's belongings. "To his reckoning."

CHAPTER FORTY-SEVEN
MAIA

This has been the week from hell.

Even after burning all of Tristan's clothes at my house, I cried. Again. I have to avoid Lyla at all costs at work because I would rather die than tell her she was right all along. The job that used to bring me more comfort than anything has now become a tightrope; turning the wrong corner and spotting her can ruin my day entirely. And it's already happened three times.

We don't speak. We give each other glances here and there. But other than that, we're complete strangers. No one, including Dr. Pagoda, asked me about it, which could be good or bad. It could mean all of their information has come from Lyla.

I don't want to be who she and the media expect me to be, but I need a night out.

If I'm not at work, I'm home. And when I'm home, even as I'm harvesting my garden and playing with my animals, I fight an onslaught of tears left and right and dodge Nina's calls at the same time. I opt for texting her instead; I just know that the act of *speaking* will make everything worse. I'm on the verge of tears twenty-four-seven and I'm really fucking tired of crying.

On Friday, I text Roman.

And I haven't decided if it's a mistake or not.

I don't want to start up with him again, but I need to get out and do something different. I haven't been to Lynx Room since early this year and it might be just what I need to unwind and let go.

I stare at my reflection, at my puffy curls and tight glittery dress. I hardly recognize this girl anymore. My circles are barely covered by concealer and my cheeks are more hollow than ever before. Tristan didn't do that. The media and my chronic illness did. Maybe I should give another stab at letting the doctors figure out what's wrong...

But I've had enough bad news to last me years. One step at a time.

I lock up the house and slide into the town car ready to take me to Kosita. Mason is usually my ride, but he's in America visiting his kids.

It's not that I don't love going out anymore. The thrill of dancing my worries away is unmatched. Music drowning out my concerns. Strobe lights blinding me to my issues that would follow the next day. I just can't keep up with myself anymore. And accepting that is one of the hardest things I've ever had to do.

Before Lyla and I stopped being friends, our group consisted of us, Roman, Jace, and their other friend Giorgio and whatever girlfriend he had at the time. Now it's just Jace, Giorgio, Roman, and me. I don't like being the only woman, but I'm just looking for a night of fun.

What I appreciate most about Roman is his inability to be awkward. Nothing makes him uncomfortable. He's not asking whether we're going to start up again; he reacts only to what I say. A horrible habit for a boyfriend, but a great one for a hookup.

Jace, being my cousin, is an added comfort whenever we go out on the town. He's been in the royal institution a lot longer than I have, and his down-to-earth nature always makes me wonder why he's friends with Roman in the first place.

He wraps his arms around me in a hug. "Hey, cous. It's been too long."

My heart twinges. I truly ignored everyone and everything during those months with Tristan. "I know, I'm sorry. I've missed you! How's Aunt Bev?"

He shrugs. "She's okay, busy as usual. Oh, how's the garden?"

He, like the rest of my family and the institution, knows the garden was supposed to cure everything; get me out of Kosita to stop me from being harassed and stalked everywhere I went and turn my focus on something that can keep me out of the press.

"It's great!" I reply. "The crowds have finally started to calm down after this summer."

He smiles a boyish smile. "Good."

"Your Majesty," Giorgio interjects with a grin, wrapping me in a hug the same as my cousin. "How are you?"

"Hi, Giorgio! I'm good, how are you?"

We've been friendly, but nothing more. He's tall, white, and lanky. Not my type. He's sweet as a peach, though I've heard the way he talks about women sometimes. Not every man but always a man, I suppose.

"I'm great. I was so happy when Roman called us to come out tonight. I've missed you!"

"Really?"

"Well, you and Lyla," he adds. "The way it was before—us as a group. We haven't done this in a while."

I offer a sympathetic smile. Lyla secretly despises Giorgio. She finds him fake and irritating. I see what she means, but I've been too busy to go out of my way to hate people.

"This year has been really hectic," I admit. "But I want to switch it up a little bit and do something I haven't done in a while."

"Glad to hear it."

Roman, who has never cared that he's shorter than me, reaches up to hug me briefly. We've been hanging out and pregaming in the lounge, a room outside of the dance floor. Most people who come here are either obscenely wealthy or high-end celebrities. It's the best and most private way to party without also being near some shady rich people who do questionable things with their money.

I suffer through more small talk before we finally pour another round of drinks and head into the room next door to hit the dance floor. One thing I love about Europe is that they play early 2000s American music. It's not hard to start dancing to *Crazy in Love* and *Hollaback Girl*.

It's different—dancing with only Roman instead of Lyla. A slice of regret bleeds through my stomach, but I have to move on.

Just because she wasn't friends with me for clout doesn't mean she was a good friend.

I'm on my third drink within one hour and there's no looking back. The room spins and I grab onto Roman in front of me for stability as we wade through the small crowd. The alcohol has numbed me enough to hide any pain for the time being. It won't last long, but I'll enjoy every moment. Music thumps through my chest as Gwen Stefani sings about runnin' 'round that track.

For a little while, I feel like my old self.

Roman is handsy. I don't mind. I need to purge every memory and touch of *him* from my body. It's as though Tristan is embedded in my skin, stitched into my soul, my heart—

My eyes.

I blink again. And again.

This is *not* happening.

Across the dance floor in a lounge chair, *Tristan* watches me. *Tristan* nudges off the man beside him, who tries to speak. The other man has a woman on his lap, and I recognize him when he shifts his face: Romèo. Tristan told me about him a while ago and showed me a picture from when they were teens. He doesn't look much different.

My heart fractures once more. I wasn't ready to see him. I'm *not* ready to see him. How did he even know I'm here? Is he here because of me? Was Romèo here, noticed me, and snitched?

"You okay?" asks Roman, noticing my halt in dancing.

Roman might be a player, but he's caring. That's why I gave him a chance. Then a second. Underneath all of his bullshit is concern for people. He just chooses to turn it off more often than not.

A wave of emotions threatens to crash into me. The final thread pulls taut—

No.

I won't let him ruin this, too.

"I'm fine," I say to Roman, spotting Giorgio over his shoulder dancing with another woman. I reach around Roman to grab the other man by his arm. "Dance with me. Both of you."

Giorgio doesn't hesitate as I pull him to the other side of me. I don't know how the woman reacts; she's not on my radar. I'm grateful for the upbeat tempo of Rihanna's *Please Don't Stop the Music.*

I shamelessly turn my gaze to Tristan as I sway my hips, sandwiched between Giorgio and Roman. I can hardly make out his expression through the dim lights, but it's clear enough he's furious.

All I keep wondering is why the fuck he's here and if he knew I would be, too.

Giorgio's head dips into my neck as the three of us dance to the beat. Blood pumps through my veins; the breath in my lungs burns. Roman's hands on my waist are tight enough to slip up my already short dress an inch or two, and Giorgio takes advantage of the exposed skin.

This isn't enough. I need Tristan to hurt like he hurt me. I need his heart ripped from his chest, stomped on, and spit on.

I lean down to Roman's ear. "Let's have sex in the bathroom."

His eyes light up. "Hell yeah."

Within seconds, we're stumbling into the empty women's bathroom and every feeling the dance floor suppressed comes rushing back; the feeling in my legs, my hearing, the air in my lungs. Roman is already kissing my sweaty neck as my ass hits the counter.

"Wait." I pull him back. "This doesn't mean anything about us. I'm just trying to make someone jealous."

It's as if I told him he won a million dollars. He smirks as a piece of his dirty blond hair falls into his face.

"Then let's make him jealous."

I try to smother my disgust when he kisses me, the taste of vodka burning my tongue. At the very least, he's familiar. I know what to expect with him: a few thrusts, some of his weird grunts, and it's over. But he has a big enough dick to make me come, so it's the little wins.

The memory of Tristan and me in the bathroom at the auction edges my vision, but I shove it away by shoving my tongue in Roman's mouth, eliciting a moan from him. He presses himself between my legs, his hands roaming my thighs.

Why am I doing this again?

The bathroom handle jiggles. We ignore it, knowing it's locked. It's not the first time Roman and I have hooked up in a place we shouldn't.

What I don't expect is the *thump... thump... crack.*

The bathroom door flies open, pieces of wood flicking off the hinge. Before I can hardly gasp, Roman is ripped off me and thrown against the wall by Tristan.

I scramble to push my dress back down as Roman throws an elbow behind him despite being half a foot shorter. Tristan stops it with his hand, using the other to grasp his wrist and slam it down on the edge of the counter.

I clamp my eyes shut just before the *snap* of Roman's bone as he cries out and crumples to the ground. Only then does Tristan back away.

My hands tremble and I can't even look him in the eyes. He's never been violent. I never thought he would be.

It's clear I know nothing about him.

I drop in front of Roman, swallowing my bile at the sight of half of his forearm dangling. The veins in his neck strain, his head falling back against the wall. "What the *fuck*, Maia?"

"Wha—*me?*"

Spit flies from his lips. "You didn't tell me you were trying to make *Tristan fucking Farrugia* jealous!" He bangs his head against the wall, fighting to distract himself from the pain. It's hard to get mad at someone who's in such agony.

Tristan nudges his way in front of me and lifts a terrified Roman to his feet like he weighs nothing. My heart tightens when I hear him speak, his deep British accent snaking into me.

"Go get that checked out, yeah?" He gives the other man a condescending pat on the cheek before pushing him out the broken door. It's only a matter of minutes before someone like Jace or Giorgio comes looking for me to ask what happened.

I climb to my feet. When Tristan looks at me, my voice catches in my throat. I want to ask him why he thinks he can break someone's arm like there's no issue, but I can't. My mind blanks as we stare at each other, the tension slipping away.

"Seriously?" he eventually asks. "Him?"

"Are you insane? You can't just *break* people's arms like that!"

Tristan scoffs.

He fucking *scoffs*. As if he had any right to do what he just did.

"You had no fucking right," I seethe. "Last time I checked, *you* were the one who fucked up. *You* were the one who lied. Who I fuck is none of your goddamn business!" I step closer, unable to stop myself from what comes next nor the crack in my voice. "I was willing to risk everything for you. My reputation, my sister's reputation, my *career*... The whole time, you were using me to boost yours."

His stony facade cracks. I haven't seen stern, business Tristan since the first few days we met. He inhales, clenching his jaw, but his brows dip low as if he's in pain.

"We shouldn't talk about this here."

It's not until his demanding energy in the room that I realize how awful the sex with Roman would have been. It reminds me of our time in the bathroom at the auction. We were explosive. He had taken care of me yet mercilessly worked my body through as many climaxes as he decided to give me.

And the thought of being with Roman—anyone that's not Tristan—dries me right up and shreds my heart all at once. We could have had everything. I *wanted* to give him everything. That might be the worst part. It's not only that I became the very person I forbade myself from becoming, but the willingness that startles me. I was ready to jump in headfirst with him, and looking back, I would have been reckless. From the moment we first hooked up, we couldn't keep our hands and hearts off each other, and it only got more intense the longer we went on. It was only a matter of time until I was thoughtless enough and was caught or it somehow leaked to the press.

None of that matters now.

My goal from the start was to protect my career, and even though it's intact, it feels like I lost everything.

"We shouldn't talk about this at *all*," I say, curving around him. "I need to go."

Before I can pass, his hand wraps around my arm snugly. I flinch at his skin against mine, more memories threatening to attack me.

With a sniff, I say, "Let me go."

"Not until I know you won't try to fuck anyone else tonight."

I grimace at his possessiveness and lift a contemptuous gaze to him. "Don't worry. This conversation dried me right up."

I rip myself away and fight the onslaught of tears as I rush down the hall. I need to get out of here. I can't be around strangers; it'll only make it worse. I need to be around someone I trust.

With blurry vision, I dig out my phone to send a text.

CHAPTER FORTY-EIGHT
MAIA

I tuck myself in a dark doorway up the street. An ambulance has arrived by now and spectators are gathering. The last thing I need is to be in the middle of that. My phone has been buzzing with texts from Jace, and I only answer his last one.

Can you at least tell me if you're okay?

I'm fine. Promise. Waiting to be picked up.

Tell Roman I'm sorry. I never meant for that to happen.

Fifteen minutes later, a black car pulls up to my location and I eagerly climb to my feet and stagger out of the grimy doorway. My feet and legs are screaming at me and I decided that coming out tonight was the worst idea I've ever had.

I slide into the passenger seat, slamming the door behind me. "Thank you for picking me up. I'm sorry to wake you up."

Wesley shifts the gear before driving off down the street. "I was already awake. Why didn't you call Mason?"

I sniffle. "He's visiting his kids in America. And I didn't trust anyone else."

He side-eyes me. "Is that Nina's dress?"

"Maybe," I mumble, knowing full well that it is. I can't help that she has cute clothes.

The highway takes us out of the city, and a semi-comfortable silence fills the space. My brother-in-law doesn't feel the need for small talk—and I appreciate that about him.

"Wanna tell me what happened?"

Spoke too soon.

"Not really," I admit. "Are you gonna tell Nina?"

I'm not quite sure *what* he would tell her. I just don't want her to think I'm spiraling (I am). I guess I'm just tired of always having something going on.

"Did you do something illegal?" asks Wesley.

"No."

"Anything capable of irreparable public scandal?"

"No."

"Was or will there be threat of physical danger toward you?"

"No."

"Then I won't tell her."

My appreciation for him swells so much so that after a long pause, I offer, "Tristan was there. So was Roman."

"Ah."

"Long story short, Tristan broke Roman's arm."

Wesley snorts.

I look at him, surprised. "What?"

"Nothing. Just reminds me of something."

Thankfully, the rest of the ride is quiet. It's almost one

in the morning and I'm starting to feel it in my bones. My body sinks into the seat, able to relax for the first time since I left my house.

When Wesley pulls the car through my gate, he says, "I know I said I wouldn't tell Nina, but she might be awake when I get home—and I won't lie to her."

"I don't want you to."

"She also knows you're avoiding her. And she's really upset over it."

I swallow my discomfort. "Yeah."

"I try to stay out of your relationship, but…"

"But what?"

"You're avoiding her because you don't want her to see you sad, but it's only making it worse. She worries more than ever." Wesley gives me a pointed look for the first time. "You need to make this right."

Even though he's the one who stopped me from chucking a vase at Tristan's head, he's never been more sincere than he is in this moment.

I nod. "Thank you. For picking me up and the—the honesty."

Wesley's words of encouragement didn't matter; my sister still banged on my front door just before noon. I open the door to reveal a very pregnant Nina with her hands on her hips and a glare in her eyes.

"Good morning," I quip, feigning cheerfulness the best I can. She doesn't say anything, so I drop the act. "Wesley told you."

She flinches in surprise at my disappointment before her grimace deepens. "Of course he told me."

"Relax, I was just asking." I shift aside for her to come on. "I didn't want him to lie."

I was planning on seeing her today; I only hoped Wesley hadn't told her so I could. I close the door behind her as my dogs pepper her with affection and greetings. "Maia, you're worrying me. And I don't just mean what happened last night."

On instinct, I say, "I'm fine."

"Bullshit!" she snaps. "You're not fine and you're shutting me out!"

My breath catches in my throat. "I'm trying to figure this out on my own without worrying you. It's always *what did Maia do now? Who did she piss off this time? How can we clean up her mess?* I'm a fuck-up, Neen. You're about to have a baby and the last thing I want is to keep being someone you have to fix and take care of!"

Nina's eyes well with tears, and the sight makes my resolve vanish.

"Don't cry," I beg, my own tears creeping up. My voice cracks. "If you cry, I'll cry."

Both of us are weeping within seconds. She throws her arms around me tightly. "I could have ten kids and it still won't stop me from worrying about you. You're my *sister*, for god's sake." She pulls from the hug and takes me by my shoulders. "Pushing me away won't make me care less. I know you can figure things out. The past few years taught me there is *nothing* you can't handle and you're so much stronger than you give yourself credit for."

The tears drip from my jaw onto my neck. Praise from Nina always makes me feel better, but this confrontation is exactly what I was avoiding. It rips open my chest in a way I'm not ready for. Perhaps it's because I knew I'd have trouble believing I'm worthy of her praise—or any praise at all—when Tristan turned me into so much of a fool.

"I still..." I shake my head with a gulp, trying to garner the courage to admit it aloud. "I still fell for him. I became the exact person I swore I wouldn't be."

Nina pouts and brushes away one of my tears. "Being in love does that to you."

"That's what Esme said."

I prided myself on being immune to his charm, on having enough self-control to stay true to my beliefs. And I ended up being duped the worst. I didn't realize how hard I fell until I crashed, and I might be shattered beyond repair.

I thought I was destined for more. I had hope for the woman I could become and here I am in the exact spot I wanted to avoid. Because I somehow believed this would be different.

With Nina and me on good terms, we crawl into my bed and turn on one of our favorite movies: *The Princess Diaries*. Despite us being extremely different from Mia Thermopolis and her life, my sister and I find ourselves relating to her becoming royalty unexpectedly.

I pause the movie when Nina winces and presses a hand against her belly. "Are you okay?"

"She's kicking. Want to feel?"

She guides my hand to the side of her stomach and lo and behold, a tiny foot—or hand—thumps against my palm.

"Does it hurt?"

"Sometimes. Feeling her move around can be the weirdest thing ever."

I shiver at the idea. As much as I already love my niece and am willing to die for her, pregnancy doesn't seem all that different than a parasite.

Our movements alert Daisy, who's already in bed with us. She snicks her nose against Nina's stomach and jerks back when the baby kicks. Her head tilts from one side to the other, her tiny yet floppy ears perking. The sight makes us laugh.

"Have you guys thought of names?"

Nina lights up with a nod. "Yeah. We want to keep it a secret but he should know by now that *we* includes you."

I prop up on my elbows. "Do tell."

"Cordelia Rose. Cori for short."

"Cordelia Rose! Oh thank *god* it's a cute name," I say, nearly pressing my nose against her belly the same way Daisy did. "Cordelia Rose, you are going to be the most spoiled baby in all of Europe. Your auntie Maia loves you more than anything in the world."

I'm so grateful my niece will have present parents, the mother we missed and the father we needed.

The dark thought of Tristan as a father hits me. At one point, I pictured him in my life for as long as possible. It wouldn't have been long before I imagined him as the father of my kids.

Nina notices my crestfallen expression. "Do you wanna talk about him?"

I stiffen. "What's there to talk about?"

"Well, you hid him from everyone, so I don't know anything about your relationship... My therapist showed me that talking about it helps. Not to fix anything, but just talking and letting it exist."

I hesitate. The last time I spoke about Tristan with her was when I was told to be cautious with him.

"I'm not going to judge you," she adds, ever so perceptive of what others might be thinking. "I promise."

"At first it was just sex... We argued in almost every

conversation—well, more like me giving him crap and him defending himself. I don't know... we just wanted to be around each other all the time. There weren't really any butterflies at first; it felt like we clicked and that was it. He spent *so* much time here—and you know I don't let just anyone in my house."

My sister nods.

"But I still made it clear that I thought being a billionaire was selfish and he could make his company sustainable if he wanted to. That's why I didn't want to tell anyone."

"He knew that was your reason?"

It's my turn to nod. "Then one time he asked me what I would do with his wealth. When I told him, he said he'd see what he could do about it—all of it. And I believed him. He donated millions just to make me happy and I feel so stupid for falling for something he should've done in the first place. I *knew* that. I reminded myself of it, but it was so hard to push when everything else seemed so perfect." My voice trembles, turning fragile as another round of tears is on the verge. "I *physically* felt better around him, Neen. He made my chronic pain go away in so many ways and it—" A sob chokes out of me and I bury my face in the pillow. "I hate that any part of my health would rely on him."

Nina doesn't say anything; she wraps her arm around me as Daisy nudges her big head between us. I swear I can't shed a single tear without my dog being up my butt.

A random memory hits me—of the one thing I couldn't bring myself to get rid of when I first tried to purge him from my heart.

That damn rock.

"He gave me a rock," I say into my pillow.

"He gave you a rock?"

"He gave me a rock." I reach over and grab it from my nightstand to show her.

She turns it over in her fingers, brows drawn. "At least it's pretty."

"I can't bring myself to get rid of it. I don't know why."

"'Cause you're a nature nerd."

I roll my eyes and take my rock back. I tuck it into my drawer for safekeeping.

"Do you want a milkshake? I can have Wesley bring us milkshakes."

I chuckle. "Milkshakes sound good."

Nina digs out her phone to call him, and suddenly says, "Oh, and before I forget, he wants me to take my dress back. The one you wore last night."

"What? Why?" I pout. "I like that dress."

She avoids my gaze with a bashful smirk. "No reason."

Then it hits me; something sexual. I recoil and shake out my hands, hoping they didn't do anything while she wore that dress. "Oh my god, ew. *Ew.* Yeah, take it back. I don't want it."

CHAPTER FORTY-NINE
MAIA

At four in the morning, the familiar chime of my front gate notification wakes me up.

My heart seizes at the thought of someone trying to break in. I snatch my phone, sleep fleeing my body like it was never there. While Poppy and Sage snooze away, Callie and Daisy sense my fear.

In the camera, I find Tristan's face magnified like in a fishbowl. I rub my eyes. What the hell is he doing here at the crack of dawn?

I swipe to the messages in my security app to inform whoever's on duty that I know the guest. They respond with a thumbs up and I switch back to the security camera.

I hit the microphone. "What are you doing here?"

Tristan flinches back as if surprised by my voice—and that's when I see it. Blood. He blinks slowly, drunk off his ass. "Whoa, didn't expect you to be that loud."

"Is that blood on your face?" Panic grips me. "Did you drive here and crash? Where's your car?"

"No, no." He gulps, a hand braced on the wall to keep himself upright. "I'm—I fell, right before I rung. A man named—named River drove me here. An odd name, but I rather like it."

"You shouldn't be here. He just dropped you off and left?"

"Can I come in?" Tristan asks, not answering my question.

This is a bad idea. He's covered in his own blood and stumbling drunk and it's honestly pathetic. But I can't just leave him out there injured. No matter how mad I am at him, I'm just not that kind of person.

Instead of saying anything, I unlock the gate.

I stuff my feet into raccoon slippers and wrap myself in an oversized cardigan, my heart thundering. I take off my bonnet to reveal two braids. It's been four days since he broke Roman's arm—and he hasn't called me since.

His silence makes me feel guilty. I hurt him. And even though he hurt me first, bringing him pain doesn't sit right in my heart.

When I open the door and step onto the porch, Tristan stops mid-stride across the courtyard at the sight of me. He wears slacks and a messy, half-buttoned dress shirt. His hands are empty and he watches me with an overwhelmed, exhausted expression.

"Hi," he says.

"Hi." I wrap the cardigan tighter around my body. "Come inside so I can clean you up."

Poppy and Daisy are ecstatic to see him as if they were never sleeping. It's weird seeing him with them, especially since he's about as excited as they are.

His presence is nostalgic yet disjointed at the same time. It's a raw wound that hurts no matter the angle, no matter the ways we try to purge each other from our lives.

I bring him into my bathroom, fighting to keep the tears

at bay as I pull out the first aid kit and wet a cloth. The emotion clogs my throat. I avoid his eyes as I cage his jaw with one hand and clean the wound with the other. His goddamn pine and musk smell nearly makes me fall apart.

"I got your package," he says in the silence.

Ah, right. I'd followed through with Esme's suggestion by mailing him the ashes of the belongings he left here.

I don't answer.

"I miss you so much," he says, angling his head to get a better look at me.

I shift him back. "Stop moving."

"Do you miss me too?"

"Don't," I snap, though my voice is a whisper. I clear my throat. "Let's not do this. What's done is done."

"You don't believe that."

"I have to."

There's so much I want to say, but it won't make any difference. He broke my trust. Our entire relationship was founded on a lie and he knowingly and purposely kept it from me. Taking me on vacation only made it worse.

I almost told him I loved him—and now I don't trust myself. I thought I was making the right calls in my life. Finally, just *finally*, I wouldn't be the first person people underestimate. I convinced myself I wasn't the person I vowed never to become, compromising my long-standing values for a man. He tried to do better, and I thought it was what he wanted.

There's no point in having that discussion with Tristan now—or ever. He's drunk and likely won't remember a thing.

Despite it all, I find myself saying, "You shouldn't have come here."

I can't help that I crave his conversation. I'm tired of

telling myself I don't miss him when I ache for his company again.

"I wanted to see you," he says. "I think about you all the time." He releases a sardonic chuckle. "Believe it or not, I'd be a bigger mess if not for Poe."

I blink. Poe? I forgot about the cat in the Maldives; I assumed he gave Poe to another shelter in the country. "You kept him?"

Tristan nods, eyes closed. "He's my best friend. I have a million pictures I've been wanting to send to you."

My heart twinges as I finish cleaning the final drop of blood from his temple to his chin to reveal a two-inch gash. The bleeding stopped so I unscrew a homemade salve with comfrey and plantain leaves.

"What is that?"

"An ointment to help with healing."

He crinkles his nose at the yellow balm. "What's in it?"

"Herbs. Now sit still." I feel him leaning into my hand as I place the ointment on the wound and I honestly can't tell if it's out of affection or trying to stay conscious. I place an adhesive bandage on his head before backing away. My throat clogs with emotion; I need distance between us.

I don't like seeing him drunk. It reminds me of Dad and is a whole other bucket of trauma that I can't deal with right now, so I bring Tristan to the couch and lay him on his side.

"Thank you, love," he mumbles, taking my hand before I have a chance to pull away. He holds it like his lifeline, pressing a kiss to my palm.

A few tears break free, and I rip away and head to my closet, needing the comfort of an enclosed space. Why do I feel that I can forgive him? My heart still aches for him, but it's my heart that landed me in this crippling misery.

I'm not sure I can admit that our breakup took a six-four no-nonsense billionaire and turned him into a bumbling drunk fool. It tells me he might actually care. And if he does—

I drop onto the ground between the shroud of my clothes. Seconds later, Daisy finds me and I cuddle her big body. I try to nap on the floor for almost two hours before getting up to make coffee. There's no use in trying to get some sleep.

My instinct is to handle this alone; I've dealt with my entire relationship with Tristan alone. But I promised Nina I wouldn't shut her out anymore. I take out my phone to call her.

"Hello?" Nina answers, her voice sleepy and slurred.

"Shit, did I wake you?" I can usually count on her being up and bright with the sun.

"I'm good," she deadpans, but I'd bet her eyes are still closed. "I'm here. It's Maia." I'm guessing she's talking to Wesley. "What's wrong?"

I glance at the kitchen threshold from my spot at the table. "Tristan's here."

"*WHAT?*"

I flinch from her loud voice. "Jeez, don't panic. He's asleep."

"Why is he there? What happened?" I hear Wesley in the background begging her to keep it down.

"He was drunk. He took an Uber or something here, but he fell and had blood all over his face. I didn't know what else to do, so I cleaned him up and put him on the couch. And then I waited for the sun to come up before calling you. He was trying to apologize and I just..." I pause, fury building inside me at the emotion pricking my eyes for the umpteenth time in the last few hours. "I don't trust myself."

"I'm coming over," Nina says without pause. Wesley immediately protests in the background.

"Wait, wait. No. What's going on?"

My sister explains the situation, and her husband tries to stop her from getting up again.

"You need to rest right now. You're about to give birth."

"I don't give a shit. My baby sister needs me right now."

Both remorse and affection flood my heart.

"I'll go," Wesley insists. "I'll just be there to make sure he leaves."

"That's fine with me," I say quickly. "You should rest, Neen. I'll come see you later this morning. Promise."

"Are you sure?"

"Yes. I really just need a cockblocker."

"Wonderful," my brother-in-law groans sarcastically.

After hanging up, I drag myself into the bathroom to put myself together. I let Poppy and Daisy outside because it certainly doesn't help to see my children are still in love with him, too.

When Wesley arrives, I let him through the gate before moving to the sleeping man on my couch. I sit on the low coffee table in front of him.

I touch his shoulder. "Tristan."

He flinches awake, tossing himself on his back. His eyes squeeze shut. My stomach tightens and so quickly do I regret calling Nina and saying yes to Wesley coming over. I want this time alone with him. My logic is telling me I shouldn't, and I know I made the right choice, but *I still want him.*

But I don't trust him.

Tristan scrubs his eyes, letting his hand fall across his face. "What did I do?"

"You showed up here drunk—and bloody."

My breath hitches when he soberly meets my gaze, his fingers drifting to the bandage on his temple. He deflates.

"Shit."

The hours-old memories come back, the sinking in my gut when I heard the slur of his voice. The faraway look in his eyes. It reminds me of my dad.

I sniffle, failing to keep the emotion out of my voice. "You know I don't like seeing you drunk."

His eyes soften as he drags himself onto an elbow. "I know, love. I'm so sorry." He covers my trembling hands with his and I can't help threading my fingers through his. "I'm sorry about all of it. I—"

"Maia."

Tristan and I flinch at Wesley's voice from the doorway. My brother-in-law eyes our joined hands. Welp. He's definitely telling Nina about that.

I jerk away with a deep breath, swatting at the barely shed tears. I turn to Tristan, but pointedly keep my eyes from his. "You should go."

His head lowers, and I knot my hands together as he pulls himself to his feet with a grunt. Awkward tension lingers as he wades across the living room, past a stern Wesley.

I jump when the front door closes behind him. Poppy and Daisy's barks outside are muffled.

"Are you okay?" Wesley asks, and I realize it's the first time he's ever asked me that question.

I sniffle, bouncing my knee from my seat on the coffee table. "No."

He folds his arms across his chest, and though it makes

him look menacing, I've known him long enough to know it's from discomfort. "I'm not quite sure what I'm supposed to say in a situation like this."

I chuckle despite the tears clouding my eyes. "Just get out, you weirdo."

"Do you need a hug?"

"No."

He exhales in relief. "Thank god."

I chuckle again, harder this time. I grab a throw pillow off the couch and launch it at him. "Get *out!*"

He catches it before flinging it my way too fast for me to block it. "Made you laugh. I win," he calls, backing out of the living room.

Okay, maybe there's half of a perk to having a brother after all.

CHAPTER FIFTY
TRISTAN

Being that close to Maia again is a wake-up call.

If I want her back, I need to work for it. Moping and hanging out with Poe isn't going to do anything.

When a car takes me home to my studio, I open my sketchbooks and rip out every drawing of Maia I completed despite my pounding headache. She doesn't know that I sketch her often. I usually make mental notes when I'm with her, remembering to add the tiny freckle beside her belly button. The scar below her knee. The birthmark behind her ear. Everyone has a million little details about their body, and I wanted to memorize each one on Maia.

I gather all of the drawings I have of her and spend hours upon hours shading and sketching a portrait. I work on the piece until my hand is cramping and covered in lead. Poe demands my attention every so often, forcing me to take breaks.

I call out of work for the following two days and ignore most of Augustus's calls as I work on Maia's piece. Eventually I'll look at pictures of her to check the proportions, but first I want to sculpt exactly how I see her. I want Maia to know what I see when I look at her.

The soft mass caves under my thumb as I sculpt the top of her eye socket. I scrape each detail and hair of an eyebrow, studying sketches and reflecting on my memories; the darkest freckle by her left eye, the extra curly baby hair by her right ear. I slice detail into every curl that blows in a frozen breeze.

Just the sculpture won't win her over. It might for the moment, but I can't ignore the inheritance again. Losing her makes me realize how little I care about Space Tech. If I could have Maia, a studio to sculpt in, and all of *our* animals together, I'm content. I don't need anything else. There's only one way to show her that.

Maia didn't steal my heart. She can't steal what she's always had. Nothing could've stopped us from being together. Whatever path ahead is meant to happen. The more I work on the sculpture, the less worried I am.

Our paths will lead back to each other. I'm sure of it.

Jazz music blares through the speakers and barely allows me to hear the incessant banging on my door. The *thump thump thump* rattles the hinges.

I pause the music, grumbling, "All right, all right," as it continues. I peer through the peephole from a distance so the rattling from the banging fist doesn't knock into my face.

"Augustus?" I unlock and open the door and my assistant barges in without another word, shoving past me.

"Okay, I know I'm already crossing a line by being here but this has gone on long enough so I need you to shut it and listen," he says. "I know you're upset and depressed, but you've got to get over it, man. I don't know what happened with you and the princess but if you're not going to pull yourself together and do something about it, you've got to look ahead because your absence is noticeable and I cannot keep lying for you—"

"Augustus—"

"I mean this with all due respect—"

"*Augustus*—"

"But in other words, get off your arse and make a decision."

I pause, waiting for him to end his tirade of criticism. He sighs, out of breath, and I watch him with crossed arms. "Are you finished?"

He gulps. "Am I fired?"

"No."

"Then yes. I'm finished." Then, he adds quietly, "Sir."

"Great. Now turn around." I nod behind him to the work in progress.

"Wha—*oh*." He squints. "Is that her?"

The pose and proportions are finalized. The entire process is laborious, but the detailing will take the longest. I clean one of my tools with a rag.

"Think she'll like it?"

"I should hope so," he says, adjusting his glasses and circling the sculpture. "It's very good."

I clear my throat, unaccustomed to praise. "I'm glad you're here because I have a few large proposals and contracts I need drafted."

Augustus creases his brows. "What kind of contracts?"

"To transfer my position as Chief Executive Officer."

CHAPTER FIFTY-ONE

MAIA

On November third, I'm officially an aunt.

Wesley called me at two in the afternoon to tell me her water broke. I had to wait to be picked up and brought to the hospital because of the crowds and press outside. But by the time I got there two hours later, Cordelia Rose was already born. I'm grateful it was a quick, smooth delivery so my sister doesn't have to endure hours of pain and labor.

I dart over to Nina the second I step into her hospital room—which looks more of a hotel room—to envelop her in a hug.

"Are you okay? How are you feeling?"

She looks weary, but somehow manages to glow. "I'm all right. Sore. Tired."

I squeeze her hand. "You did it. I'm so proud of you, sis."

She attempts a weak smile, then looks over to Wesley who I notice for the first time. He holds a bundle of blankets in his arms and it's weird to see such a large man hold something so small and fragile.

"Want to meet your niece?" my sister asks.

Let the tears begin.

I stay at the hospital as long as I can.

Aunt Beverly and the rest of our mom's side have filled the room with flowers and Dad video-chatted just before boarding a plane to come here.

Plenty of advisors and assistants have asked Nina if she wanted to make a statement and said it's tradition for royals to show the country their newborn. She, Wesley, and I shut it down before they could finish their sentences.

I take plenty of pictures on my digital camera for a photo album before giving my sister and brother-in-law privacy to adjust as a little family.

Dad stays at my house again and ever since his last visit, he has less shit to say about Nina and her decisions. Either his first grandchild softened him or Wesley said something. Both are equally plausible. While I visit my sister every day to hold my niece and help out around the house so the tired new parents can rest, Dad stops by just a couple of times.

"Where did you get this cat again?" he asks one night, when it's just us having dinner as Callie passes through the kitchen.

"The Maldives. She was a stray."

"When did you go to the Maldives?"

I hesitate, poking at my vegetarian chicken parm. "Last month."

His brows lift. "How come you never tell me about these things?"

I bite back a retort. Perhaps because he didn't tell me my step-grandmother died until months later. Perhaps because he thinks I'm some heartless hussy who leaves men heartbroken in my wake. Perhaps because he thinks my preferred pastime is telling people they're wrong. The last one might have a sliver of truth, but I stand by the rest.

Instead of arguing, I shrug.

"Whatever happened to that guy you were seeing? Tri—"

"We broke up."

His expression falls. "Oh, no! What happened?"

I shake my head, debating how honest I should be. But he always thinks I'm the one who's in the wrong, so maybe this is my one chance to get his sympathy. My one chance to get him on *my* side.

"He was using me to get his inheritance of five hundred million."

Dad's jaw drops. "*Five hundred million?* You're serious?"

I nod.

"What do you mean he was using you?"

"He needed volunteer hours and came to Felicity Gardens. He lied and told everyone he wanted to learn about the earth and environment. I was the only one who didn't trust him, so he manipulated me."

He releases a sharp breath. "Why would he do that? You could've split the money!"

Of course. Of fucking course. Does he know me at all? Does he know my beliefs, what I work toward every day?

"Why don't you ask him that?"

"Relax, Maia. It was just a question."

"It's always just a question."

"You don't need to be nasty," he argues, his tone

clipped. "Your sister just had a baby. Put aside your anger toward me for once."

I bite back my tears of frustration, grabbing my plate and rising from the table.

"Here we go," he mumbles, and I have to stop myself from throwing the food in his face as I leave the kitchen to finish eating elsewhere.

A sudden wave of grief washes over me over the fact that Dad and I may never have the kind of relationship I want. I long accepted that he wouldn't be the perfect father, but at least I had hope we would get better. Some points in time are better than others, and I'm caught between being grateful I have a father at all and wanting to preserve my peace of mind.

I need to accept the fact that some relationships won't heal. This might very well be the best we can do.

I want Tristan back.

After realizing my relationship with Dad is at the best point it can ever be, I see the potential with Tristan.

We can heal. *We* can find our way back to each other.

It might be stupid to even think that, but it's true. There's a twinge in my heart that tells me he might not be as guilty as I paint him to be. What would he have told me? How would he have framed it? Maybe I should hear him out.

I need to talk to Nina about it, but it's not the time. I push the thoughts aside to continue helping her around the house and braiding her hair in a few cornrows so she doesn't have to worry about it. Cordelia is the first baby I've held that doesn't cry from being in my arms and it makes me love this little munchkin so much more.

For two weeks, I've been so busy working, helping my sister, and trying to survive being near Dad that I have less time to mourn my relationship with Tristan. I don't know how I can get him back, but I also know I won't chase him. He was still the one in the wrong, and I can only hope that he'll try to rekindle us soon.

One Sunday, I get a text from Raven, one of Nina's closest friends from back home. She's supposed to fly out in a few weeks, but she wants my help to surprise my sister. I meet both her and husband Zafir out front while Nina is in the backyard getting some fresh air. Summers in Maldana may be brutal, but autumns and winters are perfectly bearable. It's a balmy fifty degrees outside and is perfect for leggings and a cozy sweater.

The Christmas season is rapidly approaching and to be frank, the holidays when you're rich are way more enjoyable. I can tell myself it's about the family around you that makes it special, and though it's true, I don't have the same worries I had growing up. Pretending otherwise would be ignorant.

"Oh, you cut your hair!" I whisper-yell at Raven, who once had curls almost as long as mine. Now she rocks a curly bob and it fits her look as a future lawyer. She's not far into law school. "It looks so cute and fits you so well!"

"Thanks, Maia. I haven't seen you in forever." Raven grins, wrapping me in a hug. She's the epitome of cozy with her cable knit set of matching sweater and joggers. Raven and I aren't close enough to spend time together without Nina, but I always enjoy seeing her.

"Your Majesty," says Zafir with a bow of his head.

Before he can say anything more, I wave a hand before

extending it to shake. "Please, don't bother with that. It's just Maia."

Even though Raven and Nina have been friends for years and Nina played matchmaker to get them back together, I've never met him before. They had gotten married around the same time Nina did, but I remember my sister telling me they'd eloped. Zafir reminds me of Tristan in the idea that they're both pretty-boys—a charming smile, expensive clothes.

"Wait—aren't you in the middle of your season?" I ask, remembering that he's in the NFL and November is the height of football season.

"Yeah, I'll fly back tomorrow, but I wanted to see Nina and the baby."

I smile at how my sister has touched so many people that they would put themselves through almost twenty hours of flying just to see her briefly.

I bring them inside before fetching Nina. She's typing on her phone when she walks in and flinches so hard it flies out of her hand.

"*Ravenohmygod!*" she screeches as I scramble to catch her phone. She throws herself at Raven. "What are you doing here? You weren't supposed to fly in for another few weeks!"

"I couldn't stand not being here for you after you gave birth. I can do some remote work from here. Zafir has to leave tomorrow morning, but he wanted to see you."

Nina wraps Zafir in a quick hug just as Wesley comes downstairs from putting Cordelia down for a nap. In a rare sight, his expression lights up at Zafir and Raven. They greet each other all over again and I watch, dreaming what it would be like if Tristan were here with me. Of how he might get along with my family and friends.

In the midst of conversation, Nina slinks aside to me, nodding her head. "It's okay to miss him."

"Oh my *god*," I wail. "Stop knowing literally everything I'm thinking."

She laughs. "Trust me, I wish I wasn't like this. Mom hormones mean I notice everything ten times more. You won't be able to get away with shit."

CHAPTER FIFTY-TWO
TRISTAN

Romèo suddenly decided to visit me again and it's so uncharacteristic that I have to mention it.

His reasoning for the visit includes both the women and to see his only friend. Apparently, he avoids Italian women because it's impacted his work at home.

"Don't shit where you sleep," he said.

We're at a rooftop lounge in Kosita that overlooks the city instead of going to the Lynx Room, something that gets old fast for me. I'd be perfectly content if I never stepped foot in there again.

"I've seen you more times this year than I have in the past decade," I point out as I puff on a cigar.

Romèo shrugs nonchalantly. "Making some changes."

"Mate, come on. It's me. I've known you—"

"I know how long we've been friends."

"Then what the hell is going on?" I ask, my tone equally clipped. "You dropped off the face of earth for, like, five years, somewhat reappeared, now this."

He runs a hand through his dark hair, gripping a fistful in the back. He's stiff and awkward. "Trust me when I say

367

that not telling you is protecting you. It's best if no one knows we're friends."

"The fuck does that even mean?"

"That my family isn't innocent. That I have skeletons in my closet and the Romèo you knew when we were kids was tortured out of me a long time ago."

I flinch. The first two points are understandable enough to get me to back off. But tortured?

I lean closer. "If you're in trouble, I can help you."

He offers a pitiful smile. "I appreciate the offer. My family isn't perfect, but there's nowhere I'd rather be."

I'd believe that—if I hadn't known him for over twenty years. There's a sad twinge in his eyes that wasn't there when we were kids, and it's more than learning the harsh realities of the world. Something has happened. Does he mean his own family tortured him?

We got into plenty of mischief in our childhood, but I remember him well-behaved when it mattered. Please, thank you, yes ma'am, no ma'am. He never talked back the way I would. Those few years in secondary school, he was like a brother to me. He spent more time with me and my nanny than in his home country.

"Onto better things," Romèo says, dipping a slice of rosemary bread into a bowl of seasoned oil. "You finished the princess sculpture?"

I wish he were comfortable enough to tell me what happened, but it seems we're going to be friends again for a while—meaning there will be another chance to bring this up. So I let the topic go.

"Uh, yeah, it's in the kiln."

"And you're *really* giving her the company?"

"If she wants it." I turn my thoughts to everything that's been plaguing me the last month. "It's not worth it.

Space Tech. Five hundred million. I can't stomach the idea of continuing the legacy of my grandfather anymore."

Weeks ago, I'd told Romèo over the phone what Nico had done, and he was horrified and sorry for me. Once I succeed in getting Maia back, I'm going to invest my resources in finding Danica. Even if I never see her again, I need to know what happened after my father took her.

"When are you going to offer it?"

"She's attending a private auction next week—supposedly to try and buy an artifact from a London museum and return it to some Asian country. I doubt she'll attend anything else for a while and I can forget just showing up at her house or work. She wouldn't let me in. It's my only chance."

"The queen just had a baby, right?"

I nod with another cigar drag. I imagine Maia has been doting on the baby and taking care of her sister since then. Though I've met Nina only twice, I can surmise they're fiercely protective of each other.

Maia will forgive me if everything goes to plan. Even then, I'll have to work to gain the trust of her family, too.

CHAPTER FIFTY-THREE
MAIA

The Carnegie auction is one of the rare chances for someone to buy back an oracle bone script from the Qin Dynasty.

There's been negative buzz online about the Carnegie family loaning the artifact to the British Museum instead of sending it home to China where it belongs. Alina had brought it to my attention because the family is having the auction in Maldana, where they spend the holidays. We figured it would be a good opportunity to use our wealth and influence for good. After all, my sister is in the process of dismantling a centuries-old monarch.

The institution made it clear they won't give me money to help buy it back—especially after they ended up donating more than anticipated after the auction Tristan outbid a man for me. I'll have to use a combination of my donated estate money and my take-home pay. My team will have to determine which of my causes can stand to have a temporary pause in funding.

"Your Majesty," begins Dale Carnegie—one of the many English snobs I try to keep away from. "It's truly an honor to have you attending this event. Thank you for making time in your busy schedule and please, give Her Majesty the Queen my biggest congratulations on the baby."

A year ago, I would've told him the exact reason I'm here: that I want to do the right thing he clearly won't.

But this Maia is more refined and mature. I nod, graciously accepting his respectful bow. "I will pass on the message. Thank you for allowing me to attend this evening."

I haven't been to the history museum since I came to Maldana for the first time. Nina and I have already successfully returned any artifacts we shouldn't have in exchange for loaned exhibits instead.

Alina sits beside me in the crowd and it's much different than the auction months ago. This time, there's no dinner served and it's more like a cocktail party. Lyla typically accompanies me for events like this—and the painful memory of our dead friendship twists my heart.

Upon raising the paddle once, twice, three times, I realize just how demeaning that other auction was. We raised money for important campaigns and something great certainly came out of it, but I was paraded on the stage like I was no more than a lifeless artifact from the Maldana History Museum.

After out-bidding the others, I obtain the artifact for 1.1 million euros. My team can budget it in less than a year, but it's been a while since I spent that kind of money. It makes my skin itch—and it's no big deal for most of the people in this room.

Alina and I step into the hallway and I flinch at the person before me.

"Augustus!" I blurt. "What are you doing here?"

He pushes his glasses up his nose and bows. "Your

Majesty... It's good to see you again. Uh—I was actually hoping I would run into you."

My chest tightens. Does this mean Tristan is nearby? I'm not sure if I like or hate that idea. "Really? Why?"

The first time I met Augustus, he was bumbling and nervous while I was confident. Now it's the opposite. He slides his hands into his pockets.

"Do you remember when I gave you my boss's address and you said you owed me?"

"Yes..."

He nods in the direction behind him, hinting that I walk alongside him. I dismiss Alina for the moment and follow him down the hall.

"You know I meant within reason, right?"

Augustus chokes out a laugh and I must be in another universe. He's more sure of himself than I've ever seen him.

"Yes, of course, Your Majesty."

We stride down the marble hall of the museum, elegant arches flanking us. The chattering crowds far behind us and the clack of my heels are the only sounds. My heart beats faster with each silent second and my dress is suddenly too tight to bear. The soft black fabric wraps around my neck and covers my arms, but the dip in my back helps me breathe.

Augustus reaches for a door handle just as I muster the courage to ask, "How is he?"

I haven't seen Tristan since he left my house hungover almost a month ago. I miss him so much it hurts. I miss what we were.

Augustus purses his lips in response, and I get a hint of the nerdy, awkward assistant who stumbled over his words the first time we met. He beckons me into the exhibit room.

"Not good," he says. "He's been an annoying mess, if I'm being honest..."

I only make it a few steps before stopping from the hook in my throat. My head starts spinning.

Tristan. Here. Now.

This can't be happening.

The one person I've ached to see for weeks is in front of me—I don't know if my heart can take it. I know I want him back, but I haven't prepared for it. I haven't thought about what I would say.

"Hear him out," Augustus adds as he slinks out of the room. "That's my request."

I wish my hair weren't in an updo; I feel more exposed to Tristan and I don't like it.

"Hi," he finally says, and I already want to cry.

It pains me that he looks so damn good in his crisp black button-up open just enough to reveal his gold chain and tattoos which have always been the death of me. My cheeks warm at the realization that we're matching in black.

I can't do this. I need to talk to Nina ASAP because I'm ready to throw myself at him and forget everything he put me through.

I shake my head, but Tristan walks closer, his footsteps almost silent in the display room filled with paintings and sculptures.

"Listen. Please. You don't have to speak. You don't even have to look at me," he says.

I tighten my jaw against any words I might utter, knowing that I would instantly start crying.

I stare at his offered hand, the decision staring me down. Taking it feels like I'm betraying myself, but shutting him out is killing me slowly.

I place my hand in his, the warm skin sending tingles through my body. He leads me over to a bench and gestures for me to sit down beside a stack of files someone must have left here.

Relief from the pressure of standing shudders through my legs and back. I fucking hate high heels.

My chest constricts the moment Tristan kneels in front of me, eye contact never faltering.

"Yes," he begins, "I first looked at Felicity Gardens as an easy way to get my inheritance. I went there hoping to talk you into a donation so I could move on. I already knew your opinions, but you still surprised me. You saw through my bullshit before talking to me. You were giving me attitude while wearing pig slippers and all I could think of was how beautiful you are. And we started working together and there were some comments I regret making. But I was completely shaken by your wisdom and ideas." He kisses my knuckles. "You talk a lot but I love everything you say. I love your passion. I love your intelligence. I love your generosity. I love your beauty. I love *you*, Maia. Nothing could have stopped me from falling for you."

The tears have long since freed themselves. A sob chokes out from my chest and I rip my eyes away from his. All I can remember is the pain and betrayal of the day I found out. I swallow thickly to steady my voice.

"You broke my heart."

My words break him. His face melts and his shoulders fall as he sinks toward me, reaching out to wipe my tears. "I know, my love. And I'm so sorry. I'll never forgive myself for not giving you the respect of telling you sooner. I need to show you how sorry I am and how much you mean to me."

Tristan reaches for the stack of files I thought belonged

to someone else. I notice a slight tremor in his hands as he offers the first one.

"First, the inheritance. I'd offer you the money if I thought you'd accept it, so instead I have a list of every cause and campaign the money would fund should you choose to sign. There's also all of Nico's will for you, too, so you know I'm not hiding anything." Without letting me digest this, he hands me another folder, this one much heftier. "These are the receipts and plans for everything we talked about those months ago. The compatible technology, funding agriculture restoration, renewable energy efforts, education. By the end of the month, I'll no longer be a billionaire." And just when I think my heart can't fill anymore, he hands me the last folder. "And this is a transfer of power contract for you to assume CEO of Space Technolog—"

"*Wait*—" I finally burst. "You're *giving* me your company?"

"Maia... *you* are the most important person in my life. I love *you*. I don't need a company—especially when it was created by a monster. I have enough money to retire now and I'm more than happy to spend those days sculpting. But none of that matters if you're not by my side."

My mouth opens, and I struggle to find the words. "I... I don't want Space Tech."

A smile tugs at his lips despite his worried eyes. "You don't have to accept it, love. I just need you to know it's not worth more than you. Even if you turn it down, the second folder lists all of the sustainable changes we're making, effective immediately."

"But what about the board? You said they could vote you out."

"Then they vote me out."

My heart was right.

I couldn't ignore the lying, but my gut told me there was more.

Logic betrayed me, too. I cut him off the way I should have done before we even kissed. It was way too late for that.

I close the distance between us, my lips finally finding home again. The files slip off my lap as Tristan pulls me closer.

My body burns with the suppressed desire over the last two months, and our kiss quickly turns needy.

Tristan hums against my lips. "Um, actually—I had one last thing to show you."

I pull away. "More?"

"I'm desperate, love. I wasn't walking out of here without your forgiveness."

My face warms as he guides me to my feet. I was too wrapped up in him to notice that one of the displays has a curtain around it. He rushes off to the side to operate a pulley.

The sight snatches my breath in a gasp.

I force myself to blink, unable to register the fact that it's *me*. In stone. Or clay. Or whatever he used to sculpt *me*.

I'm wrapped in a sheet like in antiquity, my hair—my curls—flying behind me in an eternal breeze with a few strewn across my face. I reach out to touch it, but flinch back in fear I'll break something. It wouldn't be the first time. I look at Tristan with tears in my eyes once more.

"You can touch it," he says.

The sculpture stops at my belly button and shows my curves, yet manages to be respectful at the same time. One arm wrapped around my stomach, the other rests on my shoulder.

I run my fingers along my nose, my lips, my cheeks. The ridges of my hair are so delicately detailed that only a true professional could complete it.

It looks *exactly* like me.

"Tristan..."

"Do you like it?" he asks, his tone quiet and hopeful as he strides toward me. "I did the majority of it from memory and the sketches I have of you."

I turn toward him just before he wraps his arms around me. "You drew pictures of me?"

He blushes. "I know you said not to—"

I slam my lips against his as my love grows for him each second, something I didn't think was possible.

There's nothing to debate. Tristan loves me; it's never been clearer or brighter. He laid himself bare and offered me everything and I finally feel safe enough to do the same. I clamp my teeth around his bottom lip and slide my fingers under his shirt collar to touch the chest I missed so much. He moans.

"Love," he mutters, "not here."

I pout.

He leans down to kiss behind my ear, setting my skin on fire. "I know, but I have a lot to make up for."

"All the more reason to take off your pants."

Tristan smirks, taking my hand to kiss the inside of my wrist. "Let's go home."

CHAPTER FIFTY-FOUR
TRISTAN

I t feels like I've been underwater my whole life and am being thrust into crisp, mountainous air for the first time.

I couldn't keep my hands off Maia if someone paid me, scratched me, or stabbed me. If not for the lack of a partition in the car, my head would already be underneath her dress. Instead, we're wrapped in one another's arms, exchanging kisses every few seconds whether it's a shoulder, a hand, a neck, or lips.

"I missed you so fucking much," I mumble into her neck. She jumps with a giggle when I nip her skin. Her intoxicating rosy smell makes me dizzy, but that's okay. Even if I'm dizzy all my life, I'll be the happiest man alive.

We rush inside her house, stopped by the utter bombardment of Daisy and Poppy. Their excitement is too much to ignore, and though I want to ask about how Callie settled in, I have other things on my mind.

"While you do that," says Maia as she saunters away, "I'll go get undressed."

I pry myself away from the animals with ease and

scoop up my woman over my shoulder. She squeals with laughter and there has never been such a calming sound. Her happiness is my peace. I've been starved of her my whole life yet she's become so ingrained in me like I've known her for centuries. Our past lives have crossed. I'm sure of it.

Once Maia orders Poppy and Daisy to leave her bedroom, I shut the door with my foot and rest her on the bed.

"Don't move," I command before rushing off to the bathroom to wash my hands. I just pet the dogs, after all.

When I return a minute later, I find Maia utterly naked and standing up on her knees. The air squeezes from my lungs and my heart lurches. Her hair is still in an updo, giving me a completely unobstructed view of her perfect body. Perfect legs, perfect hips—

If I don't touch her soon, I'm going to finish in my pants like an eager teenage boy. I un-cuff one of my sleeves and manage to say, "I told you not to move."

I was looking forward to taking her clothes off.

"We're in a relationship now," she says, and those words from her mouth make me harder. "I think we should establish up front who's in charge."

I cross the space between us and hook my arm between her legs, my hand spanning across her arse to tug her closer. My body tenses at how wet she is. Her arousal sticks to me like aloe and there's not a chance in hell I could ever be in control.

"Have I not made it clear it's you?" I ask, my voice thick. "Have I not spent my evening begging?"

A sly, sexy grin pulls at her lips. "You *were* begging."

"And I'll do it again."

Maia presses her mouth to mine, running her tongue

across my lower lip. "I don't need you to beg, Tristan. I need you to fuck me."

As if struck, I reach for my shirt and start unbuttoning frantically while kicking off my shoes. She laughs and reclines on the bed, her ankles crossed and her knees tucked to her chest to reveal her pussy. I don't hesitate to dive in, lapping at one of the things I missed most as I fumble with my pants. Her laughter quickly fades to moans, her nails raking the back of my head.

Her delicious taste elicits a hum from the back of my throat as her moans feed my own desire. My tongue finds the precise rhythm that makes her body twitch and I flick the pattern relentlessly until her chest starts to rise off the mattress. Her thighs suddenly clamp around my head, body convulsing.

Fuck, I missed this so much.

Feeling her soft skin in my hands. The vanilla scent of her bedside candle, even knocking into one of her million fucking plants. I climb on top of her, dipping my head to connect our lips.

"I love you," I mumble, grateful I can finally say it aloud.

"I love you, t—"

I cut her off by pushing inside of her for old time's sake. My eyes fall shut as I sink into euphoria. She twitches under me, releasing a moan as she gets wetter by the second and I fit so snugly inside of her that my breath leaves my body. She wraps her legs around me, her nails raking down my back.

"You're so tight," I mutter, sliding in and out at an excruciatingly slow pace.

"No, you're just fucking huge."

I chuckle and brush my thumb along her bottom lip. I

tense when she tugs it between her teeth. "I've missed your filthy mouth, too."

She holds every bit of me in her hands. We clash and move in sync at the same time and there's no universe we don't end up together. She's destined for me, and I for her.

The sounds of our moans and slapping skin fill the room and I squeeze my eyes shut again, fighting to hold off a little longer, just ten more seconds to feel this complete bliss. I fall apart entirely when she kisses me, her tongue clashing against mine.

"So you *are* a minute man," she says tauntingly.

I laugh in spite of myself, dropping my face against her neck. "I hate you."

"You love me."

"More than anything in the fucking world."

In the morning, I wake up to Daisy pouncing on my back and knocking the air from my lungs. Her paws rake across my skin as she pants wildly. She smells like the outdoors— Maia must have taken her and the other animals outside.

"*Dai-sy!*" I groan, protecting my head from her nails. The friendly giant licks my back with good-morning kisses —not quite the one I wanted them from.

I hear Maia's sweet laugh as she mocks my accent. "*Dai-sy.*"

She whistles and Daisy pushes off me as a head start off the bed. Her weight dips onto the bed and she pushes me onto my back and I've been jostled around too much for someone who woke up thirty seconds ago.

She drops onto my chest and I trap her with my arms,

blinking the sleep from my eyes. This is the first morning I wake up and she's officially and unequivocally mine.

I want this every fucking day.

"Is it too soon to get married?" I ask, brushing a curl from her face.

Her eyes widen. "Yes, it's too soon."

I huff. "Fine."

Callie hops onto the bed and snuggles against my leg. I reach down to pet her with a free hand. I wonder if she remembers me. "How's she settling in?"

Maia grins. "She and Sage hit it off right away. I've never seen her so playful before! Callie's been a sweetie from the jump even though she's already broken a few of my pots and tried eating a plant. What about Poe? I want to see those pictures you were talking about."

I grin, reaching toward the nightstand for my phone to show her the literal hundreds of pictures I have of my cat. We spend the morning discussing our pets, and it's like we created a little family I wouldn't trade for the world.

"I trust you," Nina says over the phone, "but I'm iffy. I don't like that he made you cry."

"He gave her a *rock*," Wesley says in the background, his voice echoing. "He loves her, for fuck's sake."

Of course Nina told him that.

It's still my most prized possession. I pace my backyard, a blanket wrapped around me as my dogs and ducks roam, play, and shit. Christmas is less than a week away and I decided to take off work between now and the new year.

Tristan and I agreed to make the announcement about Space Technologies at the beginning of January. The sustainable policies will be met with pushback and we want to enjoy this peaceful time together. I'm grateful Nina's on board with us being back together; her approval is what I need most.

"So he can come to the holiday party?" I ask.

"Of course! I need to threaten him to never hurt you again."

I laugh. "Okay, just go easy."

"Never. Bring Esme, too! She's married, right? Her husband can come."

"Are you sure? That's a lot of people." She gave birth a month and a half ago and is having what seems like a crap ton of people over.

"Only family will meet Cori, but for the most part she'll be away from everyone."

I imagine Wesley will be happy to sneak away from the crowds to be with Cordelia. She's the most precious newborn to ever exist, born with a full head of hair that's only getting longer seemingly by the day.

Just as Nina and I hang up, Tristan finds his way outside. "Breakfast is ready."

I wrap the blanket tighter around me as butterflies swarm my stomach. A thousand tingles erupt inside of me as he strides across the grass and dips his head to kiss me.

He's mine. Tristan is *all mine*.

His love is all-consuming. We're naturally unguarded with each other. Moths to flames. Two halves of a whole. All of those metaphors. We meet every single one because that's just it—we're *everything*.

I hate entertaining the idea that a break was good for us. Our time apart was miserable, but now there's a plan. An entire packet approaching my every concern. It shouldn't have happened this way, and I can blame Tristan for that, yet there's nothing stopping us now. It's like he was tailored just for me.

He can be too pompous for his own good, but I love him regardless. I love him in his bad and I'm enamored with his good because I know that he truly cares for people. I saw it in the Maldives during our volunteer days; his broad smile was infectious and he ended up doing twice the amount of work as I did.

"I love you," he says, and his brow lifts when I pout. "What?"

"I was gonna say that."

"You still can."

I perch on my toes to kiss him. "I love you."

"I love you, too."

We break apart at the sound of Poppy crying out from getting run over by Daisy. The sound alerts Elliot and Olivia, who flap their wings and quack loudly. In turn, Callie gears up to pounce on Olivia, and it's a good thing her nails were just trimmed. Otherwise, she would shred my ducks apart.

"You sure you want to be with me?" I ask with a chuckle, nodding toward my animals. "We're a packaged deal."

Tristan smiles before dropping another kiss on my lips. "There's nowhere I'd rather be."

It's Christmas Eve and I'm slightly grateful, albeit offended, that Dad and Ruby opted for a hotel rather than staying with me. He knows Tristan and I are back together and claims it's to give us privacy, but part of me wants to rub it in his face that in spite of his claims that no one would put up with my attitude, Tristan is happy to be with me.

Christmas dinner tomorrow will only be my sister, Wesley, Cordelia, my parents, and Tristan and me. Wesley's side of the family is traveling to Palfu to be with his grandparents, but apparently they'll be visiting before the new year to meet Cordelia. According to my sister, Wesley's grandparents have been Nina's biggest fans from the start.

I lean closer to my reflection to put the finishing

touches on my mascara. One of my favorite pastimes is getting dressed up only to pair it with cozy slippers, so in the holiday spirit, I'm wearing elf slippers with a bell at the tip. My off-the-shoulders dress is red with long sleeves and a white fur trim. It's too chilly not to wear stockings, but I'll put those on before we leave.

Behind me, Tristan lounges on my bed watching TV, one arm thrown behind his head as he waits for me. The only reason he's allowed on the bed with his outside clothes is because we haven't left yet. And Tristan has very precise hygiene habits that sometimes make me feel like a slob.

"Your phone vibrated," he calls suddenly. "You got a text."

"Who is it?"

"Uh—Roman."

"What?" Slight panic fills me; I hope he doesn't think I ever saw Roman again after that night at the Lynx Room. I shake it off and continue applying mascara.

"You can delete it."

"As in delete the message or block his number?"

I bite the inside of my cheek, slightly pleased at his possessiveness. I've been with possessive men before, but they weren't jealous because they wanted *me* to themselves; they wanted the princess.

"I mean, he's still my cousin's best friend—"

"Who you used to fuck."

I pause. Despite Roman and I actually being kind of friends, I have to consider if it's worth strife with Tristan. I don't want him to be upset.

I close my mascara and walk toward him, my slippers jingling with each step.

Tristan, with my phone in his hand, doesn't shift as I take his face in my hands and kiss him deeply.

"Block him for me. My code is Sage's birthday: 0317."

His lips catch mine again before I can leave, and I know I made the right decision. Roman isn't worth shit.

Moments after I return to the bathroom to finish my makeup, Tristan appears behind me. His hands find my hips, rubbing the suede fabric.

"Um." His nervous expression all but reveals what he's going to ask. "When we were apart... did you—"

"No," I say, turning to face him. "I didn't. And for what it's worth, I probably wouldn't have gone through with Roman even if you hadn't broken the door down."

"Probably?"

"I wouldn't have." I wrap my arms around his neck, raking my nails across the back of his head as memories of that horrible night flash across my mind. "I just kept thinking of us in the bathroom that night at the auction. And how I really didn't want any other man touching me."

Tristan tightens his arms around me, pressing his lips to mine. Even though I regret going out that night, I found out just how far he's willing to go for me. That should've been my first sign, but I was too hurt and shaken to see it.

He hoists me onto an empty part of the counter, his hands slipping under my dress. I hum against his mouth.

"Now? We have to leave soon."

"You wanted to be fucked on a bathroom counter, right?" He grips my thighs, his head dipping to my neck. "This is how he was touching you?"

My breath hitches, sparks tingling between my legs. "Yes."

The word falls from my lips subconsciously. Yes to both.

Yes to him. There's no point in resisting the feeling anymore
—I'll take him at any given moment.
     Forever.

CHAPTER FIFTY-SIX
TRISTAN

I'm nervous to meet Maia's family.

I never formally met her brother-in-law, Wesley, but he's mean-looking enough and I can only imagine how Maia described me when we were broken up.

However, when I meet Pierce Laffley, he shakes my hand and says, "It's good to see you again, son."

And I have a problem with how *little* of a problem he has with me.

Maia told him I used her. Then she told him she forgave me and included little detail about it.

And he has nothing to say about that?

Maia is worth protecting and he isn't doing a damn thing.

Wesley is indifferent and Nina is more reserved in our interactions. Maia thinks highly of her sister; it's her approval I need more than their father's.

Maia and I somehow managed to arrive early enough that we got to see Cordelia before her nap. It surprised me to learn she won't be given the title of princess, but I suppose it makes sense if the queen is dismantling the monarchy. I decline holding Cordelia, but seeing Maia coddling the baby stirs something inside of me. I lean over the two of them, shifting aside the blanket to reveal chubby cheeks.

"I like the thought of you as a mother."

Her eyes snap to mine. Even as she rocks Cordelia to sleep, she mutters to me, "Say that again and I'll give you a vasectomy myself."

I merely chuckle and kiss her temple. I'll never get tired of her ferocity.

As the party gathers and Cordelia naps, I finally find a moment alone with Wesley and Nina. Maia is off in the bathroom and the new parents are sitting on the couch with drinks in hand.

"Is everything okay?" Nina asks, and I school my nervous demeanor.

"Yes, I just—" I sit on the end of a chaise, my elbows on my knees as I tilt closer. "I wanted to apologize to both of you... I understand that it's not just Maia I have to make it up to—it's her family. And I sincerely apologize for the trouble I've caused. Especially with the timing of Cordelia's birth."

Nina looks at Wesley as if impressed, and I suddenly feel like I'm looking at Maia's parents when her real parents are in the sitting room with everyone else. Do I ask for her approval when I want to propose? I feel like I should.

While Wesley nods quietly, Nina shifts and says, "Maia isn't easy to win over. If she trusts you, I do, too." Her gaze narrows, making me bristle. "Your love for my sister is loud. And I admire that." She leans over and places her hand over mine, her diamond ring glinting in the light. From her sweet smile, I expect praise for how much I love Maia. Instead, she says, "But if you *ever* hurt her again, I *will* send my husband to silence you. Permanently."

I blink. "What?"

She pats me on the shoulder as she leaves. "Think about it."

I look at Wesley for some type of explanation, but his previously stony face has morphed into pride, his gaze following his wife.

"Threats are their way of welcoming you," he says to me, tossing back a swig of his drink. "I got a similar one from Maia. Something about breaking my neck."

I puff. "You got off easy. She threatened to slice off my balls and shove them down my throat."

Wesley raises a brow and pauses. "Did you deserve it?"

It was the night Maia and I first kissed. Looking back, I realize I had certainly gripped her arm far too tightly when I pulled her into the hallway. I had been frenzied with anger and desire.

"Grab me like that again and I will slice off your testicles and shove them down your throat."

I nod, leaning back in my seat. "Yeah, I deserved it."

The other Laffley sister comes bouncing in the room, and my heart lurches. "There you are," Maia chirps, plopping beside me. "What are you two talking about?"

"You and your sister's tendency to verbally threaten people," Wesley says.

He earns a middle finger from her.

I instinctively rest my arm behind her, eyeing the way her bronze-gold curls spill down her chest. The front strands have been pinned back, save for two spirals that frame her face. Though she looks delicious, I wish she wore something other than red lipstick. She refuses to let me kiss her lips with it on and I'm in agony.

I rip my gaze away, fully aware that I'm staring. God, I can't wait until we can go home.

We carve out another week of relaxation and preparation for plans with my wealth and Space Technologies.

We find ourselves talking about it naturally when Maia tells me about her work in the city. She comes up with plenty of ideas about projects and I help configure them into profitable models that will feed directly back into its community. We don't only do this on our days off because we're passionate, but because we enjoy each other's company. We're doing something together on equal ground and we work in sync, just like I knew we always would.

The first thing I do once I get back to work is send out the necessary proposals to every board member for our meeting in a few days. I don't want their initial reactions; they need to stew on it.

I took the liberty of putting most proposals into action already—such as immediately halting production to switch to recycled cobalt, lithium, and zinc, requesting our suppliers to commit to clean energy initiatives, and actions toward replenishing freshwater withdrawals.

Maia visits me around lunch, knowing that I'm nervous about initial reactions. I pace in front of my window despite having slept a couple of hours last night. She stops me, wrapping her arms around my neck.

"Just slow down," she coos. "Breathe."

"This could backfire quickly."

"Are you having second thoughts?"

I pull my gaze to hers. "Not a chance. I don't want to disappoint you if it doesn't work."

She flinches, cupping my face in her palm. The sincerity in her gaze stitches together a wound I hadn't realized was raw. "Tristan, it won't make me love you less; I'll only love you more for trying... You're a good man. I'm inspired by your ambition every day and your ability to get things done no matter the obstacles. Nothing is impossible to you, and I admire that more than anything. I'm so damn proud of you for how much you've grown and I love getting to experience you."

I lean my head against hers. "You really had to one-up me on that one, innit?"

She giggles. "You may as well accept defeat now because I *always* win."

After my father took Danica and left, Celine left me under the guidance of a pedophile. Though my sister had it much worse, both of us were abandoned by the people meant to protect us.

With Maia, I feel seen. Cared about.

"Fine," I say. "Even when I'm right, I promise to concede."

"We're making promises now?"

"Absolutely, because if there's one thing I've always remained truthful in, it's how madly in love with you I am. We fit so perfectly it's frightening. It's like I feel your every breath"—I peck her lips—"every word"—I kiss her jaw—"every moan"—I kiss her throat—"every heartbeat"—I bend down to kiss her chest, covered by her shirt.

She rolls her eyes, fighting to withhold a grin as her cheeks turn a deep crimson shade. Being able to make the princess of Maldana blush is the only power I ever want to hold.

"Well fuck, babe," she says, making my dick jump. "That one takes the cake."

I laugh, but can't get over that one word. "What did you call me?"

"Nothing." She turns away from me, suddenly shy as if she didn't make a declaration of love just seconds ago.

I trap her with my arms. "It's all right, love. You can call me babe."

Considering she's not a mushy, romantic person, little things that make her blush. But I understand her heart the way she understands mine. Which is why when she says, "Bite me, lover boy," I know it's just another way to say I love you.

EPILOGUE
MAIA

A year and a half later

I yelp before releasing a of string of *"fuck, fuck, fuck, fuck, fuck,"* as I drop the pan on the stove. I pout as my burned banana bread stinks up the kitchen.

"What happened—oh, love."

Tristan hurries to open the windows before the fire alarm goes off.

"How bad?" he asks.

I wave an oven mitt over the loaf to rid the smoke. "Inedible."

He comes up behind me, wincing at the black food in front of me. He wraps me in his arms, pressing a kiss to my head. "I'm sorry, my love."

"I followed the recipe and everything!"

"How long did you set the timer?"

"Two hours, just like it said."

"Two hours?"

I turn to look at him. "You don't believe me?"

"I believe you," he says, though I know he's bullshitting. I probably did get something wrong, but I refuse to admit it. He squeezes my hip. "Go lie down. I'll clean this up."

I nod, trudging toward the living room where we've been lounging for hours. We arrived home last night after traveling for almost a month for conferences and meetings about clean energy initiatives and plant conservation. It was so exhausting that both of us took off work for the remainder of the week—and it's only Tuesday.

He wants time off to be away from people. I want time off for my body to recover. We're a match made in heaven.

I wanted to be cozy by baking banana bread, but that evidently fell to shit.

The last time I tried to bake was for Cori's first birthday party. It certainly did *not* look like a puppy and was far too embarrassing to be seen by anyone other than Tristan. He held me as I cried before he found a perfect replacement cake on short notice. That night, we stayed up and ate my ugly albeit delicious cake together.

All he's done since we've been together is take care of me.

We'd spent five more months a secret before going public; the positive public reception of Space Tech's actions created good timing for both of our sakes. Wonderfully and annoyingly enough, my image repaired itself. I'm known as the *woman who changed a billionaire* when I didn't do anything but bring out the best of who Tristan is. People believe me now. And I hate that it took a man for that to happen.

Nonetheless, the media loves us. Everyone suddenly realizes how awful online buzz has treated me and they're grateful there's someone who truly advocates for me. Their theory was simply confirmed when Tristan had snatched someone by the throat for trying to pull me over the barrier as we were greeting fans in the city.

It was a terrifying moment for me, but social media loved every bit of it—of how my honor was defended—instead of being furious over the fact that a random man felt entitled enough to put his hands on me.

Tristan does what he can to distract me from the media. Every minute we've spent together is sacred, whether he's lounging on the couch with me after I burned another baked good or gardening with me on a warm June morning.

Birds chirp from the magnolia tree above me as I gently water my potted seedlings. June weather is already sweltering, but the shade makes it perfectly enjoyable.

"Babe, can you grab me the hose, please?" I glance over my shoulder to find Tristan standing behind me. "What's wrong?"

"Nothing," he says, his throat bobbing. He takes my free hand, kissing my knuckles. "I just love you."

"I love you, too, but you're acting weird."

Tristan reaches into his pocket as he lowers to the ground, on one knee—

"Oh, shit," I whisper.

"Maia Grace Laffley—"

"Oh, *shit*," I repeat, more emphasis this time. I frantically glance around for a place to set the watering can before eventually tossing it aside.

"Will you—"

"Wait!" I drop to my knees so we're nearly eye level, my hands shaking. "Are you sure?"

All I can think of is Dad telling me he's sorry for the

man I end up marrying, all the little comments from family and friends saying I scare off men.

Tristan recoils. "Am I sure?"

"*Yes*, are you sure?" My voice cracks. "I-I-I'm needy and I'm dramatic and I *never* shut up—"

"All of my favorite things about you."

"I'm bound to drive you crazy."

"That happened the first day we met."

"I burn everything I bake."

"I ought to stop eating carbs, anyway."

"I—you know I want more animals, right?"

"*Maia*," he warns, his thumb brushing my cheek. "There's nothing you can tell me that will drive me away. I love you. I love your raging opinions, your passion, your care for others. I'm a better man when I'm with you and yes, I'm sure I want a needy, dramatic, talkative wife who can't bake for shit and owns a dozen animals. Now, my love, will you please stop arguing with me and say you'll marry me?"

A sob rips out of my chest as I launch myself at him. "Yes—yes, I'll marry you!"

My dogs bark from the other side of the garden gate as Tristan and I topple to the ground. He laughs, wrapping me tight in his arms as my tears flow endlessly. I feel silly, but the words *he loves me, he loves me, he loves me* pang through my mind over and over.

Tristan is the man I'm destined to be with. In every world, every universe, we would find our way back to each other.

BONUS EPILOGUE
MAIA

Nina knew about the proposal.

An hour later—conveniently giving Tristan and me time for celebratory sex—she shows up with cake and a crying toddler. I gather a grumpy Cordelia in my arms, and my niece clings to me like a baby sloth. I ruffle her curly fro.

"Aw, someone's sleepy," I coo, rocking her side to side. I bring her to the guest room to set her down for a nap the way we always do when she's here. Once Cori is asleep, I can properly squeal and jump with my big sister. I show her the ring even though I have no doubt she's already seen it.

"You cried, didn't you?" my sister taunts, bringing us to the patio outside where the men have already set up the cake and utensils.

"Completely."

She's the only person I'll admit that to. Wesley gives me a quick congratulatory hug as Nina tests the baby monitor.

We sit and chat and toss around ideas for wedding themes. My stomach caves at the realization Lyla won't be a bridesmaid. She left Felicity Gardens for another job last year and I haven't seen her since. It's been about two years since we stopped being friends and a mournful pang hits me every once in a while. Since then, Esme and I have grown really close and I easily consider her my best friend.

"We can go somewhere outside the country for your bachelorette party," Nina says, pulling me out of my thoughts.

"Oh, yeah—um... what about Italy? I've never been to Sicily."

"That could be fun!"

"We can go to the restaurant Tristan's friend owns," I suggest, turning to Tristan beside me. "Romèo's family owns a bunch, right?"

"Yeah."

I pull out my phone to look it up for any distraction from my dead friendship. "What's his last name again? Amante?"

Across the table, Wesley freezes. He sets his drink down. "You're friends with Romèo Amante?" His accusative tone sends tension rippling through the four of us.

"They've been friends since they were kids," I say, answering for Tristan.

"Have you met him?" Wesley asks me, which is an unexpected question.

"Uh—once or twice, I guess."

Nina places a comforting hand on his back. "What's wrong? You're worrying me."

I glance at my fiancé, who doesn't say a word. He *bristles*.

What the hell is going on? What don't I know *now*?

"What's wrong is that the Amantes are one of the strongest families of the Sicilian Mafia," Wesley spits. "And Romèo Amante is their enforcer—I would know because we've done a few jobs together." He leans closer, his voice dripping with poison. "And I need to know *everything* you've told him about Nina and Maia."

"Nothing that's not already known by the public," Tristan says without backing down.

I can't help my accusatory tone. "Did you know he's in the *Mafia*?"

"*No,*" he insists, holding my gaze. "I swear it. A while ago, he told me something about his family having skeletons in their closet, but I didn't think he meant that literally. He's private; I've never even met his family."

"Has he asked anything about them?" Wesley presses.

"No," Tristan repeats. "He's quite uninterested, actually."

"When's the last time you spoke to him?"

"Not since April."

"About what?"

"Dude," I snap at my brother-in-law. "This isn't an interrogation."

He ignores me. "If I were you, I wouldn't be friends with him anymore. Other than the fact that he's rude as fuck, he's one of the few assassins I knew who loved what they did. Romèo Amante takes great pleasure in murdering people."

SOURCES

I would like to thank the scientists at Longwood Gardens for providing insight on Maia's job as a conservation scientist!

Abdul Azeez, Azhaar. (2025). *More cats taken to shelter amid rising reports of abuse.* The Maldives. The Sun.

Avtzis, Dimitrios N., (2014). *Control of the Most Dangerous Insects of Greek Forests and Plantations.* Thessaloniki, Greece.

Biology Insights. (2025). *What is Methoxyfenozide and How Is It Used?* Biology Insights.

Brewer, Grace. (2019). *Strangler figs: Killers or bodyguards?* United Kingdom. Kew Gardens.

Center for Biological Diversity. *Mining.*
No other publication information available.

Gukurume, Simbarashe and Tombindo, Felix. (2023) *Mining-induced displacement and livelihood resilience: The case of Marange, Zimbabwe.* The Extractive Industries and Society

Karanikola, Paraskevi and Tsikas, Angelos. (2012). *The most important forest insects in Greece and their management.* Evros, Greece. Dept. of Forestry and Management of the Environment and Natural Resources.

Manduna, Kennedy. (2023). *Are mining-induced displacement and resettlement losses compensable? Evidence and lessons from mining communities in Zimbabwe.* The Extractive Industries and Society.

Selvam, V. (2007). *Trees and shrubs of the Maldives.* Bangkok, Thailand. FAO Regional Office for Asia and the Pacific.

The Morton Arboretum. *Canopy Career Chronicles: Carmen, the Conservation Scientist.* Lisle, IL. The Morton Arboretum.

ACKNOWLEDGMENTS

This book was a beast to write.

It wasn't the book I planned to write, but definitely the one I *needed* to. Maia and Tristan speak to me in so many ways and their characters are very close to my heart. I'm grateful I get to share them with you.

Thank you to Josh for being my biggest fan, supporter, and hype-man. I couldn't have done this without you. You've been patient and understanding when I declined your calls because I'm in the writing zone. You've brought me ice cream and glasses of water so I can focus on working. I love you so much and I'm lucky to have you in my corner.

Ellie Blackbourne, thank you for enduring my panicked, last-second messages and for always propping me up when I need it. I'm so grateful for you and am proud to be your friend!

Thank you to Rin, Marjorie, Elwen, Robyn, Anna, and all of my betas for your feedback and support. You've helped me shape this book!

To Marina, for making us the best author-PA duo as chronically ill northeast-based Eagles fans named Marina. You've been supporting me since *Roaming Holiday*, and I'm eternally grateful for you.

To Emily, for being the best sister I could ask for. I love having you in my corner!

To Yenthe, for hitting it out of the park with your art every time!

To my family, for always showing up and having my back. I'm incredibly lucky to have you guys!

ABOUT THE AUTHOR

Marina Hill is a multifaceted author of books from romance to historical fiction with an eventual path into fantasy. With over a dozen publications of short stories, her work has been hailed as fun comfort reads while managing to discuss important topics. A New Jersey native, Marina spends her days working around books and her nights writing them.

Also by Marina Hill

Little Writer
Fumbled Love
Royal Pain

CONNECT WITH ME!

Instagram
@marinahill.docx

Website
themarinahill.com

If you enjoyed *Royal Pain*, please consider leaving a review
on your platform of choice! Reviews help authors
tremendously.